Take the Bait

S.W. Hubbard

**First in a thrilling new series of
Adirondack mysteries
featuring
Police Detective Frank Bennett**

THE CRUELEST MONTH

A palpable joy coursed through Trout Run, New York, on that first balmy Saturday at the end of April, marking the end of the winter's long siege. People shed their heavy coats and walked around wearing T-shirts and even shorts, despite that in the shade, the air was still cool enough to raise goosebumps on naked skin. Everyone was outside: babies who'd been born over the winter got their first stroller promenades, children drew hopscotch grids on driveways, gardeners dug with unchecked optimism.

And Janelle Harvey, walking the half-mile between Al's Sunoco and her home, disappeared.

TAKE THE BAIT

S.W. HUBBARD

POCKET BOOKS
New York London Toronto Sydney Singapore

This book is a work of fiction. Names, characters, places and incidents are products of the author's imagination or are used fictitiously. Any resemblance to actual events or locales or persons, living or dead, is entirely coincidental.

An *Original* Publication of POCKET BOOKS

 POCKET BOOKS, a division of Simon & Schuster, Inc. 1230 Avenue of the Americas, New York, NY 10020

ISBN: 0-7434-6653-5

First Pocket Books printing April 2003

10 9 8 7 6 5 4 3 2

POCKET and colophon are registered trademarks of Simon & Schuster, Inc.

For information regarding special discounts for bulk purchases, please contact Simon & Schuster Special Sales at 1-800-456-6798 or business@simonandschuster.com

Designed by Melissa Isriprashad

Front cover illustration by John Vairo, Jr.; photo credit: Sime s.a.s./PictureQuest

Printed in the U.S.A.

Acknowledgments

I would like to thank my fellow writers, Julie Cohen-Evans, Judy Graeff, Pamela Hegarty, Joan Migton, and Jennifer Vogel, for years of love and criticism; Denise Tiller and all the Guppies, for the final push; Pam Ahearn, for her risk-taking, keen editorial eye, and endless persistence; Micki Nuding for her guidance and patience; and my husband, for the infrastructure that makes it all possible.

For Kevin

TAKE THE BAIT

1

MAKE NO MISTAKE—spring is not a season of unrestrained joy in the Adirondack Mountains. Too late for skiers and too early for hikers, spring brings financial grief to everyone who relies on the tourist trade. At best, it's muddy; at worst, the melting snow and rain push rivers and streams above their banks, uprooting trees and flooding low roads. The same warm weather that coaxes the leaves onto the trees also draws the blackflies out of their larval state.

Still, a palpable joy coursed through Trout Run, New York, on that first balmy Saturday at the end of April, marking the end of winter's long siege. People shed their heavy coats and walked around wearing T-shirts and even shorts, despite that in the shade, the air was still cool enough to raise goose bumps. Everyone was outside: babies who'd been born over the winter got their first stroller promenades, children drew hopscotch grids on driveways, gardeners dug with unchecked optimism.

And Janelle Harvey, walking the half mile between Al's Sunoco and her home, disappeared.

• • •

Frank Bennett tried to ignore the phone ringing over the shrill whine of his table saw, but the caller's persistence got the better of him. Brushing the sawdust from his sleeves, Trout Run's police chief took the stairs from his basement workshop two at a time, arriving at the phone cross and out of breath.

"Yeah?" he rasped.

"Hello, Frank. It's me. We have a missing persons case. I think we have to get on it right away." Earl's voice was so loud, Frank had to hold the phone six inches away from his ear.

"Who's missing?"

"Janelle Harvey. Jack's daughter."

The name meant nothing to Frank. He had lived in the town for less than a year, and as small as Trout Run was, there were still people he didn't know.

"A little girl?" Frank asked, keeping his voice calm although he could already feel a knot of dread forming in his gut at the mere mention of a missing child. "What, did she wander out of her yard?"

"She's not a little kid, she's a teenager," Earl informed him. "She's been missing for four hours."

"Oh for Christ's sake, Earl!" Disgusted with himself for that moment of panic, Frank lashed out at his young assistant. "That's what you're so worked up about? Kid's probably at her boyfriend's house." Missing teenagers were not the same as missing children. They almost always had taken off in some act of underhanded or intentional defiance, and turned up again soon enough, dragging their tails.

"Uh, her father checked that out," Earl said. The slight hesitation in Earl's voice was enough to tell Frank that the kid was lying. No doubt he had been so rattled by this report of a serious crime while he was on duty that he had failed to question Jack Harvey thoroughly. "He's real upset. He wants us to help him search. He asked for you specifically," Earl added.

Frank smiled as he kicked off his work boots. Certainly no one in town would specifically request Earl. Now that the police chief's position had been filled, everybody expected to get their money's worth from Frank. "Don't worry, Earl, I won't send you out there to deal with Mr. Harvey yourself. I'll swing by the office and pick you up."

Not bothering to change into his uniform, Frank jumped into his truck and drove toward Trout Run. He'd stop by the Town Office and pick up Earl, then head out to Jack Harvey's place.

Three roads led into Trout Run. Where they intersected, a sort of haphazard town square had been formed. The village proper didn't amount to much. It had sprung up near the spot where Stony Brook widens and deepens, forming an ideal habitat for trout. The village had none of the postcard quaintness that towns across Lake Champlain in Vermont leveraged into big tourist dollars. There was no revolutionary war hero standing in a town green, no white steepled church, certainly no chintz-bedecked tea shops or pricey antiques stores.

And yet, Trout Run possessed a definite charm. Perhaps it was the way the mountains surrounded it, holding the town in their protective embrace. Perhaps it was just the carefree way children pedaled their bikes through the streets, dropping them heedlessly in front of the general store, where they went in search of ice cream and candy.

The Town Office, a little clapboard building painted barn red, sat on the north side of the square. On one side of the center hall the tax collector, water authority, and road department were each represented by metal desks.

Today the building was empty except for Earl, the civilian assistant Frank had inherited from his predecessor. When he entered the police department's side of the building, Frank fully expected to find Earl in his characteristic posture—scrawny backside perched on the edge of the swivel chair, work boots up on the metal desk, slightly grimy hands clasped behind his head. But instead, Earl was pacing the five steps from window to phone and back again.

"What took you so long?" he demanded as Frank walked in.

"I didn't even stop to change!" Frank protested, dusting wood shavings from his pant leg. Then, annoyed at himself for offering Earl any excuse at all, he snatched the incident report Earl had completed from Jack Harvey's call and scanned it quickly.

"Maybe you think I could have handled this myself," Earl said.

Frank shook his head. There was very little he thought Earl could do by himself, including filing things alphabetically, driving the patrol car without denting it, and directing traffic without causing a major pileup. "You did the right thing. Let's go out and get this settled, huh?"

Earl filled him in on the Harveys as they drove. For all his faults, Earl was invaluable as a source of background information on every citizen in Trout Run. He categorized everyone he knew as either "from around here" or "not from around here." Earl himself fell into the first group—his family had been scratching out a living in the beautiful, harsh Adirondack Mountains for over a century. Frank would forever remain in the second group. Even if he lived to be ninety-eight, he would only have spent fifty years in Trout Run, hardly enough to make him "from around here."

"Jack's in his early forties I guess," Earl began. "Works over at the lumberyard. His wife, Rosemary, died from some disease when Janelle was real little, so it's just him and Janelle. You see them around together a lot. He started up a girls' softball league and coaches it, just so she'd have a team to play on.

"Jack's sister Dorothy lives in the house right behind theirs. They inherited the property from their parents, and Dorothy built a new little house behind the old farmhouse."

"Is she married?" Frank asked.

"She was till two years ago. Her husband was coming home from the Mountainside Tavern on a rainy night and skidded right into Long Lake. Drowned."

"Sounds like a family with a lot of bad luck."

"Maybe not so bad in that case. Dorothy's husband was real mean. Drank a lot and never worked much. Seems like she supported them and their son, Tommy. Everyone kinda felt she was a lot better off without old Tom."

"What about Janelle—you know her well?"

"Not really. She started high school a year after I graduated."

"You're twenty-one, so, that makes her seventeen."

"Yeah. Tommy's a year older, but they're both seniors. I think she skipped a grade in grammar school. This is the driveway," Earl added as they were nearly past it.

They pulled up to the house with a squeal of tires and a cloud of dust, providing the kind of drama that Frank knew Earl enjoyed.

The Harveys' house, tucked back on a side road branching off Stony Brook Road, was plain and square and white, with a big front porch. The grass was a little tall and there were no flowers, but Frank could see a vegetable bed being prepared for planting in the side yard. He knocked on the storm door and peered through to the tidy hall and living room as he waited for someone to answer.

"I've been calling Janelle's friends and no one's seen her," Jack Harvey said as he walked down the hall to the door. He was a well-built, competent-looking man, but his voice carried a high-pitched edge of panic. "Dorothy's out driving around now looking for her, but she said I better wait here for you."

"Good, good." Frank clapped him on the back. "Let's sit down and go over this right from the beginning. I'm sure there's nothing to worry about."

There was something reassuring in Frank Bennett's appearance and manner that made people want to believe what he said, even when there was no good reason to. At forty-eight, his short hair was still quite dark, and his arms and legs were strong, although he was not a big man. It was only recently that he had accepted the expansion of his waistline to a size thirty-four. The addition of a few wrinkles had not significantly altered his midwestern farm boy's face. His brown eyes could be both kindly and stern—small children recognized him as a pushover, but one icy stare could silence the protests of speeders and barroom bullies.

Jack Harvey's hunched shoulders visibly relaxed. "I was repairing our lawn tractor and Janelle was keeping me company while I worked. I thought I was closing in on the problem, but then I realized I hardly had any gas, and I didn't want to start her up and then have to stop again to fill it. Tommy was out in Dorothy's car, so Dorothy had borrowed my truck to go to the supermarket. I asked Janelle if she'd mind walking up to Al's Sunoco to get some gas. I told her just fill the can halfway or it'll be too heavy to carry. It's less than a mile.

She's been walking up there since she was a little kid to buy candy and sodas." Jack's tone had turned plaintive, as if someone had accused him of intolerable cruelty for asking his daughter to run this errand.

"When she didn't come back by twelve-thirty, I started to wonder what was keeping her, but I figured she ran into someone she knew and lost track of time."

"Did she go back in the house before she left? Maybe she called someone to meet her," Frank suggested.

Jack shook his head. "When I asked her to go she took right off. I called Al and he told me she got there at about quarter to twelve and bought the gas and a candy bar. He said he could see her walking back until she turned the corner onto Stony Brook Road. That's when I started getting worried." Jack's upper lip, covered with weekend stubble, trembled slightly. He clenched his teeth for a moment, took a deep breath, and continued in a steady voice. "By one Dorothy came home with the truck. We've been looking for Janelle ever since."

"What about your nephew, Tommy?" Frank asked. "Is he still out? Maybe Janelle's with him."

"No!" Frank thought Jack answered a little louder than necessary. "I mean, he got back right after Dorothy did. He hasn't seen Janelle."

"Is he looking for her now, too?" Earl asked.

"No, he's out back." Jack jerked his head to indicate the expanse of yard that separated his house from Dorothy's. "Building something."

Rhythmic hammer blows echoed through the quiet spring air. Frank hadn't registered them before. Apparently Tommy wasn't as worried about his cousin as the adults in the family.

Frank rose. "Let's go talk to him—he must know all the kids' hangouts."

"That's a waste of time!" Jack objected. "I told you Tommy doesn't know where she is. I want to show you where I found the gas can on Stony Brook Road."

Frank brought his head up sharply. "Did you leave it there?"

"Yes. Otherwise I thought I wouldn't remember exactly where it was, " Jack answered.

"Good. All right, let's go there now before someone disturbs it. We can talk to Tommy later."

Jack gazed intently out the car window, keeping up a rambling monologue without any prompting from Frank. "Janelle's had a very busy week: softball practice, cheerleading, lots of homework. She must've gotten tired, the can was too heavy for her, so she set it down. And then . . ."

Frank nodded. Then, keeping his eyes focused on the road ahead, as if driving on this deserted country lane demanded his full concentration, he asked, "Did you have any, uh, disagreements with Janelle lately? Could she be staying away just to assert her independence a little?"

There was no immediate answer, and Frank cast a casual glance at his passenger. Jack seemed stunned into silence, so Frank continued, "It's not unusual. Just a teenager's way of letting her parents know they're not totally in control."

The reaction, when it came, was explosive. "My daughter is not playing some prank to teach me a lesson!" Jack screamed. His fair face turned bright red so quickly, you could almost see the blood coursing beneath the taut skin. His hands formed tight fists and he pounded the dashboard. "She wouldn't do that to me!"

Frank offered no response, just drove slowly until Jack's fury played out. He'd expected maybe indignation or annoyance, not rage, and he wondered how often

Jack's fuse was lit. Although tall and strong, Jack had come across as gentle, even sensitive. But Frank no longer trusted first impressions. They could set you off down the wrong path, and by the time you realized it, the opportunity to turn back was gone.

He stopped the car a quarter of a mile down Stony Brook Road, when Jack made a mute gesture. Frank got out and stared at the red metal gas can, which stood upright about six feet from the edge of the road. A straggly bush shaded it but did not completely conceal it.

"You didn't move it at all? It was standing like that when you found it?"

Why would the can be so far back from the edge of the road, almost, but not quite, hidden? A vague uneasiness niggled at Frank.

Jack nodded. "I told her a million times never to hitch-hike." He gave the ground a ferocious kick. "I can't believe she would."

"It's doubtful she was hitching. She would have taken the can with her if she was looking for a ride home. Earl, watch where you're walking," Frank added, not missing a beat.

Earl gave a guilty little leap backward, mostly out of reflex, since he almost never knew what Frank was yelling at him about. Frank paused to examine the ground where his assistant had just stepped, along the shoulder of the road. There were no footprints leading up to the gas can. Janelle, mindful of the spring mud, had apparently walked on the macadam road.

"These your tire tracks?" Frank asked.

"Yeah. When I spotted the gas can I pulled off the road and stopped real sudden," said Jack, explaining the deep grooves in the spongy earth.

The wide truck tires were the only visible disturbance

of the spring mud; no other vehicle tracks marked the ground.

Frank made a broad loop through the meadow that bordered Stony Brook Road, and approached the gas can from the opposite side. Jack watched him work, continuing a shouted conversation from the road.

"So if you don't think she was hitchhiking, you think someone followed her from the gas station and grabbed her?"

Frank lay flat on his stomach and viewed the area around the can at eye level. "What kind of shoes was Janelle wearing?" he asked, in lieu of answering the father's question.

Jack hesitated. "Running shoes, I think. What difference does it make?"

Frank grunted. In the area where the muddy berm left off and the grass and weeds of the meadow began, he could see the faint but distinctive waffle weave pattern of a small running shoe. "You see, she carried the can over here and put it behind this bush," he said, more to himself than to either of his companions. He tried to picture Janelle doing this; to imagine what set of circumstances would make placing the can here the logical thing to do. He drew a blank. In another part of his consciousness he was dimly aware that Jack was talking to him, and refocused his attention.

"I said, someone must have followed her and grabbed her," Jack repeated.

"Don't go jumping to conclusions." Frank walked back through the meadow to where Jack and Earl stood. "Stranger abductions are actually very rare. And there's no sign of a struggle. That's a good thing." He didn't add that an abductor would hardly be likely to order Janelle to walk fifteen feet away from him to put her can behind a bush.

"But if it's not that—" Jack began to protest, but Frank held up his hand for silence.

"Let's just take one step at a time. Someone's bound to have seen something." And Janelle's friends might know something they weren't telling her father. If she was up to something, the friends might be covering for her. He'd check it out, but there was no point in getting Jack riled up again.

Frank got some yellow tape from the patrol car and roped off the area around the gas can. He marked exactly where the can sat, then put a stick under the handle to carry it. "Who lives over there?" Frank pointed to a small house on the other side of the street as he put the gas can in the patrol car trunk. Perched on the side of a hill and painted dark green, the small house was barely visible through the trees.

"Old man Lambert," Jack answered, with a certain disgust in his voice.

Frank glanced at Earl.

"He's blind,"came the clarification.

"All right then, let's go talk to Al," Frank said.

Al Jewinski was a man of very little imagination, except for when it came to diagnosing the source of strange rattlings under car hoods. He emerged from his garage as soon as the patrol car pulled in and seemed surprised to hear they had not come to buy gas.

Al began to repeat what he had told Jack. "Janelle got here at eleven forty-five. I know that for a fact, because I made a note of the time so I'd know how much to charge for the labor on that transmission job." He nodded toward a car up on the lift in the garage. "I got her gas and a candy bar—she was a nickel short but I told her she could owe it to me—and she left."

So Janelle had been penniless at the time of her disappearance. That made running away seem less likely, but Frank asked the next question anyway. "Did she seem like her usual self? Was she nervous or excited?"

Al's dim gray eyes grew dimmer, and he hooked his thumbs in the belt loops of his dirty green work pants. "No, she was friendly, just like always."

"You said you saw her walk away until she turned onto Stony Brook," Frank prompted him.

"Yeah. I watched her walking while I was filling a car."

"You had another customer right after Janelle? You didn't tell me that!" Jack said.

"You didn't ask," Al replied, straightening his angular frame from its perpetual hunch.

"Who was it? Anyone you recognized?" Frank asked.

"I'm thinking, I'm thinking. I get a lot of customers in a day."

This seemed unlikely, given the remote location of the Sunoco station, but Frank supposed that when you moved as slowly and thought as slowly as Al, four or five customers filled up your day quite smartly.

"What kind of car was it?" Earl asked, thinking rightly, for once, that Al had a better memory for makes and models than for names and faces.

"A green Ford Taurus—that's right, it was Joan Haddon's car," Al proclaimed.

"And which way did she pull out?" Frank asked.

Al looked puzzled again.

"Did she go off in the same direction as Janelle?"

"Oh. Oh, yes she did. She turned right."

"Now we're getting somewhere," Frank said as he put the car into gear, leaving the dazed Al to ponder their departure. "Where would we find Joan Haddon this time of day?"

"She works over at Mr. Foley's real estate agency,"

Earl said. "It's not five yet. She's probably still there."

When Frank pulled up to the small frame bungalow that Mr. Foley had converted into an office, the green Taurus was parked out front. Working for Mr. Foley for twenty years had given Joan an unflappable disposition, so she seemed unsurprised to see Frank, Jack, and Earl troop into her office at the end of a working day. "What can I do for you gentlemen?" she asked.

"Did you see my daughter this afternoon walking on Stony Brook Road?"

"Why, yes I did. I offered her a ride."

Relief passed through Jack's body like a liberating army. His eyes lit up, his shoulders unknotted, and his posture straightened now that he knew that Janelle had merely been driven somewhere by kind, familiar Joan Haddon.

"Where did you take her?"

"No place."

"What do you mean?" Jack shouted, leaning over Joan's keyboard, his anger returning as fast as it had dissipated.

Joan used her desk chair to roll away from him. "I mean she turned me down. What's going on here?"

Frank pushed Jack gently into a chair. "No one's seen Janelle since around noontime, and Jack's getting worried. Can you just tell me exactly what you and Janelle said to each other?"

"Sure. I had filled up at Al's, and then as I turned onto Stony Brook Road I saw Janelle walking along, carrying a can of gas. So I stopped and asked her if she wanted a ride home. She said it was a nice day and she needed the exercise. She thanked me and I drove off."

"Did she seem insistent that you not take her, like she had someplace else to go?" Frank asked.

"No. She just seemed like she was enjoying being outside now that the weather's finally nice."

"Where were you going?" Frank asked.

"Out to the Eggerts' cottage on Long Lake. They're coming up this weekend, and I had to make sure everything was ready for them."

"Did you see anyone behind you as you drove away?"

"No one that I noticed. I came back the same way about an hour later," Joan continued. "I didn't see her anywhere along the road then."

Looking at their worried faces, Joan, too, knit her brow. The she gave herself a little shake, as if to physically dispel the anxiety creeping over them all. "Kids lose track of time. She probably went over to a friend's house." The men turned to file out and Joan followed them to the door.

"My Heather did that to me once. Two hours late from school. I was worried sick. Turned out it was cheerleader tryouts and she never mentioned it." Her voice trailed off as she stood in the door and watched them get into the patrol car. "Try looking at the baseball diamond," she called as they pulled away. "They all hang out at the baseball diamond."

But Janelle was not at the baseball diamond. Nor was she at the library, Malone's diner, or the Teen Center of the Presbyterian Church. As each place was checked without success, Frank felt a dread rising in his throat. The frenetic activity brought to mind the case of little Ricky Balsam. The case he couldn't close; the case that had precipitated his "retirement" from the Kansas City force and led him here to lie in wait for speeders on Route 9, investigate a few break-ins at vacation homes, and calm the occasional domestic dispute.

It was nearly two years now, but not a day went by when thoughts of what he should have done, what he should have known, didn't plague him. Eleven-year-old

Ricky Balsam had left his home in a quiet neighborhood in Kansas City one afternoon, selling candy bars to raise money for his soccer league. When dinner came and went with no word from Ricky, his parents had called the police. Intensive searches and house-to-house questioning had turned up only one clue: an elderly woman reported buying a candy bar from Ricky at two-thirty, just as her favorite soap opera came on the air. Then the trail went cold.

Frank still remembered the faces of Ricky's parents when, about six weeks after the disappearance, he went to their home to tell them that hunters had found Ricky's candy order form. The mother's face had lit up, certain that this was good news. But the father had looked deep into Frank's eyes and let out a low moan that built into a keening wail. The next day, searchers found Ricky's decomposed body buried under some leaves in the same area. Frank had investigated the case for what it so obviously was: an abduction and murder. And he had been wrong, so wrong. . . .

Frank tried to push from his mind any thoughts that the Janelle Harvey case would turn out the same way. It couldn't.

He wouldn't let it.

Not again.

2

BY DINNERTIME word of Janelle's disappearance had spread throughout town, and friends and neighbors turned out in scores on the green in front of the Town Office, waiting for their orders.

"It's one of them pedal-files that snatched her," Augie Enright opined to anyone who would listen. "They look normal, but they get these uncontrollable urges."

"Shut up, Augie," hissed Lydia Barton. "We'll find that girl safe and sound." Lydia's opinion carried some weight, but still, a current of fear coursed through the crowd, and Augie found plenty of sympathetic ears for his theories until Frank's emergence from his office stilled all the murmuring.

Frank walked up the steps of the gazebo in the center of the green and gazed out at the anxious, upturned faces before him. He could almost feel their fear and worry transfer itself to his shoulders. *Here, take this. Fix it and make everything all right again.* He didn't want to let them down. They had done a lot for him, without even realizing it. Given him a place to go every morning, things to do, words to say at a time when he'd felt that the very core of himself had crumbled away. When suddenly he had found he was no longer a husband, no longer a detective commander.

He wanted to show Trout Run he could do what they'd hired him to do—keep them safe. But he wasn't sure it was within his power. All afternoon he'd played out best-case and worst-case scenarios in his mind. The best case was that Janelle had run away, but that was beginning to look less and less likely. It wasn't that easy to run away from Trout Run—not without a lot of planning. The nearest train station was forty miles east in Essex, and the Trailways bus stopped just once each day in Keene Valley, twenty miles to the south. He'd checked both—no Janelle. That she could have hitchhiked off with a stranger without a penny in her pocket seemed extremely improbable. But teenagers were impulsive, and if she had been angry or distraught she might have set off without thinking what her next step would be.

Was Janelle the impetuous type? It was too early for him to know. In these frantic hours since her disappearance, no one had anything but kind words to say. Janelle was a wonderful girl. Jack was a wonderful father. Everything about their life was wonderful, wonderful. With time he might turn up a different story, but right now it didn't seem that Janelle had any reason to run away.

So, the worst-case scenarios won out. First, the theory everyone here probably believed: that Janelle had been abducted by a stranger—a sexual predator or serial killer. If that were true, she might well be dead already. And searching for her killer—a person with no link to his victim or logical motive—would be like searching for the proverbial needle in the haystack. He might never make an arrest, might never even find her body. He saw nothing but grief and failure for everyone if Janelle had been abducted by a stranger.

The alternative was both better, and much worse: Janelle had gone off with someone she knew, and for whatever reason, could not—or would not—come back. That scenario offered the possibility that Janelle was still alive and could be rescued if they found her fast enough. Even if she were dead, Frank was confident he could uncover any killer who knew his victim. So that kind of case could be solved—but at what cost?

Frank looked out at the crowd before him, supposedly his allies, here to offer him every assistance. What would happen if they realized he suspected one of their own? Would they fight him every step of the way? Would they turn on him, then turn him out? He'd lost his last job by failing; he might lose this one by succeeding.

But right now, Trout Run had turned out to search for Janelle, and Frank had to let them do it. So with no preamble, he began barking out orders.

"Joe, Augie, Dave—I want you to take your pickups and drive all the back roads between here and Verona. Look for any vehicles pulled off the road. It's possible that Janelle could be trying to make it back home.

"Ned, Vinnie, George," Frank called on some of the younger men in the group. "Take these flashlights—it'll be getting dark soon—and walk the whole length of Stony Brook from where Janelle disappeared to the bridge. Look for any signs of her clothes or other belongings." What he didn't say was, "Look for signs of a shallow grave." He wouldn't shout that out in front of the crowd, not with Jack pacing anxiously beside him. Tomorrow, if Janelle still hadn't been found, he would search the meadow and brook again.

"Ladies, I want you to divide the phone book between

you and call every family in Trout Run, Verona, and John-sonburg," Frank told a group of women that included Janelle's Aunt Dorothy and Joan Haddon. "Ask if they've seen Janelle, of course, but also ask if they were any-where in the vicinity of Stony Brook Road around noon. Write down the name of anyone who says they were, and I'll go talk to them. They may have seen something important without realizing it."

A group of teenagers milled on the fringe of the crowd, not certain whether they were considered part of the problem or part of the solution. Frank recognized most of them—he'd spent the latter half of the afternoon talking to all the kids Jack had identified as Janelle's clos-est friends as well as her boyfriend, Craig Gadshaltz. He'd interviewed them separately, and they had been remarkably consistent in their answers. No one had seen or spoken to Janelle since the night before, when most of them had gone out for pizza following the baseball game. Janelle had been her usual self—not moody or nervous. She had not mentioned any special plans for today. He didn't get the sense that any of them were covering for her. They'd all seemed so ingenuous, so awed that they were being questioned in a disappearance.

The boyfriend, Craig, had seemed bewildered and wor-ried. Frank hadn't been able to tell if the boy was holding something back, or if it was just typical teenage inarticu-lateness that made him so quiet.

Now Frank could see that some of the girls had been crying. They clung to one another, clutching twisted tis-sues in their hands. Occasionally one of the boys offered a clumsy hug in consolation.

"Hey, guys!" Frank shouted, waving them closer. "I want you all to drive over to Lake Placid and show Janelle's picture around in all the pizza joints and ice cream parlors and other places kids hang out. Show her picture to kids you don't know—someone may have seen her there."

"But Janelle never—" One of the girls, he thought her name was Kim, started to protest, but the others over-ruled her.

"C'mon—divide up. Craig and me can drive," a tall boy named Jerry took charge, and the others followed.

Frank noticed that Janelle's cousin Tommy was not among the teenagers, nor was the boy with Dorothy and Jack. The absence might not have registered, if not for the fact that his interview with Tommy that afternoon had been so odd. He'd found Janelle's cousin hammering away in the barn behind Jack's house, and the kid would've kept pounding through their conversation if Frank hadn't asked him to stop. He soon understood why Jack had told him not to waste his time talking to Tommy. All Frank's questions about Janelle's possible whereabouts were met with a resolute blankness and a slow shake of the head.

Finally, Tommy had spoken. "Uncle Jack's always up Janelle's ass. She probably just wants a little time to her-self." And then he added, "When I go off, no one calls the cops to look for me."

By now Tommy must realize that Janelle hadn't just slipped off for a little private time, but he hadn't joined the search. Was he simply jealous of all the attention being shown his cousin, or was there something more there? Frank didn't have time to worry about it now.

"Earl, I want you and . . ." He scanned the crowd, looking for someone who could handle authority. Reluc-tantly, he settled on a man he didn't personally like, but whom he knew could be trusted. ". . . Clyde Stevenson to run a roadblock on the main road to Lake Placid. Stop every car and show them Janelle's picture."

Jack Harvey turned to go off with Clyde and Earl, but Frank laid a restraining hand on his shoulder. "Jack, you come back to the office with me."

"But I'd rather help Clyde with the roadblock. That seems like the best bet."

"No, I need you with me," Frank insisted. He nodded to Clyde and Earl to get them moving, then led Jack, still protesting, back to the Town Office.

"We've been together all day—you know everything I know," Jack said. "I want to be *doing* something to find Janelle."

"I understand," Frank answered as they walked into his office. "But if some news comes in, it'll be best to have you right here."

Jack tensed. "You mean if they find her body, you want to keep me from doing anything crazy." It was not what Frank had meant, but he was glad Jack had leaped to that conclusion. The truth—that Jack must still be considered a suspect—would have upset the distraught father even more.

"You've seen a lot of this stuff where you come from, haven't you?" Jack continued. "You know she's dead." His voice cracked, and he didn't bother to hide his tears.

"I don't think that at all," Frank lied. "It's only been a few hours. We'll find her." *But you might not like how we do it.*

Jack sprawled in the hard wooden chair across from Frank's desk, staring up at the water-stained ceiling, but his eyes were focused on something only he could see. "Janelle is more than a daughter to me. She's my life. We did everything together. Since I lost Rosemary, Janelle is all I have." He slumped forward, cradling his head in his hands. "This can't be happening. Not to us. Not here."

"Where is she?" Jack enunciated each simple word. "One minute she was walking along Stony Brook Road, the next minute she's gone—how can that be? Why didn't anyone see anything, hear anything?"

Frank had interviewed everyone who lived on Stony Brook Road with remarkably little success. The houses there were widely spaced and set well back from the road. Two families had not been home at the time of Janelle's disappearance. The other three could remember nothing about any cars that might have driven by. Certainly they had heard no screams or shouts. Frank had even stopped by at Mr. Lambert's house, which, ironically, had a perfect view of the stretch of road from which Janelle had gone missing. Frank had hoped the old man might have had a visitor who'd seen something, or that Lambert himself might have heard something. But the adage about the blind having a keener sense of hearing was not true in this case. Mr. Lambert kept his radio tuned at an ear-splitting decibel, and spoke in the raised tones of the nearly deaf.

"I can't stand to think of her out there alone, in the dark, hurt, afraid," Jack said softly, to himself. He looked up and met Frank's eyes directly, and his fear passed like a current into Frank's gut. "What if you never find her? What if I never, ever know what happened to her? I won't be able to bear it."

Frank returned Jack's gaze without blinking. "I won't let that happen. I promise you."

He was a father, too. He knew what it was to love a child more than your own life; knew what it was to lose a wife, and to have nothing left of her but what you had created together—a daughter. But even though Estelle was gone, taken from him so suddenly by a brain aneurysm in that last dreadful year in Kansas City, his daughter Caroline was safe and sound in her home downstate in suburban Westchester. His little grandsons, Ty and Jeremy, were where they were supposed to be, not missing, or abducted, or dead.

And he was here in Trout Run, with a crime to solve. He pulled away from Jack Harvey and his web of pain. He couldn't let himself get tangled there, not this time, not ever.

By nine-thirty Saturday night, virtually every family in Trout Run, Johnsonburg, and Verona had been called. Janelle's friends had shown her photograph at every store, movie theater, and restaurant in Lake Placid. They even took the photo out to the Burger King on the New York Thruway, more than thirty miles away. Everywhere, people intently studied the picture, which showed the engaging if slightly startled smile of a girl caught too soon by an impatient school photographer. The fine strawberry blond hair had, for the occasion, been coaxed into poufed wings on either side of her high-cheekboned face. The hazel eyes, unsullied by anything the cosmetics counter at the local drugstore had to offer, were wide and ingenuous. But everywhere people shook their heads, without even a moment of hesitation to give a moment of hope.

Now Frank sat in the Town Office surrounded by Reid Burlingame, Ardyth Munger, Clyde Stevenson, and Clyde's son, Ned. The first three were members of the town council. Frank didn't know why Ned felt the need to be there, but he chose not to make an issue of it. "I'm going to call off the search for tonight," he told the group as he replaced the phone receiver in its cradle. "Lieutenant Meyerson from the state police barracks in Malone will be here at daybreak with two investigators and a K-9 team."

"Well, I'm glad the state police finally *realize* we have a serious crisis here," Clyde fumed. "They certainly don't *hesitate* to accept our tax *dollars*, but they are certainly reluctant to do any *work*."

Clyde spoke in a strange syncopated rhythm whose logic was clear only to him. He was not the man an outsider would have pegged as the most powerful person in Trout Run. On the short side of average, Clyde carried no extra weight, but a tendency toward wide hips made him look dumpy and vaguely effeminate. His facial features were unremarkable except for one detail: he had uncommonly long and meaty earlobes. Whenever Frank spoke to Clyde, he found his eyes irresistibly drawn to these fleshy pendulums, which quivered and shook in sync with Clyde's odd cadences.

"Since there were no obvious signs of foul play, we had to be certain she hadn't run away before the state police would get involved," Frank explained. "They're prepared to give us their full assistance in the morning."

"Well, I think it's *premature* to call off our own *efforts*," Clyde protested. "Don't you agree, Reid?"

Reid opened his mouth to reply, but Frank cut him off. He didn't appreciate this decision making by committee, and he intended to squelch it fast. "It's dark and we haven't discovered anything. The last thing we need is for one of the volunteers to get lost or hurt. There's really nothing more that can be done tonight by the searchers."

Ardyth looked out the window, through fine droplets that clung to the glass. "I don't know. It's starting to rain and the temperature's really dropped. Hypothermia's a real possibility if the poor girl is out there in just a T-shirt," she said.

Frank massaged his temples, struggling to keep the edge out of his voice when he answered. "Well, Ardyth, I'd agree except Janelle didn't get lost on a hike in the woods. We have no reason to believe she's out in the open."

"We have no reason to believe she's *not*, either," Clyde insisted. "Most *likely*, her abductor has dragged her off into the *forest* and is holding her there."

This time Frank didn't even attempt to restrain his irritation. "There is absolutely no evidence to support that statement, Clyde. I'll thank you not to go getting everyone more upset than they already are by spouting off theories that have no basis in fact."

A shocked silence engulfed the room. Frank could hear his own blood pounding through his arteries, propelled by a heart beating much too fast for a man his age. Then support came from an unlikely corner.

"I think we're all a little too tense to accomplish much more tonight," Ned said as he rose. Although taller than his father, Ned was still several inches shorter than Frank. Dressed for the search in hiking boots and a ratty University of Pennsylvania sweatshirt, he looked younger than his thirty years. "Chief Bennett has probably organized many searches in his career—let's let him do his job," Ned said, dropping a casual hand on his father's shoulder. He directed an affable smile at the rest of the group, revealing perfectly even teeth. To Frank's amazement, Clyde stood without another word and left the room with Ned following.

Ardyth and Reid stared at the door that had just closed behind the two Stevensons. Finally, Ardyth found her voice. "Boy, I never saw Clyde back down like that. Maybe you're right, Reid. Ned's coming back home does seem to be having a good effect on the old goat."

Ever diplomatic, Reid let this characterization pass without comment. At seventy-two, he still practiced law and had a reputation for being both even-handed and even-tempered. "Better get out there and call in the searchers, Frank," he said as he put on his jacket. "You see, I would've agreed with you if you'd just given me the chance." His smile took the sting out of the words. "We'll see you in the morning."

After Reid and Ardyth left, Frank trudged across the green, the fine, cold mist coating his face and penetrating the shoulders of the uniform he had changed into when he realized this would be a working day like no other. The chill barely registered compared to the cold knot of tension lodged within. What had possessed him to snap at Clyde like that? There had been no call to be so defensive, as if Clyde were accusing him of incompetence.

And who was to say Clyde's ideas might not be right? Keep an open mind, listen to other opinions—if he hadn't learned *that* from the Balsam case, he hadn't learned a thing. But the hell of it was, tolerance didn't come any easier here in Trout Run with Clyde, than it had in Kansas City with Detective Rob Perillo.

Clyde and Rob Perillo had nothing in common, except that Frank didn't like either of them, and he let it show. He'd allowed his contempt for Perillo, the man—his poofed-up hair and pumped-up biceps, his constant bragging about chicks and wheels and scores—to blind him to the value of Perillo, the cop. When Perillo said he sensed something "off" in the story presented by Ricky's father, Frank had ignored him. What could a punk like Perillo know about a pillar of the community like Steve Balsam? And when Perillo had kept digging, Frank had rebuffed everything the detective had brought him, until Perillo had gone over his head and brought it to the chief.

And then he'd had no defense, because Perillo had been completely, entirely right. It was Perillo who'd noticed that no one outside of Ricky's family had seen the boy since the day before they reported him missing. Perillo had discovered that the old lady who claimed

Ricky had sold her a candy bar got the day wrong. Perillo had uncovered the long history of visits to different emergency rooms by all the Balsam children. Perillo had carefully built the case against Steve Balsam, but by the time he got anyone to take him seriously, crucial forensic evidence had been lost, opportunities squandered. The father couldn't be successfully prosecuted, but Frank had been tried in the court of public opinion and found guilty. He was lucky to be able to "retire" with some shred of dignity intact.

Now, over a year later, he'd built a life for himself here in Trout Run. It was a dim shadow of the life he'd lived before, but it was more than he believed he could ever hope for when he'd first left Kansas City. The rebirth had been painful, and one thing he knew for sure—he didn't have it in him to do it again. If he couldn't succeed as police chief in Trout Run, he'd hole up somewhere far away and wait for Alzheimer's to overtake him.

Frank shook himself as he headed toward the lights of Malone's diner, shining with deceptive cheerfulness in the otherwise dark town square. No need to get maudlin—things weren't that bad yet. Probably by tomorrow Clyde would have forgotten their little set-to.

Regis Malone had agreed to keep the diner open late, giving the volunteers a place to tank up on coffee between assignments. Earlier in the evening, Frank had told all the volunteers to report back to the diner by nine-thirty. As he drew closer, he could see the place was now jammed, with more cars parked out front than there were on a Saturday morning in deer season. At least Jack wasn't there—he'd persuaded the father to wait at home by the phone. Taking a deep breath, he pushed open the door and stood silently in the entranceway. It only took a few moments for the buzz of conversation to peter out.

"I'd like to thank everyone for turning out to help today," Frank began. "I don't think we can be very productive in the dark, so I'm calling off the search until tomorrow. The state police will be here at daybreak with the K-9 team. Anyone who's able to help tomorrow should report here to Malone's and follow instructions from Sergeant Vigne." Frank paused. He didn't want to say the next two words but knew he had to. "Any questions?"

Immediately, the diner turned into a babble of raised voices and waving arms. Frank patiently sorted through the questions inspired by a day of unchecked production from the rumor mill. No, no fragment of Janelle's clothing had been found. Yes, he'd heard about the car with Connecticut plates seen circling the green three times, but they had turned out to be elderly tourists looking for the Adirondack Craft Center. No, it wasn't true that Janelle had been spotted hitchhiking on the Thruway. And so it went, for nearly half an hour.

Finally, Frank wound it up with a little pep talk. "We have every reason to be optimistic. The fact that we haven't discovered any signs of foul play encourages me to believe that we will find Janelle unharmed." He smiled. "Now, go home and get some rest."

As he crossed the green back to his office, Earl appeared, breathless, at his side.

"Is your car over here?" Frank asked. "I didn't see it outside the office."

"Nah, it's over by Malone's. But I thought you might have something else for me to do." Earl emphasized the "me" slightly, distinguishing himself from the general mob of townspeople who had been dismissed from the search.

"Afraid not, Earl. I'm going home soon myself."

"Oh. Okay, then." Earl stopped walking, letting Frank go ahead.

In a few more steps, Frank stopped, too, and glanced back over his shoulder. Suddenly, he wanted company. He'd been surrounded by people all day long, yet he'd been all alone. He opened his mouth to call out to Earl, then closed it again before any sound escaped. He didn't want Earl now. He wanted someone to share all his contradictory ideas with. Someone who would just listen and not tell him what sounded right or wrong or crazy. He wanted what he could never have. He wanted Estelle.

He felt the familiar surge of emotion that had plagued him since Estelle's death. Strange that he should be so angry with her in death, when he rarely had been in life. Unbidden, that final scene in the hospital came to him. Estelle in a coma, tubes and wires running into and out of her like some appliance. Caroline holding her mother's hand, telling her softly how much she loved her. And there he was at the foot of the bed, consumed with rage, wanting to grab Estelle by the shoulders and shake her, screaming, "Come back! Come back here right now, do you hear me?"

Later that day she died, and at the funeral people kept saying how wonderful that he'd been with her at the end. It was all he could do to keep from punching them, the flaming fools.

He swallowed his anger now, sending it down to join the anxiety and fear already roiling his belly. When he went to meet his maker, it wouldn't be his heart or lungs or brain that brought him down, it'd be his digestive tract—he was sure of that.

3

"A COFFEE AND A POWDERED." Reid Burlingame dropped four quarters into the cigar box on the counter and went to join the group gathered around the big Formica table in the front window of the Store. "They sure did devote a lot of time to Janelle on the news out of Plattsburgh this morning. Announced a toll-free number and everything."

The Store had been "The Mack Bros. Store" for the first fifty years of its existence, until the death of both Macks had caused its sign to be truncated by the thrifty new owners, Stan and Rita Sobol. Their slogan was still, "The Store that has most everything . . ." The locals snidely completed the sentence with, "except what you really need." Everyone drove to Plattsburgh or Lake Placid to do their serious grocery shopping, but the Store was a handy stopgap. And Rita did make a mean cup of coffee. Every morning, the Store hosted the Coffee Club, a gathering of Trout Run's sharpest eyes and tongues.

Frank, who had entered the Store through the back door precisely because he wanted to avoid the crowd at the front, now eavesdropped on them from the other side of the bread rack. He had come in search of a decent cup of coffee after a long morning of bringing the state police up to speed and coordinating their efforts with his own.

"You know who's paying for that phone line?" Bart Riddle proceeded to answer his own question. "Clyde Stevenson. They say he's offering a ten-thousand-dollar reward for information that helps find Janelle."

Reid nodded, running his hand through his thick silver hair. "No matter what you might think of Clyde, you have to admit he's a good man to have on your side in a crisis."

Frank snorted. He'd never go that far; the only benefit lay in *not* having Clyde against you.

Jeanne Arnott, picking up her copy of the Plattsburgh *Press-Republican,* added her two cents' worth. "Jack's worked for Clyde for twenty-five years—it's the least he could do. I tell you, I hardly slept last night, thinking of Janelle out there with some pervert."

"It don't much matter—he won't have to pay out. People don't want to get involved these days." Augie Enright hooked his thumbs into his belt loops, adding more downward pressure on pants already sorely strained by the weight of his large belly.

"Now, now Augie. People report information to those hot lines all the time," Reid insisted.

Good old Reid, Frank thought. Always the voice of reason.

"Just crackpots who want attention. No, they'll never find her. Just look at that." Augie pointed toward the big plate glass window.

Bart obediently peered through it. "Look at what?"

"Look at all those goddamn trees! Look at the mountains!"

The view from the Store was spectacular, Frank had to admit. Mount Marcy loomed in the distance, and several smaller peaks nestled at her feet. Vivid green flushed the trees at the foot of the mountains, while at the crest they still struggled to shake free of their wintry brown. The birches and maples were almost chartreuse this early in the season, while the deep green pine trees provided swathes of contrast. Not one building, not one clearing, interrupted the flow of the forest.

"Janelle could be anywhere out there," Augie continued. "What's one hundred-and-five-pound girl compared to all that? She could be stuffed in a cave or weighted down in a lake. This is probably the best place on earth to hide a body. And no one would ever see you. Why, I've gone fishing in these lakes and never seen another soul all day long. If you knew where you were going, you could fix it so that body would never be found in a million years."

Augie's words expressed Frank's fears all too accurately. What if he came up with a suspect, but not a body? No body, no crime—he likely wouldn't be able to prove a thing. Frank drew a deep breath. He had to stop second-guessing himself, looking for similarities to the Balsam case at every turn. He decided to challenge Augie.

"What makes you think Janelle's been murdered?"

The men at the table twisted in their seats at his voice. Frank stepped out from behind the bread rack and, without waiting for an invitation, claimed a chair at the table.

"I didn't say she's been *murdered*," Augie said, hastily backing away from his comments.

"Well then, what's your take on Janelle's disappearance, Augie?" Frank prompted as he fixed himself a cup of coffee and tossed fifty cents in the box.

"Oh, she's been kidnapped, sure enough. I hear that Meyerson fella from the state police was asking Jack, did Janelle have any problems, like she run away or something."

"The state police should just butt out if that's all the more help they're going to be," Martha Feeson, passing by en route to the dairy case, interjected. "What do we need them here for?" She shot Frank a significant look before beginning her struggle with the perpetually jammed sliding door of the refrigerator.

"First of all, I'm the one who asked the state police to join in the investigation. Earl and I can't handle this by ourselves. And Lieutenant Meyerson doesn't believe Janelle's run away. We just have to talk to everyone Janelle knows. It's all part of the investigation."

"You should be talking to—"

The jangling of the string of bells hung on the front door interrupted Augie's advice. Clyde Stevenson stood on the threshold of the Store and surveyed the scene before him.

"If you're all just sitting *around* here drinking coffee, you might just as well come across to the old *flower* shop and help us." Although the florist business had been defunct for several years, the empty building was still known by its previous name. Normally unused, today a steady stream of human traffic flowed up and down the sloping wooden steps.

"I noticed people going in and out over there. What are you up to, Clyde?" Bart asked.

Frank knew full well what Clyde was doing and was sure everyone else in the Store did too, but they all waited to hear Clyde's self-promotion.

"Elinor has taken it *upon* herself to organize the concerned *citizens* of Trout Run to assist in the search for Janelle." Clyde fixed Frank with a ferocious glare. "Ned will be back from Plattsburgh with the fliers *shortly*, and we'll need volunteers"—his glare shifted to the members of the Coffee Club—"to hang them *up*. I just came in here to get some snacks for our workers."

"Well, that's a real good project for your family, Clyde," Frank said as he drained his coffee cup. "I think I'll head back over there with you and check out your operation." Although the little man irritated him mightily, Frank had learned that by maintaining an air of cheerful obtuseness to Clyde's barbs, he could return the irritation in kind. He waited patiently while Clyde pored over the selection of boxed coffee cakes, then longer as he painstakingly counted out exact change for his purchase.

Finally, Frank headed across the green with Clyde, remembering to shorten his customary stride so that the lumberyard owner wouldn't have to trot to keep up. His courtesy did not extend to making small talk. It was no secret that in the search for a new police chief, Clyde had preferred a local man that he could control, as he had controlled Frank's predecessor for the past twenty-five years. But in a rare show of independence, the other six members of the town council had resisted Clyde, arguing that they would never find anyone else with Frank's experience. Besides, his pension from the Kansas City police made him available at an unbeatable price, a rationale that Frank suspected ultimately swayed the frugal little entrepreneur.

There was no love lost between the men. Frank found Clyde absurd, and in his early days on the job had made some wisecracks that soon came back to haunt him. He had failed to appreciate how deeply Clyde Stevenson's economic power pervaded the town. As owner of the lumberyard, he controlled three hundred jobs, and the income from those jobs in turn helped local businesses like the Store and Al's Sunoco and Malone's diner stay afloat. So while he sensed that no one else in town genuinely liked Clyde any better than he did, Frank had learned that he'd best keep his smart remarks to himself if he wanted to gain the respect and cooperation of the citizens of Trout Run.

Silently, the two men entered the old flower shop, and the buzz from twenty workers' voices immediately ceased. They all stared at one another for a moment until Ned spoke up. "Dad, Frank, is there some news?"

"My only news is that the Store is out of donuts already so I had to get *coffee* cake." Clyde turned to his companion. "Perhaps Chief Bennett here has something more relevant to tell us."

Forty eyes switched their focus from Clyde to Frank. Filled with fear and worry, they pleaded with him to tell them that this was all some horrible mistake, that Janelle was on her way home.

Frank took a deep breath and started talking. "As many of you know, I called in the state police today, after Janelle had been missing overnight." He rattled on about missing persons bulletins, roadblocks, and background checks. He could see that none of it brought the slightest reassurance to the volunteers, mostly mothers and grandmothers who no doubt believed their efforts at the old flower shop would somehow protect their own offspring from mortal danger.

He wound up with an exhortation to keep up the good work, which sounded lame even to him. Ned Stevenson listened, then set his jaw in a disapproving clench and returned to pounding the keyboard of his laptop computer. He had recently returned to Trout Run from finishing his MBA at Wharton and never missed an opportunity to show his contempt for the provincialism that surrounded him.

"Couldn't one of the ladies do all that typing?" Clyde asked his son.

"I'm setting up a database of appropriate places to send these fliers," Ned replied without raising his head from his work. "I've downloaded a list of highway travelers' information desks across the country and I've written a cover letter asking them to post our flier. By the time I teach anyone here how to do the mail merge, I can have it done myself."

Clearly flummoxed by his son's jargon, Clyde retreated to the door but preserved his dignity with a parting shot, "Well, don't spend all morning here. Remember, I want to review all the orders you're placing with Calverton before you send them off."

A twitch of annoyance passed over Ned's even-featured face. Neither Clyde nor his wife, Elinor, was particularly attractive, but their genes had combined to produce a son whose pleasant looks fell just a little short of handsome. His brown hair, styled carefully at a unisex salon in Lake Placid or maybe even Albany, concealed some incipient thinning at the crown. Sporty clothes chosen from catalogs made him look a little more rugged than he really was.

"I'll be up by eleven," Ned replied without looking at his father.

Frank supposed he should be grateful for the involvement of people like Clyde and the group he had rallied around him, but he could not shake the feeling that their efforts, and perhaps even his own, would be fruitless. Augie Enright had been surprisingly perceptive—this was one of the best spots on earth to hide a body.

A burning pain gnawed below Frank's rib cage as he crossed the green to his office. He hadn't felt it since he had left Kansas City, and he took it as an ominous sign that this case was not going to resolve itself easily or soon. The doctor had called the pain irritable bowel syndrome, which was his way of justifying a $150 fee for telling Frank he had a bellyache that wouldn't kill him and there wasn't a damn thing anyone could do about it. Well, he was irritable all right. This wasn't the kind of work he'd expected when he'd agreed to take the chief's job in Trout Run. He didn't need challenges anymore; just a little routine, a reason to get out of bed in the morning.

Frank trudged past Meyerson's state police car, parked beside the Trout Run patrol car. Maybe Lew would have some new information.

"Didn't they have any?" Doris, the town secretary, demanded as soon as Frank walked through the door.

"Have any what?"

"Coffee filters! When you went out for coffee I told you to pick some up!"

Frank looked down at his hands, surprised to see that they were indeed empty, but Doris had already stormed off. "I'll just have to use a paper towel. Don't complain to me if there's grounds in the pot," she called back over her shoulder.

Doris's coffee was consistently dreadful, and he didn't think a few loose grounds would affect her results one way or the other. Crossing the hall, he opened the heavy wooden door that separated the police department from the other town offices. Two heads snapped up to greet him.

Earl, with his general air of a dog recently rescued from the pound, and Lieutenant Meyerson, an ex-Marine of almost painful cleanliness, were not destined to be boon companions. They looked equally relieved to see Frank.

"Bennett. Glad you're here. Reports are in on every car stopped by troopers on the Northway Saturday and yesterday. Nothing suspicious. Ditto with the report on recently released sex offenders. No one in this area."

Frank nodded. "Thanks, Lew. I wasn't really expecting much, but you can't be too careful. What about you, Earl, did you talk to Dell Lambert's niece?"

Celia Lambert checked in on her blind uncle every day, so they had hoped she might have seen Janelle.

"Yeah, I caught up with her this morning. She says she left old man Lambert's by eleven-thirty yesterday. Didn't notice anything. Now what do we do?"

"It's time to start reinterviewing Janelle's friends and the neighbors, plus her teachers, coaches, everyone that knows her at all well."

"What's the point of that?" Earl asked. "The friends and neighbors already told us everything they know. And what could her teachers possibly know about where Janelle was on Saturday?"

Frank and Lew exchanged a glance.

"What?" Earl asked. "What don't I understand?"

"We think Janelle must have known whoever she got in the car with," Meyerson explained.

"How can that be?"

"Think, Earl," Frank said. "Why was the gas can set behind that bush? It seems as if Janelle herself put it there—hers is the only footprint leading up to it. A kidnapper wouldn't have ordered her to do that."

"But why does that mean she went off with someone she knew? She couldn't have been planning on meeting someone and running away. She didn't have any money with her. She didn't even know she would have to go up to Al's for gas."

Frank nodded. "That's right. I struggled with that all yesterday. But what if she ran into someone she knew there on Stony Brook Road, and she *didn't want* that person to drive her home, so she set the can back off the road, intending to come back for it later?"

"Why wouldn't she want the person to drive her home? Her dad was waiting for the gas," Earl objected. "She could've dropped it off and gone back out again."

"Not if the person was someone her father didn't approve of—someone she wasn't supposed to be with," Frank answered.

Understanding spread across Earl's face. "Oh, so you think she went off with him, thinking it would be for just a few minutes, and then she never came back!" Earl sat back, pleased with himself. Then distress replaced satisfaction on his pliable face. "Wait a minute! Then what happened? If she's with someone she knows, why hasn't she come back? She's gotta know by now how worried everyone is."

Frank sat silent.

Earl shoved his hair out of his eyes, as if seeing Frank more clearly would help him understand. "You mean you think this guy tied her up, or, or hurt her or something? Someone she *knew*? Someone from *Trout Run*? No way. No way!"

Frank turned away from his assistant's incredulous face. Unfortunately, there was a way. There were many ways. Making neat piles of the papers on his desk, he began speaking again, as if Earl had never mentioned a thing.

"Yesterday, we asked people the basics. Now, we have to find out about her friends, her relationships. See if we can figure out who she knows who could be a suspect. Or see if there's anything in her life that could possibly provide a motive. Before we get started, though, I want to stop by to see Jack Harvey."

"But if there's someone Mr. Harvey doesn't like Janelle hanging around with, wouldn't he have told us that right away?" Earl protested.

"Maybe, maybe not. Never be afraid to ask about the obvious—you may look foolish, but you look even more foolish if you don't ask. Besides, there's some rumbling over there at the Store that we're not handling this thing right. I want to keep Jack posted on what we're doing. Word will spread soon that we're asking questions over at the school."

Meyerson compressed his thin lips until they virtually disappeared from his angular face. "We're operating totally by the book, Frank. We don't need his permission to investigate."

Frank's voice took on an edge. "I'm not looking for permission. We just need to hold his hand a little."

Meyerson's frown grew more pronounced.

"Look, Lew, hand-holding is what the people of this town pay me for. If they wanted the state police code read to them for every incident, they could turn this office over to you boys, just like in Johnsonburg and Verona."

Lew gave a curt nod. "I'm going out to check on the K-9 teams. Talk to you later."

"What are you smirking at?" Frank asked as they listened to the front door of the Town Office slam. Earl quickly rearranged his expression as Frank continued. "Meyerson's a good cop. He's just a little too caught up with procedures—probably all that time he spent in the Marines. Estelle always said it was a good thing I pulled a high lottery number in the draft and never had to go to Vietnam. I probably would have been court-martialed for insubordination."

"What's that?"

Frank smiled. "Thinking you know more than your bosses."

"You don't have a boss here."

"That's where you're wrong, Earl. I have to answer to the whole damn town."

As Frank walked up the Harveys' back porch steps, through the screen door he could see Jack sitting at the kitchen table, a cup of coffee and an untouched donut before him. Unshaven and gray-faced, he had the look of a man who'd been kept awake by torturous pain. The only relief morning had brought was that he was no longer obliged to lie in bed.

Ardyth Munger and her sister-in-law, Grace, stood at the sink washing and drying dishes. Ceramic casseroles and foil-wrapped plates of all sizes covered the counter—the ladies of Trout Run responded to every crisis with an outpouring of lasagna, chicken divan, and oatmeal cookies.

Frank knocked on the door and walked in without waiting for an invitation. Jack brightened.

"Frank! What brings you out here? Have you heard something from the state police?

Frank shook his head.

"*You've* discovered a new clue?"

"No, sorry. I just wanted to fill you in on what we're doing." Frank pulled a chair up to the heavy old oak kitchen table and glanced up at Ardyth and Grace. "Would you ladies mind giving us a few minutes?"

"Of course, we were just finishing up. Grace, put that tuna noodle in the freezer. Jack, tell Dorothy to pop this lasagna in the oven for tonight—it just needs reheating. Or do you want me to tell her?" Ardyth asked.

"No, no. I'll remember. Thanks for coming." Jack rose shakily to accept an awkward hug from Grace. "Tell everyone I appreciate all the food."

"It's nothing. You let us know if there's anything you need, anything at all, you hear?"

The ladies left and Jack sat back down across from Frank. "Well?"

"The state police have checked the status of recently released sex offenders—there's no one in our area. Clyde's organizing volunteers to post fliers with Janelle's

picture. And her description has been circulated nation-
wide. Now we'll start interviewing Janelle's teachers,
friends—that sort of thing."

Jack's calloused hands tightened around his mug. "But
you already talked to her friends; what more do you need
to ask them?"

"We need to see if anything was going on in Janelle's
life. You know, figure out how she was thinking, who she
was involved with . . ."

"What's that supposed to mean? She wasn't 'involved'
with anyone."

"Many times, in cases like this, someone the victim
knows is mixed up in the disappearance. That's why I
have to take the time to really get to know your daughter."

Jack sat back in his chair and squinted at Frank
through red-rimmed eyes. "What in God's name are you
talking about, man? You think someone from Trout Run
kidnapped Janelle?"

Frank shook his head. "I just want you to understand
that we'd be falling down on the job if we didn't look into
the possibility that this could be a local thing."

Jack leaped up from the table, sending his chipped coffee mug into a slow roll. "The people in this town have
known Janelle since she was a baby—why, they've known
me since I was baby! Maybe where you come from, people
do terrible things to their neighbors, but not in Trout
Run!"

Frank watched Jack continue in a restless loop around
the sunny, old-fashioned kitchen. He felt as if he were
about to kick away a lame man's crutch, but he took a deep
breath and went on. "Jack, there's something bothering me
about the way Janelle seems to have walked over and put
the gas can behind that bush—almost like she was setting
it out of the way until she could come back and get it."

"She must've got tired. The can got too heavy for her, so she decided to walk home without it," Jack said.

"We found it only fifty yards beyond where Joan Haddon says she stopped to offer Janelle a ride. If she was energetic enough to turn down Joan's offer, she wouldn't have got so tired that she'd abandon the can in just fifty yards."

Jack opened his mouth as if to protest, but Frank didn't give him the chance. "She might have gone for a ride with someone she knew," he continued, "then intended to come back for the can and walk home. Now the question is, why wouldn't she just let that friend drive her home? I'm thinking it's because she knew it was someone you didn't approve of."

"Didn't approve of?" Jack sputtered. "There's no one she knew that I don't approve of! Janelle's friends are all the nicest kids. They play sports, they're in the church youth group. They have good clean fun together. Not like this crap you see on TV—drugs and guns and hanging around on street corners. You know there's nothing like that here in Trout Run. "

"I didn't say it had to be someone from Trout Run—I said it might be someone she knew. Maybe someone she met in Lake Placid or Plattsburgh."

"I didn't allow her to hang out there. She would just go to Placid or Plattsburgh to go shopping. She was always with her aunt or me—she was just learning to drive."

"Did she ever get any calls from someone you didn't recognize, or act cagey about where she was going?" Frank persisted.

"Are you suggesting that my daughter *lied* to me?" Color crept up Jack's neck and suffused his cheeks.

"Of course not. It's just that you can't expect a teenage girl to confide everything to her dad. My daughter certainly didn't," Frank answered.

Jack leaned across the table until his face was inches from Frank's. "I don't know how you brought up your girl," he growled. "But I brought up my daughter to tell the truth. Janelle is an angel. She never gave me one moment of trouble."

"We have to look at every angle, Jack." Frank found a sponge on the counter and began mopping the puddle of spilled coffee on the table as he talked. "If Janelle was really abducted by some maniac, then I gotta tell you, there's not much we can do." Frank hesitated, but pushed on. "Maybe weeks or months or years from now, some hiker or park ranger will find her body. To be honest, there's not much hope for Janelle if that's what you think happened."

"What the hell does that mean—you're just going to give up!"

Frank continued as if he hadn't been interrupted. "Crimes like that have no motive. Usually, the way we end up catching these serial killers is through some fluke. They get picked up for a traffic violation or something, and start boasting about what they've done." Frank's eyes hardened. "It's not a pleasant thought, but if someone from around here was involved in her disappearance, our chances of catching the person are a lot better than if this was just some random act."

Jack sat and stared ahead impassively.

Frank spoke quietly. "No one's blaming you, Jack. No one's saying you're a bad father, that you weren't watching out for her. I have to investigate it this way, whether you like it or not. It would just be easier with your support."

Jack let out a slight snort at this last remark. He remained silent for a long time, then finally said, almost inaudibly, "Go ahead and see what you can do."

"I'd like to start by looking at her bedroom again."

"You already did that on Saturday," Jack protested.

"Nothing's missing. All her clothes are there and the ten dollars her aunt gave her for her birthday is still in the card."

"I know that. I'm looking for something else."

"What?"

Frank shrugged. "I'll know it when I see it."

"All right." Jack led him down the hall to Janelle's room. "I haven't touched anything."

The room looked as if Janelle had just stepped out of it. Three stuffed animals stood guard on the twin bed. A poster of four surly young men dressed in black—some rock group, Frank presumed—adorned one wall. The bulletin board was a jumble of cartoons and funny buttons, award ribbons for cheerleading and 4-H, and photos. One showed a laughing group of teenagers on the ski slopes at Whiteface Mountain. Another showed Janelle in a long pink dress with a ruffle at the bottom, holding the arm of a tall, thin boy who looked distinctly uncomfortable in his suit: Craig Gadschaltz, her boyfriend.

Frank turned his attention to Janelle's desk. Posted on the wall where she would stare directly at it if she were sitting at the desk was a square of heavy white paper covered in elaborate black script.

"Isn't that beautiful?" Jack asked proudly. "Janelle was teaching herself calligraphy. She did that all herself."

Frank nodded and bent to read the text:

The scarlet letter was her passport into regions where other women dared not tread. Shame! Despair! Solitude! These had been her teachers—stern and wild ones—and they had made her strong, but taught her much amiss.

—Nathaniel Hawthorne,
The Scarlet Letter

Frank raised his eyebrows. It seemed like a somber sentiment for a happy seventeen-year-old. On the desk he found a stack of index cards covered in Janelle's round, even handwriting.

"Those are for a paper she's been writing for school. She spent a lot of time on it." Jack still referred to his daughter in a disconcerting mix of the present and past tense.

Next Frank examined the bookshelves. There he found a couple of current fashion magazines. He remembered their names from when Caroline was a teenager, but the stories advertised on the cover certainly seemed to have changed in ten years. "What's sexy now!" one headline proclaimed. "The Shattered Love Life of Gwyneth Paltrow." "Is Your Relationship Too Hot to Handle?" Frank picked the magazines up. Perhaps he should browse through them just to catch up on what young women were concerned about these days.

In contrast, Janelle's bookshelves were filled with reading material of a loftier nature. Janelle apparently had a compulsive streak, for the novels were arranged alphabetically by author. On the top of the waist-high bookcase, five books were set apart between brass bookends: *Tess of the D'Urbervilles*, *The Portrait of a Lady*, *Anna Karenina*, *The Scarlet Letter*, and *Middlemarch*. They meant nothing to him, and he wondered why Janelle had given them a place of honor.

Finally Frank took a perfunctory look through the drawers and closet. His earlier search had revealed no diaries or letters, and none of Janelle's clothes were missing. He turned to Jack. "I'd like to take the magazines, the note cards for the school report, and those five books there."

Jack shrugged, but didn't object. Following Frank out

of the house, he stood on the front porch. As Frank started up the car, Jack shouted something. "What was that?" Frank asked, sticking his head out the window.

"I said thanks."

Frank drove slowly up the rutted drive. He didn't know what to make of Jack's abrupt mood swings. The man seemed genuinely distraught by Janelle's disappearance, but then, Ricky Balsam's father had been genuinely distraught, too. Distraught because he'd known all along that his son was dead. Was Jack responsible in some way for whatever had happened to Janelle? Or did he just blame himself, as all parents do, for everything from cavities to car crashes? Frank's gut told him Jack was all right but his gut could no longer be trusted.

The bark of the radio interrupted his train of thought. "Trout Run One, give your location." The voice certainly did not belong to Doris. Despite repeated instructions on radio procedure, she always quavered, "Frank, Frank, can you hear me? Where are you?" It must be the state police dispatcher.

"Trout Run One. I'm on Baxter Road headed north, over."

"Meet Lieutenant Meyerson on Stony Brook Road. The K-9 team has found a body."

Frank's hands tightened on the wheel. So, it was to be a murder investigation after all.

4

FRANK ARRIVED MINUTES LATER to find Stony Brook Road mobbed with state police cars, dogs, and dog handlers. The center of activity seemed to be a stand of birches and low bushes directly down the hill from old man Lambert's house. To Frank's great annoyance, Earl had taken it upon himself to leave his post at the office and now stood making a great show of holding back a small group of local onlookers.

"What are you doing here?" Frank snapped. Pushing through the crowd with Earl trailing after him, he located Lew Meyerson standing next to a blue tarp. Frank watched Earl's eyes grow saucerlike as he registered what must be beneath the heavy plastic. Thank God the body was covered—he hadn't even given a thought to the fact that Earl had never been present at the discovery of a corpse before.

The trooper finished barking orders into a radio, then hung up as Frank and Earl approached. "Dogs were searching both sides of the road when they picked up a scent," Meyerson said. "Bit of a surprise that this was what they found."

Frank lifted the corner of the tarp and heard Earl gasp as Dell Lambert's eyes, sightless in death as they had been in life, looked up at them. Lambert's frail, pajama-clad body lay curled on the sloping ground, his head cocked at an angle that would have been natural only for an owl.

"When did he die?" Frank asked.

"I'd guess early this morning," said Meyerson. "Rigor's just beginning to set in. M.E. can't get here for another forty-five minutes, but I'd say he broke his neck. There's no blood."

"So he must've tumbled all the way down the hillside from the edge of his yard. I wonder what he was doing outside?" Frank said.

Only a small square of lawn surrounded the house; trees, shrubs, and ivy covered the rest of the steep property as it ran down to the road. Years ago, some large stones had been set into the hillside to make steps through this woodsy area. The body lay at the foot of them. Frank began to climb, nodding his head to Meyerson to follow. "You stay here, Earl," he said, and for once, Earl obeyed.

The slope was steep enough to make Frank's breath ragged by the time he reached the top, although he noticed with some irritation that Meyerson seemed unaffected. The last step, higher than the others, was part of a little retaining wall that had been built to extend and support the level lawn area.

"The old man must've stepped off this edge and just kept rolling down," Meyerson said.

"I don't like it, Lew," Frank replied. "What would he be doing out here alone, early in the morning, still in his pajamas?"

Meyerson shrugged. "He heard something. He wanted some fresh air. Old people all wake up early."

"But he knew the yard dropped off—that it would be dangerous for him," Frank objected.

"What are you getting at, Frank?" Meyerson sounded impatient. "Whatever the reason, he was out here and he tripped."

"Or . . ." Frank made a pushing motion with his hands.

"Oh, come on. Why would you think that?"

Both men turned to look down at Stony Brook Road. Even through the trees Frank could clearly see the meadow and the bush where Janelle had left her gas can. "A disappearance and a death in the same location less than twenty-four hours apart. I don't believe in coincidences like that."

"But you interviewed him yourself. He was blind and hard of hearing. He wasn't a witness to whatever happened to Janelle. Why look for trouble—you've got your hands full with this missing girl."

Frank turned and started walking toward Lambert's house. Meyerson might be right, but it couldn't hurt to stay open to all the possibilities. "What if whoever took Janelle noticed Lambert up here looking down at them, and came back and killed him?"

"I thought we were working on the assumption that Janelle went off with someone she knew, in which case, she'd have said that Lambert was blind and no threat."

Frank nodded, conceding the point.

"And why wait until the next morning to come back and kill him? You'd have to figure by now, he's already told the police anything he might know."

"Not necessarily. Whoever took Janelle wouldn't know when we first considered her disappearance suspicious, or who we talked to first." Frank reached out to open Lambert's front door. "Let's go in and look around."

The door opened into a hall that led straight back to the kitchen, bathroom, and two bedrooms. To the left was a sunny living/dining room, dominated by a huge picture window with a spectacular view of Stony Brook Road and the Verona Range beyond.

All the furniture hugged the walls, leaving a wide, clear path to the kitchen. No books, magazines, or newspapers filled the shelves. Instead, Lambert had a large boom box and a stack of books-on-tape. A small TV sat on one shelf—Frank had commented on it yesterday, and Mr. Lambert had cheerfully confessed to being a news junkie. "I got one of them dishes just so I can listen to CNN and those Sunday morning news shows," he had said. Well, he'd missed them today.

He caught a movement from the corner of his eye and spun around to face the window. A bevy of goldfinches had settled on a large bird feeder that hung outside. Had that been there yesterday? He couldn't recall, although he'd certainly looked out the window, checking the view of the road and meadow. Why would a blind man keep a bird feeder outside his window? A rectangular table with two deep drawers stood under the window. He opened the top drawer and pulled out a large pair of binoculars. Holding them to his eyes, he focused on the crowd of people still milling on the road. The ambulance was here now, loading the body. He could actually read the name tag on one trooper's uniform. Crouching down, he reached into the back of the drawer and pulled out a book—*Peterson's Guide to Eastern Birds*.

"Hey, Lew—what if our witness could see?"

Returning to the beehive of activity at the bottom of hill, Frank saw a slender woman struggling with a state trooper trying to keep her off the path leading up to the house. "It's all right, Pierson," Frank shouted, and Celia Lambert broke free and ran up to him.

"What happened? The neighbors called me. Where's my uncle?"

She looked at Frank through her stylishly shaggy bangs. Celia struck him as a little sharper than the average local girl, as if she'd been out in the world and chosen to come back.

"Your uncle had an accident," Frank said. "He seems to have stepped off that ledge at the edge of his yard and rolled down the hill."

Celia breathed in sharply. "Is he all right? He's not—"

She knew the answer to this. Frank knew she knew—they always did. But they always made you say it.

"I'm afraid he didn't make it. He may have, uh, broken his neck. I'm sorry."

Her large dark eyes stared at him, unblinking. Then the tears spilled over and she buried her head in her hands. "Oh, I should have come to see him this morning. If only I had, this wouldn't have happened."

Frank hated this. You never got used to doing it, no matter how many times you had to. At least it hadn't been a child or a husband, although Celia seemed pretty cut up about the old man. "Don't blame yourself. He probably went out right after he talked to you—he was still wearing his pajamas."

Still weeping softly she said, "He must've gone out to—" She stopped.

"Gone out to do what?" Frank asked.

Celia found some tissues in her purse and blew her nose. "To get some fresh air. He hated to stay in the house all day."

"Wouldn't he have gotten dressed first?" He was sure Celia had been about to say something quite different.

Celia smiled weakly. "My uncle is—was—a little eccentric. Sometimes he stayed in his pajamas all day."

Frank hesitated. He wasn't ready for everyone to know he suspected a link between Lambert's death and Janelle's disappearance. "Celia, was your uncle *totally* blind?"

"He could see light and dark, shadowy outlines. He was supposed to count his steps when he went outside. Never go more than twenty steps from the house." She began to weep again.

"Celia, I found a pair of very powerful binoculars in your uncle's house. Why would he have had them?"

Celia began to twist her tissue. "Where?" Was that fear he heard in her voice?

"In the drawer of the table under the window," Frank replied.

Celia's shoulders relaxed and she went back to mopping her eyes. "My uncle had always been a great bird-watcher, before he lost his sight. He still liked to know the birds were being fed. He liked to hear them out there—recognized all sorts of bird calls."

That still didn't explain the binoculars, but Frank let her ramble on.

"Whenever we'd go over there we'd tell him what birds were on his feeder. It gave us something to talk about. My brothers and I used the binoculars to scan the woods for big birds—hawks, flickers, owls. You could even see a blue heron down at Stony Creek with those things."

She sniffled. "I liked our visits. I'll miss him."

"I'm very sorry for your loss. Would you like me to drive you home? Earl's here—he could drive your car back."

Celia shook her head. "I'll be okay. Where did they take my uncle?"

"The medical examiner," Frank explained. "There will be an autopsy, then they'll release the body to you."

"Autopsy!" Again the flash of fear, or was he imagining it? "Why? I thought you said he broke his neck?"

"Just my guess. I'm not a doctor. The M.E. will be in touch."

Frank watched as Celia stumbled back to her car, turning twice to look back at her uncle's house.

Her explanation of the bird feeder made sense, and even the binoculars, but still, she had seemed jumpy. Why had she asked where he'd found the binoculars? If she was the one who used them, surely she knew where they were kept. And when he'd said the drawer, she had seemed relieved.

And the autopsy, why had she objected to that? Frank sighed. He was reaching too hard. Lots of people didn't like the idea of their loved ones' bodies being cut up. Perhaps the simplest explanation held true here. Perhaps Dell Lambert really was a blind old man who hadn't seen anything happen on Stony Brook Road, and who died when he lost count of the steps he'd taken from his door. Still, he intended to find out more about the nature of Lambert's blindness.

The crowd around Lambert's house had finally dispersed, and Frank and Earl prepared to leave. As Frank got in the patrol car he said, "Lew, have the forensic team go over this whole area, especially up at the top."

"Looking for . . . ?"

Frank didn't care for the tone of Meyerson's voice. A little snide, he thought. "Any sign that someone other than Lambert was up there this morning. And get someone to talk to the neighbors—see if they noticed anything."

"You want me to pull men off the search for the girl for that? Forget it!"

"It's related," Frank backpedaled. He had to remember he didn't have a staff anymore. Meyerson didn't work for him, he was helping him out. "Please."

"Frank, the neighbors didn't notice the girl disappear from the middle of the road in the middle of the day. What could they see up here at dawn?"

"All, right, all right. I'll get Earl to do it. But the forensics guys, please?"

Meyerson scowled. "Fine."

"Thanks, Lew. I'll catch up with you later."

"How did Lambert lose his sight?" Frank asked Earl as they drove back to the office.

"Mr. Lambert worked for years at Stevenson's Lumberyard. One day some kid operating a crane with a load of these twenty-foot pine beams swung it around too fast, and a beam hit Mr. Lambert in the head. He was in a coma for like, a week, and when he woke up he couldn't see."

"Even though his eyes themselves weren't hurt," Frank clarified.

"Yeah, 'cause the problem was in his brain or something."

"So then what?"

"It's been ten or twelve years—I was just a kid. I think Clyde said he'd give Mr. Lambert early retirement and some extra money to help him out, and Mr. Lambert was all set to do that, when somehow this lawyer got mixed up in it and he told Mr. Lambert to sue. In the end, Mr. Lambert got a whole pile of money and he bought that house. And some people said it wasn't right, but others said it all came from the insurance company so why not—"

They rounded a sharp bend, and a flash of red appeared on the side of the road. A little boy shot out of the hedges, directly into the path of the patrol car.

"Look out! That's Jeffrey Maguire!" Earl shouted.

Frank slammed on his brakes and swerved, missing the child by inches, and skidded to a stop.

The squeal of tires was loud enough to bring the boy's father, Mac, running down the driveway. Taking in the scene at a glance, he ran to his son, but as soon as he determined that the child was unhurt, set about doing his own damage.

"What's wrong with you?" he shouted, shaking the boy hard enough to make his head flop. "You know better than to run out in the road like that!"

"I thought I saw Benjamin." Jeffrey, about eight years old, pointed to a patch of tall weeds across the road and began to pull away from his father.

"It's not bad enough that rabbit's gone; do you think I want to lose you, too?"

Mac looked at Frank and explained, "Jeff woke up this morning to feed his new pet rabbit and the thing was gone. He must've left the damn hutch unlatched. That's why he's carrying on so much."

Jeffrey spun around and stomped his small sneakered foot on the pavement. "I did not leave his cage open!" he screamed.

"That bunny didn't just reach his paw out and open the door himself," Mac countered.

"I think someone stole him!"

Father and son had clearly been through this discussion before. Jeffrey took off into the scrub-covered empty lot across the street, calling "Benjamin" and peering under bushes.

"Well, good luck finding the little fellow," Frank said, putting the car in gear.

"At least Benjamin's only a rabbit. Jeffrey'll get over it

before long." Mac looked down the road toward town. "Not like Jack."

"Messages, Doris?" Frank demanded as they entered the office.

"Let's see. Oh, yes. Mrs. Gadschaltz called and asked could Craig come in to talk to you and Lew tomorrow instead of today, because he has to study for a big test he has tomorrow in math, or did she say Spanish? Anyway, she doesn't want him getting all upset before it. He's got to keep his grades up to stay on the baseball team. So I said tomorrow would be fine. I told her it's not that important, they're just wanting to talk to all Janelle's friends, not to worry ab—"

"Doris! I wish you'd let *me* decide what's important and what's not," Frank said. Doris had insisted on working on Sunday during this crisis, but if this was all the help she was going to be, he might just as well send her home.

"Well, excuse me. You're always telling me to just make a decision, so I do, and look at the thanks I get. I'll just call up Mrs. G. and tell her my boss says I overstepped my authority."

"Never mind. That's it for messages?"

"Yes, except Clyde was in here looking for you."

"Great," Frank muttered as Earl trailed him into the office.

"How come you didn't make Doris call Craig's mother back and make him come in today?" Earl asked. "You would've made *me* do it."

"Oh, for Christ's sake, Earl. The interesting thing is, why is Craig more worried about his Spanish test than his girlfriend? Isn't that a little odd?"

"You think Craig knows something he's not telling?"

"No!" Frank regretted his tendency to think aloud in front of Earl. "Look, you'd better get this straight right from the start. We're going to be following up on hundreds of leads, and ninety-nine percent of them aren't going to amount to anything. So I don't want you shootin' your mouth off that we suspect this or we suspect that. Everything we talk about in this office is strictly confidential, you understand?"

"You don't have to tell me that," Earl sulked.

Unable to bear Earl's presence after this dressing-down, Frank abruptly changed his tone.

"Say, I have an important job for you. Go over to Stony Brook Road and talk to the neighbors again. See if they saw anything going on at Lambert's house this morning. A car going in or out of the driveway, shouting, anyone walking along the road. Take down everything they tell you—don't judge what's important and what's not. I want to see everything, okay?"

Earl nodded. Frank could practically see the "why?" forming on his lips, but the boy bit it back. He was learning.

With Earl and Lew both gone and the phone mercifully silent, Frank finally had some time to collect his thoughts.

If whoever had been involved in Janelle's disappearance had really come back and pushed Dell Lambert down that hill, then it meant he wasn't afraid to kill. Janelle was in great danger, if she wasn't already dead. But people in town were hysterical enough already—he didn't want them to think there was a murderer in their midst until he was absolutely sure.

Who had Janelle ridden off with? Jack might believe that it wasn't anyone she knew, but fathers of teenage girls are all clueless. Her girlfriends—that's who he needed to talk to again. Janelle's two best friends, Kim Sorenson and Melanie Powers, had been scheduled to come in right after Craig. He hoped Doris hadn't taken it upon herself to reschedule them, too. Just as he reached for the phone to check, the intercom squawked. "Kim and Melanie are here," Doris announced.

He went to the outer office, where two girls stood, shifting their feet. Dressed almost identically in jeans and thin sweaters, they couldn't have been more unalike. A pixieish tomboy with short, dark hair, Kim had the physique of an Olympic gymnast, but certainly not the dazzling smile. Her frown seemed permanent, not inspired by the circumstances. Melanie, on the other hand, was the stuff of which X-rated cheerleader fantasy movies were made. There was something almost awe-inspiring in watching her impossibly high, round breasts straining against a sweater that, on Kim, was quite shapeless.

"Thanks for coming in, girls." Frank ushered them into his office. "Have a seat."

Kim stood behind one of the straight-backed visitor chairs, clutching it tightly. "We already told you everything on Saturday."

"I just need your help on a few more things."

Kim perched on the edge of her chair, as if it were hot. Melanie plopped down and looked around with unabashed curiosity at the drab little office with its institutional green walls and worn linoleum floor. "I've never been in here before. Cool—are those the wanted posters?" she asked, pointing to the bulletin board.

Frank smiled. "Yep. Any reason I should put your picture up there?"

"Nah, I'd be too nervous to rob a bank or anything. I'd probably—"

"What was it you wanted to ask us?" Kim interrupted.

Well, she's all business—the other one's the talker. He turned to Melanie. "It must've been hard for Janelle not to have a mom to confide in. Someone to talk to about boys, that sort of thing."

"I guess. Well, I mean, it was sad her mom died, but then, I don't really talk to my mom about boys, so . . ."

Melanie's voice trailed off and Kim jumped in to fill the void. "She got along great with her dad."

"What about Tommy? How did she get along with him?"

Melanie and Kim exchanged glances. "Tommy's a little weird," Melanie said. "But, you know, you could never say that to Janelle. Like sometimes she'd complain about him, but then, if you agreed, even, she'd get mad."

Frank crossed his legs and leaned back in his chair. "What sort of things did she complain about?"

Kim picked up on his interest and tried to quash it. "Nothing, just little stuff. You know how it is with families. I can call my brother a dork, but no one else better."

Frank nodded and turned the conversation back to Jack. "So even though Janelle and her father were close, she probably didn't tell him everything. Like maybe she had a friend who wasn't a school friend that she didn't want him to know about."

"Janelle didn't know anyone who would kidnap her," Kim said.

"That's not what I'm asking." Frank kept a patient smile on his face and focused his eyes on Melanie. "Did she have any friends other than school friends, someone a little older maybe, who she found interesting, someone who might, uh, influence her?"

"No, except for Pastor Bob," Melanie said with a gleeful giggle.

"Melanie!" Kim barked. "That's a horrible thing to say, and you know it."

"You mean Bob Rush at the Presbyterian church?" Frank asked.

"He's a very fine man," Kim answered hotly.

"I'll say," said Melanie with a leer. "Ver-r-ry fine. It's a shame such great looks are wasted on a minister."

"You know, just because you're an atheist doesn't give you the right to insult other people's religion, " Kim said, turning on her friend.

"I was just joking, really." Melanie turned to Frank, confusion etched on her good-natured face.

"How well did Janelle know Pastor Bob?" he asked.

"We were both in the youth group that he leads. That's all," Kim spat out. "Come on, Mel, let's go."

Frank watched through the window as the unlikely friends made their way across the green.

5

FRANK SURVEYED HIS PANTRY with satisfaction: cream of celery soup, tuna, egg noodles—all there. The milk and Velveeta were in the fridge. Though he didn't enjoy cooking or solitary dining, tonight he almost looked forward to spending an evening alone and going to bed early— although sleep was problematic.

He was about to start buzzing open the cans when the phone rang.

"Hello, Frank. I'm glad I caught you. It's Edwin." Edwin Bates and his wife, Lucy, were the first people Frank had met in Trout Run. They had left Manhattan to run the Iron Eagle Inn, a two-hundred-year-old farmhouse in a perpetual state of disrepair. Caroline had booked Frank into the Iron Eagle for the fishing trip in the Adirondacks she had planned to rejuvenate him after Estelle's death and the thinly disguised firing from his job in Kansas City. Left to his own devices, Frank would have stayed at the Trim 'n Tidy motel in Verona—real sportsmen did not stay in bed-and-breakfasts. But Caroline's insistence on overpriced quaintness had paid off in the long run.

Frank had been unable to resist giving Edwin advice on the restoration of the inn. And Edwin had persuaded Frank to apply for the police chief's job in Trout Run as an alternative to spending the rest of his life wallowing in self-pity.

They had nothing in common except that they'd both been thrown out of jobs that they loved—Edwin had been an English professor at NYU before he lost his tenure bid. Being an innkeeper had brought Edwin out of his funk, and with the fervor of a convert, he'd been determined to rescue Frank. An unlikely friendship had been born.

"We were wondering if you'd like to join us for dinner tonight. Are you free?" Edwin asked.

Frank's face lit up. "You caught me just in time."

A quick shave, a clean shirt, and Frank was on his way to the Iron Eagle. He got all the way out to the car when a thought occurred to him, and he doubled back to the house. Edwin could probably offer some insights on the books Janelle had been reading. He picked up the stack of five novels and the magazines and set off again for his dinner date.

Frank surveyed his plate with caution. It contained a piece of pink fish in a big puddle of green sauce, what appeared to be two withered brownies, and a heap of miniature purple and green vegetables that could have passed for refrigerator magnets.

"Poached salmon in a coulis of basil and yellow pepper, grilled buckwheat polenta with shitake mushrooms, and steamed baby eggplant and pattypan squash," Edwin announced with a flourish.

"It looks marvelous, darling," Lucy gushed.

"It certainly is colorful," Frank offered. He reminded

himself before picking up his fork that any meal eaten with friends had to be better than a meal eaten at home alone.

"Hey, this is good," Frank declared after two bites of salmon and a tentative stab at the polenta.

"You needn't sound so surprised," Edwin responded.

Frank grinned sheepishly and changed the subject. "I was over at the Harveys' house this afternoon and I brought back some books I found in Janelle's room. If you could give me an idea what they're about, it might help me get more of a feel for the kind of girl Janelle was. Is," he corrected himself.

This was met with silence. Suddenly Lucy and Edwin seemed inordinately preoccupied with eating.

"Edwin?" Frank prompted.

Edwin took a large swig of wine from his glass before answering. "Sure, anything I can do to help. But, you know, I was in the Store today and I overheard some talk."

"I know, I know. Everyone in town thinks I'm mishandling the case." With a show of unconcern, Frank speared a pattypan squash and popped it in his mouth whole. The effort of choking it down nearly brought tears to his eyes. "What were they saying?"

"Well, they seemed to think you should be focusing more on tracking down strangers seen in town."

Frank banged his water glass down, precipitating a shower of forsythia petals from Lucy's centerpiece. "Let me tell you about the strangers who were lurking in Trout Run yesterday. First, three people called to report a Peeping Tom looking in the windows of the Seavers' house—turns out it's Mr. Seaver's nephew, come over from Saranac Lake to help take down their storm windows. Then about fifty people called to report three black men—if you can imagine that—were seen having lunch at the Mountainside. Seems they're a group of investors from Boston thinking of opening a fast-food franchise outside of Lake Placid. Then—"

"Calm down. You asked what they said and I told you."

"I'm sorry. I guess this has me a little touchy."

"What's this I hear about Mr. Lambert falling—did he really die?" Lucy asked in an obvious bid to change the subject.

"I'm afraid so. Stepped off the edge of his little lawn area and tumbled down the hill." Frank had no intention of confiding his suspicions even to Lucy and Edwin.

Edwin shook his head. "Poor old guy. I used to run into him at the Feast and Fancy sometimes. What a character—he had an opinion on everything under the sun."

"The Feast and Fancy?" Frank said. "What's that?"

"Oh, sort of a cross between a health food store and a gourmet shop outside of Lake Placid. I get my French roast beans there, in bulk."

"And what was Lambert doing there?" Frank couldn't resist probing. "Was he alone?"

"No, of course not. Always with Celia."

When he got a free moment, he might go over there. The store was far enough away from Trout Run that the old man might have let his guard down about his vision in front of the clerks.

"So whatever happened with your taxes?" he asked instead. "Did you get an extension?"

"Yep, and I called in Bertha Calloway. Since the Stevensons got rid of her, she's being doing taxes for people. The way she figures it, we're getting seven hundred dollars back."

"Sounds too good to be true," Frank said. "Maybe Bertha can't handle such complicated work anymore. You know Clyde never gets rid of anything before it's totally worn out."

"Bertha knows the tax code like I know Dickens," Edwin said. "It wasn't Clyde who got rid of her. Ned computerized everything at the lumberyard when he joined the business. Since Bertha does all her calculating on an old adding machine, Ned said she had to go. I think that stinks."

"Oh, you can't blame Ned for wanting to modernize that place." Frank found himself in the unaccustomed position of defending one of the Stevensons. "Before Ned computerized the inventory, Clyde and Randall Bixley were the only ones who ever knew what was in stock and how much things cost."

"I suppose. But you know me, I like everything old and falling apart."

"Guess that explains why you like me," Frank said.

Afterward, in the parlor with coffee and triple fudge cake, Frank produced the stack of novels. "What would you say about a girl who was reading these books?"

"I'd say she was a pretty serious seventeen-year-old, especially for Trout Run. This is tough sledding for your average high-school senior. Especially *Portrait of a Lady*. Hell, I taught with people who wouldn't touch Henry James."

While Edwin was examining the books, Lucy had been leafing through the magazines. "Say, look at this!" she interrupted, shoving one of the magazines in front of Frank. "These fashion magazines always have quizzes. This one's called 'Is Your Relationship Too Hot to Handle?' and it looks like Janelle has circled some answers."

Frank picked up the magazine and held it at arm's

length, squinting. "Here, Lucy, you read it to me. I don't have my glasses."

"Okay. Question number one, 'What do you think is most important to a successful relationship: (a) great sex or (b) great conversation.' Janelle has circled (b).

"Two. 'What do you think is most important to your man: (a) great sex (b) great conversation.' Janelle has circled (a). Uh-oh, a little strife there."

"All that proves is she has a normal boyfriend," Edwin interjected.

"You men all stick together. Three. 'Do you ever feel pressured to keep up with you man's sexual desires?' God, who writes this stuff? The choices are 'always, sometimes, never' and Janelle has circled 'sometimes.'

"Four . . . this is the last one she's answered. 'If you could call a one-month moratorium on sex, what do you think would happen to your relationship: (a) it would improve (b) we'd break up.' And Janelle has circled (b). What do you think, Frank . . . is it significant?" Lucy asked.

"Oh for heaven's sake, all it proves is that her boyfriend was hornier than she was. Show me a teenage boy who doesn't fit that profile," Edwin objected.

"I didn't ask you, I asked Frank."

"I think it gives me some background to use when I talk to her boyfriend. But what about the books? What are they about?" Frank asked.

"About? About? They're what all great art is about—the human condition."

Lucy rolled her eyes. "Come on, Edwin, give Frank a break. He wants the Cliff Notes plot synopsis."

Edwin grimaced. "Oh, all right. "*Portrait of a Lady* is about an idealistic young heiress who's manipulated by her husband and his former lover. Anna Karenina is a woman who sacrifices everything for love then throws herself under a train when it doesn't work out. Dorothea in *Middlemarch* is another idealist who marries an old intellectual only to find out he's a fraud. Tess of the d'Urbervilles is a poor girl raped by a nobleman. And in the *Scarlet Letter*, Hester Prynne takes the fall when the holier-than-thou preacher knocks her up."

"Geez, there's as much sex in these classics as there is in the magazines," Frank said.

"Oh, nineteenth-century novels are brimming with it. It's just all right beneath the surface. What else is there to write about? Love and sex, greed and ambition, that's what all great novels boil down to."

Frank nodded. "That's more or less what's behind all crimes, too."

6

High Peaks Regional High School, a squat, red-brick legacy of a Depression-era work program, sent out buses for thirty miles in every direction to round up three hundred students to fill its classrooms. Its students were largely the children of 1970s alumni, and in twenty more years the desks would be filled by the sons and daughters of those who sat in them today.

Frank planned to spend Monday morning in the teachers' lounge, catching Janelle's instructors as they came in for coffee on their free periods. The project began without much promise—the only information Frank gleaned from Mr. Felson, the stern-faced trig teacher, was that Janelle would probably not excel at college-level calculus. Mr. Unckles, the history teacher unaffectionately known to his students as "Cry Uncle," nervously assured Frank that Janelle had never given him any trouble. The women who taught Janelle French and chemistry also insisted that they had not seen anything amiss with their student; had never noticed her talking to any strangers, young or old, male or female; had never suspected personal problems of any kind.

Frank paced restlessly around the stuffy little lounge. "Who else do we have left to see, Earl?"

"Mrs. Carlstadt. She had Janelle for American Studies— that's an advanced humanities elective," Earl said, clearly marveling that Janelle would have chosen to take this class rather than a study hall.

"Do you know where her classroom is? Let's go there."

In Mrs. Carlstadt's class, Frank sensed an encouraging atmosphere. The students pulled their desks into a circle, and Mrs. Carlstadt, petite and plump, sat among them. Her benign, rather rumpled appearance belied a keen perception as she skillfully wove threads of history, politics, and economics into a discussion of Steinbeck's *Grapes of Wrath*.

When the bell dispersed the kids, Frank said, "That's quite a class you run there."

"They're a great bunch of kids, but you didn't see them at their best. We're still in shock over Janelle." The teacher shook her head. "A *kidnapping*—I never thought I'd lose one of my kids that way."

"What kind of student was Janelle?" Frank sensed the possibility of tears and headed them off with practical questions.

"She cared passionately about the material we were covering this year. She was quite vocal in the class discussions—always leading us into deeper waters." Mrs. Carlstadt sighed and shook her head again. "Janelle was one of the finest minds I've encountered in ten years of teaching here."

No one else, not even her father, had spoken this glowingly of Janelle's intelligence. "Funny, this is the first time I've been given the impression that Janelle was so smart," Frank said.

A flash of annoyance crossed Mrs. Carlstadt's kindly face. "Janelle went to great lengths to hide it. It's very common with teenage girls. Their brains are at odds with their hormones—they're afraid they'll scare off all the boys if they come across as too smart. Luckily, there was no one Janelle was trying to impress—or perhaps I should say not impress—in this class, so she let herself go."

"Janelle's boyfriend, do you know him?" Frank asked.

Mrs. Carlstadt nodded. "Craig Gadschaltz. Nice kid. Decent student."

"But not in Janelle's league."

Mrs. Carlstadt ran her dainty fingers through her already disheveled hair as she attempted to explain. "Janelle wasn't considered one of the brains—there were other kids who had better averages. She just loved knowing things for the sake of knowing them. To my way of thinking, that made her an intellectual." Mrs. Carlstadt's eyebrows disappeared under her curly bangs. "Of course, there's not much room for *that* at High Peaks High School."

"So you think she kept that part of herself hidden most of the time so she'd fit in?" Earl piped up.

"Exactly."

Frank nodded slowly and gazed at the drab walls and tattered window shades of the classroom, apparently the only place in which Janelle had felt free to be herself. Janelle, who had been rather generic up to this point, began to take shape as someone more complex, a real person with ideas and dreams and fears of her own.

"I found some books in Janelle's room." He turned to a page in his notebook. "Was she reading these for your class?"

Mrs. Carlstadt barely glanced at the list; clearly she

knew the books Frank was referring to. "That's an example of Janelle when she was knocking herself out. We read *The Scarlet Letter* in class last semester and Janelle was so fascinated by the theme of—well, I guess you'd call it the woman betrayed—that she wanted to read other novels that dealt with the same issue. So I recommended some, and as she read them she would come and discuss them with me after school."

"Would you say those talks were . . ."—Frank searched for the right word— ". . . revealing . . . in any way?"

Mrs. Carlstadt rose from her seat and began packing books into a canvas tote bag as she thought about her answer. "Janelle was a very astute reader," the teacher replied eventually. "She was quick to pick out that in all these books, the heroines' lives are shaped by men—that their successes and failures are all controlled by the men in their lives."

Frank straightened up in his chair. "Don't you think that's kind of an unhealthy fascination?"

"I wouldn't call any student's interest in great nineteenth-century literature 'unhealthy,'" Mrs. Carlstadt said laughing. "She simply identified with the heroines. Show me any seventeen-year-old girl who doesn't feel stifled by her parents and paralyzed with love for her boyfriend."

"I suppose." Frank slumped back. "So did she ever confide in you any of her problems with her boyfriend? Could there have been another man in her life besides Craig?"

"I have no idea. We never talked about her love life. I think she liked to think that our relationship was loftier than all that."

Frank untangled himself from the student desk. "So if she were in trouble, she wouldn't necessarily have come to you?" he asked, stamping life back into his numb right leg. "She didn't think of you as a mother substitute?"

"Oh no, certainly not that. Although she did ask my advice about the problems she was having with her father about college."

Frank snapped to attention again. "What problem? All I keep hearing is how she and her dad were devoted to each other."

"I think they honestly were," Mrs. Carlstadt replied. "That's what made this disagreement so difficult for Janelle. You see, she wanted badly to go straight to the State University in Albany, but her father wanted her to go to Mount Marcy Community College for two years, and then transfer. He said he couldn't afford four years at SUNY, and he was adamant that she not take out any student loans to pay for her education.

"But if you ask me, I think he just couldn't bear to think of her leaving home so soon," the teacher said with conviction. "He saw community college as a two-year reprieve. But Janelle would have just withered there, stuck with a bunch of kids studying hotel management or wildlife preservation. She would have been bored and probably would have done badly. I was worried that she'd drop out and never finish college at all. I offered to speak to her father about it, but she said no. That it might make things worse."

Frank nodded. A father who wanted to keep his daughter close to home; a girl who wanted to stretch her wings—hardly a new story. But Jack hadn't seen fit to mention it. Was it because he considered it too trivial, or too significant? "When did all this happen?" he asked Mrs. Carlstadt.

"Let's see, it was the beginning of March, because that's when Janelle heard she'd been accepted at the State University."

"And did she mention it to you again—like in the week or two before she disappeared?"

"No, she seemed sort of resigned, so I assumed she had given in on going to community college."

"But she didn't tell you one way or the other? Didn't you ask?" Frank demanded.

Mrs. Carlstadt spoke emphatically. "No, I didn't ask. I figured it would just upset her to bring up something that she couldn't do anything about. When I first started teaching I was always rushing off on my white horse, trying to save one student or another. But I soon learned that you really can't do much to change the way parents choose to raise their kids. So now I make myself available to my students if they need me, but I try to stay out of the middle of their relationships with their parents."

Frank had wandered over to a bulletin board and was engrossed in the display entitled "Ordinary Americans Who Changed History." "What if you suspected a child was being abused?" he asked casually as he crouched to read the bio under Rosa Parks's picture.

"Well, that's a different story. Of course, then I would be obligated to intercede."

"But you didn't think that was the case with Janelle?" Frank continued, now absorbed by a photo of Woodward and Bernstein.

"Heavens no!" Mrs. Carlstadt jumped down from her seat on the table and marched across the room to confront her questioner. "Do you have any reason to think her father abused her?" she asked, drawing herself up to her full height, which still put her head level only to Frank's shirt pocket.

Amused by the teacher's terrier ferocity, Frank suppressed a smile. "I don't know what to think," he said with a gentle shrug. "Right now I'm just trying to figure out a good reason why Janelle should disappear. That's always a possibility."

Mrs. Carlstadt's tone grew frosty. "I have to tell you, I think you're barking up the wrong tree."

"Well, Mrs. Carlstadt, I've found that if you start off an investigation ruling out all the trees you're not going to bark up, pretty soon you're left with no trees at all. Thanks for all your help," he said as he shook the teacher's reluctantly offered hand. "We'll let you get back to work now. Come on, Earl."

In the silence of the empty school halls, Earl lowered his voice to a throaty stage whisper. "Why did you tell her you thought Mr. Harvey was abusing Janelle?"

"I didn't say I thought he was. I just said it was a possibility."

"What if she goes and tells Mr. Harvey that?"

"What if she does? I'll probably be able to tell quite a bit from the way he reacts to the news," Frank said.

Earl was still baffled. "I thought you liked Mr. Harvey?"

"There were people who liked the Boston Strangler. There were people who liked Ted Bundy. What the hell's that got to do with it?" Frank lashed out. There had certainly been lots of people who had liked Steve Balsam. Like all the people he'd worked with at his fancy corporate office. And all the people he'd ushered with at church. He'd been so likable, so respectable, just so damn *nice*, that he'd flown right under Frank's radar. That wouldn't happen again; he'd already had one of Meyerson's men check out the emergency room records at the small hospital in Elizabethtown and talk to the Harvey family doctor in Verona. Janelle had been exceptionally healthy, but that still didn't rule Jack out.

"You'd be surprised at the people I liked that I've arrested," Frank told Earl in a gentler tone.

Earl accepted this silently. "Where are we going now?"

"To get some lunch," Frank said as they arrived at the door of the cafeteria.

"Here?"

"Why not?" Frank grabbed a plastic tray and started sliding it along the metal rails in front of the steam tables.

They took a table in the far corner of the cafeteria and watched as, thirty seconds after the bell rang, a tidal wave of teenagers rushed through the doors. Earl picked at his turkey gingerly, but Frank made short work of his.

Before diving into a slab of cake encrusted with pink icing, Frank surveyed the room. He spotted Craig Gadschaltz at a table in the center of the cafeteria. Two boys and three girls sat with him as he received condolences—awkward punches in the arm or pats on the back—from a steady stream of students.

Earl saw Frank scanning the crowd and made a contribution. "There's Tommy over there at that table by the window." The table was empty except for Janelle's tall, lanky cousin. He ate steadily with his head lowered, as if to conserve the energy required to cover the distance from plate to mouth. His longish brown hair fell forward, practically dragging in the turkey gravy, and obscuring Frank's view of his face. As he and Earl watched, another boy, this one wearing headphones connected to a small tape player, came up to the table and sat down. Tommy lifted his head briefly—the extent of his greeting—but the other kid was no friendlier, and sat silently, bobbing his head to a beat only he could hear.

"Kind of funny that no one's going up to Tommy to

ask about Janelle, don't you think?" Frank asked. "And he wasn't in any of the search groups yesterday."

"He's kind of shy. I don't know him that well, but I don't think he hangs around with the same kids Janelle does," Earl explained. "Are we going to talk to her friends now?"

Frank looked again at the table of Janelle's friends and found Craig staring at him. Craig quickly dropped his eyes, and none of the others seemed aware of Frank's presence. "No, I think we'll wait and try to catch up with them after school. I don't want to make a big production out of this." He concentrated on systematically folding his paper napkin into smaller and smaller squares. "Who coached the cheerleading squad?" he suddenly asked.

"Huh?"

"The cheerleading squad. Janelle was a cheerleader, right? Who's the teacher in charge of that?"

"Oh. Miss Powell, I think."

"Let's go talk to her."

They found Miss Powell in a tiny, glass-walled office off the gymnasium. Upon being introduced, she grasped Frank's hand with a firmness that bordered on painful. Her palms were leathery and dry, but smooth. Not the kind of girl you'd get a kick out of holding hands with.

It soon became clear that Miss Powell considered cheerleading very serious business indeed. Her squad had been about to compete in the state championship and now Janelle's disappearance had knocked them out of the running. Her tone seemed to imply that she thought it very inconsiderate of Janelle to get herself abducted on the eve of this big event.

"She was the top of the pyramid," Miss Powell said.

"The what?"

"When we formed a pyramid, Janelle was at the top.

She was the lightest one. Aside from that, she was just an average athlete. In fact, she probably wouldn't have made the cut except for her sparkle. She used to have loads of sparkle, and the judges do look for that."

"Used to?" Frank noticed that people had begun speaking of Janelle as if she no longer existed, and he wondered if that's what Miss Powell was doing.

But she wasn't. "Janelle used to be brimming with enthusiasm when she cheered, but lately, it just wasn't there. I used to say to her, 'Janelle, we're here in the gym. Where are you?' Because she would just tune out. Go on autopilot."

"When did you first notice this?"

"Well, let's see. She was all right through football season. And even into the beginning of basketball. I think it was right after we lost that real close game in overtime to Lake George that she seemed to lose heart. We were all disappointed. There were only two games left after that, so I just let it slide. But she kept it up right into baseball season, so I had to speak to her about it."

"What did she say? Did she offer any explanation?" Frank asked.

"No. She just promised to do better. And at the games, she did. She seemed to be making a conscious effort. But like I said, at practice sometimes she just tuned out."

"And that didn't worry you? You didn't try to find out what was the matter?"

Miss Powell seemed to grow larger in her chair as she placed her hands flat on the desk and leaned forward to glare at Frank. Earl tried to shrink himself in his seat. "Mr. Bennett, I'm their coach. My job is to push them to be the best that they can be. I can't do that if I'm forever letting them cry on my shoulder about some silly fight they've had with their boyfriend, or some squabble they had with their parents about their prom dress."

Frank was conciliatory. "No, of course you can't. I understand. But if Janelle was worried about something, that could be significant."

Miss Powell studied him with narrowed eyes. "Why? The child was abducted. What do her petty little school problems have to do with that?"

"Maybe they weren't so petty." Frank was about to elaborate, but Miss Powell cut him off.

"Now you look here." She tapped her desk blotter with the whistle she wore around her neck. "You didn't hear it from me that there was something wrong with Janelle. All I said was that she was a little distracted. I'm sure it was only senior slump. You know they start looking forward to graduation so much that they lose interest in the here and now."

Frank offered her a tight little smile. "I suppose. Did you ever notice her talking to anyone at the games— maybe a guy who was a little older, someone not from around here?"

"Certainly not! I tell my girls cheerleading is a serious responsibility. There's no time for flirting or carrying on during a game."

"But afterward," Frank persisted. "Did you ever notice who she left with?"

"Her father, of course. He came to every game." Miss Powell stood up. "My next class is waiting for me," she said as she glanced out at a group of chattering girls sprawled on the gym floor.

"I won't keep you," Frank said. He turned back as he reached the door. "Just out of curiosity, do you still have the basketball schedule? When was the game against Lake George?"

Miss Powell rustled around in her desk and produced it. "January twenty-second. You really think that's important?" she asked, clearly wishing she had never mentioned Janelle's slump.

"Could be. When's the next home baseball game?"

"Today at four. Why?"

"Oh, Earl and I are great baseball fans. Maybe we'll see you there."

After leaving the high school, Frank sent Earl off to finish talking to Dell Lambert's neighbors while he answered a call from Carla Sweeney, who'd reported seeing a strange man lurking around her neighbor's house. The prowler turned out to be the neighbor himself, wearing a new hat and jacket as he checked the condition of his gutters. A waste of time, but he couldn't blame Carla. The whole town was jumpy.

Upon his return, Frank could hear Meyerson's distinctive staccato voice issuing commands before he even reached his inner office. Doris, clearly intimidated by the state police presence, sat with her back to Frank's open office door, pounding her keyboard with unusual speed. Frank suspected that the computer screen might reveal "The quick red fox jumped over the lazy brown dog," typed over and over again.

Meyerson hung up the phone and brandished some file folders at Frank by way of greeting. "Forensics reports. They found squat at Lambert's place. No fresh footprints. No fresh tire tracks. And the rain we had Saturday night would've washed away old ones. No pieces of fabric stuck on the bushes."

Frank detected a note of sarcasm in Meyerson's voice and he didn't appreciate it. Lew probably thought he was squandering state police resources, but he wouldn't be embarrassed into cutting corners. He would work on the assumption that nothing was as it appeared, until he had conclusive evidence showing him otherwise.

"Thank you, Lew," Frank said in a voice entirely without inflection, as he took the reports. He read them over, if for no other reason than to show Lew that he wasn't willing to accept his judgments unconditionally. "What about you, Earl?" Frank asked. "What did you learn from the neighbors?"

Flustered, Earl pulled a tattered notebook from his pocket and began to read, with some difficulty, from his own notes. "The Seiverts slept late—the sirens are what woke them up. Mr. and Mrs. Lanterman were asleep, but the kids were up watching cartoons." Earl paused. "I asked to speak with the kids, but Mrs. Lanterman said a bomb could go off while they're watching Scooby-Doo and they wouldn't hear it, so . . ."

Frank waved him on.

"Mr. Paulson woke up early and drove into Placid to get the *New York Times,* but he said he didn't pass another car until he was outside Trout Run. He didn't notice if Mr. Lambert's lights were on. And the Zwickles are still away," Earl concluded.

"Good work, Earl," Frank said and watched the tension drain out of Earl's face. Then he turned back to Meyerson. "What about the medical examiner's report?"

"Autopsy's today. We'll have it tomorrow." Meyerson then launched into a detailed recitation of every trail, field, and pond his searchers had covered, which Frank listened to while lost in his own thoughts. Janelle took a new shape in his mind's eye. The guileless face that stared out from all those posters the Stevensons made had been replaced by a Janelle who was a little sharper, a little sadder, a little more worldly.

• • •

Across the green from the Town Office, the Presbyterian church sat: a rectangular red brick building notable only for its huge parish hall, the only space in town big enough to hold a wedding reception, the volunteer fire department annual pancake breakfast, and the concerts put on by the Trout Run Independent Cultural Society.

So though Frank was not a member of the church, he'd been there many times, and he knew just where to find Bob Rush. Taking advantage of a brief lull, he popped across the green and entered the church through a side door. Disregarding a sign requesting visitors to announce themselves to the church secretary, he headed straight back the hallway, past the Sunday school classrooms, to a door marked simply, PASTOR BOB.

Frank tapped on the door, then marched in without waiting for an invitation. Bob Rush leaped from the easy chair where he had been reading, sending two books and a sheaf of papers scattering across the Oriental carpet on the floor. For a split second Frank saw a flicker of irritation cross the minister's face, but in an instant his features had composed themselves in an expression of welcome.

"Well, hello Frank. What brings you here today? Nothing serious, I hope?"

"Might be serious, might not. I was hoping you could take a minute to talk to me. Do you have the time right now?"

"I always have the time to serve this community, Frank," the minister answered earnestly.

Frank controlled the urge to roll his eyes. There was something he found irritating about this man. For one thing, he was better looking than any minister had a right to be. Six feet tall, broad-shouldered yet trim, Bob Rush had the look of an outstanding athlete. In his mid-thirties, his wavy brown hair showed no signs of gray or thinning, and his skin was rosy. But the most riveting thing about Bob Rush, everyone who met him agreed, were his eyes. Although startlingly blue, the usual adjectives "icy" or "piercing" did not apply—perhaps because the eyes were offset by long dark lashes, the likes of which no woman could ever hope to duplicate with makeup.

Whenever anyone spoke to him at length, Pastor Bob had a tendency to keep his eyes cast down, as if he were concentrating so hard he couldn't bear to catch sight of any distractions. Then, when he answered, his eyes would fly open and he'd fix you with those baby blues. Women seemed to find this disarming, but Frank thought it was all a bit much.

"I'm here about Janelle Harvey," Frank said, settling himself in a pretty but rather uncomfortable bentwood rocker. "Her friends said you were close. I was wondering, did she ever tell you that anything was bothering her?"

Pastor Bob focused his eyes on his folded hands, listening to Frank as if he were a priest hearing confession. Slowly he raised his head, fixed Frank with "The Look," and said, "She was a member of our youth group and she was a fine young woman."

Puzzled by this non sequitur, Frank tried again. For a man with a Yale degree hanging on the wall, Bob Rush seemed a little obtuse.

"Look, I know the buzz around town is that Janelle has been kidnapped by a stranger, so I suppose you probably think any problems she talked to you about aren't relevant. But I'm very sure there was something happening in her life, and that it might have a bearing on her disappearance. If I knew what it was, it might help me find her. Can you tell me if she confided in you?" Frank repeated.

Bob simply shook his head.

"She didn't, or you can't tell me?" Frank asked.

"As a minister, I cannot reveal the privileged confidences of my parishioners," Pastor Bob said, rising from his chair. He spoke down to Frank from his full height. "But I'm quite certain that nothing Janelle discussed with me has anything to do with her disappearance."

"Are you, now? Well, I wish I could be so confident. Without knowing what happened to Janelle, I kind of have a hard time saying for sure what's not important. You don't happen to know where she might be, do you?"

"There's no need to be sarcastic, Mr. Bennett."

Frank observed that Pastor Bob did a good job of appearing righteously miffed as he busied himself stacking his books neatly in a corner of his desk.

"Heck, Bob, I'm sorry." Frank struggled to match the minister's own earnest demeanor. "It's just that I'm so worried about that kid. She could be in danger. And her poor father is just heartsick, not knowing what's happened to her. What if betraying a confidence meant that we could bring Janelle back home safely and end her father's misery? What would you do then?"

"I'd pray to the Lord to guide me. Just as I pray every day that He will see fit to return her to us. But I assure you, there's nothing I can do to help."

Clearly, nothing was to be gained from gentle persuasion. As he rose to go, Frank took a parting jab. "Melanie Powers says Janelle had a crush on you. That wouldn't be what she confided in you, would it?"

The potshot hit like a bullet between the eyes. Bob's handsome face turned a blotchy red and his upper lip trembled. He summoned all his dignity to reply, but his voice came out half an octave higher than normal. "I would think, Mr. Bennett, that an experienced police officer would know better than to listen to the idle fantasies of a girl like Melanie. And now, you'll have to excuse me. I have a sermon to write."

Frank left without another word. He was beginning to feel that a girl like Melanie knew more than people gave her credit for.

"So, do you know these girls, Kim Sorenson and Melanie Powers?" Frank asked at four as he and Earl drove over to the baseball field to talk to Janelle's cheerleader friends again.

"Yeah, sort of. Kim's older brother was in my class, but he was a real jock." Which meant, Frank knew, that he would have had nothing to do with Earl. "And Melanie, well, everyone knows Melanie."

"Yeah, I bet."

When they arrived, the High Peaks team was down 5–0, and the cheerleaders were making a halfhearted attempt to get the twenty or so fans in the bleachers to show a little team spirit. There had been talk of canceling the game in light of Janelle's disappearance, but the teachers and coaches felt it would be best to keep the kids occupied.

Lithe Kim performed some effortless handsprings, but the show really belonged to Melanie. She just jumped up and down, shaking her pom-poms, and as she leaped into the air, her breasts fell; as she landed they rose, doing their own part to urge the team on to victory. Frank found his eyes drawn back to her with less than professional scrutiny.

A pop-up fly to right ended the game and Melanie's mesmerizing performance. Frank intercepted Kim and Melanie as they left the field.

"We already told you everything yesterday," Kim stated before he could even get a word out.

Frank smiled at her in a way that he hoped conveyed fatherly benevolence instead of the irritation he felt rising. She really was a suspicious, sour little thing.

"There's something else I needed to clarify with you," he explained.

"Sure," said Melanie.

"I have to go straight home," said Kim simultaneously.

Melanie turned on her. "Kim, he's trying to find Janelle. We've got to help him!"

Kim pressed her lips into a firm line of disapproval. "My mother said I wasn't to hang around after the game."

"Oh, for God's sake, Kim. He's a policeman. What, do you think *he's* going to kidnap us?"

Kim said nothing but the look on her face implied that she didn't think this out of the realm of possibility.

"Well, I'll stay," Melanie said.

Kim wavered. "I guess it would be okay if it's just a few minutes," she said finally.

"Do you remember the High Peaks–Lake George basketball game?" Frank asked. "Did you notice that Janelle was particularly moody or unhappy around that time?"

"We were all unhappy—we lost," said Kim.

"No, I mean even before the game."

Kim stared straight ahead in stony silence.

"That was around—" Melanie broke off in midsentence, stopped by her friend's ferocious glare.

"That was what?" Frank asked. "Melanie, if you know something you need to tell me, now."

Melanie looked from Kim to Frank, trying to size up who posed the greater threat.

Finally, positioning herself on the bleacher so she

wouldn't have to see Kim's stern disapproval, Melanie said, "I think that was around the time she broke up with Craig."

"Everyone's been telling me that Craig's her boyfriend— no one mentioned that they'd broken up." This was it, the opening he needed! If Craig wasn't in the picture, there must be another man.

"Only me and Kim knew," Melanie answered. "And Craig wouldn't accept it. He kept acting like they were still together."

"Why did she break up with him?"

"When we asked her, she just kept saying it wasn't working out. But the thing is, they never had a fight or anything before that."

"And you're absolutely sure there was no one else?"

"That's what made it so weird. By the end of senior year, everyone's all paired up. There's no one left but the geeks and dweebs."

Earl slouched down even farther than usual.

"How about someone not from school?" Frank persisted. "Someone she met in Lake Placid, maybe, or at the mall in Plattsburgh?"

Melanie and Kim kept shaking their heads. "When we go there we're always together. We go to the movies, we come home. We go shopping, we come home. There's no one to *meet* there," Kim said firmly.

Frank found that hard to believe. The sidewalks of Lake Placid were packed every weekend, winter, summer, and fall. "What about college boys who come to town for skiing or skating or bobsledding?" he prodded.

"They come with their own friends. They're not interested in us."

"Yeah. Unfortunately," Melanie agreed. "And the kids who go to Lake Placid High School and North Country

Academy are all so stuck up." Now Frank understood. The kids from Trout Run were at the bottom of the social ladder. The wrong shoes, the wrong jeans—all those things that meant so much when you were seventeen. So they kept to themselves.

"So there was no one not from around here that she ever talked to?" Frank asked.

"Well, there were those Butterheads," Melanie giggled.

Even Kim cracked a smile. "Not Butterheads, Bruderhof," she corrected.

"Bruderhof? What's that?" Frank asked.

"That goofy term paper she was writing . . ."

"On Utopian Religious Communities?" Frank remembered the note cards he'd taken from Janelle's room. He hadn't looked closely at them yet.

Melanie nodded. "Janelle saw these people one day when we were out by Stult's Farm. They were getting ready to hike up Mount Ursa. The girls were all wearing long skirts and these dorky scarves on their heads. Serious style crisis. And Janelle, like, recognized them."

"Not the people themselves," Kim said, taking over the story. "She recognized from the way they were dressed that they must be Bruderhof. You see them around here sometimes. They come together in a bus to go hiking. Anyway, Janelle had read about them for her term paper and she started talking to them. Asking them about their group, religion, whatever you want to call it."

"And what did they tell her?" Frank leaned forward as he listened to Kim. A religious cult—there was a possibility that had never occurred to him. They'd had some trouble with Moonies recruiting on college campuses in Kansas City, but that had been years ago.

Kim shrugged. "The girls were kinda shy, but one of

the men talked to her for a few minutes. I didn't listen to what they were saying. Then they went on their hike and we went home. That's it."

"So where are these people from?" Frank asked. "You said you'd seen them before."

Kim squirmed on the hard bleacher, clearly exasperated by all Frank's questions. "I don't know where they live—ask up at the Store. I've seen them in there."

"Did the man give Janelle any literature on their group? Did she—"

"What's all this got to do with who kidnapped Janelle, anyway?" Melanie interrupted.

"He doesn't think anyone *kidnapped* her," Kim snapped. "I heard him talking to Miss Powell at school. He thinks she ran away." She scowled at Frank, daring him to deny this.

Understanding crept slowly over Melanie's face, rearranging her features from curiosity to shock. "But Janelle wouldn't run away. If something was bothering her that much, she would have told us. Why do you think she ran away?" she asked Frank. When he didn't immediately answer, she turned to her friend, "Why does he think that?"

"Because he doesn't know how to catch the creep that kidnapped Janelle, so he's trying to make her look like a runaway. C'mon, Mel. I told you this would be a waste of time." And the two girls got up and left.

Frank could feel Earl's eyes drilling into his back, willing him to turn around and offer some explanation.

When none was forthcoming, Earl cleared his throat then plunged ahead. "Uh, you don't really think Janelle ran away, do you?"

Frank shrugged. "Something was going on with her, and then she disappeared. I'm not a big believer in coincidence. Now I find out she broke up with Craig, so there could be another guy in the picture. And then she knew these Bruderhof people—she could've gone off with them."

Earl dismissed this idea with a wave. "Nah, I've seen them around, too. They're not weird. I mean, they are weird, but not scary weird. They're like those people in that old Harrison Ford movie—whatsitcalled—*Witness*." Earl used a substantial portion of his salary to pay for a satellite dish and had become an expert on old movies.

"Well, we'll have to check them out," Frank said. "But even if they're a dead end, I keep coming back to that gas can. At first I thought this boyfriend, or whatever, just happened to drive by when Janelle was walking home and she sticks the can behind that bush so no one will bother it, and goes off for a spin. I figured she's expecting him to drop her back in the same spot to pick up the can and finish walking home. But he never does."

"Right."

"But what doesn't make sense to me is, why not take the can with her, and let the boyfriend drop her off at the top of her road, where it connects with Stony Brook Road. Jack still wouldn't be able to see her from there."

Earl shrugged. "Maybe she was afraid someone passing by on the road would notice them there."

"But all of Stony Brook Road is out in the open. The place where she left the can is just as noticeable as the top of the Harveys' road. No, it's starting to look to me like she left the can there because she knew she wasn't going to need it. Because she wasn't going back."

"But why put it behind the bush? Why not leave it right at the edge of the road?" Earl objected.

Frank didn't answer. That part puzzled him, too.

"And remember, she didn't have a penny in her

pocket," Earl continued. "No one would run away without any money."

"She *told* Al she didn't have any money. We don't know for sure."

"But if she lied to him, that would mean she planned it in advance."

Frank's eyes met Earl's and did not blink.

"Wait a minute! Janelle didn't know she was going to be walking to Al's. Her father didn't know he'd run out of gas. How could she make a plan to meet someone?"

Frank rose and began to walk across the muddy baseball field, his hands shoved in his pants pockets. "Janelle was a very smart girl. She could've realized that if she disappeared when she told her family she was going to visit a friend or something, that we'd be more likely to suspect she'd run away. But disappearing while you're on a spontaneous errand—that's a good plan." Even as he said the words, Frank wondered if Janelle were really that clever. It took more than intelligence to pull off a good con.

"But how did whoever she went off with know when and where to pick her up?" Earl persisted. "Jack said she didn't go into the house before she left, so she couldn't have called anyone in advance."

"I can't explain how she worked it yet," Frank replied, his voice a little louder than necessary. He wasn't confident himself in this theory, but he didn't appreciate Earl shooting holes in it. "Maybe the accomplice was watching her, just waiting for the right opportunity."

Earl hunched his shoulders, as if to ward off an expected blow. "You're skatin' on thin ice, Frank. Awful thin."

7

"COFFEE MADE YET?" Frank grumped by way of greeting Earl the next morning in the office. "I just can't wake up. I got involved in looking over Janelle's term paper notes last night—it looks like she did most of her research at the community college library. Then, I stayed up late reading that damn book."

"Which one?"

"*The Scarlet Letter*. It's not that long, but I dropped off to sleep before I made it to the end. Now I'm dying to know what happens to poor old Hester and that spineless preacher boyfriend of hers. I guess I'll have to wait 'til tonight to find out.

"So, what are those incident reports in front of you about? What do we have to do today?" Frank asked. Despite the frenzy caused by Janelle's disappearance, the citizens of Trout Run still expected their usual level of service from the police department.

"Oh, the principal at the elementary school called to say people are speeding in the school zone again."

"Okay, I tell you what we're going to do, Earl. How about you go over and park the patrol car behind that stand of trees near the school and catch yourself a few speeders, and I'll stop by the Harveys' and see Jack, then go over to Mount Marcy College to see what I can find out about the Bruderhof. I'll meet you back here after lunch, okay?"

Earl was clearly thrilled—running the speed trap was his favorite assignment. He set off immediately with Frank's warning echoing after him. "Don't get carried away, Earl. Four or five tickets ought to get the message out."

Frank was about to follow Earl out the door when the buzz of his intercom brought him back to his desk.

"Frank? Craig Gadschaltz is here with his mother. Do you want to talk to him now?"

"Yes. I'll be right out."

"Hi there, Craig, " Frank greeted the boy. "Thanks for dropping him off," he said to Mrs. Gadschaltz. "I'll see that he gets over to school after we talk—why don't you just have a seat in my office there, Craig."

Craig's mother, a bosomy, square-bottomed woman in jeans and a sweatshirt, interposed herself between her son and the office door. "You can't talk to him without me being there. I know my rights!"

Frank mustered his best look of astonishment. "He's not being *interrogated*. I hope I didn't give you that impression. It's just a few more things have come up since we first talked to him the day Janelle disappeared, and I need some clarification. But you're welcome to stay if you think he needs your help."

As Frank expected, Craig immediately said, "Go ahead, Mom. You better get to work. I'll be fine."

Mrs. Gadschaltz took one faltering step backward.

"He won't miss more than half an hour of school," Frank reassured the reluctant mother.

"He better not." She glared up at him, years of hard work and worry about money and family shining fiercely in her eyes. "He's up for a baseball scholarship. He needs to keep his grades up and play good when the scouts come around. I won't let the trouble with this girl ruin it for him."

Frank patted her on the shoulder. "No, of course not," he said as he propelled her out the door.

"All right, Craig," Frank boomed, closing his office door behind him, "this won't be any worse than sitting through Cry Uncle's history class."

But his show of good cheer did nothing to put Craig at ease. The young man dropped his gaze to the clenched hands in his lap. His mouth opened, but no sound came out. Craig was absolutely unremarkable looking. Light brown hair, pale blue eyes, clear skin marked only by a rosy flush beneath the cheekbones. Frank supposed that teenage girls must consider Craig handsome, mainly because he had none of the common flaws of adolescence. No big nose, jug ears, or zits—just a simple face that had not yet been marked by life. Not, at least, until now.

Frank leaned across the desk in an effort to get low enough to meet Craig's downcast eyes. "I know you want to talk to me about Janelle," he said softly. "I've been wanting to talk to you, too. I thought maybe together we could get some ideas about what happened to her."

"You don't think she was kidnapped, do you?" Craig asked.

"Let's just say I don't think a stranger snatched her off the street."

Craig sighed, as if he found this to be discouraging news. "Neither do I."

"Why not?" Frank tried to keep the eagerness out of

his voice. This was the first time anyone he'd talked to had agreed with him.

"Janelle had been acting weird."

Frank waited, but to no avail.

"Weird in what way?" he finally prompted.

Craig shrugged.

"When did you first notice she was acting different?'

"The middle of January," Craig answered unhesitatingly.

"Right after the basketball game with Lake George?" Frank asked.

"Yeah, how did you know?" Craig straightened up and looked at Frank with new interest.

"Miss Powell said Janelle seemed to lose her enthusiasm for cheerleading right around then."

Craig nodded, as if this made sense, but volunteered nothing further. Either the kid was intentionally obstructionist, or he simply belonged to the class of male who would remain forever baffled by emotions. Women would be a mystery to him throughout his life, and even his own feelings would be so foreign to him that he wouldn't recognize them unless someone else gave them a name.

"Do you know why? I understand the two of you broke up around that time," Frank probed.

"I didn't break up with her. She broke up with me. I still loved her!" Craig set the record straight with surprising force. Having apparently startled himself, he slumped down in his chair again and began scuffing the heel of his sneaker against the worn brown linoleum.

"Do you know why she wanted to call things off?"

Craig focused his eyes on a crack in the office wall above Frank's head. Again, his mouth opened soundlessly.

Frank's usual method with recalcitrant suspects was

to let the silence hang heavy in the air until the person being interrogated couldn't stand it and started talking. But Craig clearly had a high tolerance for silence. The kid needed an occasional explosive charge to move the discussion along.

"Were you and Janelle sleeping together?"

"Who told you that?" Craig demanded.

"No one. It's my job to put two and two together."

Craig seemed relieved by this. "We never really did it. We were going to, but we didn't," he muttered into his shirt collar.

"What do you mean you never *really* did it?" Frank dropped his paternal air. The sex quiz that Janelle had filled in had been in the December issue of the magazine. Had she been thinking of Craig when she answered those questions, or some other man? He might as well play it as if it had been Craig and see where that led. "I have reason to believe Janelle felt pressured by your sexual demands."

Color consumed Craig's entire face. "Demands! I didn't make any demands. She wanted to as much as I did, but then . . ." Craig stopped.

"Why don't you tell me what happened," Frank suggested softly.

"We were at Janelle's house. No one was home. But then she thought she heard something. She was afraid it might be Tommy. It was nothing. But then we were, you know, too nervous."

"Tommy? I would think she'd be more worried about being caught by her father."

Craig shrugged. "I guess she knew her dad was definitely out. Besides, Tom's a little crazy. He doesn't like me much. Not since Janelle and I have been going together."

"But before then, you were friends?" Frank asked.

"Kind of. We were in Boy Scouts together for a lotta years."

Frank brought the conversation back to Janelle.

"So you think this incident upset her enough to break up with you? When did it happen?"

"Before Christmas. I told her it didn't matter," Craig continued pleadingly. "I told her we never had to do it again."

Fishing for a reaction, Frank let out a snort of disbelief. "That's not the impression I got."

"Got from who?" Craig's teenage baritone shot into soprano range. "It was Melanie wasn't it? She just assumes that everyone screws around as much as she does." Craig met Frank's eye squarely. "It's not like I forced her. I didn't."

"But still, she insisted on breaking up?" Frank asked.

Craig nodded. "She claimed it wasn't that, but she wouldn't say if there was anything else. Then she'd start crying and I thought she'd change her mind, but she didn't. Finally she just stopped talking to me. Wouldn't take my calls, walked right past me in the halls at school. I couldn't believe it. It just wasn't her." Craig's voice trailed off and he looked like he might start to cry right there.

Frank stood up and walked over to the window to give Craig a minute to compose himself. With his back still turned he asked, "Were you two using any, uh, protection, the night you were together?"

"I told you, we didn't actually do it," Craig answered.

Now it was Frank's turn to squirm in embarrassment. "You know, Craig, you don't actually have to penetrate— get all the way inside a girl—to get her pregnant. Even if you're interrupted, there could be enough semen present to get her pregnant."

Craig was shocked. "No way! You think she ran away 'cause I got her pregnant! No way, man. No way!" He jumped up from his chair and headed for the door. Before he left he paused and shouted over his shoulder. "You're wrong!"

The office door vibrated with the slam Craig gave it on his way out. Frank regarded it without satisfaction. He imagined Craig driving along Stony Brook Road; seeing Janelle and pulling over; begging her to get in the car with him so that they could talk things over. The picture was clear up to this point. Then what? Craig drives the car to some quiet spot; Janelle tells him she's pregnant and her father insists they get married; Craig sees his future going down the drain. And he strangles her with his bare hands? Hides the body so well it hasn't turned up in four days of searching? Frank shook his head. Did young men kill for that reason in this day and age? It seemed to him they just walked away from their responsibilities without a backward glance. And even if Craig were passionate enough to kill, was he clever enough to conceal it for long?

The need to talk to Jack Harvey was more pressing now. He called, but the phone rolled over to an answering machine on the fourth ring. Hanging up, Frank decided to drive over to the Harvey house anyway. Perhaps Jack would have returned by the time he got there.

County road 518, in the stretch between Birch Lane and the unnamed drive that led to the Harveys', contained one of the most impressive vistas in all the Adirondack Park. Right after Birch Lane, the road took a sudden veer to the right and climbed sharply. Upon cresting the hill, the entire expanse of the broad, shallow valley was suddenly visible, and at the far side of the valley, five of the High Peaks stood shoulder to shoulder.

Frank couldn't help but pause every time he came to that spot in the road—he view was different every time. On a sunny day like this one, the mountains were so big and close it seemed you could reach out the car window and touch them. But on misty days you could barely discern the outline of each peak, and they seemed as remote and mysterious as mountains in Tibet. The mountains changed the weather patterns, so often you'd see an expanse of azure sky behind them, while black clouds between you and them dropped rain on the road you were about to drive over. Today the mountains looked benign, as if they harbored no secrets and wouldn't harm a soul, but Frank knew it wasn't so.

He let the truck pick up speed as it coasted down the hill, and raised a considerable racket as he rattled down the Harveys' drive. Bounding from the truck, he proceeded to pound loudly on the door.

Harvey didn't answer Frank's knock, but as Frank turned to leave the front porch, he saw Jack's sister approaching along the drive that continued back behind the house. He gave her a big wave and shouted, "Hi, Dorothy, I just stopped by to talk to Jack for a minute."

She nodded, and the furrow of concern etched permanently in her forehead grew deeper. "Jack's not home. Is there some news on Janelle?" When Frank shook his head, Dorothy's lip trembled and he thought she might start to cry. "I just feel so helpless." She shrugged her shoulders. "I wander around all day not knowing what to do with myself."

Frank put his hand on Dorothy's shoulder but said nothing. His supply of reassuring platitudes had just about run dry.

Dorothy slipped away from his touch. "Jack went to help the volunteers up at the flower shop. You could catch him there."

He was just as glad that Jack was not home—it gave him a chance to size up this woman whom everyone considered fortunate to be a widow. "Say, could I ask a favor? Could I just use your bathroom before I take off?" Frank asked.

"Oh, sure," Dorothy hesitated. "If you have to."

They walked toward the small house that sat behind Jack's. A one-story rectangle, punctuated at regular intervals by square, double-hung windows, the house had been built by an able, albeit unimaginative, carpenter. The front door opened directly into the living room, and as Frank stepped into the house, the reason for Dorothy's reluctant hospitality became apparent. Tommy was sprawled across a brown vinyl recliner, engrossed by the antics of some game show contestants on the blaring TV.

"Tommy's, uh, home sick from school today. This bug has been going around . . ." Dorothy's explanation trailed off. Clearly Tommy was perfectly healthy, unless chronic sullenness could be considered a medical malady.

"Hi, Tom," Frank bellowed over the TV, but Tommy merely lifted his gaze momentarily and gave an imperceptible nod.

"The bathroom's this way," Dorothy said, hurriedly steering Frank to a hallway at the far end of the room.

Dorothy disappeared into the kitchen and Frank headed toward the bathroom at the end of the hall. On the way, he unashamedly stared into the two bedrooms that opened off the hallway. One contained a neatly made double bed with a faded flowered bedspread. Above the plain pine dresser was a large mirror with a discolored streak. Clearly this was Dorothy's room, although it bore none of the more obvious signs of feminine habitation.

Across the hall was a door with an orange DANGER—KEEP OUT road sign hung on it. The door was partially open and in the dim light that penetrated the partially drawn curtains he could make out the usual astonishing clutter of a teenage boy's bedroom. From the posters on the wall, it seemed that Tommy's interests were divided between cars and martial arts. Two room fresheners gave off a pine scent that could not mask a strong chemical odor. He opened some drawers, looking for airplane glue or spray cans, and soon found both. So, Tommy huffed—a great way to kill off whatever limited quantity of brain cells he'd been born with.

Frank ducked out of Tommy's room and went into the bathroom, where he flushed the toilet, ran some water, and popped back out again. In a few moments he had parked himself at Dorothy's kitchen table and was inquiring about the possibility of coffee.

Dorothy clearly didn't know what to make of Frank but she was not a woman accustomed to giving a man an argument, so she obediently set about filling the percolator. Frank watched her as she worked: she had the kind of even, delicate features that can make a woman either quite plain or quite beautiful. The Dorothy of today fell squarely into the former category, but Frank imagined that she could have been very pretty once. Just how long ago that would have been, was hard to judge.

Dorothy was curiously ageless. Hair of no particular color—not blond, not brown, not gray—lay in aimless waves that stopped around her chin. She was thin, but more haggard than lithe. Still, Frank noticed, she was not flat-chested. There was a figure there somewhere, although she made no effort to display it. Frank watched her hands as she measured the coffee. The nails were bitten to the quick, but there were none of the knotty veins that gave away the age of even the most well-cared-for women.

Frank guessed that she was perhaps thirty-eight—maybe twelve years older than his Caroline. But what a world of difference! Caroline seemed to him—even with a husband and kids—to be the perpetual teenager. Always bouncing around, full of ideas and laughter. Always sporting a new haircut and some outlandish new outfit. In a hundred years, Caroline would not look like Dorothy did today.

"So, Dorothy, you've lived in Trout Run all your life, I bet," Frank said to get the conversation going.

"Oh yes. So did my parents and grandparents. Harveys have lived on this land for one hundred and twenty years," Dorothy told him, her voice revealing a little animation for the first time.

"Well, this sure is a pretty spot," Frank said as he looked through Dorothy's kitchen window at the meadows that ran away from the house until they hit the Verona Range. "You think Tommy and Janelle will want to keep the land in the family for another generation?"

Dorothy looked at him curiously. "What do you mean?"

"Oh, you know how hard it is to hold kids back today. They want to get away and see the wide world."

Dorothy shrugged. "Tommy likes it fine right here in Trout Run."

"What about Janelle?" Frank pressed. "Did she ever express an interest in going somewhere else to live someday?"

Dorothy's expressionless face seemed to close down even more, if that were possible. "No, she didn't. She loved her home and her family. Why would she want to move away?"

"Her teacher, Mrs. Carlstadt, mentioned that Janelle wanted to go to the State University at Albany, and that Jack didn't want her to go. Did Janelle ever talk to you about that?"

Dorothy looked genuinely surprised. "No, no she didn't."

"What about this disagreement she was having with Craig Gadschaltz; do you know what was going on there?"

Dorothy began rooting around in a drawer, her soft voice drowned out by clattering silverware.

"What?"

"I said, I don't know anything about any disagreement."

"But wouldn't she have come to you with a problem like that?" Frank persisted. "I mean with her mom being dead, she must have turned to you for advice. Clothes, boys, you know, girl talk."

Dorothy did not return the smile. Instead she gave a deep sigh. "I don't think my brother encouraged her to talk to me about things like that. I'm not exactly the best—whaddayacallit—role model when it comes to romance."

Dorothy dropped into the battered chair across from Frank and spoke while biting a hangnail. "Janelle would come over and visit with me. She could talk up a blue streak when she wanted to. But I got the feeling that she was never telling me the important stuff. Lots of times she would want me to talk. She'd say, 'Tell me about my mother.' She was so young when Rosemary died. I think she was forgetting her. So I'd tell her stories about when her father and mother were going together. How they

were the best-looking couple in school. That was a real
love story—Jack and Rosemary." Dorothy's face relaxed,
and for a moment Frank could see the shadow of a pretty
young girl. Then the pain seemed to snap back into place
and the beauty was extinguished. "There are so many
miserable marriages. Why God had to step in and break
up such a happy one, I'll never know."

Talking to Dorothy, Frank understood why Janelle
didn't confide in her. To unburden yourself on a woman
who carried so much sorrow inside her would be cruel
indeed, and Janelle, from all accounts, was not an unkind
girl.

"Well, Dorothy, thanks very much for the coffee. I
won't hold you up any longer."

He stood up from the kitchen table. "If you could just
mention to Jack that I came by—I'll try to catch up with
him later."

As he passed back through the living room, he saw
Tommy still rooted in his chair. Frank paused and
crouched down beside the TV, putting himself in
Tommy's line of vision. "You don't mind if I turn this off
for a minute so I can ask you a few questions?"

Tommy's glance implied that he minded very much
that he would now not know whether Joel or Charlene
would win the $10,000, but Frank snapped off the TV
anyway. "Tommy, did Janelle ever mention to you where
she wanted to go to college?"

The young man shrugged, but said nothing, apparently
thinking that this was an eloquent enough answer. It was
hard to say if he was intentionally avoiding Frank's eye,
because his own were hidden beneath long dark bangs.
Lean but strong-looking, he had incongruously big hands
and feet, like a puppy that promised to grow into a very
large dog.

Frank did not like disrespect from young people and was not used to getting it. When he repeated his question, his voice had an edge that made Tommy straighten up a bit in his chair and find his voice.

"No, we never talked about that," he said.

"What did you talk about?"

Tommy shrugged again, then realized that this would not be an adequate response. "School, sometimes. But we didn't really hang with the same people."

"Did she ever talk to you about Craig Gadschaltz?" Frank could not be sure if he imagined it, but Tommy's eyes seemed to shift and his hands grew restless at the mention of the other boy.

"No, I mean I know they went out, but she didn't talk about him to me."

Clearly, Tommy didn't intend to volunteer one iota of information. "You know, Tom," Frank leaned closer to the boy, "a few people have mentioned that you don't seem all that upset about what's happened to your cousin."

Tommy sat up straight. Finally, some show of emotion. "People should mind their own business," he said through clenched teeth. "You don't have to be crying and carrying on to be upset. Everyone wantin' to act like big heroes, going off in those search parties. They ain't going to find her like that."

Frank happened to agree, but he wondered why Tommy thought so. "Why not?"

"Because they're far away from here by now. No point in sticking around."

The flat certainty in his voice disturbed Frank. "Tommy, do you know who has Janelle?"

"How would I know? I'm just saying, you watch *America's Most Wanted* and shows like that, you know these guys always take off. They don't hang around close by."

Tommy slumped back, as if all this communication had exhausted him.

"Okay. It's been good talking to you, Tommy." Before he was out the door, Frank heard the TV come on again.

On his way to the flower shop, Frank reviewed his encounter with Dorothy and Tommy Pettigrew. If she was better off now than when her husband was alive, it was hard to imagine how bad she must have looked then. And Tommy seemed to have accepted the premise that Janelle had been kidnapped. Was it wrong to assume he didn't care because he appeared so remote and sullen? Between the glue fumes and the TV, his mind was shot—maybe he'd lost the ability to express emotion. But, as Estelle had often pointed out to him, he was a pessimist.

8

As Frank pushed open the door to the old flower shop, the buzz of conversation abruptly stopped and the six women gathered around a folding table turned their heads toward him in one motion, like a flock of birds following some imperceptible signal.

"Good morning, ladies. I'm looking for Jack Harvey—his sister said he might be here." As he spoke, Frank scanned the room for Clyde Stevenson, but mercifully, his nemesis seemed to have abdicated leadership of the volunteers to his wife.

With her no-nonsense Dutch boy haircut and broad shoulders, Elinor Stevenson did not exactly project an air of feminine compliance, but she was still preferable to Clyde. "You just missed him. Why? Is there some news?" she asked.

"No, no. I just wanted to ask him something."

"About what?" Elinor demanded, with no pretense of subtlety.

Frank was spared having to refuse to answer her when Laureen Nicholls, sitting closest to the window, announced, "Here comes Ned with the rest of the flyers."

Frank opened the door and Ned staggered in, carrying a large box, which he dropped on the table in front of his mother. "The printer ran out of the yellow paper the other flyers were printed on, so these are different." Ned held up a sheet of sickly green paper, from which poor Janelle stared out bravely.

"Oh Ned! They're dreadful! Why did you agree to this?" Elinor wailed.

"Mom, he's printing them for free. I can't argue about what he gives us."

"I just can't do everything myself. I can't! But look what happens when I trust someone else." Elinor leapt up from the table, tears streaming down her face, and ran to the little office at the back of the store, where she could be heard weeping.

The volunteers exchanged looks of surprise, then everyone turned to Ned, expecting some explanation.

"Sorry about that. It's just that it's the twenty-first."

"Ah," some of the ladies said, and they all turned back to folding and stuffing flyers as if nothing had happened. Frank found this even more astonishing than Elinor's outburst.

"What's the twenty-first?" he asked Ned.

"Today."

"Yeah, and . . . ?"

"She's always a little touchy on the twenty-first of every month."

For a horrified moment, Frank thought Ned was confiding the timetable of his mother's menstrual cycle, but surely Elinor was past all that.

Seeing his confusion, Laureen piped up, "The twenty-first is the anniversary of when her little dog Leo had his accident."

Frank was beginning to feel like he was in a surreal

dream. Could it be that Elinor broke down because her dog had peed on the carpet on the twenty-first? "What accident?"

"You surely must be the only person between Albany and Plattsburgh to not know about Leo's accident." Charlotte Venable said this quite neutrally, but Frank knew her to be a sensible woman and reassured himself that she intended some irony.

Ned, however, was clearly racking up this gap in knowledge as an example of Frank's gross incompetence. "You must have noticed my mother's little dog, Leo, in the store of the lumberyard. He came to work with her every day for twelve years."

Frank recalled the creature now—an irritating, yipping little dog who was invariably underfoot when you were looking for something on the shelves. Now that he thought about it, he hadn't encountered Leo lately. "What happened?" he asked.

"For some reason Leo wandered out of the store, which he'd never done before, and he got into shed number four," Ned explained. "One of the men found him out there. A stack of two-by-fours had fallen on him."

"Mmm, a lumberyard's a dangerous place," Frank murmured, in the closest approximation to sympathy he could muster. While Ned had been talking, Frank heard Sylvia Hansen answering the phone, and it sounded like Clyde was on his way. He had no desire to be caught here discussing Leo's demise when the old man arrived. "Well, I'll be in the office for a while," Frank announced to the room at large. "If you see Jack, send him over."

Frank walked into the office to find Earl regaling Doris with his tales of glory in running the speed trap.

"You should have seen the look on Millie Hartmann's

face when I gave her that ticket. Forty-seven in a twenty-five zone—that's a sixty-dollar fine."

"You might have just written her up for thirty-nine in a twenty-five—that would have made the fine only thirty-five dollars," Frank reminded him.

Earl was shocked. "But she was going forty-seven—I had her on the radar!"

"For Christ's sake, Earl, she's the principal's sister. There'll be hell to pay for this tomorrow."

"Well, he shouldn't ask to run a speed trap in front of his school if there's certain people he wants to let go as fast as they please," Earl sniffed. It was not often that he occupied the moral high ground in a discussion with Frank, and he was enjoying the view.

Earl's lecture on justice for all was interrupted as Jack Harvey burst through the door.

"I was picking up my mail and they told me you were looking for me. What's up?" Jack asked with pathetic eagerness.

"I haven't come up with anything concrete yet, Jack," Frank answered. "I just wanted to ask you about some things I've found out about Janelle."

The father's face contorted as he slammed his body into the already wobbly wooden chair across from Frank's desk. "Why are you wasting your time investigating my girl? Why aren't you looking for who took her?" Jack's voice was loud enough to bring Doris's typing to a halt.

Frank walked across the office and shut the door. "Jack, we've been over this," he resumed. "There's no concrete evidence to suggest this was a stranger abduction, but I seem to be turning up more and more indications that Janelle was worried about something recently."

"Like what?" Jack's large hands clenched the bills and advertising flyers he'd carried over from the post office, as if these alone had the power to keep him afloat in heavy seas.

Frank made a calming gesture with his hand. "Nothing terrible. It's just that Mrs. Carlstadt mentioned that you and Janelle had been having a little disagreement about where she was to go to college, and she thought Janelle might be upset about it."

Frank wondered if Jack would scrape the entire mailing label off his JCPenney catalog before answering. Finally, without raising his eyes, he began to speak. "Janelle wanted to go to the State University in Albany. I thought it was too far away and too big a school for her. She doesn't know anything about getting around in a big city like Albany. I wanted her to go to Mount Marcy Community College. Then if she wanted to finish up in Albany in two years, that would be okay."

"Did you argue about it?"

Jack's head snapped up and his voice took on a plaintive edge. "You know how kids are. She kept on after me about it. Begging, pleading, telling me she'd take out a loan to pay for it. Ha! She's doesn't know what it means to be in debt. Finally I told her to stop—she could go to Mount Marcy or no place at all. And that seemed to settle it. She didn't mention it anymore. I didn't know she told Mrs. Carlstadt about it."

He was quiet for a moment, then looked at Frank suspiciously. "What did she say?"

"Who?"

"Mrs. Carlstadt. I guess she thinks I'm some dumb hick who won't send his daughter to college, huh?"

"Not at all. She said she thought you wouldn't let Janelle go to SUNY because you'd miss her too much."

Jack turned his head toward the wall, but Frank could see his left eye blinking rapidly. In a moment he resumed speaking, and his voice was steady, but wooden with pain. "I guess that was it. I was too selfish to let her go. I couldn't imagine life without Janelle. It seems like just yesterday that I was carrying her around on my shoulders, and to think that she would be leaving home in the fall—I wasn't ready for it.

"If Rosemary were still alive this would never have happened. I was never one much for school, but Rosemary, she was the smartest. Janelle gets her brains from her mother. Rosemary would have let her go to Albany. But I just couldn't. I couldn't bear to lose her. She's more than a daughter to me; she was all I had left of Rosemary.

"But what's this got to do with anything?" Jack jerked himself back to the here and now. "Are you trying to say she ran off to Albany? What would be the point in that— she hasn't even graduated high school yet."

Frank turned the conversation without answering Jack's question. "Did you notice any change in Janelle's behavior around the third week in January?"

"What kind of change?"

"Did she seem distracted or depressed?"

"Why?"

"It's when High Peaks lost to Lake George in basketball, but that's also when Miss Powell says she noticed a change in Janelle. Said she wasn't as perky as usual. Seemed distracted, not focused on what she was doing."

"Let me think. January. Well, somewhere around there is when Janelle and her boyfriend Craig split up."

Frank raised his eyebrows. "You knew about that? Why didn't you tell me?"

Jack shrugged. "I couldn't figure out exactly what was happening. All I know is he would call a lot, and sometimes she would make me answer it and tell him she wasn't there, and sometimes they would talk and she would seem happy, and other times she would talk to him and hang up in tears. I asked her what was going on, if he was hurting her, but she insisted that it was all her fault, that she didn't know what she wanted. But that's all I could get her to say. Then after a few weeks he didn't call much anymore, and she seemed okay. I was just as glad, really."

"Why, you didn't like the boy?"

"Oh, no. Craig is a very nice kid. Good family. But, you know how it is, I didn't like the idea of her getting too serious with one boy just yet."

"Mmmm," Frank murmured noncommittally. "You and your wife were high school sweethearts, weren't you?"

"Things were different then. Besides, we waited a year to get married. Not like my sister and Tom Pettigrew. I just didn't want what happened to Dorothy to happen to Janelle."

"What was that?" Frank asked.

Jack seemed sincerely surprised that there was anyone in Trout Run, no matter how recent an arrival, who did not know Dorothy's story. "You may not believe it now," he began, "but my sister could have had her pick of guys when she was young. But she started going with Tom Pettigrew in tenth grade and she never looked at another boy from then on. Our parents tried to break it up, but that only made it worse."

"Why didn't they approve?"

"Tom was real jealous and had a nasty temper even as a kid. He and Dorothy were inseparable, and then, just what you'd figure would happen, happened. Dorothy got pregnant, and in those days you had to get married and drop out of school, so they did.

"When our folks died, they left everything to me and told me to take care of Dorothy. They knew if Tom got hold of any of the money he'd just drink it away. I said I'd help Tom build a house. He was a pretty good carpenter when he was sober.

"So they moved there behind Rosemary and me and things were better for a little while, but it didn't last. He drank more and more, and then I found out he was beating her. She tried to hide it from me, but one day he knocked one of her teeth out. I went after him, and he pulled a knife on me. I was in the hospital for a week. By that time, Rosemary had started to get sick. I couldn't afford to get tangled up in my sister's problems anymore. I had to think about taking care of Rosie and Janelle. It ate me up inside that I couldn't do anything to help her."

"Why didn't she leave him?" Frank asked.

"And go where? She lived all her life here. She's a shy person. She could never go off and live by herself in a strange town. And how would she make enough money to support Tommy, working in a store or something? She was trapped."

"Couldn't she have had the police arrest him?" Frank inquired.

Jack looked as if Frank had suggested consulting a witch doctor. "And hang out all our dirty laundry for everyone in Trout Run to see? The Harveys don't operate that way."

"So she finally escaped when Tom drove his car into the lake, huh?"

"Yeah, but by that time he had destroyed her. She's nothing like she used to be. She's got no life left in her. You know, she actually cried when he died?" Jack shook his head. "So you can see why I didn't want Janelle rushing into anything. I always told her, 'You have plenty of time for boyfriends when you get older. Look at what falling for a boy did to your aunt. Don't let what happened to her, happen to you.'"

Frank's thoughts ranged back to the years when Caroline had been dating. When she was seventeen, Frank had been so certain of his daughter's innocence that the possibility that she could be the object of a boy's sexual desires—and worse, that she might reciprocate those feelings—was entirely beyond the realm of his imagination. But once she had been away to college, the truth was harder to evade. He still remembered the moment when his eyes, seeing the packet of birth control pills lying on the bathroom counter, fought a mighty battle with his mind to suppress the obvious: his little girl, in a moment of carelessness, or perhaps conscious cruelty, had left them there.

No father wants that knowledge of his daughter. So he sympathized with Jack, which made it all the harder to have to ask the next question.

He drained the cup of tepid coffee on his desk and cleared his throat. "You don't think that could be it, do you? That Janelle *did* make the same mistake as Dorothy and was afraid to tell you?"

"Absolutely not." Jack's reply came almost before Frank had finished. "Why are you asking me all this?" his voice rose sharply. "The other day, you told me you thought someone Janelle knew might be mixed up in her disappearance. But now it sounds like you think she ran away."

Frank could feel Earl's eyes on him, but he stayed focused on Jack. "Something was bothering her, and then she disappeared. Janelle's a smart girl. She may have planned this to look like an abduction, just to throw us off the track."

"My daughter did not plan anything!" Jack flung his chair back and leaped up. "My daughter did *not* run away!"

9

FRANK HEADED OUT to Mount Marcy Community College after his disastrous talk with Jack, hoping to find the librarian who'd helped Janelle with her research on the Bruderhof, or at least find some of the books she'd been using.

Entering the nondescript beige bunker marked Downing Memorial Library, Frank followed the signs to the reference department and saw a tall, slender woman in a shocking pink dress showing someone how to use the microfiche reader. He could not hear her words, but her face was animated as she turned the knobs of the machine, then gestured over to a row of storage cabinets. The librarian returned to her desk without noticing Frank, then looked straight up at him as she heard him approach. In shock, he took in her face and the nameplate on her desk at the same moment: Penny Stevenson, Ned Stevenson's wife.

"Why, Penny," he stammered, "what the heck are you doing over here? The last time I ran into you, you were waiting tables over at the Trail's End."

Penny waved a long elegant hand, on which a sizable

diamond ring slipped and shined. "Oh, that was just a temporary job to keep me out of trouble—my degree is in library science. It drove my father-in-law crazy to have a Stevenson 'slinging hash' as he put it"—Penny grinned wickedly—"so in a way, I hated to give up waitressing."

Frank's smile broadened in response. For a Stevenson, Penny wasn't half bad.

"Mrs. Parkes's death was a terrible way to get a job," Penny continued, "but I must say, I love the work." When Frank looked perplexed she explained in a hushed tone, "Mrs. Parkes, my predecessor, had a heart attack in the stacks in March."

Frank groaned to himself. Great—not only did the librarian who probably had helped Janelle not work here anymore, she was no longer even on this earth.

Penny gave her stylishly bobbed dark hair a toss and evaluated Frank with her slightly almond-shaped eyes. She was not conventionally beautiful; her jaw was a little too strong, her mouth a bit too wide. Using Estelle's term, Penny was "striking." "So," she said, "you must be here to do some research on the Harvey case."

Frank coughed. "What makes you say that?"

A broad smile consumed Penny's face. "All I hear about at home is how you're mishandling this case. I'm sure the library is the last place Clyde thinks a cop working on a kidnapping should be; therefore, you're here."

Frank flopped down into a chair and extended his long legs in front of him. Taking Penny into his confidence was probably like a cobra asking a mongoose for help. Still, there was something irresistibly likable about her. On the other hand, she had chosen to marry that pompous ass, Ned, which tended to call her judgment into doubt. But he had no choice but to show his cards; she had called his bluff before he could even offer it.

"All right, Penny, here's why I came." Frank leaned forward and held up his hands, as if to physically ward off the objections he felt sure were to come. "Janelle was working on this paper on utopian religious communities when she disappeared, and I want to check on her sources, and find out more about this group, the Bruderhof. Her friends said Janelle talked to some of them one day, and I want to find out where they're from. "

Frank pulled out Janelle's note cards, and for the next half hour Penny searched out the books and magazine articles Janelle had used, helped Frank make photocopies, and even used her own card to check out some books for him to take home.

"Here's something," Penny said, reading aloud from a thick book. "Apparently the Hutterites are an outgrowth of the Anabaptists. They're named after Jakob Hutter— he was burned at the stake in the 1500s."

"How does that help us?"

"This word 'bruderhof' means 'dwelling place of the brothers,' and that's what they call their communities. The book indicates there are Hutterite colonies in Montana, South Dakota, and Canada, too."

"Anything about a community near here?" Frank asked.

"Well, let's keep going and maybe we'll see." Penny was on a roll and not about to quit. "Oh, wow, here we go! A guy named Eberhard Arnold wrote some theological books in the 1930s, and that was the foundation of the Bruderhof movement. They're similar to the Hutterites, in that they both forbid private ownership of property. But the Bruderhof split with the Hutterites in the early 1990s. There are Bruderhofs all over the world, but look at this—a book about Arnold is published at a bruderhof in Silas, New York."

"Silas!" Frank sat up from his slouch. He'd passed Silas many times as he drove the Thruway south to Caroline's house. "That's what, two, two and a half hours from here?"

Penny nodded. "You think Janelle is there?"

"No, don't get that rumor started." Frank stood and paced in front of Penny's desk. "I just want to see if I can find the people who spoke to Janelle. It's more a matter of eliminating them as a possibility."

Penny studied a photo of some Bruderhof women sewing a quilt. "Yeah, they don't look much like kidnappers." She smiled up at him. "Don't worry—I'm not tapped into the Trout Run gossip network. I'm an outsider here too, remember."

Frank nodded, but he wasn't reassured. He didn't lump Penny in with all the old hens in town, but he couldn't very well ask her not to mention any of this to Ned. That would look too paranoid. Best to just act casual.

"Thanks, Penny, I really appreciate the time you've taken on this," he said.

"No problem. I hope it helps."

As Frank reached the door, he impulsively glanced back and saw that Penny was looking at him. "Good luck," she called, suddenly serious.

"Thanks. I'll need it."

By the time he got back to the office, the Lambert autopsy report had arrived. As Lew suspected, Lambert had died of a broken neck. Frank waded through the dry medical language of the report, searching for any indication that Lambert had been involved in a struggle, but although the old man had sustained other broken bones in the fall, there were no defensive wounds on his hands or arms, and nothing under his fingernails.

When Frank reached the portion of the autopsy report that concerned Lambert's brain, something caught his attention and he reached for the phone. After a protracted period on hold, Dr. Hibbert, the county medical examiner, came on the line. Frank read aloud the part of the report that had confused him. "What exactly does that mean?"

"Just what it says," Hibbert answered perversely. "His brain showed signs of a previous major trauma."

"Could you tell if he was blind because of that?" Frank asked.

"Well, it was in the part of the brain that controls vision, if that's what you're asking."

"Lambert was supposedly blinded when he got hit in the head by a wooden beam. I suspect that he might have been faking," Frank explained. "Could you tell if he really had brain damage that would cause blindness?"

"Well, his doctors at the time would certainly have been able to tell." Hibbert went off on a tangent about MRIs and brain scans. "But," he concluded, "I can't tell from looking at his corpse."

"Is it possible that his sight could have come back, after the initial loss?" Frank continued.

"Sure, it's possible. Neurology textbooks are full of miracles." Hibbert started rambling about the unpredictable regeneration of neural pathways.

Frank felt a surge of vindication. "Is it likely?" he interrupted.

"Oh, I wouldn't go that far. But definitely possible."

• • •

"My cousin Donald and I went to the Mountainside last night," Earl said, apropos of nothing. Frank didn't think this required an answer.

"Ray Stulke was there."

"Oh," Frank murmured, continuing to read a report.

"He horned in on our darts game."

Frank threw down his report. "Do you mind? I'm trying to read."

"Sorry." Earl began to pace around the office, like a cat who hears a mouse in the walls.

"Willya cut that out! What's the matter with you?"

Earl stopped in front of him. "Look, Frank, I just gotta tell you this. I've been worried about it all day. Don't get mad, 'cause I wasn't blabbing about the case, but Ray started talking about Janelle, and he said something that I think might be important."

Ray Stulke was the Mountainside Tavern's resident lout; twice Earl's size with half his powers of reasoning. Frank couldn't imagine a worthwhile contribution from this quarter. "Spit it out, Earl."

"Ray started ragging on me, calling me 'Dick Tracy of the North Country' and stuff, but I didn't let him get to me. Finally, he said he knew what happened to Janelle. That she was a real little slut and probably ran off with some guy."

"Oh, come on, Earl. That cretin talks that way about all women."

"I know, that's why I kept ignoring him. Finally he said, 'If you don't believe me, ask her cousin. Tommy Pettigrew says Janelle's a whore, sneaking out at night when she's in heat.'"

"Ray said that Tommy called his own cousin a whore and said she was sneaking out at night to meet a man?" Frank repeated.

"Yeah, he said Tommy was sick of his old lady always saying, 'Why can't you be good like Janelle.' He said if her and Jack only knew the truth, they wouldn't think Janelle was so great."

Frank sat twisting the cap on his marker.

"Well, what do you think?"

"I think I have to have another talk with Tommy."

"Don't tell him Ray told me and I told you!"

"Don't worry, Earl. We have to approach this carefully. Very carefully."

10

FRANK SPED SOUTH on the Thruway toward Silas in his pickup, listening to Patsy Cline. Free of billboards and fast-food joints and even other cars, the highway was a joy to drive: smooth, and for a mountain road, surprisingly straight.

Maybe he really would find her today at the bruderhof. It wasn't totally out of the question. From what he'd read in the books Penny had found for him, they certainly didn't appear sinister in any way. But maybe Janelle had convinced them she needed refuge and they had offered it. If she were there, how easy would it be to get her back?

He had dressed in khakis and a plaid shirt. He'd see how far he could get posing as someone interested in the community. If he had to, he could always pull out his I.D. About twenty miles after leaving the highway, Frank saw a large wooden sign announcing the Silas bruderhof.

He started up the small paved road, expecting at any moment to be stopped by a chain or a guard house. But he was able to drive all the way up to a cluster of large, freshly painted buildings before a middle-aged, bearded man in a bright blue shirt and suspenders hailed him with a friendly wave.

"Hello, there. Can I help you?"

"Well, I sure hope so!" Frank offered his best mid-western farm boy smile. "I've been having quite a time trying to find this book on Eberhard Arnold. Someone told me you publish it here. Am I in the right place?"

"Oh, yes indeed! Park over there and we'll walk to the publishing office. You are interested in the life and work of Eberhard Arnold?" his guide, who introduced himself as Henry Bruckner, asked eagerly.

"The book's not actually for me. It's for my brother, Bill. He's a pastor out in Missouri; teaches theology at a small Lutheran college," Frank said, blithely appropriating the life of his erstwhile neighbor in Kansas City. "Bill's very interested in the Bruderhof movement. He's been telling me about your communities. This is quite a place you've got here."

Frank looked around with unabashed curiosity as Henry led him down a wide, grassy path toward a white and blue frame building. Everyone they passed seemed to be busy with something: two women carried a huge basket of laundry between them; another woman supervised a group of children who had been berry picking; some men in the distance were working in a large vegetable garden. All the buildings were plain, but in good repair.

Henry smiled bashfully. "Yes, visitors are often surprised at the size and prosperity of our community." They had reached the blue and white building, and Henry stepped forward to open the door. "Here we are at the publishing office."

Inside, Frank was startled to see several women sitting

in front of computers—typical office workers in every respect but one. Like all the women he had seen so far, they wore identical black and white polka-dotted head-scarves, and shapeless, calf-length dresses. They worked steadily, uninterested in their visitor, while Henry went back among the racks of books and pamphlets in search of the volume Frank had requested.

When he returned, Frank feigned enthusiasm as he forked over eight dollars for the book, which featured a dour old German man and his wife on the cover. As they left the building, a loud bell started to toll.

"It is lunch time," Henry announced. "Perhaps you would like to be our guest in the dining hall?"

"Thanks, I'd love to," Frank said, amazed at his luck. All over the bruderhof, people poured out of buildings and headed toward the large dining hall at the center of the complex. A great place to check for Janelle.

Inside the cavernous building rows of long tables filled quickly with an orderly procession of Bruderhof members. Except for the youngest children, all the girls and women wore those scarves. A sea of black and white heads bobbed up and down over white blouses or gingham dresses. It was amazing how the headgear made all the women, regardless of age or coloring, look virtually identical. Frank scanned the room, on the off chance that he would see the fringe of Janelle's strawberry blond bangs under a babushka.

Henry kept up a cheerful chatter throughout lunch, and afterward offered to take him to meet Michael Heine, the community steward.

On the way down the dirt lane to the steward's office, Frank and Henry encountered four little boys standing on the rails of a fence that enclosed a small herd of goats. The goats maa-ed excitedly, pushing one another aside as they tried to reach the boys' out-stretched hands.

"Children!" The harshness in Henry's voice surprised Frank. "You know that is against the rules!"

The boys hopped off the fence, their heads hanging guiltily.

"Now, go back to Anna and tell her what you have been up to."

Frank watched as the boys scurried off, then observed his formerly genial host. His irritation seemed out of character. "Are those goats important to what you do here?"

"They are valuable animals; we've been breeding them selectively."

"I guess you don't want the kids getting too attached to them, huh?"

"We do not keep animals as pets, or assign them human qualities. Animals are a resource that God has given to Man." Henry answered him politely but still seemed distracted by what the children had done.

Henry snapped out of his mood as they stopped before a small, square building. "Well, here we are," he said. "The steward works here."

There were certainly no perks attached to the steward's leadership position, for his office was as spartan as any low-level bureaucrat's might be. Michael Heine sat behind a large beige metal desk. Frank marveled at the man's orderliness: three stacks of manila folders awaited his attention, but the only paper visible was the spread-sheet he was currently evaluating.

"Michael, I have brought Mr. Frank Bennett to meet you. He has driven here all the way from Trout Run to buy the book of Eberhard Arnold's writings."

Michael stood up immediately and extended his hand

in greeting, his eyes alight with pleasure. "So, you are interested in our founder."

"Yes, and in your community here." Frank was eager to head off any long historical discussion. "Henry invited me to lunch, and then we saw some of your gardens and your farm animals on the way over here."

Henry nodded to Frank. "I am very happy to have been able to show you some of our work. Now, I will leave you with Michael. Good-bye."

"Please, sit down and make yourself comfortable." Michael sat in a hard wooden chair opposite Frank. "Tell me how you came to be interested in the Bruder-hof."

Frank was about to launch into the tale of his brother the minister back in Missouri again, but the steward's sincerity and genuine goodwill brought him as close to embarrassment as he was capable of getting. He glanced away from Michael's placid, gray gaze. "Look . . . I . . . haven't been entirely truthful with you. I said I came here looking for this book—" Frank lifted it from his lap—"but really, there's this young girl, Janelle Harvey, who's been missing from home for almost a week."

Michael looked at him quizzically. "The name sounds familiar. I think I have seen a sign, perhaps in the hard-ware store in New Paltz."

"That's right. She's from Trout Run, but the fliers are posted all over the state."

"And you are her father?" Michael asked with concern.

Frank hesitated. How could he tell the man that he was a police officer working undercover to infiltrate their community? No matter how he tried to explain, it would come out sounding ridiculously suspicious and sordid in these idyllic surroundings. "No, I'm . . . a family friend."

Before Michael could inquire too closely about this, Frank pressed on. "You see, before Janelle disappeared, she had been writing a school paper on Utopian religious communities. We found a mention of your bruderhof in her notes, and we know that she spoke to some folks from your community who she met hiking around Trout Run."

Michael looked puzzled, so Frank elaborated. "She had been worried about something at home. We thought it might be possible that she asked you for help—maybe came here for refuge."

"You think we would harbor a runaway child at Silas!" Anger animated Michael's serene face, then, as quickly as it had appeared it was quashed. "I am sorry that I raised my voice, but you must understand some things about our community. First, one must be an adult to join. Even our own children do not become members of the community until they are grown and can make the proper judgment and commitment of their own free will.

"We get many curiosity seekers here," Michael continued. "People think we are some sort of cult—they wonder about our way of life. That is why we take such pains to instruct outsiders in our beliefs.

"Infrequently, outsiders come to us wishing to join, but no one is permitted to join the group, even as a novice, unless they are certain that living in community is the true path that God has called them to." Michael spread his large, strong hands, as if showing Frank the path. "People who are at loose ends . . . who do not know which way to turn . . . they are not in a position to make a lifetime commitment."

Frank nodded. He believed the man. After all, if the Bruderhof had been harboring Janelle or trying to brainwash her, they would hardly have been so open in inviting him to look around.

"I'm sorry, Michael. I can see now that I was mistaken," Frank said. "But I wonder, would it be possible for me to meet the group that Janelle spoke to in Trout Run?"

Michael regarded Frank with some skepticism.

"I'm just curious what she might have asked them about," Frank went on. "It might help me . . ." His voice trailed off. What? He wasn't sure himself.

But Michael's essential generosity won out over his doubts. He gestured for Frank to follow him and explained as they walked that the young people in the community were very fond of hiking. They took day trips all around the area to hike—winter, summer, spring, and fall. In a barn filled with tractors, trucks, and a large van, Michael introduced Frank to a young man who looked a few years older than Janelle.

"Lucas always drives the van on hiking trips. Perhaps he will remember this young woman you are looking for," Michael said.

Lucas listened intently as Frank showed Janelle's picture and described the location where Kim and Melanie said the encounter with the Bruderhof hikers had taken place. Before Frank had finished speaking, Lucas began to nod. "Yes, I remember the young woman. She was very friendly."

"What did she ask you about? Do you recall?"

"She asked if we had been raised in the community. I told her, yes. And she asked if anyone from outside ever joined, or if anyone ever left. And I said yes again. And then, this was funny, she asked did the men and women get married and live as families?" He laughed. "And I said, yes, what other way is there?"

• • •

"*Chief* Bennett, *may* I have a word, please?"

Doris had launched into an elaborate and wholly incomprehensible pantomime the moment Frank walked into the Town Office after returning from the bruderhof, and now he understood why. Clyde Stevenson stood inside Frank's office, his arms crossed and his foot tapping.

"Sure, Clyde," Frank said with a slightly forced smile. "Has Doris given you a cup of coffee?"

"This isn't a social call, Bennett," Clyde said as he shut the door pointedly in the secretary's face. "I'm here to find out *what* could possibly justify your slanderous attack on Bob Rush!"

"Attack? All I did was ask him if Janelle Harvey had ever confided in him about her problems." Frank struggled to keep his voice level and almost succeeded.

Clyde chose to ignore this. "You *implied* that there was something improper going on between them." Without waiting for a reply he rattled on. "Do you *know* how lucky we are to have a man of Bob Rush's caliber as our pastor here? Do you *realize* how long our church was without a minister before we were fortunate enough to recruit Reverend Rush? For *two years* we had to depend on Reverend Sikes from the Bristol Presbyterian church to drive over here to lead one quick service a week. Why, when he married Katie and Paul Malone, he forgot their *names* in the middle of the ceremony.

"Anyway, that's all beside the *point,*" Clyde said, as if someone else had been doing all the talking. "I want to know what you think you're trying to *prove,* alienating our minister when you're supposed to be finding out who kidnapped Janelle Harvey!"

Frank exhaled slowly before he allowed himself to

speak to the little man pacing up and down in front of him. "I'm obligated to follow up every lead that I get, Clyde," he said. "When I learned that Bob Rush might have been someone Janelle would turn to with her problems, naturally I had to ask him about it."

"And who, may I ask, provided you with this so-called *lead?*" Clyde demanded.

"Melanie Powers," Frank said wearily, anticipating Clyde's reaction.

"And you would accept the idle gossip of that, that *person* over the word of an ordained minister?"

"I have news for you, Clyde. A big part of police work is based on so-called idle gossip, because it's human nature to talk. And it's my job to listen—to everything."

Clyde pursed his thin lips so tightly that they all but disappeared in his pale face. "Rumor mongering," he hissed, "is *not* what the town council hired you for. We thought we were getting an experienced law enforcement *professional.*"

Frank did not deign to defend himself. This two-bit town had gotten far better than it deserved when they hired him. One mistake, one mistake in a twenty-year career, and now he had to put up with idiots like Clyde second-guessing him at every turn! He went on the offensive. "Just why is it that Bob Rush came running to you to complain as soon as we had our little conversation?"

"Pastor Bob did not come *running* anywhere. I just happened to be at the church for a finance committee meeting and he mentioned it to me. As an elder of the Presbyterian church and a member of the town council, I felt it was my *duty* to speak to you about the way you're running this investigation."

"Well, consider me spoken to," Frank replied. "Now, if

you'll excuse me, I think there must be some reports of masked intruders on the outskirts of town that I need to look into."

"I *do* not appreciate your *sarcasm*, Mr. Bennett." Clyde glared at him through his steel-rimmed glasses. "The council will expect a *full* report from you at the next meeting. And there better be some real progress on this Harvey case, or we'll just *see* about breaking your contract!"

11

"HEY!"

Walking back to the office with coffee and a sticky bun from the Store to comfort him after the encounter with Clyde, Frank heard the cry, but assumed it was directed at someone else.

"Hey, Mr. Policeman!" This could only be meant for him, so he stopped to look around. The green was deserted.

"Over here." The high-pitched voice was not particularly loud, but it carried. Frank finally traced it to a tiny figure leaning on the fence of the house that faced the west side of the green. Etta Noakes and her house were even more immutable fixtures in Trout Run than the Store. She had been born in the mansard-roofed Victorian nearly one hundred years before, and had lived there all her life. The house itself predated her by another half century, or at least the front of it did. About thirty feet wide, it had grown to twice that depth as various lean-tos and porches had been added on, enclosed, and gradually subsumed into the main structure. Like her house, Miss Noakes was cloaked in an air of genteel decay.

As he walked toward her, the old lady said, "Agnes tells me you're good at finding things."

Frank had found Agnes Guttfreund's stolen lawn mower last summer, and the old biddy had been singing his praises ever since. "Well, if I were half as good at finding people as I am at tracking down lawn mowers, Janelle Harvey would be home by now."

"Oh, her." Miss Noakes waved a gnarled hand as if shooing a blackfly. "She'll come back. Those girls always do."

Frank plopped into a weather-beaten Adirondack chair and studied the old woman curiously. Her pure white hair stood up around her head like a dandelion gone to seed, and the motley assortment of cardigans, shawls, and socks she wore made her seem even smaller than she was. "What makes you so certain?" he asked.

"Young people always think their troubles are tied to a certain place. They expect to outrun their trouble. But when they get where they're going, they find their problems are there, too, so they come back," Miss Noakes said simply as she looked past Frank's shoulder to study the comings and goings on the green.

The old gal was sharper than she looked. He only hoped she was right about Janelle.

"So, what is it that *you* want me to find?" Frank asked.

"Petey, my cat."

Frank watched as a gray tiger-striped cat threaded his way carefully through a tall stand of pussywillow in Miss Noakes's overgrown garden. He revised his judgment; maybe Etta just had momentary flashes of lucidity. "He's right there," Frank said gently, pointing the cat out.

Miss Noakes did not even turn her head. "That's Mr. Tibbs. Petey is the one who's been stolen. He's solid white, with a black tail. I always say that somewhere there must be a black cat that got Petey's white tail."

"Well, he probably just wandered off ma'am—cats do roam. He'll be back. I'll sure keep an eye peeled on my rounds in case the poor fella got . . . well . . . hit or something." Frank put his hands on the arms of the low chair, preparing to rise, but the look of withering scorn that Miss Noakes fixed on him caused him to sink back into his seat.

"Agnes said you were a little slow to catch on, but that eventually you'd figure things out. Petey is not a young, foolish cat. He's lived here next to the green all his life, and he's never been hit by a car. As for roaming, a few years ago that young vet fella fixed him"—Miss Noakes made a hacking motion with her hands—"and since then Petey's never had the urge to leave the yard. No, he's been stolen, sure enough, and I want you to find who did it."

Frank knew when he'd been checkmated. "All right, Miss Noakes. I'll look into it. But don't get your hopes up. A cat could be"—Frank sighed and looked at the mountains that surrounded the green—"anywhere."

"That's what you said about Agnes's mower, and you found that, didn't you?" Miss Noakes got up and marched back into her house.

Frank walked glumly back to the Town Office. The coffee he'd bought would be cold by now, and what good was a sticky bun without a decent cup of hot coffee? He'd be forced to drink some of Doris's sludge, he supposed.

"That was an awful long coffee break," Earl reproached Frank as he entered the office.

"I was taking a citizen complaint. Miss Noakes thinks I'm the man to find her lost cat." Frank slid down in his chair and balanced his coffee cup on his chest. "The council may want to fire my ass, but the little old ladies of this town think I've got the touch. If worse comes to worse, I can spend the rest of my career tracking down lost crochet hooks and missing eyeglasses."

Frank continued to gaze into the crystal ball of his coffee cup. "Hey, Earl." He sat up with a lurch. "When Clyde was in here defending Bob Rush, he made a big point of how lucky Trout Run was to get him. How *did* a little church like ours get a minister from Yale?"

"My Aunt Thelma was on the selection committee—she never shut up about it. Bob was associate pastor at some big, fancy church in Westchester. Said he got tired of ministering to the rich and wanted to be the head pastor of a small church, so he accepted the call. Why?"

Frank's answer was interrupted by the sound of a truck screeching to a halt outside the building, followed by slammed doors and pounding footsteps. Frank rose to open his office door, sure that whoever had arrived at the Town Office in such a hurry had come to see him.

Jack Harvey practically fell into Frank's arms as the door swung in. "Look what came in the mail today!" he gasped, breathless from his sprint. "It's a ransom note! Now you'll believe me when I tell you Janelle was kidnapped!"

As Frank took the envelope, Jack's and Earl's excited chatter receded in the background. "How many people have handled this?" he asked as he crossed to his desk and took out a pair of disposable latex gloves from a box. He struggled to put them on, his fingers suddenly feeling huge and clumsy. Could he have been totally off base after all? Time seemed to have stopped and he had the oddest sensation of watching himself sit down at his own desk.

"No one's touched it but me," Jack said. "I picked up the mail on my way home from work, and came straight here after I read that."

Despite Jack's impatience, Frank took the time to study the outside of the envelope: plain white, low quality, standard number 10 size. Jack Harvey's address was typewritten on the front, with no return address. The letter was postmarked from Saranac Lake, with yesterday's date.

Carefully, Frank removed the single typewritten page from the envelope. Earl leaned over his shoulder and they read together:

> Dear Mr. Harvey,
>   I got your daughter. She ain't been hurt yet. It will cost you $10,000 to get her back. She says you ain't rich, so you can have some time to raise the cash.
>   On May 2 at dawn, put it in a red napsack and leave it under the porch of the old deserted ranger's cabin on Mt. Henry. If all the money is their, I'll let Janelle go.

Earl looked up in awe when he finished reading, but Frank kept his head down, studying the document without comment for almost five minutes. Jack, unable to contain himself any longer, finally broke the silence.

"Well, what do you think? What're you going to do?"

"I'm going to take this right over to the state police lab. They'll dust it for prints, examine the paper and the typewriting, and look for any other identifying marks. It's unlikely that anyone at the post office in Saranac will remember this letter, but we'll ask anyway."

Frank returned to scrutinizing the letter.

Jack tolerated this for a minute or so. "Then what?" he asked.

"Hmm?"

"The ransom! The ransom! How are we going to give him the money and make sure he gives us Janelle?"

Frank sat back and studied Jack as he circumnavigated

the small office. Jack had run his hands through his hair repeatedly, and this, combined with years of bad haircuts from the Verona barbershop, gave him a crazed appearance that warned Frank to weigh his response carefully.

"We'll have a few troopers dressed like hikers go in and look at the cabin," Frank said, authoritatively. "When May 2 comes, we'll set up a stakeout with Lieutenant Meyerson."

Jack searched Frank's face for reassurance. "What if you blow it? What if you scare him off?"

"I don't think we're dealing with an Einstein here, Jack. He'll be no match for the state police. Now you go home, and don't tell anyone about this. Not even your sister."

"But what about the money? I don't have that kind of cash. The only person I could get it from would be Clyde Stevenson. I'm sure he'd let me use the reward money he's put up."

Frank studied the desperate father closely, then nodded slowly. "Yeah, go ahead. Tell Clyde about the letter."

The ride to the state police headquarters in Ray Brook took nearly forty minutes, time that Earl spent in nonstop speculation about the ransom note and how the state police would handle what he called "the drop."

"Do you think they'll find any prints on the letter? Would anyone be dumb enough not to wear gloves? Where do you think he's hiding Janelle—in the woods on Mount Henry? That might not be too safe—there's a lot of hikers out this time of year. Do you think the state police will let you and me go on the stakeout? Where will we hide . . . up in the trees? You know, I saw this thing on *Crimebusters* once, where the cops wore these special glasses that let them see in the dark. Do you think the troopers have those?"

Most of Earl's questions required nothing more than a grunt or a nod from Frank, and finally, twenty minutes into the trip, he wound himself down and fell silent. They rode like this for another five minutes, when Earl spoke hesitatingly. "Are you worried that Mr. Stevenson will want to fire you now that it turns out you were wrong about Janelle running away?"

Frank jumped, roused from a waking dream. "Huh?"

"I said, are you thinking that Mr. Stevenson will want to fire you now that it turns out you were wrong about Janelle running away? "

Franks lips twitched. "Hell, no, I'm not worried. Besides, what makes you so sure I'm wrong?"

"What!" Earl twisted to face Frank as best as his seat belt would allow. "How can there be a ransom note if she ran away?"

"Nothing strikes you as strange about that note?" Frank asked. "Why do you think he would wait three days before sending it? And why offer Jack such a long time to raise the money?"

Earl shrugged. "I dunno. Maybe it's his first kidnapping . . . or something."

"Yeah—it's the 'or something' that I'm wondering about."

Earl undoubtedly would have pursued this further, but the appearance of state police headquarters, and all the marvels it contained, saved Frank from further explanation.

12

THURSDAY DAWNED CLEAR AND BRIGHT, with a few fluffy white clouds on the horizon to give the sky some interest. Arriving at a minute past six, Frank was first in line at Malone's for the lumberjack's breakfast: two eggs, two sausages, two pancakes, two slices of toast, and, of course, as much coffee as you could get up and pour for yourself. Thus fortified, he returned home to tackle a job that had been crying out to him all winter long—replacing the chronically stuck bathroom window.

He knew that this was politically unwise; he should at least give the appearance of frantic investigative activity. But there was little to be done until the lab reports came back in the afternoon. He had intentionally not discussed the note in detail with Meyerson, curious to see what conclusion the trooper would reach on his own. So he left Earl in charge for the morning, with instructions to call him at home if any new information came in.

He wasn't long into framing out the new window when he realized he needed a gutter cap. He'd have to make a trip to Venable's Hardware. On the quick trip down the hill and across Stony Brook, Frank noticed that the clouds were piling up, obscuring the peak of Mount Marcy. He thought of the gaping hole in the front of his house and hoped that he hadn't picked the wrong day to tear out that window. But the Adirondack weather was always unpredictable. Sometimes the sky went from crystal blue to black and back again without a drop of rain ever falling. The weather report, even from the radio station in Lake Placid, was about as pertinent as the daily horoscope that immediately followed it.

Frank intended to be in and out of Venable's in five minutes, but he forgot to allow for the fifteen minutes of unsolicited advice from Rollie Fister that came with every purchase, no matter how small. By the time he got back into his truck, the first heavy drops of rain were dissolving the dust on his windshield. A dagger of lightning, so perfect it could have been drawn by a cartoonist's hand, reached down from the black clouds on the horizon. A tremendous clap of thunder followed seconds later, then the skies opened up.

The rain fell in solid sheets. Frank could see the road only in split-second intervals as his wipers worked futilely to clear the water away. He was uncertain of just where he was on the road until he felt it descending toward the new steel bridge that carried truck traffic over Stony Brook. In the vivid illumination of the next lightning flash, Frank saw a hunched figure loping along the side of the road. Immediately he beeped his horn and leaned across to throw open the passenger side door. "Get in," he shouted.

"It's not safe to walk across that bridge in a storm," Frank said as his passenger straightened out the sweatshirt he had pulled over his head in a vain effort to stay dry. It was Tommy Pettigrew.

"Yeah," Tommy agreed. Then, as an afterthought, "Thanks."

They sat in silence for a few moments, Frank concentrating on his driving, and Tommy staring out at the storm. When they reached the other side of the bridge, it occurred to Frank that the weather was cooperating with him after all, delivering up Tommy Pettigrew for an impromptu chat.

"Listen, Tom, it's raining too hard for me to drive you all the way home now. But it can't keep up like this for long, so we'll just wait it out at my house, then I'll run you back," Frank said, turning the truck in the direction of his own house. Tommy, in no position to argue, grunted glumly.

Pulling up in front of the cottage, Frank and Tommy got drenched in the time it took to run the ten feet from the driveway to the back door. Frank went immediately to the front of the house and surveyed his rainswept bathroom.

"Geez, would you look at that! I'll go down to the basement for a tarp and you can help me cover up that opening," Frank said. Tommy neither agreed nor disagreed, and upon returning with the tarp, Frank found the boy just where he had left him, leaning against the bathroom door frame.

As they struggled with the tarp, Frank tried to get his reluctant guest to loosen up. Twenty years of volunteering with the Police Athletic League had given him plenty of experience in communicating with sullen teenagers, but Tommy was proving to be an exceptional challenge. Frank peppered him with questions: sports, cars, music, his summer plans—every subject was greeted with an indifferent shrug or a few muttered monosyllables.

When they finished and moved to the kitchen for lunch, Frank wracked his brain for another topic to try. Suddenly, the image of the posters in Tommy's bedroom popped into Frank's mind, and he said, "I caught that movie *Enter the Dragon* on the *Late Show* last week. Boy, that Bruce Lee really is terrific."

"Bruce Lee sucks!" Tommy set down his baloney sandwich and straightened from his perpetual slump, shaking the hair out of his suddenly animated gray eyes. "Brandon Lee, his son, could have been the best of all time if those stupid assholes hadn't killed him while he was making *The Crow*."

"Oh, yeah, I read about that. Someone accidentally put real bullets in the gun instead of blanks."

"It wasn't no accident," Tommy corrected Frank authoritatively. "Brandon had enemies—they were out to get him."

Uninterested in paranoid conspiracy theories, Frank took a different tack. "Funny how kids can get to be better than their parents at things. I hear your father was a pretty fair carpenter, but I bet you're probably even better."

If talk of kung fu stars had ignited a spark in Tommy, talk of his father lit a crackling blaze. "No, I'm nowhere near as good as he was. He built our whole house by himself."

"I'm just a hack, myself," Frank said deprecatingly. "Your dad probably would've had that window all nailed in by now."

"Oh, yeah," Tommy agreed as he reached for more potato chips. "He worked real fast, and he never made mistakes. 'Measure twice, cut once,' that's what he always said. I helped him all the time. He taught me how to miter corners when I was only nine years old. I have all his tools." Suddenly Tommy's voice hardened. "My Uncle Jack wanted to sell them, but I wouldn't let him."

"Good tools are hard to come by," Frank sympathized.

"Not if you're willing to spend a little money," Tommy lectured. "Uncle Jack was always buying cheap shit from Sears 'cause his old lady wouldn't let him buy expensive tools. He was pussy-whipped by Aunt Rosemary. Not like my dad—he was a real man!"

Frank knew that Tom Pettigrew Sr. had displayed his manliness by beating his wife and son, yet Tommy's pride in the man didn't surprise him. He had seen this kind of pathetic loyalty time and again. As social workers carried them out of the house, kids would stretch out their arms and cry for the parents who had whipped and kicked and burned them. Frank guessed there weren't many people who were willing to listen to Tommy sentimentalize the cruel drunk who had been his father.

And by letting the kid run on, he'd seen a pattern in Tommy's conversation. If you asked Tommy a question he clammed right up, but if you made a definitive statement, his natural contrariness compelled him to set you straight.

"Too bad your cousin didn't know a little about martial arts," Frank said as he set a plate of Oreos on the table. "She's such a sweet kid—I'm worried that she's being taken advantage of."

Tommy took the bait without hesitation. "Janelle's not the little princess Uncle Jack makes her out to be. She can take care of herself."

"Maybe," Frank said, dunking his cookie in a glass of milk. "But an innocent young girl with no money—I just wonder how she can survive on her own."

Tommy snorted. "She'll survive the way all bitches survive—by opening her legs."

Somehow, Frank doubted the boy had much direct experience in the behavior of women. Was this bravado just talk he had learned from Ray, or did he really know something incriminating about Janelle?

He began clearing dishes from the table. "Yeah, I guess girls always have that to fall back on, huh? Still, I'd hate to think of Janelle being forced to earn her way like that."

"She'd enjoy it. They all do."

"You seem to have sort of a low opinion of your cousin. Was there bad blood between you?"

"She just pissed me off sometimes. She thought anything *she* did was all right, but anything anyone else did was . . ." Tommy used his thumbnail to pulverize a cookie fragment. "A big fuckin' deal."

Frank took a calculated risk. "Yeah, I could see where that would get under your skin, especially when you knew she used to slip out of the house at night without her dad knowing."

Tommy's eyes narrowed. "Who told you that?"

"Oh, I just heard it around town."

"The rain stopped," Tommy said abruptly. "You don't have to drive me home. I'll walk."

"No, no. I'll drive you; it's no trouble," Frank insisted, desperate to keep Tommy talking.

"I said, I'll walk. I got things to do."

Frank laid a restraining hand on Tommy's arm, all pretense of casual conversation abandoned. "Look, if you know who Janelle was meeting at night, you need to tell me. It could be our only hope of finding her."

"I don't know who Janelle was sneaking around with, or where she went. But I'm glad she's gone." And with that, Tommy bolted out of the house.

Frank stood in the doorway and watched the boy's angular frame, shoulders hunched as if he were still battered by rain, slouching down the road until he disappeared from view.

By two the new window had been nailed in, and Frank was back at his desk. He called his daughter, Caroline, to see if she could find out anything about Bob Rush's tenure at the Presbyterian church in Rappahonack, a town not far from her home in Chappaqua. She promised to check and get back to him. After he had hung up, Meyerson called with the lab results.

Frank cradled the phone against his shoulder, stretching back as far as his ancient swivel chair would allow. He took notes on a pad propped against his knees as he listened intently to Myerson's report.

"I'm sorry to tell you, there's not much to go on," Meyerson began. "No prints on the letter except Jack Harvey's. Cheap envelope available in every discount store in America. Letter paper is twenty-pound bond of the type used in every copier in America. Letter written on a PC and printed with an ink-jet printer, again of the type found in virtually every office and half the homes in America. No one at the Saranac Lake post office remembers anything, and there's been no unusual activity at the ranger cabin on Mount Henry."

Frank grunted. "I figured that's what you'd say."

"Then I faxed a copy down to Dr. Steinmetz—he's the shrink at headquarters in Albany. He's worked a lot of kidnappings, serial killers, hostage situations—the guy can look at the smallest details and tell you what kind of nut you're dealing with. So I sent this down without giving him any background on the case, just to see what he'd say. And you know what?"

"What?" Frank responded cautiously.

"He asks me, are we sure this is a real kidnapping."

Frank straightened up in his chair and put the pad on the desk. "I knew it! What reasons did he give?"

"Steinmetz says most ransom notes warn against calling in the police. Also, the writer didn't offer any proof that he actually had the kid, so it could just be some lame effort to cash in on Harvey's misfortune, which is what I thought when I read it. But the doctor said something else was weird: all the punctuation in the note—commas and everything—was correct, which leads him to believe the grammatical errors and misspellings were intentional."

A slow smile spread across Frank's face.

"Hey, are you still there?" Meyerson wanted to know.

"Yeah, I heard you. So, what do you make of that?"

"It's some jerk trying to cash in on Janelle's disappearance, who thinks ransom notes should look like they come from illiterate nuts."

"Maybe," Frank answered.

"Maybe? What else could it be?"

"What if someone wrote the note to get us to start looking at this case as a kidnapping?"

"You figure Jack thought this would light a fire under us?" Meyerson hesitated. "I don't know. I don't think he's that good an actor."

"Neither do I."

"So, who else would want us to think she's been kidnapped?" Meyerson asked.

"Think of it from a slightly different angle, Lou," Frank instructed. "Who wants us to *stop* looking for a runaway?"

After a slight pause, Lew's low, throaty chuckle escalated to full-fledged laughter. "Oh, man, Frank. You got your hands full with this one. Just how do you plan on telling Jack Harvey that his daughter's behind her own ransom?"

Frank reclined in his BarcaLounger. His back and shoulders throbbed from the day of lifting and nailing. Normally a job well done brought him enough pleasure to counteract his aches and pains, but his mishandling of Tommy Pettigrew had ruined any satisfaction the new window could offer.

If only he'd hung back and let Tommy bring the information to him. But no, he had to charge right in like the hounds of hell were on his tail. Now he was even further away from knowing who Janelle was meeting, and why Tommy held her in such low regard.

And the gratification of being right about the ransom note had evaporated when he contemplated all the unanswerable questions the note raised. Why had she sent it now? Maybe Janelle knew he was on to her? But for that to be true, she must be in touch with someone in town who was keeping her posted on the direction of the investigation. It was bizarrely comforting that she thought he was closing in—at least she had confidence in his ability.

He shut his eyes and tried to call up a mental picture of Janelle. Her sweet, eager face reproached him from telephone poles, bulletin boards, and store windows everywhere. The more he learned, the more elusive she became. Intellectual, whore, daddy's girl, schemer—who was the real Janelle?

Nothing in his long career had prepared Frank for this: a case where everyone pressured him for results, but no one wanted him to pursue any of the leads. In fact, someone wanted him to spend the next nine days going down a blind alley. Then the phony ransom drop would explode in his face and the Town Council would demand his resignation. Unless he did some major ass kissing.

To hell with them—he'd resign before he let Clyde and Jack dictate how he ran this investigation. And then he'd find that kid just to spite them all—Janelle included.

13

THE SHOUTING MATCH taking place in the Town Office was loud enough that people crossing through the green could hear the raised voices, although, try as they might, not the precise words of the combatants.

Frank paced around his desk, his vow to be more patient slipping away. He had carefully constructed a strategy that would allow him to follow up on Tommy's assertion that Janelle was meeting someone at night, while still appearing to believe in the ransom note. But things weren't playing out as he'd expected.

"Why are you fighting me on this?" he asked Jack Harvey, keeping his voice level while crushing a blameless soda can.

Jack's face, already red from a morning spent loading trucks at the lumberyard, was now flushed deep maroon in rage. "Why? Why? Because I can't get you to believe she was kidnapped, even when we've got a goddamn ransom note that says she was!"

"I explained it to you—the person she was secretly meeting might be the guy who wrote the ransom note. That's why we've got to figure it out before Saturday."

Jack leaped up so suddenly that his hard wooden chair rocked back on two legs and came down again with a resounding thump. "We don't agree on shit!" he roared. "My daughter's friends are all welcome in our home. Janelle didn't have to *sneak around* to meet anybody."

"Your own nephew is the one who said he saw her slipping out at night!" Despite his best intentions, Frank's voice took on its angry edge again.

Jack snorted. "Tommy's a liar. He gets more like his old man every day."

"But Jack, think. What reason would he have to make this up out of the clear blue?" Frank sat down behind his desk and stacked loose papers into neat piles without looking at them. "Did he and Janelle fight? Was there some animosity between them?"

"Tommy's just jealous of her because she does so well in school."

"Oh, come on. Tommy doesn't strike me as the type who cares much about school one way or the other. There's got to be more to it than that."

Jack stared out the window blankly. Finally, he spoke. "When Tommy and Janelle were little kids, they were inseparable. Living out where we do, there weren't many other kids around, so they played with each other all day. Tommy was Janelle's hero—he called all the shots and Janelle did whatever he said. But he was real protective— saw that she never did anything dangerous. We used to say that Tommy and Janelle were like brother and sister. That they'd look out for each other, just like Dorothy and me always did."

He paused, lost in his memories. "Things changed when the teachers decided Janelle should skip a grade. She got put into Tommy's same class at school then, and it wasn't long before she went straight to the top of the class. Tommy always had trouble in school. Janelle said the other kids made fun of him sometimes. I think he was embarrassed to have his little cousin see him struggle.

"At home, she still tagged around after him like a puppy, but he pushed her away often enough that she finally left him alone. At the time, we just figured he was going through a stage where he wanted to spend more time with other boys, but the truth is, he never did have many friends. By the time they got to high school, it was like they hardly knew each other anymore."

Jack looked Frank straight in the eye. "So that's why I say Tommy wouldn't know what Janelle was doing or who she was seeing."

Eager for a change of scenery after his latest run-in with Jack, Frank headed out to answer a call at Harlan Mabely's place just off Route 53. Just when he began to worry that he must have missed the turnoff, a hand-painted wooden sign warned, WHOA, SLOW DOWN! A second command soon appeared: HEY KIDS, DON'T MISS THIS! The third and final sign rewarded passing motorists' anticipation: GENUINE ADIRONDACK PETTING ZOO. MEET BART THE FRIENDLY BEAR.

Harlan Mabely's petting zoo was the kind of roadside attraction that used to break up long hours of car-bound tedium, before the Interstate system turned family vacations into a hopscotch game from one fast-food outlet to another. Frank pulled up in front of a little green-painted log cabin peppered with signs in contrasting yellow: OFFICE, GIFT SHOP, ALL VISITORS CHECK IN HERE, LAST TOUR: 4:30, NO UNACCOMPANIED CHILDREN.

Before Frank had even opened the car door, Harlan emerged to greet him. A wiry little man with very few teeth, he always sported a two-day growth of beard. Frank marveled at the man's consistency, since stubble implied at least occasional shaving, yet Harlan never appeared fresh-faced.

"Someone cut a hole in Martha's fence!" Harlan shouted, trotting down the two steps from the office porch with his gray work pants flapping around his spindly legs. "Come right this way." He waved for Frank to follow him down a gravel path that led into some sparse woods where the animals were kept in pens.

The Adirondack Petting Zoo was a flea-bitten menagerie of abandoned, displaced, and wounded animals, who, with the exception of Bart the Bear and a couple of de-scented skunks, were not native to the Adirondacks at all. As they passed the cages, Harlan kept up a non-stop patter filling Frank in on each animal's provenance. Finally, they arrived in front of a fenced-in patch of dirt with a shed in the corner. A five-foot-tall bird with droopy gray feathers regarded them balefully through the chain-links.

"There's my sweet girl," Harlan crooned in a high-pitched singsong. "A lot of people think she's an ostrich, but she's an Australian emu. I got her when a zoo in Florida closed. She was real sickly when she first came, but I take good care of her, don't I, sweetheart?"

The bird emitted a throaty cackle that Frank was hard-pressed to interpret as agreement. Still, a flightless bird stuck on the wrong continent didn't have many options open to her. Directly in front of the emu's food dish, the fence had been cut with wire cutters and bent back, leaving an opening about three feet high and two feet wide.

"See what they done!" Harlan pointed dramatically at the hole. "Lucky for me, the thief don't know much about emus. You can't get 'em to squeeze through a little hole. They just won't go. Stubborn, aren't you Martha?" The bird moved toward Harlan and he stroked her scrawny neck.

"So there was never any danger of her getting loose because of this?" Frank asked, examining the cuts in the fence.

"No, but who's to say they won't come back and cut all the way through? I can't afford to lose one of my star attractions." Harlan wagged a grimy finger at Frank. "You know what I think? I think there's someone out there tryin' to build a herd of emu. There's money in raising them for their meat and their hides. Yessir, there surely is."

Emu rustlers in Trout Run seemed highly unlikely. "Look, Harlan, it's getting close to graduation and the kids are up to all kinds of pranks, but they don't mean any harm. I tell you what—Earl will sit here from nine to eleven for the rest of the week. Once they know we're taking this seriously, they'll give up on trying to steal Martha."

"All right," Harlan agreed. "But don't fall asleep on the job. Remember, that bird's worth a pretty penny and I don't have insurance on her."

As Frank returned to town along Stony Brook Road, unconsciously, irresistibly, his eyes were drawn to the spot where Janelle's gas can had been found. Surveying the meadow, he noticed three large black birds wheeling in the sky over the farthest part of the field. Occasionally one swooped down to the ground, then rose again, wings flapping languorously.

Turkey vultures, feeding on some carrion. His heart raced. But it couldn't be Janelle; this field had been searched, and her body would have been spotted. Besides, this was the first time he'd noticed the birds— they were obviously after a fresh kill. He was about to drive on when some niggling seed of doubt pulled him back. What if Janelle *had* been abducted and her killer had returned to dump her body here, as some sick flourish?

Frank got out of the patrol car and waded through the meadow grass, swatting at the bugs that dived into his head and cursing himself for getting all bitten up for the sake of what was likely to be some half-eaten rabbit corpse. Still, he hesitated when, as he came within a couple of feet of the birds, one of them flew up in front of him, dangling a piece of gory flesh from its beak. Frank steeled himself to look; his stomach still churned at crime scenes.

In the flattened grass lay a small bloody mass. It was clearly not human, and Frank turned away in relief. Then, something black peeking out from a clump of flowers caught his eye. Frank found a stick and pulled it forward. A long black cat's tail lay before him, and now he noticed tufts of white fur amid the bloody pulp of the corpse. Against all odds, he had solved another case.

14

AFTER LUNCH Frank decided to stop into the store out-side of Lake Placid where Edwin had run into Dell Lambert. The Feast and Fancy was far enough out of the way that Lambert might have felt comfortable letting down the charade of blindness. A long shot, but if he didn't get any useful information, he could at least get some of the coffee Edwin raved about.

Located in a small strip mall, the Feast and Fancy shared unpretentious space with a dry cleaners, a drugstore, a hair salon, and a gift shop. As he opened the door to the gourmet/health food shop, the scent of fresh-ground coffee energized him. Showing the clerk a picture of Lambert that had run in the *Mountain Herald* obituary, he asked, "I think this man was a customer of yours. Do you recognize him?"

"Sure, that's Mr. Lambert," the woman answered. Then, realizing the picture was part of an obituary, she gasped. "Oh, my goodness . . . he's dead?"

"I'm afraid so," Frank answered, not bothering to elaborate. "Did he shop here often?"

The clerk shrugged. "A couple of times a month. He came in with a woman—I think it was his niece."

"Never alone?"

"Oh no—he was blind, you know. He needed her help."

"This is important, uh, Nancy," Frank said, glancing at her name tag. "Did Mr. Lambert ever do anything that would make you think that maybe he really could see? Like push the shopping cart, say, or read a label or count his change?"

Nancy cocked her head to one side. "That's a weird question. No, no—he always walked with his hand on his niece's arm, like you see blind people do on TV. And she put everything in the cart, and she paid."

Frank nodded. "Thanks for your help." He turned as he reached the door. "Say, how much do you charge for that coffee?"

"Nine dollars a pound."

Frank's eyes widened. No wonder Edwin couldn't turn a profit at the Inn. He let the door swing shut behind him. It looked like Lambert's death really might be a coincidence. He turned to head back to the patrol car when a sign in the Nature's Way gift shop caught his eye. SQUIRREL-PROOF BIRD FEEDERS!

Every square inch of Nature's Way, including the ceiling, displayed something nature-related. If Lambert had shopped in here he would have had trouble holding Celia's arm—two people couldn't walk side by side in the jam-packed maze of merchandise. But when Frank showed Lambert's picture, the genial, gray-haired man at the counter immediately recognized him. He volunteered a wealth of information before Frank could even ask a question.

"Poor old Dell—I heard he passed away. He really

knew his birds. Loved to come in here and pass the time while his niece was getting her hair done."

"So he walked around in here alone?" Frank kept the excitement he felt out of his voice. No way a blind man could navigate through this tangle of stuff.

"No, he'd hang around the counter here with me. He was blind, you know. If I got busy, I'd put him back there in Books and Music to listen to the CDs of nature sounds."

Again, the logical explanation. But Frank persisted. "You never saw him do anything that would lead you to believe he really could see?"

"Of course not! Why—" A gasp and a crash from the back of the store sent the man running. Frank sighed and wove his way along crooked trails toward the door. As he rounded a pyramid of insect collection boxes, he nearly tripped over a young man unpacking a box of butterfly nets.

"Whoa, sorry! I didn't see you there."

The kid stared up at Frank for a moment before he spoke. "It never really struck me until I heard what you asked Charlie, but once, when Mr. Lambert was sitting over there"—with a nod he indicated an easy chair next to a stereo with headphones—"I saw him get up and change the CD. He pressed all the right buttons and everything."

Bingo! I knew it. I knew I was right. But as Frank returned to the patrol car and sat thinking, the thrill of vindication faded. This made it more likely that he *could* have witnessed what happened to Janelle. And more likely that he had been killed to silence him.

But if Janelle had staged her own disappearance, did that mean she was complicit in Lambert's death? Frank massaged his temples. The alternative wasn't much better. If whomever Janelle had left with had come back and killed Lambert, that meant Janelle herself was in great danger. The stakes were suddenly a hell of a lot higher.

When Frank got back to the office, Doris waggled the phone receiver at him. "Just in time. Your daughter's on line two."

He listened as Caroline's animated voice provided him with new information. Then he hung up and stared unseeingly at his phone. A few hours ago, he would have thought this message had solved all his problems. Now, he didn't know what to make of it.

Frank braced himself for his next task and headed across the green to Etta Noakes's house. Before he left, he told Doris to call the Presbyterian church and make an appointment for him with Bob Rush. He'd do everything by the book so Clyde couldn't accuse him of harassment.

The sagging porch and drooping shutters that faced him as he approached Etta's house should have been an affront to Frank's passion for square corners. But the porch swing and the wisteria vine that shaded it reminded him of old farmhouses from his youth. Miss Noakes, unaware of his coming, pulled weeds as best she could without getting down on her knees, framed by an arbor overrun with honeysuckle.

Afraid of startling her, Frank scuffed his feet on the sidewalk and rattled the garden gate. Miss Noakes turned with a smile of welcome, but it faded quickly from her face as she saw Frank's expression.

"You've found Petey, and he's dead, isn't he?" she said unflinchingly.

She's a tough old bird, Frank thought. She's making it

easy on me. "Yes, ma'am, I'm afraid so. I found him over in that big meadow along Stony Brook Road. "

"The same place the Harvey girl disappeared from?" Etta tossed down the weeds clutched in her hand. "What made you look there?"

"Well, I was driving along and I noticed some birds circling overhead . . ." Frank trailed off uncomfortably.

"Vultures," Miss Noakes said. "How do you know it was Petey, then?"

"I found his black tail. They hadn't, uh, touched that. And there were some clumps of white fur . . . around. I buried him out there, Miss Noakes. I thought you would've wanted that."

"That was nice of you. You can't blame the vultures for doing what they do. It's just nature's way of cleaning up," Miss Noakes said philosophically. "Well, you found him, just like Agnes said you would. Now, do you know who stole him and killed him?"

Her question took him by surprise. "I assumed a fox had got him."

"A fox doesn't kill what she's not going to eat." Miss Noakes folded her hands on the knob of her walking stick and fixed her eyes, which were still a clear blue, on Frank. "No, someone killed my Petey and left him there for the birds, and I want to know why."

"Yes, ma'am." He might have known it wouldn't be that easy to write off Miss Noakes. The old gal had a point, though—a fox would've eaten its kill. And why had he found the cat on Stony Brook Road, of all places? Just another supposed coincidence, like Dell Lambert's death? "I'll keep working on it."

Something about the droop of his shoulders as he left must have prompted Miss Noakes to take pity on him. "Don't worry so much about that Harvey girl," she called out. "She'll come back, just like her mother did."

With his hand frozen on the garden gate, Frank turned to face the old woman. "What do you mean by that?"

Miss Noakes hobbled toward him so she wouldn't have to shout. "Rosemary Harvey took off for a while when that child was just a baby. No one knew about it—they covered up by saying she went to take care of her sick aunt in Saranac Lake. Of course, Rosemary's mother's sister was as healthy as a horse—I knew her quite well. Rosemary wasn't gone long—couple of weeks. I suppose the baby brought her back. Picked up her life here like nothing ever happened."

"But why did she leave?" Frank asked.

Miss Noakes shrugged. "None of my affair. I'm just telling you; she left, she came back. It's in the blood."

The next hour passed with the speed of sap dripping from a maple tree. Frank sent Earl to look into a complaint that garbage cans had been overturned at the Stop'N'Buy convenience store, while he feigned interest in Reid Burlingame's strategy for traffic management during the Annual Volunteer Fire Department Parade and Carnival. By 3:30 Frank was looking anxiously at his watch, and by 3:40 he was nudging Reid out of the office. Then he set off across the green to the Presbyterian church.

This time Frank allowed Melba, the church secretary, to formally announce him, so Bob Rush was sitting authoritatively behind his desk when Frank entered. The minister's earnest blue eyes met Frank's shrewd brown ones directly. Frank ignored his host's offer of a chair and instead began to prowl around the office.

"This is a nice little table," Frank remarked. "I bet it's an antique. Did you get it over at Martin Deurr's barn?"

Deurr's barn, an astounding tangle of broken-down furniture and worthless gimcracks with a GARAGE SALE sign perpetually posted out front, was what passed for an antique shop in Trout Run. Bob Rush's delicate mahogany table was as unlikely to have turned up there as a Renoir among the paint-by-number landscapes at the church bazaar.

A flicker of condescension passed over Bob's face so quickly that it might almost have gone unnoticed. "It's a piece that's been in my family," he said.

"Ah. You're not from around here, are you? Connecticut, I think someone told me."

"That's right."

"And what brought you up to Trout Run? There's not much here for an eligible bachelor like you," Frank asked.

"The same might be said for you," the minister parried, matching Frank's lighthearted tone.

"Oh, I moved here to be closer to my daughter," Frank confided. "She lives in Chappaqua, but that's too rich for my blood." He watched Pastor Bob closely for some reaction, but detected nothing. "You used to be at the Rappahonack Presbyterian church, right near there, huh?" In answer to Bob's pleasant nod, Frank continued, "I'm surprised you'd want to leave it. Caroline loves that area because it's so close to the City—museums, concerts, theater. Seems like that sort of thing would be right up your alley."

Either Bob Rush was a consummate actor or he had nothing to hide, for he showed not the slightest discomfort at Frank's questions. "I grew restless ministering to a wealthy congregation. Someone's got to do it, but that's not how I wanted to serve the Lord."

"Got tired of trying to push those camels through the needle's eye, huh?"

"Exactly. I'm happier in Trout Run."

"I imagine you are." Frank suddenly went for the jugular. "There's no Ashley Manning here."

Bob's handsome face became as solid as marble. All that gave away his shock were his ears, which had turned a vibrant red. "I don't know what you're talking about," he said levelly.

"I think you do. Ashley Manning was a sixteen-year-old girl in your youth group in Rappahonack. She accused you of forcing yourself on her sexually. Nothing was proven, but the congregation decided it was best for you to leave. They gave you a good recommendation so they could get rid of you.

"Now you come to Trout Run," Frank continued, "and a year later a pretty seventeen-year-old girl—who I understand was quite taken with you—has vanished into thin air. She had been slipping out to meet someone late at night without her father knowing. What am I supposed to make of that?"

Any pretense at self-control was gone. "You cannot *possibly* think I had anything to do with Janelle's disappearance!" Bob dropped his head in his hands and wove his fingers through his thick hair. "My God, will this thing follow me the rest of my life?"

"I'd be interested to hear your side of the story," Frank said, unmoved by Bob's show of despair.

"Ashley Manning was a very unhappy young lady, desperate for attention," Bob began. "She started by making suggestive remarks to me that I tried to ignore. But her behavior kept getting more . . . inappropriate. I knew I had to speak to her. I should have called her parents, but I didn't—I just talked to her alone. She was upset—I suppose she perceived it as a rejection. Two days later, she came out with these accusations that I had . . ." Bob's voice faltered. "Touched her, come on to her.

"Everyone who knew me well at Rappahonack knew that these accusations were completely groundless. But the atmosphere of hysteria surrounding clergymen who take advantage of children sexually—well, all it takes is for one kid to say something, and your career is over. I was lucky to be able to leave quietly."

Bob shook his head and gazed at the Japanese woodblock prints on his wall. "At first, I felt like I had been exiled to Trout Run. Forced out of a good position and into a little church where I could quickly be forgotten. But in a few months, I began to really enjoy my work here. I feel that I'm making a genuine contribution to people's lives. So I started to see the incident in Rappahonack as one of the mysterious ways that God guides our lives. I feel that I was meant to come here, and God acted through Ashley to achieve that."

Frank regarded the minister dubiously. It sounded like revisionist history to him. Still, many people *were* unjustly accused of abuse and had no way to defend themselves. But it was just as true that thousands of kids really were abused and their attackers went unpunished. How could he know if Bob was telling the truth?

"What about Janelle?" Frank asked. "Last time we talked, you said she told you something that you couldn't tell me. I think you better drop the sacred confession routine now."

Too weary to put up an argument, Bob said, "I didn't really know Janelle all that well, although I could see that she was different from the other kids. More serious, more inquisitive. She did seem drawn to me—but, not in the way Ashley had been," he hastened to explain.

"Did you ever meet her alone at night?" Frank asked.

"Good Lord, no!" Bob said. "I never saw her outside youth group. She liked to ask me challenging questions about the Scripture passages we were studying. Or about ethical issues like capital punishment or euthanasia. She was grappling with the realization that right and wrong are not always so easy to determine. Then one evening after youth group, she said she needed to speak to me privately."

"When was this?" Frank asked.

Bob paused to think. "Early February, I would say. It was clear she wanted to stay behind to talk after the other kids had left. But I was so spooked by Ashley's accusations, that I had no intention of being left all alone with Janelle at night. So I told her to stop by my office after school the next day, when I knew Melba and other people would be around."

"And did she come?" Frank inquired.

"Oh, yes." Bob sighed, reluctant to go on.

"Well, what happened?" Frank prompted him.

"I'm not proud of the way I treated her. I felt the need to maintain some distance between us—physically and emotionally. When she came in, she closed the office door behind her, but I got up and opened it again. I made some excuse that I had to keep an eye out for Mr. Enright, the handyman."

"What did she *say*?" Frank asked, trying to hold his exasperation in check.

"She started out by asking me what to do when God didn't hear your prayers. I said God always hears our prayers, we just don't always understand his answers. I explained that God doesn't always give us what we ask for.

"Janelle seemed very dissatisfied with my answer,"

Bob continued. "But I really believe what I told her. When I was going through my ordeal with Ashley, I prayed constantly that God would reveal the truth and my name would be cleared. But instead he answered my prayers by bringing me here. At first I didn't see the wisdom in that, but now I do."

"But you were hardly in a position to share that example from your life with Janelle," Frank responded, unconcerned by how callous he sounded.

Bob seemed to think he deserved whatever Frank had to dish out. "No, I didn't do a very good job of helping Janelle to understand God's ways. She blurted out that she didn't believe in God anymore, because if there were a God, he wouldn't let terrible things happen."

Finally, something of substance! Frank leaned forward. "What terrible things?"

Now it was Bob's turn to pace around the room. He stood looking out the window with his hands buried in his pockets. "Then Melba popped her head in to ask what kind of rolls she should order for the men's breakfast, and Janelle ran out," Bob answered flatly.

Frank kicked the tasteful little wicker wastepaper basket beside Bob's desk and sent it skittering across the floor. "And you didn't think any of this was worth mentioning until now?"

Bob shrugged defensively. "She kept coming to youth group and she seemed okay. I suppose in retrospect, she was a little cool to me, and I was subconsciously relieved. But if I really thought she was having a personal crisis, I would have reached out to her," Bob pleaded.

Compassion was not forthcoming. "But she said, 'God wouldn't let *terrible* things happen.' "

"I thought she meant things like famines in Africa or terrorism attacks, not something in her own life. I presumed she was just coming to terms with the central mystery of faith—how to reconcile a loving God with the existence of evil."

"Oh, spare me the theological claptrap," Frank said in disgust, as he rose to leave. "That kid was crying out for help and you ignored her."

15

FRANK STALKED ACROSS the green with his gaze fixed on the patrol car parked in front of his office. If he could just make it there without anyone stopping him to offer advice, or complain, or seek his services, he could get away for a minute and think. The sound of the door slamming and the engine starting brought Doris to the door, but Frank pulled out fast, ignoring her waving arm in the rearview mirror.

Cruising out of town, oblivious to the glories of the Verona Range reflected in the clear, still waters of Diamond Pond, Frank let his mind wander. As irritating as he found Bob Rush, the minister's story had the ring of truth. If Bob wasn't the other man in Janelle's life, who was? *Was* there even another man? Why did he believe a sullen, glue-sniffing kid with a chip on his shoulder, when Kim, Melanie, and Jack all claimed it wasn't so? What if the mystery man was the blind alley, the false lead?

What terrible thing had happened before Janelle ran? Certainly it wasn't some petty squabble with Craig, or even her father's refusal to let her go away to college—

she wouldn't have laid that at God's feet. No, it had to be something really big that made her desperate to get away. Everyone she knew claimed not to have the slightest idea what could have been troubling her. But one of them—Tommy or Jack or Dorothy or Kim or Melanie—must know, *had to* know.

And why wouldn't that person tell? Because he—or she—was part of the problem? What was Janelle was running from?

That line of reasoning seemed to take him right back where he didn't want to go. To Jack, and this matter Miss Noakes had brought up. Of course he didn't think running off was "in the blood"—but abusiveness tended to be passed down from generation to generation. Despite carrying on about how terribly Tom Pettigrew had treated Dorothy, had Jack been just as cruel to Rosemary? And had he then transferred the cruelty to Janelle? Oh, he didn't beat her—that much Frank knew. But sexual abuse could underlie the devotion everyone spoke of.

And then there was that odd business with Petey the cat. Miss Noakes thought he had been stolen, and someone else had recently claimed their pet had been stolen. Who was that? Frank tried to think but came up blank. Someone had cut through that pen at Harlan Mabley's petting zoo, but nothing had been stolen.

Pens . . . cages . . . something was coming to him. Yes, the little boy he'd nearly run over, Jeffrey Maguire. He'd kept insisting that he hadn't left his rabbit's cage unlocked; that someone had come along and stolen him. Why would anyone want a cat, an emu, and a rabbit? He wondered if Jeffrey's rabbit had ever turned up—he'd have to call.

A huge flatbed truck carrying part of a prefabricated house interrupted the seamless flow of Frank's thoughts.

Pulling onto the road ahead of him, the truck moved at a snail's pace and blocked his view. Someone in Verona must be getting a new house, and Frank had no intention of following it all the way there. Passing on the twisting road when you couldn't see oncoming traffic could be deadly, so Frank simply turned off on a side road at his first opportunity, figuring he'd find a way to wind through back roads to his destination.

He found himself on Blascoe Road—a funny name, and one that stuck in his mind, for some reason. Then it dawned on him. Celia Lambert lived along here some-where; talking to her was on his "to-do" list. A woman out working in her garden told him Celia's place was four more houses down, on the right.

He might have found the house even without the directions. Bird feeders and birdhouses of every size and shape hung everywhere—from the house, from poles in the yard, nailed to trees. And Celia herself stood among them, filling one with tiny black seeds from a large sack at her feet.

She smiled and waved as Frank approached. "Thank you for sending me that copy of the coroner's report," she said. "You don't know how reassuring it was to find out my uncle died instantaneously and didn't lie there suffering." Frank nodded and let her natter on about what a good job Bob Rush did at the funeral and all the nice cards she'd been receiving.

Finally she paused for a breath, and Frank could get a word in. "Celia, your uncle sometimes visited the Nature's Way gift shop, didn't he?"

"Yes, do you know I even got a card from . . ." Sud-denly it seemed to strike her odd that Frank should ask that question. Odd that he had even come to call. The wariness of their last meeting returned. "Why?"

"A young man who works there told me he once saw your uncle get up unassisted and change the CD in the player."

"That's ridicu—"

Frank held up his hand for silence. "The coroner discussed your uncle's case with me. He said it was possible that with a brain injury like his, sight could start to come back." Frank omitted all Hibbert's qualifiers and disclaimers. "Your uncle could see, couldn't he?"

Lying didn't come naturally to Celia Lambert. Presented with a direct challenge to her story, she dropped the ruse without a moment's hesitation.

"I told him he could never keep it up! I knew he'd slip up and it would all come out!" Celia began to cry. "He *was* blinded by the accident," she said through her sobs. "He *did* have pain and suffering. But about three years after it happened, his sight gradually started coming back. He was afraid if he admitted it, no one would believe that he'd ever been blind, and that he'd have to give back the eight hundred thousand dollars from the lawsuit. And by that time, most of it was already gone."

"He went through all that in three years?" Frank asked. There certainly had been no sign of extravagant living at Lambert's little house.

Celia sighed. "The lawyer got a big chunk of it. Then Uncle Dell put me through college, paid for my brother to go to podiatry school, and bought my other brother a truck. He gave my father money to pay him back for what my father called his freeloading. And he invested money in some stupid real estate deal in Florida. He never could hold on to money—that's why he lived with our family all those years.

"Finally, the lawyer set up a trust fund so my uncle would have something to live on. That's all that was left.

That and the house. He was terrified of losing the house; it would have meant going back to live with my dad. I told him to talk to his lawyer about it—that he probably wouldn't have to give the money back, in any case. But Uncle Dell was too scared even to tell the lawyer. I'm the only one who knew."

"So if he had seen what happened to Janelle, he wouldn't have admitted it, would he? He had too much to lose," Frank said.

Celia squirmed "I told him if he saw something, we could write an anonymous note. But he swore to me he didn't see anything."

Frank caught her eye and held her gaze for a long moment. "But you can't be positive he was telling the truth."

Celia shrugged and gnawed on her thumbnail. "There's, there's something else. Ever since New Year's, he's been a nervous wreck. He was convinced that Ned Stevenson suspected he could see and was spying on him, watching for him to slip up."

"Why did he think that?" Frank asked.

"He saw Ned's SUV driving past his place a couple of times a week."

16

FRANK AWOKE before the alarm went off on Monday. Instinctively he reached out for Estelle, but his hand came up empty. It had been nearly eighteen months now, and still there were times that he forgot she was dead.

Morning had been their special time. Both early risers, they would lie in bed in the gray predawn light and talk—the gutters that needed cleaning, the friend who had cancer, Caroline's math test, Frank's latest investigation. Sometimes, after listening for any sound of Caroline stirring, they made love.

Now, lolling in bed had lost all its pleasure for him. The rising sun seemed to reproach him for all the things he'd left unsaid and undone in twenty-five years of marriage. He hadn't appreciated Estelle enough—never told her what a fine job she'd done raising Caroline, making a comfortable home for them, earning money teaching heavy-handed children the piano, and playing "I Honestly Love You" at countless weddings so that Caroline could go to Princeton.

And he'd never given Estelle flowers—never once in twenty-five years. Half the time he forgot their anniversary altogether, but occasionally when signs in store windows reminded him of the approach of Valentine's Day, he'd go into the florist's to inquire. When informed of the price of a dozen roses, he'd stagger out again, determined not to be manipulated into paying high holiday prices. He'd just wait and surprise her with them some other time. But he never got around to it. And now it was too late.

Frank escaped the bed before his demons got the better of him. Unable to face the prospect of yet another bowl of Cheerios, he headed out to Malone's diner. He arrived so early that the glass door was still locked, but he could see Marge in there, making coffee and filling creamers. His persistent knocking finally gained him entrance.

"The grill's not hot yet," Marge said, in lieu of good-morning. "So don't be clamoring for eggs."

"I'm in no hurry. I'll just sit here and read the paper and drink coffee until you're ready to feed me," Frank said. Somehow, just sitting in the steamy brightness of Malone's with Marge and Regis going about their routine lifted his spirits. Nearly half an hour passed and the sun was fully up when the next customer entered.

Ned Stevenson came in and took a seat at the far end of the counter from Frank.

Marge glared at him. "Do you have to sit clear down there, Ned, and make me trot back and forth when there's just the two of you?"

Ned forced a smile. "Why sure, Marge, I'd be happy to move down next to Frank. He just looked so absorbed in his paper, I hated to disturb him."

Frank patted the empty stool next to his. "Make yourself comfortable, Ned."

While an encounter with a Stevenson this early in the morning wasn't particularly good for his digestion, he did want to ask Ned about Dell Lambert. He slid his open copy of the weekly *Mountain Herald* toward Ned. "Quite a turnout for old man Lambert's funeral, huh? I didn't realize he had so many friends."

"He was a fixture around town." Ned studied the breakfast menu, as if he didn't already have it committed to memory. "I suppose his cronies will miss him over at the Store."

Frank nodded. "He lived a good, long life. Too bad the last few months of it were unhappy."

"Why's that?" Ned obligingly allowed himself to be set up.

"Celia said he seemed to think you were spying on him."

Ned met Frank's steady gaze without blinking. "Spying on him? Why would he think that?"

"He noticed your car cruising back and forth in front of his house. His sight had been gradually coming back over the past few years, and he thought you were on to him."

Ned's mouth actually dropped open, giving him a rather foolish expression. He lifted his coffee cup to his lips, but his hand shook, and coffee splashed on his clean khakis. "Well," Ned said finally, "I wouldn't have given Mr. Lambert credit for being so sharp. But I did suspect that he could see. And I was keeping an eye on him. No crime in that, though, is there?" He rose and tossed two dollars on the counter. "I better get to work."

Marge emerged from the kitchen in time to see the door close behind Ned. "What happened to him?" she asked, setting Frank's eggs and hash browns before him. "I thought he wanted breakfast."

"Guess he changed his mind," Frank answered. "Could I get a little jelly?"

He hadn't really known what to expect when he confronted Ned about Mr. Lambert, but it certainly wasn't that. There was a lie in there somewhere, but he was damned if he could figure out what it was.

Later, standing on the steps of Malone's diner, his stomach comfortably full, Frank watched a school bus rumble past the green on its way to High Peaks High School. Tommy Pettigrew would be on that bus—assuming, of course, that he was attending school today. Impulsively, Frank decided to head over to the high school and catch a word with him before the school day began.

He didn't even have to pull into the school driveway to find the boy. Tommy was leaning against a telephone pole at the edge of the school property, smoking a cigarette. Frank parked on the side of the road and walked toward Tommy, who watched him approach with a flat-eyed stare.

"Hi, Tom—got a minute?" Frank asked.

"Not really. School's starting soon."

"Well, I know you wouldn't want to be late. I just want your opinion—won't take long." Frank smiled. "You know, I've been talking to Kim and Melanie, and I get the feeling that those two didn't truly *know* Janelle, the real Janelle, you know what I mean?"

Tommy snorted. "That's for sure. All they care about is themselves, those stuck-up bitches."

"But it was different with you and Janelle—after all, you're blood relatives. You understood her, even if you don't hang around with the same kids anymore."

Tommy nodded. Some of his usual bravado seemed to dissipate.

Frank proceeded cautiously. Maybe, just maybe, he was getting somewhere. "You could probably tell each other things that you wouldn't want other friends to know."

Tommy didn't answer. His eyes had a faraway look, focused on the mountains surrounding the school. Suddenly Frank saw him as vulnerable, almost wistful. Maybe Tommy really did miss Janelle. Maybe he'd read Tommy all wrong. When the kid had said he was glad Janelle was gone, perhaps he'd meant she was better off gone, he was glad she was safely away. Could Tommy have been covering for Janelle all along?

"Tom," Frank said softly. "It's all right to ask for help."

Tommy's eyes met his for the first time in their conversation. Frank waited, but the boy said nothing. He remembered something Jack had said about the Harveys not washing their dirty linen in public. "If Janelle's in some kind of trouble, some kind of danger—from anyone—we can straighten it out," Frank went on, afraid to say too much.

Tommy ground out his cigarette.

"I know something was troubling her. Maybe something to do with her family," Frank forged on. Tommy's boot stopped its obsessive grinding, but he kept his eyes focused on his feet.

Frank knew he was pushing the limits, but he didn't see any way around it. "She asked Pastor Bob, 'Why does God let terrible things happen?' What did she mean by that, Tom?"

Tommy took a step backward. "How should I know? What did *he* say?"

"He didn't know. They were interrupted before Janelle could tell him."

Up on the hill, a bell rang faintly. Tommy grabbed his backpack. "I gotta go—school's starting."

Frank grabbed the boy's arm. "What terrible thing happened?"

Tommy pulled away angrily. "There was no terrible

thing! Leave me alone!" And he loped up the school driveway, blending in with the crowd of hurrying teenagers.

Frank gazed listlessly out his office window, tormenting himself with what he could have done differently. Should he have come straight out with it? *Tommy, was your uncle sexually abusing Janelle?* Tommy would've denied it and complained to Jack. Jack would be outraged and complain to Clyde. And no one in town would side with him. Why should they? He had no concrete evidence to back up the accusation.

A little red Mazda entered his field of vision, pulling into the parking lot alongside the post office. He watched, mesmerized, as a pair of strappy sandals emerged, followed by two slender, tanned legs. Immediately he perked up—those legs could belong to only one person in Trout Run.

He smiled as he watched Penny Stevenson bounce up the steps to the post office. Those long legs were wasted behind a library desk. They must have been more of an asset in her hash-slinging days at the Trail's End. The place had a slightly raffish reputation, mostly because it was run by Laurel Matson, an aging hippie from downstate, and had some odd vegetarian dishes on the menu. Frank's smile broadened as he imagined what Clyde's reaction must have been when he first learned his daughter-in-law was passing out plates of tofu to backpackers.

The scene evolving in Frank's mind's eye grew more detailed; he could see the interior of the Trail's End quite clearly. When certain faces revealed themselves to him, he raced out the office door, hoping to catch Penny before she got back to her car.

Luckily, post office workers were no faster in Trout

Run than anywhere else, so he arrived beside the little red car just as Penny did.

"Hi, Frank." She flashed him that big grin. "Did you run over here to give me a parking ticket?"

"Nah, I'm saving my summons for when Clyde parks in front of a hydrant." They chuckled together. "Seeing you made me think of something," Frank told her.

"You need more research done?"

"No, it actually has more to do with your previous job."

Penny's megawatt smile seemed to dim a bit, but she kept up her cheerful banter. "You want to know how to carry three cups of coffee and a piece of pie in one trip?"

"No, I just wondered—do any of the local kids ever hang out at the Trail's End? Maybe coming in to hear the music?"

Working her softly colored agate beads through her fingers, Penny studied the ground for a long moment. "Unaccompanied minors aren't allowed in the bar. Laurel almost lost her license a few years ago, and now she's very strict about that."

A heavy silence hung between them. Frank waited.

"I knew I should have spoken up sooner." The words erupted from Penny like soda from a shaken bottle. "Ned thought it wasn't important, that I'd only stir up trouble for Nick Reilly, the bartender, and give my in-laws another reason to be pissed at me." She brought her head up and faced Frank squarely. "Do you ever feel that you lose perspective living here? I mean, everyone knows everyone else's business." She spread her arms in a graceful arc. "Everyone has an opinion on how you ought to be living your life. But then when something bad happens, the heads all go straight down into the sand. And after a while, you start thinking *you're* the one who's

crazy." She ended her speech with a thump of both mani-
cured hands against her chest.

Even though she was obviously distressed, Frank
could not help smiling. He wondered how long Trout
Run, and Ned Stevenson, could withstand the force of
her personality. "Believe me, Penny, you're one of the
sanest people I know. Now, start at the beginning and tell
me what's troubling you."

Penny took a deep breath. "Back in March, when I was
still working at the Trail's End, Janelle came in one night
with two girlfriends to hear the band that was playing in
the bar. At the time I didn't know who she was, but with
her face plastered all over town on those posters, it came
back to me that I'd seen her there."

"I knew that damn Kim was keeping something from
me," Frank stewed.

"I'm not surprised. The rule about no unaccompanied
minors in the bar really is strictly enforced. But Laurel
was out of town that weekend, and Melanie Powers is
Nick Reilly's niece. So he agreed to let them come to
hear the Blue Mountain Stompers if they would just
drink Coke and not take up a table from paying customers.

"It was really busy that night so I didn't pay much
attention to them. But I remember seeing Janelle apart
from the other two, talking to this intense-looking guy
with a ponytail. It wouldn't have stuck in my mind,
except that she had a pen and she was taking notes."

Frank's grip on his pen tightened. "Go on."

"That's it. When Janelle disappeared, I asked Nick if
he didn't think we should tell the police that we had seen
her talking to a strange man. But Nick said he knew the
guy. That his name is Pablo; he comes into the Trail's End
every few weeks, and it couldn't be important. So I let it

drop." She chewed on her lower lip, scraping off the deep red lipstick. "Then I got the job at the library and I put the whole thing out of my mind. But when you came in, I started thinking about it again. And when you told me Janelle was supposed to do primary research for her paper, it struck me that she might have been interviewing this Pablo guy."

"Interviewing him about utopian communities? You mean, you think he lives on a commune or something?" Frank asked.

Penny shrugged. "Could be. You can tell from looking at him that he's not an investment banker. Of course, that doesn't mean he's some kind of freak."

Frank glanced at his watch. "Nick Reilly on duty now?"

"Yes," Penny said, "but wait until after the lunch rush, when Laurel will be back in the kitchen talking to the cook about dinner. He'll know that I sent you, but it would help if you could keep Laurel out of it."

Frank put his arm around Penny's shoulders. "You did the right thing," he reassured her.

Penny offered him a smile that trailed off to a grimace. "Yeah, then how come I feel like the proverbial stone has just shifted from one shoulder to the other? "

"I asked you a question and you answered it. Surely the Stevensons don't expect you to lie to the police."

Penny sighed. "I can't seem to figure out what they expect of me. I guess that's my problem. I don't know how to be a good Stevenson wife." She gazed off at the mountains. "My parents were killed in a plane crash when I was five. My mother's cousin was my guardian, and she shipped me off to boarding school as soon as she could. When I first met Ned and he described this place, it all sounded so perfect, so Norman Rockwell. I guess I fell in love with the whole package—the small town life surrounded by a big family. But I can't seem to get this family solidarity thing right." Penny smiled ruefully as she climbed into her car. "I guess it's like royalty," she said, buckling her seat belt. "You have to be born into it."

Frank watched the little red car zip out toward Stevenson Road, trying to suppress the image of old man Stevenson as he heard what his daughter-in-law had done.

17

THERE ARE ALL KINDS OF BARTENDERS: suave ones who work at fancy French restaurants; sexy young men and women who mix drinks at singles bars; avuncular types who tend neighborhood pubs; and salty, tough guys who pour shots and beers at working men's hangouts. But all successful bartenders share one quality—they're bullshit artists. Nick Reilly was no exception.

Frank entered the bar at the Trail's End at ten after three and found Nick polishing glasses and cutting lemons in preparation for the dinnertime rush. He greeted Frank cordially; if he felt any twinge of concern at having a cop leaning on his bar, he didn't show it.

"Hey, Frank, how you doin'? Some kinda weather we've been having, huh? Not nearly as buggy as usual," Nick said as he set a stein of beer in front of Frank.

"No, it's great weather for hiking or working in the yard. 'Course the fisherman all hate these clear, sunny days. Fish bite better in the rain."

"Ain't that the truth. Say, you ever pull anything out of that stretch of the brook that runs behind your house?" Nick asked.

"Yeah, I caught a beautiful brown trout a couple of weeks ago. I haven't fished since then—quit while I'm ahead."

"You fly-fish?" Nick inquired.

Frank waved dismissively. "Naw, none of that fancy stuff for me. Just a worm on a hook . . . and I eat what I catch, too."

"Hey, I'm with you, man! What's the point if you don't eat 'em, huh?" Nick grinned, slapping the polished oak bar for emphasis. His smile revealed two slightly overlapping front teeth, an imperfection that, along with a smattering of freckles, lent a permanently youthful air to a face that was pushing forty.

Frank was smiling, too. He remembered being in the Trail's End with Edwin just a few weeks back and overhearing Nick talking to some fly fisherman at the bar. On that occasion Reilly had been agreeing that anyone who did not release what he caught should be split and fried himself.

"So, you going to have a band in here tonight?" Frank asked, nodding to the right of the bar, where two straight-backed chairs sat on a small raised platform. In recognition that musicians might need a little more light than candles stuck in wine bottles could provide, someone had carelessly tacked a single spotlight to the exposed beam that crossed over the stage. Performers weren't coddled at the Trail's End.

"No, Jim and Mary Weaver will be here Saturday," Nick explained.

"You get a pretty good crowd in here on Saturdays, even in the winter, don't you?"

Nick shrugged. "Depends—some groups always pull them in."

"I hear the Blue Mountain Stompers have a regular

following," Frank said. "I've never heard them, but the kids all seem to like them. They must play rock, huh?"

"No, it's more like bluegrass—they call it Adirondack Country. You should come." Nick checked a schedule that was taped up next to the cash register. "They'll be here again August tenth."

"Yeah, maybe I will. There's one of their fans I wouldn't mind running into," Frank said as he casually studied a framed photo of the previous year's Talent Show Night.

"Oh, who's that?" Nick asked, his green eyes entirely guileless.

"A fellow named Pablo—I don't know his last name. I hear he hangs out here sometimes."

The first flush of understanding crept across Nick's ingenuous moon face. He struggled to maintain his casual tone as he filled bowls with salted nuts. "Pablo? Yeah, name sounds familiar, but I meet so many people here . . ."

"Sure, I understand," Frank said as he helped himself to the nuts. "This particular guy was seen talking to Janelle Harvey a few weeks before she disappeared. Does that ring a bell?"

Nick craned his neck to look beyond the huge fieldstone fireplace that divided the room from a small service area leading back to the kitchen. Apparently seeing no one, he propped his elbows on the bar and looked Frank square in the eyes. "You've been talking to Penny Stevenson, haven't you?"

Frank lowered his usually resonant voice to a hoarse whisper and leaned so close that his head nearly touched the bartender's. "Listen, I don't care about you letting those girls into the bar. I just think this Pablo guy could tell me something about Janelle's disappearance. There's no need for Laurel to know anything about it."

Nick emitted a sharp guffaw that sounded like a terrier's yelp. "Are you kidding? If you go into Malone's and order a piece of pie, those old farts sittin' in front of the Store know about it before you've finished up the crust. It won't be long before they find out why you're here."

Nick began to pace behind the bar. "When I got out of high school, I worked as a logger for a while. Every night, I came home feeling like I'd been hit by a freight train. Then a friend did me a 'favor' and got me in as a prison guard at Dannemora." Nick stared unseeingly at the array of liquor bottles beside him. "Jesus, the stuff I saw there! People told me I'd get used to it. But I didn't want to be the kind of guy who could get used to things like that, so I walked out. When Laurel hired me fifteen years ago I was flat broke; working odd jobs and crashing with friends. Now I have a little house over in Verona and a new car . . ." Nick's voice trailed off, and he threw down his bar rag in disgust. "What do you want to know?"

The thrill of elation Frank felt when he realized that Nick Reilly was going to cooperate suffocated every spark of compassion within him, and he began to pepper the bartender with questions. "How well do you know this Pablo? Where does he live?"

"He's been coming in maybe once a month or every six weeks for over a year now. The reason he first stuck in my mind is he always drinks cognac"—Nick pointed to a bottle of Hennessy—"even in the summer. He nurses one glass for hours, then he leaves. He always has a book with him. Never says much to me—guess I'm not highbrow enough for him—but he usually strikes up a conversation with someone at the bar. Once he got a bunch of Canadians riled up, talking about Quebec separatists. Then he managed to start a thing on affirmative action with the only black customer we've had in here for months."

Frank rolled his eyes. "Sounds like someone who could clear out a bar in fifteen minutes."

"Yeah, a couple of times I've had to ask him to tone it down. People don't come in here for that bullshit. They want to relax. But he never gets the hint. Comes in the next time and starts up all over again."

"So on this night last March, he was talking with Janelle. Did you overhear their conversation?" Frank asked.

Nick shook his head. "I was really busy—the place was packed and the band was playing. But they weren't arguing. She seemed to be eatin' up whatever crap he was handing out."

"So how old is this guy? Is he attractive?"

Nick grinned and shrugged. "Not *my* type. He's in his early thirties, I'd say. Got long brown hair in a ponytail—I guess chicks go for that nowadays. Sort of high cheekbones and thick lips, and real blue eyes. Girls *definitely* go for that."

"*Blue* eyes? I thought he was Hispanic," Frank said.

"No, why? Oh, you mean because of the name? No, he's as American as you or me. Somehow I don't think that's his real name. His parents probably christened him Bill Smith, but he always introduces himself as just Pablo. You know, like 'Madonna' or 'Cher.'"

"I'm liking this guy less and less," Frank said. "But he sounds like the type Janelle might have been drawn to. She'd think he was exotic, not like the high school boys from Trout Run."

"Oh yeah, there's no doubt he's not from around here," Nick agreed.

"So where does he live?"

Nick shrugged. "I never asked him. Can't be too close by or he'd probably be in here more often."

Frank nodded and looked around the Trail's End, as if seeing it for the first time. The bar area had rough-hewn oak tables scarred by two decades of patrons' carved initials and declarations of love. The marginally more refined dining room had honey-pine paneled walls decorated with oils and watercolors by local artists. Tucked in the corner of each frame, a discreet little price tag attempted to lure diners into taking home some artwork along with their doggie bags. The faded ink and yellowing tags suggested that no one was ever tempted.

"I wonder why he comes in here?" Frank mused.

"There's not too many places in the North Country where a guy like Pablo can order a cognac and spout off the way he does, without getting beat up. Laurel has a soft spot for weirdoes. Somehow they're drawn to this place."

Frank's eyebrows shot up. "Laurel knows this guy?"

Nick raised a cautioning hand. "No, no. Honestly," he reiterated. "I just meant Laurel's got this liberal 'live-and-let-live' attitude that sets the tone around here, and it attracts a certain kind of customer."

Frank conceded the point, then cocked his head expectantly. "If she's so tolerant, how come you're certain she's going to can you over those girls in the bar?"

Nick's face remained grim. "The Trail's End is her baby: her work, her home, her family all rolled into one. Back in '82 when she nearly lost her liquor license, she was crazed. She called her old man—this hotshot Manhattan lawyer who she hates—and had him pull some strings. It tore her up to have to crawl to him, but that's how desperate she was to save the place. Her tolerance stops at anybody she sees as jeopardizing the Trail's End."

Frank rubbed his temples and rested his chin on his

hand. Why were the Powers That Be conspiring to keep him from ever enjoying a moment of pure satisfaction in this case? He honestly believed this Pablo lead was solid, but what if it turned out to be nothing, and it cost Nick Reilly the job he loved?

"Look, Nick, I really appreciate what you've told me. If it turns out that we find Janelle with this Pablo character, then you'll be a hero. Laurel won't be able to hold up her head in Trout Run if she fires the man who brought Janelle Harvey home."

Nick tossed his bar rag in the sink. "I hope you're right."

Frank could hardly wait to get back to the office. The information from Nick Reilly was like a huge present that couldn't be unwrapped until then. On the short drive from the Trail's End to the center of town, he prioritized his to-do list: first, call the state police to see if they had anything on Pablo; next, talk to Kim and Melanie about that night at the Trail's End; and finally, start nosing around to find Pablo.

Frank had barely placed his foot over the threshold of the Town Office when his plans began to disintegrate.

Doris came running out to greet him. "You gotta get straight out to Harlan Mabely's place," she said breathlessly. "There's been a murder!"

The news hit Frank like a blast of wind at the lookout tower on Whiteface. "Harlan's dead?"

"No, no. Harlan called it in. He was so hysterical, all I could make out is that it's a woman named Martha."

"Martha's not a woman, she's an emu." Frank pivoted in the doorway and headed back out to the patrol car. "But I'm sure Harlan's very upset. I'll go over there; you tell Earl to hold down the fort here." Frank sighed. Thank

God the old man was alive, but that overgrown chicken of his couldn't have picked a more inconvenient time to get its neck caught in a fence, or whatever it did to take itself out of this world.

As soon as he passed the first sign announcing the Adirondack Petting Zoo Frank switched on the lights and siren, to reassure Harlan that he was taking his call seriously. He'd calm the old fart down, dispel the murder theories, and be back in his office inside the hour.

The scene that greeted Frank soon scuttled that plan.

Harlan shot out of his office so quickly that Frank had to slam on his brakes to avoid running him down. The old man's hands were covered with blood, which had smudged onto his face and clothes, making him look like an extra in a low-budget horror film. But the pain and terror in Harlan's eyes were all too real.

"Come," he wailed, tugging on Frank's clean shirt sleeve, oblivious to the dried blood that was rubbing off. "Come see what they done to my poor girl!"

The first sign of carnage appeared on the path leading back to the animal pens. One of the emu's long, spindly legs had been hacked off and lay on the path like a grotesque road sign.

Harlan stopped and pointed piteously at the disembodied limb. "We're closed on Mondays. I came over to do the evening feeding, and I saw that. At first I thought it was just a big stick; I had to get right up close before I realized what it was. Even then, I couldn't believe that my Martha was dead. I ran back to check on her . . ." Harlan's sobs choked off his speech. He grabbed Frank's arm and led him wordlessly back to Martha's pen.

Despite Harlan's condition and the mutilated leg, Frank was not prepared for what awaited him. Feathers were everywhere; the wind pushed them around the pen like the remnants of some obscene pillow fight. The other leg was woven through the chainlinks of the fence, and Martha's plucked torso, unrecognizable as a bird, lay in front of her shed. The bare dirt inside the pen had been disturbed, and something protruded from it. Reluctantly, Frank stepped forward for a closer look, then recoiled. Martha's head had been buried in the ground and her severed neck emerged from the earth, a hideous stalk craning toward the light.

The carnage at the petting zoo disturbed Frank as deeply as any murder he'd ever investigated. This was no prank—Martha's murder had significance. Was it linked to Janelle's disappearance? If Janelle was with whoever had killed Martha so sadistically, she certainly wasn't safe. Frank's thoughts tumbled through his mind as he drove back to the office.

Now he saw Miss Noakes and the Maguires in a new light. What if someone really had taken Petey from the safety of the old lady's garden and killed him in the meadow? What if Jeffrey Maguire really had remembered to latch his rabbit's cage? Another thought flitted around the periphery of his mind, like a mosquito he could hear but not see. Something else about animals . . . what was it?

He made his mind go blank, then slowly let information reenter. Benjamin Bunny, Petey the cat, Martha the emu—odd that they all had people names. It hadn't dawned on him before. It seemed he knew of another animal with a human name like that. Whose pet was he thinking of?

Frank cruised around the green and passed the old flower shop, which had once again fallen into disuse. Gradually, the volunteers had given up on their work, divided by their doubts over whether Janelle had been abducted or not. Suddenly Frank braked. Leo! That was it. Elinor Stevenson's little dog Leo—he remembered hearing about his death when he had been in the flower shop with the volunteers. He pulled the car over and let his head fall back against the seat. What was it they had told him? Leo had been found crushed under some lumber in the yard, even though he had never before left the safety of the store. Not an accident; another victim.

Frank shook himself. There was no point in speculating on worst-case scenarios. He would catch Martha's executioner, although the crime scene had yielded precious little information to go on. In the meantime, he had other work to do.

Frank wanted to catch Janelle's friends away from the inhibiting presence of their parents. He headed to the Pizza Haven and in his first lucky break of the day, he found both girls there. Melanie was taking orders behind the counter in a blouse no bigger than a pocket handkerchief, while Kim sat alone in a booth with a magazine and a slice.

Frank dropped into the seat across from Kim. She looked up with a smile, which disappeared when she saw who had joined her.

"Now what?" she asked, her eyes returning to the page opened before her.

Frank had given up on trying either to win Kim over or to intimidate her. "Tell me about the night at the Trail's End when Janelle met Pablo," he said levelly.

Kim had just taken a bite from her pizza, and began coughing so hard that customers at the other tables looked over in concern. "Who told you that?" she asked, her voice still raspy from her choking fit.

"Never mind who *did* tell me. I want to know why you *didn't* tell me. Now you just start at the beginning and explain how that whole evening went down."

Kim deflated, her usual self-righteous confidence hissing away. Suddenly she looked much younger than eighteen, a frightened child caught in the act by an unforgiving parent.

"I never wanted to go," Kim began defensively. "It was Melanie's stupid idea, and Janelle was in on it. By the time I realized where we were headed, there was nothing I could do. Mel was driving and I had no other way to get home, so I went along. My parents would *kill* me if they knew I went to the Trail's End to hear a *band!*"

Frank studied Kim's scared-rabbit face. It was hard to fathom a kid whose idea of vice was so pathetically benign.

"When we went in, the band was already playing," Kim continued. "Nick gave us all Cokes and told us not to sit at a table. At first, we were all standing together. Then Mel started talking to some guys. I was worried that she'd let them buy her a beer—I didn't want her drinking when she had to drive us home. So I kept following her through the crowd, to keep an eye on her. And that's when I lost Janelle."

Kim sighed as if she were recalling how her friend had fallen overboard into high seas. "Finally I spotted Janelle sitting at a table talking to this older guy with a ponytail and an *earring*."

"Did you go over to her?" Frank asked.

"No, she seemed to be okay. I thought it was best to stick with Melanie." Kim prodded the congealed cheese on her pizza.

"Then what happened?" Frank prompted.

Kim shrugged. "The band stopped playing; Janelle

came over and found us. It was almost midnight—even Melanie knew we had to go. So we drove home, and our parents never found out about it."

Frank could have cheerfully picked Kim up by the heels and shaken her senseless. "But what did Janelle *say* about this guy? What did you talk about on the way home?"

"*I* didn't talk about anything," Kim asserted, her air of superiority returning. "I was mad at both of them for tricking me. Mel was going on about those boys from Paul Smiths College. I don't remember Janelle saying much."

Frank dropped his head in his hands and massaged his temples. He could just imagine the scene in the car that night. Kim in a snit, giving her friends the silent treatment to punish them. Melanie giddy with success from her flirtations. And Janelle, always the elusive one, keeping her own counsel.

Just then, the table lurched against his knees as Melanie slid into the booth next to her friend. "What's going on?" she asked brightly.

"He wants to know about the night we went to the Trail's End," Kim informed her.

Melanie's cheerful face clouded. "Oh no! You're not going to arrest my cousin, are you?"

Frank was getting more than a little disgusted with the way everyone worried about their own self-interest in this case. "I don't give a damn about that. I want to know what Janelle was talking about to that guy, Pablo, in the bar."

"Oh, that's easy," Melanie said in relief. "They talked about that paper she was writing. Can you imagine meeting a guy in a bar and talking about your school term paper? That's Janelle for you!"

"So, what did she say?" Frank asked impatiently.

"I'm trying to think." Melanie gazed up at the grease-stained ceiling tile above her head. "Oh, I remember. She said, 'I met the most *extraordinary* man.'"

"That was one of Janelle's words—*extraordinary*—she was always saying that," Kim interjected.

"Yeah," Melanie agreed. "Then she said, like, 'He's actually living the life that I'm writing about.' I don't know exactly what she meant by that, 'cause most times I couldn't make heads or tails of what she was saying about that paper.

"Oh, and there was one more thing," Melanie added. "I said wasn't the band great, and she said too bad it was so loud because she had a hard time hearing everything this guy said. But she said he agreed to meet her again so they could talk some more."

She cocked her head and leaned forward so that her breasts rested on the red Formica table. "Do you think that's important?"

18

Nick Reilly spent Tuesday afternoon at state police headquarters, reviewing volumes of mug shots, looking for Pablo's face. When this proved fruitless, he worked with the police sketch artist, who produced a dead-eyed portrait that managed to be at once menacing and bland. After Nick grudgingly conceded that the picture bore a resemblance to Pablo, Frank sent it off to be printed in the Plattsburgh and Albany newspapers, and broadcast on the local news. The statement said the man pictured was wanted for questioning in connection with the disappearance of Janelle Harvey, but was not a suspect.

With that accomplished, Frank moved on to the other items on his to-do list. He intended to get to the bottom of the business between Ned Stevenson and Dell Lambert. Cornering Ned at work where it wouldn't be so easy for him to weasel away seemed like the best approach, so he drove over to the lumberyard.

Slipping past the customer service desk with a casual wave to the clerks, Frank cut through the aisles crowded with woodworking tools, stains, varnishes, hinges, and screws until he came to a small office at the back of the store. Ned had his back to the door, staring at a computer screen full of numbers. He swiveled at the sound of Frank's light tap on the door, but not before pressing a key that brought the screen saver pattern back up on his terminal.

"Frank! Come on in. Have a seat." Ned gestured to a chair, then came around from behind his desk, closed the door, and sat beside him. Their knees almost touched.

Frank pressed back in his chair. He hadn't expected to be quite so close to Ned in the cramped office. In fact, he'd have pegged Ned for the type who would prefer to keep the more authoritative position behind the desk.

"Sorry to disturb your work," Frank said. "I just wanted to clarify something with you. Remember yesterday morning in Malone's, when I asked you about Dell Lambert—"

Ned glanced down at his loosely clasped fingers. "I figured that's why you were here." He lifted his head and looked Frank straight in the eye. "I guess I must have come off as pretty suspicious, jumping up and leaving like that."

Frank only raised his eyebrows.

"Let me begin at the beginning. The business with Lambert's accident and the lawsuit has been gnawing at my father all these years. He just has trouble letting go."

You can say that again. Frank kept his face blank.

"Dad really felt terrible that Dell lost his sight—that's why he gave him the original settlement. He thought he'd been fair, but if Dell needed more money, he could have come and talked it over with Dad, and I know they could have worked it out. Instead Dell got the lawyers involved and started suing and dragged OSHA into it . . ." Ned shook his head.

"So your dad got his back up a bit," Frank said, his

eyes tracking around the room, taking in the spartan decor. Only one personal touch caught his eye: a lovely photo of Penny, her face lit with joy as she clowned for the photographer, presumably Ned. Go figure.

Ned smiled. "That's putting it mildly. His blood pressure went through the roof, and Mom made him settle because she thought a court battle would kill him. What still rankles him is that the case made Stevenson's look like some shoddy operation that doesn't care about its employees, when nothing could be further from the truth."

Frank made a "hmming" sound that struck a balance between honesty and agreement as he noticed the titles on Ned's bookshelf: *Small Company/Big Dreams*, *Re-Engineering the Family Business*, and *Pruning Dead Wood*. He'd had enough of Ned's defensive posturing; time to cut to the chase. "So, what made you suspect that Lambert actually could see?" he asked.

Ned grew absorbed in adjusting the lead in a mechanical pencil he'd pulled from a U Penn coffee mug on his desk. "I, uh, I'm not sure. Just little things . . . the way he acted at the Store. People would bring him his coffee but he seemed to know just where they were. I wasn't at all certain about it. I just had a niggling little doubt. So I started to, you know, watch him."

Frank observed Ned for a long moment. So far everything he'd said made sense, but something was still a little off.

"How long had you been watching him?"

Ned shrugged. "I don't know—January, maybe."

"So then why did you look so puzzled when I said Lambert knew you were spying on him?"

Ned gave an uncomfortable little laugh. "Well, I guess it was that word *spying*. I didn't really think of what I was doing as spying—I was just keeping an eye peeled, driving by occasionally. Sometimes when I took the deposits to the bank in Verona, instead of going directly there on Route 9, I'd go the long way along Stony Brook Road past Lambert's house. I just thought of it as taking a little detour."

"And if you happened to come upon him taking target practice in his front yard one day, just what did you plan to do?"

Ned arched back in the chair, rubbing his eyes. He looked up at the ceiling and began to talk. "When I was a kid, we had a dog named Scamp who loved to chase squirrels. He never got tired of going after them, even though they always escaped up a tree. Then one day he caught one. You never saw a dog so surprised in your whole life. He stood there with the thing squirming around in his mouth until he couldn't take it anymore. Then he just opened up and let him go." Ned grinned at Frank. "I guess I'm like Scamp. The chase became like a game to me, but Lambert had nothing to fear. I wouldn't have tried to get the money back."

"Oh yeah? Why not?"

"Think about it, Frank—it'd be a public relations nightmare. Stevensons taking away the money an old man needed to live on. At the most, all I wanted was to set the record straight. To make everyone realize that it was Lambert who cheated, who played dirty, not Stevensons."

Frank nodded. Ned and Clyde both had a need to be right just for the sake of being right. Then he had to smile—*takes one to know one.* "So why didn't you just tell me all this in Malone's?" he asked.

Ned plucked at a loose thread on his shirt. "I was embarrassed. You caught me totally off guard. All I could think of was to get out of there before Marge overheard us. If you hadn't come in here today, though, I would've stopped by your office on the way home tonight just to get it off my chest."

Frank rose with a smile. "Looks like I saved you a trip."

Next, Frank headed out to Harlan Mabely's petting zoo. The old man had been so hysterical at the time of Martha's death that Frank hadn't been able get a coherent sentence out of him. He hoped today Harlan would be calmer.

On the way there, he thought about what Ned had told him. He'd found himself almost liking the younger Stevenson today—being caught red-handed had made Ned drop his usual air of amused superiority, and Frank found the slightly sheepish Ned a lot easier to take. He'd always known Ned couldn't have pushed Lambert, because both Stevensons had been helping to organize the early morning search parties on Sunday when the old man had died. But if Ned had figured out that Lambert could see, then maybe the secret wasn't so well kept after all. Did Janelle know? Had she told this Pablo character?

Frank put that problem out of his mind as he pulled into the drive, but for once, Harlan did not run out to greet him. Frank found the old man sitting dejectedly in his little office, surrounded by yellowing postcards of the zoo, flimsy T-shirts with slightly crooked lettering, and an array of cheesy toys that today's jaded children wouldn't even bother to clamor for.

"You arrest anyone yet?" Harlan asked, already knowing the answer.

"No, I just came by to ask you a few more questions, now that you're feeling a little better," Frank explained.

"Have you ever noticed anyone—someone from around here, I mean—showing an unusual amount of interest in your animals?"

Harlan pondered this for a full minute, ultimately shaking his head. "I don't get much business from locals, except every year all the grade school kids come on a field trip."

"And you do all the work around here yourself? You've never had a helper?" Frank asked.

"It's just me. Always has—" Harlan cut himself off in midsentence. "Wait a minute. Last fall I dislocated my shoulder, and the doctor told me no lifting for a month. So I hired this kid to haul feed and help clean out the pens. What was his name? Oh, I remember—Dennis Treve."

"A teenager?" Frank asked.

"Yeah, he was always wearing those damn music things." Harlan passed his gnarled hands around his ears. "Drove me nuts. I had to shout and wave my arms to get his attention."

"You weren't happy with his work, then?" Frank probed. "Did you fire him?"

"Well, I wouldn't say that," Harlan answered. "He knew when I took him on it was only temporary. I told him a month, but in three weeks I felt better and I thought, why pay him when I could do it better myself?"

Suddenly Harlan seemed to grasp the drift of Frank's questions. "Wait a minute! You think Dennis killed Martha because I let him go a week early? Why, I oughta chop one of *his* legs off—see how he likes it!" Harlan dug around in his pockets, finally producing a dingy handkerchief to wipe his watery eyes.

"Don't go jumping to conclusions—it's not that likely. I'll go talk to him, and let you know what happens." Frank backed out of the office quickly. He was sure the old man was mostly bluster, but he regretted putting ideas in his head.

"Who's Dennis Treve?" Frank asked as he strode into the office.

Those three words elicited complete background information. "Lives over on Valley Road," Earl reported. "The whole family kind of keeps to themselves. We saw him in the cafeteria that day we went to talk to Mrs. Carlstadt. The kid sitting with Tommy Pettigrew, wearing the headphones. Why?"

Frank felt a little rush of adrenaline. A connection between Martha's death and Janelle. Tenuous, but still. . . . He glanced at his watch. "Five-thirty—shouldn't you be getting home?"

Earl studied him a moment before answering. "I guess I should. If you don't need me for anything."

Frank shook his head and busied himself with some papers. He wasn't in the mood to spell things out for Earl, although he had to admit the kid seemed to be picking up on things a little quicker these days.

Fifteen minutes later, Frank pulled up in front of the Treve home, a ramshackle affair that had been haphazardly expanded over the years. Black paper peeled off the most recent addition, as if siding were a needless extravagance. Conveniently enough, Dennis sat in a sagging porch swing, eyes shut but foot tapping, the omnipresent headphones blocking out the sound of Frank's arrival.

Frank mounted the porch and stood before Dennis to no effect. Finally he reached over and pressed one of the buttons on the tape player, figuring the music would either stop or be elevated to such a shriek that even Dennis couldn't endure it. Either way, he'd have the kid's attention.

Sure enough, Dennis's eyes flew open in chagrin. "What did you do that for?"

"I want to talk to you a minute. You heard that one of Harlan Mabely's animals was killed?"

"Yeah, so?"

"You worked for Harlan for a while. Maybe you didn't like it that he let you go."

Dennis burrowed into the corner of the swing and looked up at Frank nervously. "Nah, it stunk over there and the pay was lousy."

Frank eyed Dennis. The kid was so scrawny and apathetic, he hardly seemed to have the energy to kill Martha. "You know, you're right. That petting zoo sure is smelly. But Harlan's just crazy about those animals, isn't he?"

Dennis rolled his eyes. "I think it's weird. Talking to them in baby talk like he does."

Frank nodded in agreement. "I bet you and Tommy Pettigrew had a few good laughs about that, huh?"

Frank watched as Dennis's face registered agreement, then surprise, then suspicion in rapid succession. He looked as if he wanted to lie but couldn't quite figure out why he should. He shrugged.

"Tommy ever meet you over there?" Frank asked. "Did you ever tell him what the feeding schedule was, mention when Harlan went home?"

As comprehension sank into his head, Dennis's slight body went rigid. "You go talk to Tommy yourself," he said as he scuttled toward the front door. "I don't know nothing about it."

"I'm tired of saying this. I don't know nothing about where Janelle went," Tommy Pettigrew said as soon as he caught sight of Frank.

After parking his car in Dorothy's driveway, Frank had followed the sound of a power saw and discovered Tommy in the barn behind his house.

"I believe you. Actually, I'm here about something else. I can't spend all my time working on Janelle's disappearance, you know."

Tommy just stared straight ahead, too disinterested to even ask "what?"

Maybe a direct confrontation would provoke Tommy into talking. "I wanted to see what you knew about Harlan Mabley's emu getting killed over at the Pettting Zoo."

No spark of uneasiness. "Why should I know anything about that?"

"You're friends with Dennis Treve."

"So."

"He used to work with Harlan. Said you two joked about the way the old man fussed over his animals."

"So."

Frank studied his suspect for a moment. Tommy showed none of the nervousness, even fear, that these questions had aroused in Dennis. Usually teenagers began to spill their guts at the first sign that the police were on to them. Some even had the disconcerting trait of confessing to more than they had done. Frank felt a perverse admiration for Tommy—he kept his composure like a practiced criminal. Either that, or he really did know nothing about the animals. But Frank wasn't ready to concede that yet.

"Have you ever had a pet, Tommy?" Frank changed direction abruptly.

"Not anymore. My mom's allergic."

"So maybe it bothers you when some people make such a fuss over their pets, treat them like children, call them by human names?"

"If people want to act like assholes, it's none of my business." Tommy flicked the hair out of his eyes and looked longingly at the power cord Frank had unplugged when he entered the barn.

"You know, Harlan's emu hasn't been the only pet to die recently. Before her there was Miss Noakes's cat Petey, and Benjamin, the rabbit who belonged to the Maguire kid. It's strange that these things are happening now, since Janelle has been missing."

"Some old lady's cat runs away and you're wasting time lookin' for it? No wonder Clyde Stevenson's talking about firing you," Tommy said with more animation than he usually displayed.

"Oh, Petey didn't run away, Tom. He was killed—no doubt about it. I found his body." Frank watched with interest as Tommy's bravado faded into nervous picking at the rough edges of the board he'd just cut.

"And you know where I found him?" Frank continued. "Guess."

Tommy only shrugged.

"In the meadow on Stony Brook Road where Janelle disappeared. That's a real coincidence, huh? Except I don't believe in coincidences, do you?"

Frank didn't expect an answer and was satisfied with Tommy's escalating agitation. The boy had gouged at the piece of wood so much that one of his fingers was bleeding.

Frank decided to take a chance with an idea that had come to him. "You know what bothers me, Tom? That cat wasn't just killed, it was torn apart, like Harlan's emu." He couldn't be sure of this—the vultures had already been at work on the cat when he'd found it. But why else would the tail have been separated from the rest of the body?

"What would make a person do that, do you think?" Frank asked, his voice growing softer as he closed in on Tommy. "It's almost like it meant something, was some kind of ritual."

"Stop it!" Tommy screeched, hurling the chunk of wood he'd been holding across the barn. It sailed by Frank's ear and crashed into a shelf full of old canning jars. In the moment of silence that followed the shattering of glass, Frank and Tommy stared at each other. Then the door flew open and Dorothy ran breathless into the barn.

"What is it? What happened? Are you all right?"

"It's nothing," Tommy answered. "Just an accident. I'll clean it up." But his shaking hands and trembling voice made it obvious that something was terribly wrong.

Dorothy turned on Frank, her usual passivity replaced by a fierce protectiveness. "What's the matter? What did you say to him?" Before Frank could open his mouth to respond, she continued, "Why do you keep bothering Tommy about what happened to Janelle? He doesn't know anything. I won't have him upset!"

"Actually, I came to talk to him about something else," Frank answered. "One of the animals at Harlan Mabely's petting zoo was killed. I thought Tommy might know something about it."

"Why should he?" Dorothy's eyes darted from Frank to Tommy, who by now had pulled himself together and was methodically sweeping up the broken glass. "Tommy, have you ever been out there?" Dorothy asked.

"Not since third grade," Tommy said, his eyes focused on the floor, determined not to let one shard escape his broom.

"There," Dorothy said with her hands on her hips. "He can't help you."

"Where were you on Monday after school, Tommy?" Frank asked.

"I don't remember."

Dorothy interrupted. "You were home with me from the time you got off the bus. You had that history test coming up and I helped you study—remember?"

"Oh, yeah. That's right," Tommy affirmed, his confidence returning.

Dorothy turned to Frank. "You better go now—Jack will be home soon. I have to make dinner."

Seeing that he'd get nowhere further with Tommy tonight, Frank nodded. "Bye, Tom," he said. Catching the boy's eye, he added, "Be careful."

Frank expected the news stories showing Pablo's picture to trigger a flood of phone calls, but he was not prepared for the steady stream of purported sightings that had to be followed up. All across upstate New York, people called to report their fifty-year-old mailman or their fifteen-year-old neighbor. Even after the obvious crackpots were weeded out, Frank and Meyerson interviewed twenty-two ponytailed, thirtyish men, none of whom turned out to be Pablo.

But after all that work, Frank found himself no further along than he had been the day he found out about Pablo. In fact, he might be even further away from finding Pablo than before. Instead of turning the guy up, all the publicity might have alerted him to stay out of sight.

Frank sat at his desk, considering his options, when a tentative knock disturbed his thoughts. He looked up, expecting the visitor to have entered; most people just pounded on the door and walked in. The knock came again.

"Come in," Frank called, and the door opened slowly.

In every respect—hair, face, height, weight—the man was Jack Harvey. And yet, in some very essential way, he was not Jack.

Sensing the change, Frank rephrased his command as an invitation. "Come on in. Sit down."

Jack crossed the room like someone making his first trip down a hospital corridor after surgery. He eased himself into a chair and looked at Frank as if he had forgotten why he'd come.

Although he had spoken to Jack on the phone to tell him about Pablo and to get permission to search for the notes Janelle had made at the Trail's End, Frank hadn't seen him since their blowup in the office. When Frank had gone out to the Harvey home, Dorothy had let him in and watched passively as he emptied the leather backpack and examined its contents: two sticks of sugarless gum, a tube of lipstick, some crumpled tissues, a ticket stub for a movie that had been playing months ago in Lake Placid, and a dried-up black pen. Frank assumed Dorothy had told her brother that the search yielded nothing, and that he had then returned to question Tommy again. Not relishing another lecture from the irate father, he had stayed out of his way.

Now Frank was seized with the sudden fear that Janelle had been found dead, and that he was the last to know. "What's the matter, Jack? Has something happened?"

His legs splayed, Jack propped his elbows on his knees and cradled his head in his hands. "I don't know what's happening," he said softly. "Maybe you've been right all along. How can that be?" He raised his head sharply. "How can you know things about my daughter that I didn't know myself?"

Frank shifted his weight; his chair suddenly seemed

uncomfortably rigid. Jack Harvey wasn't just gradually realizing his daughter's loss of innocence, he was having his face rubbed in it.

Frank opened his mouth, then shut it again, uncertain of how to begin.

"How could she have gone off to a place like the Trail's End? *I've* never even been there. And then to talk to some low-life creep, and make plans to meet him again—why would she do that? And what the hell's wrong with those girls, not saying anything about this 'til now?" Jack kicked halfheartedly at Frank's battered desk. "Though what's the point of blaming them? It's Janelle that took up with this guy."

Jack slumped back in his chair. His role as the victim, outraged by a random crime, had supported him in his grief. Now that consolation was stripped away, and he was nothing but a baffled, lonely, frightened man.

Frank went over to his file cabinets and began to rustle papers aimlessly to give Jack a moment to compose himself. He spoke cautiously. "You know, Jack, maybe there's something that Janelle did or said that didn't seem significant before. Can you think of anything?"

Jack shook his head. "I've been going over and over everything that happened since January, but there's nothing. But why ask me?" he snorted. "I obviously don't know my own daughter any better than I know that girl who calls out the lottery numbers on TV."

Frank felt like he was inching along a branch that wouldn't hold his weight. He seemed to have regained Jack's trust, but he could lose it again instantly if he revealed his concerns that Janelle might be connected somehow with the animal murders and Dell Lambert's death.

"What about Tommy, Jack?" Frank kept his voice gentle,

chatty. "You know, I've talked to him a few times and I just can't get over this feeling that he knows something he's not telling me. Maybe you could talk to him."

Jack rubbed his eyes and gazed up to the ceiling. "If he won't tell you, he sure as hell won't tell me. He hates me because he knows I despised his father. Dorothy says she can't think of anything, either."

Frank crossed the room and rested his hand on Jack's shoulder. "Don't go blaming yourself. At least we have a solid lead now—we'll find her."

Jack lifted his head. For a moment he was silent, as if he were about to speak in a foreign language and wanted to get the phrasing right before he uttered the words. "Do you think," he asked finally, "that this guy took her away, and sent that ransom note? Or do you think she went off with him on her own?"

Frank scratched at a nonexistent spot on his pants. "I'm not sure. I think the note was sent to distract us, not to get money for Janelle's return. But we'll follow through with the ransom drop, just to be certain."

"Rosemary ran off on me once, you know." Jack's eyes were fixed firmly on Frank's bulletin board. "Janelle was a baby. No one knew about it."

Except Miss Noakes. "Why did she leave?"

"I drove her off," Jack answered, his gaze never leaving the clutter of posters and memos pinned to the cork. "I loved her so much. She was so beautiful. I didn't want anything to happen to her. I wouldn't let her drive the truck at night, or go to the lake without me, or take the baby into Placid with her girlfriends. Finally it got to be too much for her, and she just took off." Jack stood up and finally looked Frank in the eye. "And now I've done the same thing to Janelle."

Guilt pricked at Frank as he watched Jack trudging

back to his truck. No wonder the poor man had been so adamant that his daughter hadn't run away. He'd lost sight of the real pain Janelle's disappearance had caused. Finding her was more than a professional challenge. Now that he suspected she was with Pablo, and that he—or worse, both of them—had something to do with the killing of those animals, and with the death of Dell Lambert, he needed to find Janelle fast. Janelle was in danger. Either that, or she was dangerous.

The sound of the outer door opening and slamming shut again shook him from his reverie. Quick, light footsteps crossed the floor, and after a brisk rap, the door opened and Ned Stevenson's professionally cheerful face appeared in the doorway.

"Frank," he said as he strode across the room with his right hand extended, "I hope I'm not disturbing you. Do you have a minute?"

Frank accepted the outstretched hand warily. The old smug Ned was back. "What can I do for you?"

Ned produced the same smile Frank had seen him use when trying to sell a contractor the highest grade pine paneling that the lumberyard produced. "I just came in to share with you a little—well, advice is too strong a word." Ned laughed. "I only wanted to mention that maybe you shouldn't let all this stuff Penny's been telling you influence you so much. I love her dearly, but," Ned leaned forward confidingly, "she's a little high-strung."

"Really," Frank said. "She doesn't strike me that way at all."

Ned sat back and crossed his legs casually. He wore khaki work pants like the other men at the lumberyard, but his were crisply creased. Unembarrassed by his slight paunch, he rested his hands on his belly. "Oh, don't get me wrong. I didn't mean to imply that she's neurotic or anything. She just has quite an imagination—*quite* an imagination. And I find that very attractive." Again, the salesman's smile. "But you just have to understand where Penny is coming from."

Frank felt the same urge to throttle that he had experienced twenty years ago, when a man implied that Caroline had missed a fly ball because she was a girl. "And where, exactly, is she coming from?"

"Naturally, Penny loves books. But I'll let you in on a little secret that not many people know: she's done a little acting. College plays and things, even been in a few TV commercials. And that tends to make her see ordinary, innocuous events in a more, well, *dramatic* light."

"Ordinary events like a teenage girl talking for hours to a strange man in a bar and then disappearing a couple of weeks later?" Frank asked.

Ned kept his smile pasted in place, but his eyes narrowed. "Look, Frank, I know you're under a lot of pressure to solve this case, especially from my father. Just leave my wife out of this. I don't want her upset."

Before Frank could say anything that he'd regret, the phone rang and he snatched it up, turning his back on Ned. Recognizing that he'd been dismissed, Ned left, shutting the door rather more firmly than was necessary.

19

WATCHING THE STREAM OF COFFEE falling from the basket of his coffeemaker to the pot below, Frank waited until the coffee reached the two-cup mark, then pulled the pot out gleefully. Immediately, the stream of coffee stopped. He chuckled and poured himself a cup. This was just about the best birthday gift Caroline had ever given him, surpassing even the fish-shaped tie rack she had made the year she insisted on taking wood shop instead of home ec.

Frank had a contentious history with coffeepots, blaming them for coffee that was either too strong, too weak, too bitter, too cool, but always too slow in coming. Much to the annoyance of everyone he had ever shared a pot with, his impatience for fresh coffee led him to interrupt the pot in midbrew while he attempted, with varying degrees of success, to catch the onrushing coffee with his cup. This new gadget obviated the need for that—the perfect gift for the man who has everything but patience.

He took his cup and settled down in his recliner. Although it was after eight, Frank didn't worry that the coffee would keep him up at night. He was inured to caffeine; it was the uncertainties of the Harvey case that kept him tossing and turning.

Janelle's term paper research—the stack of books and articles on utopian religious communities that Penny had assembled for him—stood on the end table. He had put it aside while he searched for Pablo, using state police databases, drawings, and descriptions. Now, with nowhere else to turn, he went back to it. This was what Janelle and Pablo had been discussing at the Trail's End. If he set himself the task of knowing everything Janelle had known when she had walked into the bar, would he be able to deduce what she had learned when she left?

Frank imagined the three friends coming in, nervous and excited at their illicit adventure. He saw Melanie immediately drawn to the laughing, beer-drinking college boys, with Kim trailing after her as chaperone. And Janelle, did she approach Pablo? No, he saw her only as heading away from what had attracted her friend.

Then he pictured Pablo, with his unerring ability to strike up a controversial conversation. Why had he settled on Janelle? Probably he had recognized easy prey in a young girl out of her element.

And then they had started to talk . . .

Frank turned to the stack of books beside him and began to read. A heavy tome told him more than anyone could want to know about the Mennonites; a slimmer volume related the more interesting saga of a group in Iowa that allowed no interaction between the sexes and had, understandably, died out around the turn of the century. He read on, finding the parallels among the utopian communities: a charismatic leader; a profound faith in God; a vision of a better life achieved by shutting out the larger world; trials and persecutions; success in a few cases; in most of them, failure of the dream.

Why was Janelle so fascinated by this? If Bob Rush could be believed, she was questioning her faith. According to Mrs. Carlstadt, she wanted to break out of Trout Run and see the big city, or at least Albany. Frank studied the pictures of stoic, placid-faced women in long dresses making quilts and tending gardens. It hardly seemed the life Janelle aspired to.

Frank pictured Janelle digging through her bag for something to use to capture Pablo's pearls of wisdom. Using her pen to jot down his thoughts on the back of a napkin or an envelope. How could he hope to ever find those notes?

And then, reading the note cards, he suddenly saw the whole picture, where before he'd seen only disconnected dots. Getting up from his chair, Frank began systematically making piles on the hearth rug of books, articles, and index cards. Within minutes, his sorting paid off. He went to bed and slept dreamlessly till morning.

"So what does that word mean, anyway?" Earl asked.

"What word, *utopia?*"

"Yeah, I mean, I've heard it before but I was never sure what it meant."

In a rare relinquishment of control, Frank had allowed Earl to drive the patrol car back from a call and was using his opportunity as passenger to speculate aloud on Janelle's term paper notes.

"*Utopia* means a place where everything is perfect and there are no problems," Frank explained. After a pause, "What do you usually do if you don't know what a word means?"

"Ask you."

"What if I'm not around?"

Earl shrugged.

"Don't you look it up in the dictionary?" Frank insisted.

"I don't have one," Earl answered, in the same tone he might have used to explain his lack of a cell phone or a cappuccino maker. "Hey, that was a pheasant that just ran past," he added, craning his neck to watch the movement in the tall grass on the shoulder.

"Keep your eyes on the road," Frank said reflexively. "Doesn't it bug the hell out of you not to know something?"

"No." Earl was nothing if not candid.

Frank studied his assistant in profile: the unquestioning gray eyes; the slight overbite that had gone uncorrected; the wispy mustache he was cultivating in the mistaken belief that it made him look older. For the hundredth time he reminded himself that Earl was not his son, and that it was not his job to prod the boy on to higher levels of achievement. He sighed. "Well, Earl, one thing's for sure—you're never going to get ulcers."

Earl shot his boss a quick sideways glance, trying to determine whether an insult lurked somewhere. Then his usual placid half-smile returned, dismissing the very possibility of snide intent. "So, go on, you were telling me about the utopian groups."

Frank didn't require much prodding. Talking to Earl was like thinking aloud. "The one thing we know about Janelle's meeting with Pablo is that they talked about her term paper. And Penny thought she saw Janelle taking notes on their conversation."

"But you looked for those notes and you couldn't find them," Earl interrupted.

"I know, but I was sure that if I could figure out what

Pablo told her that night, I'd know where to find him, and maybe Janelle, too. So last night, I went over in my mind everything that must have happened in the Trail's End that night. And I think I found her notes."

The urgency in Frank's voice was strong enough to pull Earl's admiring gaze away from a new extended cab truck with monster wheels parked on the shoulder ahead of them. "Where? I thought you stayed home last night and went to bed early."

"I did. They were right there under my nose all the time, mixed in with the other index cards."

"You must've looked at those things a million times already," Earl objected.

"But I didn't see the Pablo notes because I wasn't looking specifically for them. Last night I sat there imagining how Janelle must've got interested in what he was saying, and probably started digging around in her backpack for something to write with. And I remembered that I'd found a dried-up black pen in her pack," Frank said, leaning over from the passenger seat to honk the horn at the car ahead of them hesitating at an intersection where there was no stop sign.

"So . . ."

"Most of Janelle's note cards are written in black ink; the rest are in blue. And all the note cards have citations at the bottom referencing the book or article that Janelle got the information from—that's how Penny was able to find me all the material Janelle used. But when I went back over the cards again, I noticed that there was one that didn't have any citations. And this is the clincher— the handwriting on that card is messy, like she was taking down the information in a hurry. *And* the card's got all these little scribbles on it—"

"—like you make when your pen's running out of

ink," Earl finished Frank's sentence, his head bobbing in agreement like a float on one of his fishing lines. "Sure. That makes sense. What does the card say?"

"'Secular spirituality,' 'contribution by ability,' 'segregation of the sexes,'" Frank read aloud. "And this is the clincher: 'living in community.'"

Earl glanced over at him, waiting for the punchline. When it didn't come, he said, "That's it? What does it mean?"

Frank brought his gaze back from Howard Jenks's roof, which he realized was finished in two different colored shingles. Amazing what you noticed when you weren't driving. "I'm hoping they can tell me at the bruderhof."

"The bruderhof! But you already went down there. They didn't know anything about Janelle."

"Right. But I didn't ask them about Pablo." Frank ground his heel in the floorboard, searching for a brake pedal as Earl careened around a corner. "This Michael, the leader, kept going on about how you had to make a commitment to live in community. He used that phrase 'in community' a couple of times, yet I didn't find it in any of the books Janelle took out. And it shows up in the notes Janelle took that night when she talked to Pablo. So I think he must've got it from the Bruderhof. Maybe he visited there. Maybe they know him."

Earl frowned. "That's a stretch."

The words, uttered so casually, hit Frank like a punch in the jaw. "Damn it, Earl! All police work's a stretch. What d'ya think, the answers are going to be spelled out for you like skywriting? You have to be willing to—" He stopped in midtirade, suddenly realizing what had set him off. That phrase, "that's a stretch" were the very words he'd used to blow off Perillo when he'd come up with his idea. The odd but brilliant idea to verify the day on which the old woman had claimed to have seen Ricky Balsam, by reviewing the plot lines of the soap opera she'd been watching when Ricky had called. And here he was, yelling at Earl for doing the very thing he'd done to Perillo.

The words "I'm sorry" rose to his lips. But just then the car drifted left as Earl turned his head toward the brand-new fiberglass fishing boat parked in the Pickneys' driveway. "Stay in your lane!" Frank said.

Frank's drive to the bruderhof that afternoon offered none of the pleasure of the first trip. He barely noticed the scenery flashing by. Anxiety sat in his stomach, along with a slice of pizza he'd grabbed before leaving. He had too much invested in this idea that the members of the bruderhof would know Pablo. But Earl had been right—it was a stretch. Worth checking out, but not worth counting on too much.

When Frank arrived, he went straight to Michael Heine's office. If the steward was displeased at seeing him again, he didn't show it. He pushed aside the one paper that had been occupying his attention and waited for Frank to speak.

His legs stiff from the drive, Frank paced around the small office. "I know I was totally off base thinking that Janelle could've come here to live. But you say that the curious do come to visit." Frank pulled out the composite sketch of Pablo. "We think she learned about your community from a man named Pablo: midthirties, light brown hair, blue eyes. Has he ever been here?" Frank's sentence ended on a note of hopeful inquiry.

Michael studied the picture with the same careful deliberation that Frank had noticed him apply to every question, great and small. After a moment his work-roughened finger tapped the drawing. "This is not a very good likeness, but there was a man named Paul Connor who was once a novice here."

Frank stopped pacing and pulled out his notebook. Pablo's real name—things were looking up! "That's C-o-n-n—"

"Unfortunately, we discovered after he left, when we were filing our taxes, that he had given us a false name and Social Security number."

Frank closed his eyes for a moment. He might have known getting Pablo's real name was too much to hope for. Still, the man had been here. "When was this? What happened to him?" he asked.

Michael stretched back in his chair and half-closed his eyes. Apparently these questions required a good deal of reflection before they could be answered. Frank choked back his impatience with difficulty.

"It has been almost four years, I think. He came to us in the summer. Said that he had been in seminary but had grown disillusioned with the worldliness of the other students. After careful consideration, we agreed to admit him into our community as a novice." Michael shook his head slowly. "But it was a mistake. He was not suited to our way of life."

When Michael said no more, Frank prodded him. "He was a troublemaker—couldn't follow the rules?"

The steward chuckled softly. "Our life may seem restrictive to you, Mr. Bennett, but really we have very few rules. Paul took to our daily routines without a problem. He was a good and willing worker. But to truly live in community you must be prepared to surrender yourself completely. Your personal wishes and plans and ideas must die. You must give yourself up completely and find yourself again in Christ. This, Paul was not able to do."

Frank looked around. A quiet hum of industry pervaded the place. Outside the communal kitchen, three women sat peeling potatoes, making conversation only intermittently. In the shop, the only sounds were the noise of power tools. Even the children playing happily on the swings and slides outside the nursery school seemed surprisingly low-key. Frank had built his own mental image of Pablo, and however skewed it might be, he found it hard to imagine the man in this setting.

"I'll bet he had a hard time keeping quiet, huh?" Frank wagered.

"We have no prohibitions against talking here, Mr. Bennett. But yes, Paul's problems did center around his conversation. You see, the bruderhof is not a democracy—the majority does not rule. Instead, we debate important questions until a consensus is reached. If everyone is not in agreement, we postpone the decision, and then we keep working to bring everyone together. We never 'agree to disagree.' This is the fundamental underpinning that makes community life possible.

"Paul could not accept this," Michael continued. "He kept debating issues that had already been settled. He could not relinquish his own ideas. Worse still, he sometimes criticized other brothers and sisters while not in their presence. This we do not tolerate, and he was admonished several times."

Michael sighed, gazing out into the lush green woods that surrounded the buildings. "Adapting to life in community is not easy—we all struggle sometimes. The only thing that makes such continual self-surrender possible is acceptance of Jesus Christ as your savior. Paul tried to repress his ego through sheer willpower, and of course, he could not succeed. Finally, we agreed that he should leave."

"There were hard feelings?" Frank inquired.

"No, not at all. Paul admitted that his belief in the Christian life was intellectual, not spiritual. He went off to pursue his beliefs in his own way."

"Where did he go?" Frank could hardly bear to ask the question, anticipating the answer he would get.

Michael shook his head. "I don't know. We gave him a small amount of money to tide him over until he got reestablished in the outside world. A few weeks later he sent the money back. That was the last we heard of him."

"Where was the letter mailed from?" Frank pleaded with the urgency of one who knows his cause is hopeless. "Was it from somewhere in New York?"

Michael rose from his seat and turned back toward his desk. "Really, I cannot remember."

Recognizing that he'd been dismissed, Frank rose and thanked Michael. As he reached the door he turned back. "One other thing—the last time I was here, you and Henry were upset because the children had been feeding the goats. Why was that? Are those animals important in your religion?"

Michael furrowed his brow. "We are Christians, sir. What role could goats possibly play in our faith?" He went on without waiting for an answer. "We have had some success selling our goat cheese to restaurants and markets. But the flavor is affected by what the goats eat. They must not eat the children's food."

Frank knew he risked offending Michael, but he couldn't let go of the idea that Pablo was somehow behind the deaths of the pets in Trout Run. "We've had a few animals die in, um, unusual circumstances lately. This Paul never let on that maybe he believed in, uh, you know . . ."

"Animal sacrifice! Mr. Bennett, you try my patience. You do not seem to hear what I tell you of our life here. I think it would be best if you leave now."

Frank went back out into the afternoon's bright sunshine. Too overwhelmed to begin the long drive home, he sat down at a nearby picnic table to think over what he had learned. He felt like a man who against stratospheric odds has actually managed to find the needle in the haystack, only to drop it back among the stalks again.

He had no idea how long he had been sitting there; perhaps only minutes, perhaps nearly an hour, when five men emerged from the workshop and settled themselves around the table. They nodded and smiled in Frank's direction but seemed quite uncurious about his presence among them. Seconds later, a woman appeared carrying a box of cookies, a large thermal jug, and some cups. She greeted them briefly, then left. They passed the box and jug, solemnly from man to man, including their guest in the circuit. Frank, teeth poised around a cookie, hurriedly set it down when he realized one of the men was preparing to say a prayer over their modest snack.

After effusive thanks were given for what proved to be exceedingly watery lemonade and gingersnaps that had grown spongy in the spring humidity, the men began to talk.

"Looks like we'll have five rocking horses ready for the big show next week," one young man with thick black glasses commented.

"That's good. They always sell. The horses and the table and chair sets are very popular," an old man agreed, his dentures clicking rhythmically as he chewed his gummy cookie.

The younger man turned to Frank and offered an explanation. "We're taking some of our wooden toys and children's furniture to the big crafts festival outside Lake George next week."

Frank made an effort to hold up his end of the conversation, despite his black mood. "Do you go every year?"

"The community exhibits every year. Only four of us can go—we take turns. I went last year, and Ralph will go this year," he explained. The men continued to eat in silence.

Frank would have liked to start the trip home, but pinned in by the Bruderhof men on either side, he urged himself to sit still. It wouldn't kill him to wait until their afternoon break was through.

Leaning over with his elbows on the table to conceal the two cookies he had no intention of eating, the pictures of Janelle and Pablo he had stuffed into his breast pocket flopped forward. Their presence ate at Frank, goading him to act. With a furtive glance over his shoulder to be certain Michael was not nearby, Frank pulled the pictures out and laid them in front of the friendly young man with the glasses. "This fellow Pablo—Paul—used to be a novice here," he said, not caring that his remark came entirely out of left field. "Were you friends with him; maybe you've gotten a letter from him recently?"

Taken aback, the young man stared at Frank curiously. "We do not get personal mail here. All letters are to the community as a whole."

Three of the others nodded in confirmation.

"I have seen Paul since he left us." It was Ralph who spoke, the taciturn man due to travel to the crafts fair. "The last time I worked at the fair was the year Paul left.

I saw him there. He said he was forming his own community, a secular community."

Frank dug his nails into the soft wood of the picnic table as he fought to control his excitement. "Where? Did he say where it was?"

Ralph stroked his wiry beard. Again, this ponderous rumination—it was enough to make an active man scream. "Saranac Lake," he said finally. "He said it was somewhere north of Saranac Lake."

Frank, Lieutenant Meyerson, and one of his staff, Trooper Pauline Phelps, sat staring at a large wall map of the Adirondack Park. Frank had driven straight from Silas to state police headquarters, knowing that he would need their resources to locate Pablo's compound.

"'Somewhere north of Saranac Lake' doesn't narrow it down much, Frank," Meyerson complained. "The Saint Regis wilderness area is some of the wildest terrain in the park."

"I know, I know. But isn't most of that land state owned?" Frank asked. "They couldn't get away with squatting for long."

"A lot of it is, but there are little pockets of privately owned land sprinkled all through there. That's what makes it so hard." Meyerson turned to his colleague. "Pauline here's been patrolling that area for three years now. She knows it as well as anyone."

"Wherever your man is, he hasn't been the subject of any citizen complaints, or I'd know about it," Pauline said. "My strategy would be to show the artist's sketch around at every little market and gas station in this area. They have to buy stuff somewhere."

"We've got to be able to do more than that."

Pauline stood and tapped the map twice with a

pointer. "There's also two wilderness canoe outfitters who might be able to help. Those guys know the back-country like my mom knows the layout of her favorite supermarket."

This seemed like a more productive possibility. "All right, so Pauline will work that angle?"

Meyerson nodded. "I'll brief the Saranac Lake police, see what they can come up with. You may as well get back to Trout Run. I'll see you tomorrow, for the stakeout at the lean-to."

Frank rolled his eyes. "I can hardly wait. I have to warn you—Clyde and Ned plan to come along. They seem to think that providing the ransom money gives them the right to supervise the operation."

"We can't have civilians involved! It's against regulations," Meyerson protested.

Frank waved off the trooper's objections. "If this were a legitimate ransom drop, I'd agree, but there's no harm in letting them tag along on this charade. It's a lot easier for me to just humor them."

Meyerson said nothing more. Frank took this as assent and left while he was ahead. The sun was making its final descent in the west, casting a warm glow over the apple orchards and dairy farms, fishing ponds and five-building hamlets that he drove past, but Frank was oblivious to the scenery.

It seemed typical that Pablo would think he could improve upon a system that the Bruderhof had been living by for over seventy years. Would his community merely be a secular mirror image of the Bruderhof community? Or would he somehow corrupt the Bruderhof vision to create something more sinister?

He was plagued by the notion that what had happened to Martha and the other dead and missing animals in

Trout Run was linked in some way to Janelle's disappearance. What if Pablo saw the slaughter as a sort of warning not to lavish so much attention on domestic animals? Was his influence over Janelle so great that she would actually help him in this awful work? Did she get Tommy involved, too? Was that why he was acting so coldly about her disappearance?

He still wanted to think of Janelle as a victim, but this case had shaken his confidence to the point where he believed anything was possible.

20

"THIS IS A COLOSSAL WASTE OF TIME," Frank complained, although no one was near enough to hear him. Earl was positioned beyond a clump of black raspberry bushes, Meyerson crouched behind a large fallen log, and the Stevensons were well out of the way, shielded by a huge rock formation. A cold drizzle fell, dampening even Earl's enthusiasm for the stakeout at the lean-to. They had been in their places since four-thirty in the morning, waiting for the alleged kidnapper to pick up the knapsack with the ransom at dawn. In all that time, the only activity had been the steady work of a chipmunk gathering seeds.

Now it was close to eight o'clock, and Frank was stiff, wet, and irritable. He calculated how soon he could decently call an end to this and declare the whole thing a hoax. The sharp sound of a stick snapping pulled his attention away from his wristwatch. A man in a hooded anorak moved briskly along the trail and entered the clearing.

Frank watched in astonishment as the man slowly circled the lean-to, then dropped down on his knees to peer under the little structure. A moment later he had pulled the red knapsack out and sat staring at it, as if uncertain what to do next. Shocked by this turn of events, Frank stood rooted to the spot while Meyerson leapt out from his hiding spot and confronted the man.

"State police!" he barked. "Drop the bag, stand up, and keep your hands over your head."

The man jumped in surprise, then grinned. "Wow, cool. Are you making a movie or something?" The smiled faded from his face as he saw Meyerson's gun leveled at his heart. Slowly he rose and followed the trooper's instructions, his eyes never leaving the gleaming weapon.

Meyerson reached out and pulled back the man's hood, exposing a limp brown ponytail. "All right, Pablo, the game's up. Where do you have Janelle?"

"Why are you calling me Pablo? Who's Janelle?"

"That dumb act won't take you too far, buddy," Meyerson said. "Are you going to tell me you don't know what *this* is?" He pulled open the red knapsack, revealing the wads of cash it contained.

The man jumped back, as if the bag had contained a live creature. "It's not mine."

Meyerson seemed to construe this as an attempt to flee and immediately moved to handcuff the suspect.

With the kidnapper safely restrained, Ned, Clyde, and Earl emerged from their hiding places. Clyde marched right up to the man and, undeterred by the fact that the suspect was a good foot taller than him, took his usual authoritative approach. "I *demand* to know where you are *keeping* that poor young girl."

"What girl?" The man's head swiveled back and forth in dismay. "You can't just handcuff me like this for no reason."

"You're under arrest for the kidnapping of Janelle Harvey. You have the right to remain silent . . ."

230 · S.W. HUBBARD

"Kidnapping!"

The suspect's startled exclamation didn't stop Meyerson's droned recitation of the Miranda warning. He concluded with a brusque command to sit on the floor of the lean-to until the backup troopers arrived.

Ned, ever affable, waited until the suspect had settled himself, then smiled encouragingly. "Pablo, it'll go a lot easier for you if you just tell us where she is."

"Why do you keep calling me that?" the man protested. "My name is Jason Klein."

Clyde planted his hands on his hips. "The *nerve!* To keep lying in the *face* of such overwhelming evidence! We all *know* who you are."

Frank did not share Clyde's certainty. Ponytail notwithstanding, the man didn't really look like the sketch of Pablo. His face was rounder, and he appeared to be in his midtwenties, not thirties. Though police sketches were notoriously inaccurate, this one had been good enough for the men at the bruderhof to have recognized Pablo.

But there was no point in speculating. "If Nick and Penny can pick him out of a lineup, we'll know we have our man," Frank reassured Clyde.

"Wait a minute! I won't have Penny involved in this. It could put her in danger." Ned's good humor evaporated, as Frank had noticed it was often prone to do.

"Your wife will have to view the lineup," Meyerson replied. "Nick Reilly can say whether this is the man he knows as Pablo, but only Penny can verify if he's the man she saw Janelle talking to."

"What about Kim and Melanie?" Ned challenged.

Frank snorted. "They were precious little help with the sketch artist. All they could agree on was the ponytail and earring. And I hope," he continued, "that you're not suggesting two minors should do something you consider too dangerous for your wife."

"Hey, look at this!" Earl saved Frank from what promised to be another nasty confrontation with the Stevensons by waving a small rectangle of white paper over his head. He had apparently picked it up from the path where Jason, aka Pablo, had entered the clearing.

Walking toward his assistant, Frank experienced one of those moments of dissonance when the mind, quite aware of what the eyes are seeing, nevertheless refuses to accept it as real. At a distance of three feet, he could distinguish the unmistakable pattern of Janelle's meticulous calligraphy. Two steps farther and he could read the words as Earl held the paper before him:

> On the mud they saw again the traces of their horses side by side, the same thickets, the same stones in the grass; nothing around them seemed changed; and yet for her something had happened more stupendous than if the mountains had moved in their places.

"This matches the paper you found in her room?" Meyerson had appeared at his side and read over his shoulder.

"No doubt about it," Frank confirmed.

"Can you explain how this got here?" Meyerson asked their suspect.

The man looked up at the five inquiring faces that surrounded him. Understanding dawned in his eyes and he straightened up from his slumped position. "I want a lawyer."

The suspect made one phone call, to a lawyer named Peter Stratton in Albany. It would be at least two hours until Mr. Stratton arrived, so the young man was locked up in Trout Run's only cell to wait.

Frank's effusive thanks to the Stevensons for their assistance at the stakeout, offered with the intention of dismissing the meddlesome pair, hadn't had the desired effect.

"You'd *better* find Nick Reilly; we'll need him for the *line*up," Clyde ordered as he planted his wide bottom firmly in one of Frank's visitors' chairs.

Frank wondered how noticeable his annoyance was. "A very good idea, Clyde. Earl, why don't you give Nick a call."

Earl reported no answer at Nick's home; then called the Trail's End and learned that Nick would be in at five.

"Five! We can't *wait* until five! You'd better go *out* and search for him."

"There's really no rush, Clyde. We won't be able to put a lineup together before that, anyway. We need four or five other men."

"Why, Lew and *Earl* can be in it. And just round up a few of those *fellows* who sit around at the Store all day. Let them do something *useful* for a change."

"The other participants can't be people that Nick already knows," Frank explained. "That wouldn't be fair."

"Why *that's* outrageous," Clyde protested. "Just *another* example of how our criminal justice system coddles *criminals*."

"Frank's right, Dad. He can't rig the lineup. And if this lawyer's smart, he'll probably insist on having five men with ponytails and earrings. That could take a while to come up with around here, huh?" Ned smiled at Meyerson for confirmation.

"Hopefully, the lawyer will talk some sense into this guy and he'll realize he'll be better off to cooperate. Then we won't have to proceed to a lineup at all," Meyerson replied.

"I think it's a good sign that he's not willing to talk without a lawyer. He must have something to hide," Ned said. He clapped his hand on Clyde's shoulder. "Well, Dad, what do you say we head home? It doesn't seem there's much more for us to do right now." He turned to Frank. "I'm sure you'll keep us posted on developments after Mr. Stratton arrives."

"Oh, certainly."

Clyde stood up reluctantly. "And just where did you put that knapsack filled with my ten thousand dollars? It's not just lying *around* here, is it?"

"It's locked up in the safe, Clyde. We still need it for evidence."

Clyde scowled but permitted his son to steer him out the door. "We'll be at home if you need us," Ned called back over his shoulder.

"Jesus H. Christ!" Frank sagged back in his chair, rubbing his temples.

"The old man's a pain in the ass, but the son's not so bad," Meyerson said.

Frank was not so sure he agreed but was too tired to argue. "What the hell do you think is going on here? When Jason, Pablo, whatever his name is, walked into that clearing, I thought he was just some poor hiker who stumbled into our stakeout. Until this turned up." Frank raised the plastic envelope that now contained the white parchment covered in calligraphy. "Tell me again exactly when you first noticed this?" he asked Earl.

"It was after Lieutenant Meyerson handcuffed the guy and made him sit in the lean-to. I was just looking around and the white caught my eye."

"And it wasn't on the trail before?"

"It might have been. I wouldn't have been able to see it from where I was."

"Will they be able to lift prints from this?" Frank asked.

"Hard to say," Meyerson answered. "It got pretty wet out there. And then Earl handled it."

Earl occupied himself with some papers, acting as if he hadn't heard this.

Frank sighed and read the writing again. Although smeared by the rain, it was still quite legible. There were no quotation marks or attribution, as there had been on Janelle's extract from *The Scarlet Letter*, but still it sounded like a quotation from something. If Janelle were writing about herself, why would it be in the third person?

Frank pulled the phone toward himself. "I'm going to call Edwin and see if he knows what this is from."

Edwin listened as Frank read the quotation over the phone. "Boy, there's not a lot to work with there. I'll have to study the style and syntax and see what I can come up with. I'll call you back, okay?"

"Sure, thanks."

They all sat in silence. The minutes dragged. Finally, Earl offered to go to Malone's diner for sandwiches and coffee. Meyerson, probably not trusting Earl to keep quiet about the suspect in custody, went with him.

They had been gone quite a while when the phone rang.

Frank picked it up and listened to Edwin's report. "You figured it out already? Great! *Madame Bovary* . . . what's that about? A woman who commits adultery and kills herself! I don't know. I don't have time to think about it now." Frank craned his neck to look out the window. A large navy blue Mercedes had just pulled up. "I think my suspect's lawyer has arrived."

• • •

The heat in the parish hall of the Presbyterian church on Monday night was enough to drop a moose. Having not expected more than the usual four or five supplicants at the monthly town council meeting, Augie Enright had failed to set up the large floor fans. Now, with over three hundred people crammed into a space meant to hold half as many, the atmosphere was suffocating.

Reid Burlingame, the current president of the town council, stood at the lectern, tapping his gavel in a futile attempt to gain the attention of the crowd. After a minute or so of this, Clyde pushed him aside and, inserting his fingers in the corners of his dour little mouth, let out a whistle that sliced through the babble of conversation and drew everyone's attention to the dais.

"The town council originally intended to take up the *matter* of why our police chief has made such a shocking *lack* of progress in the Janelle Harvey kidnapping," Clyde began. "But in light of what has happened in the past forty-eight hours—when the prime *suspect* in the kidnapping was allowed to walk free *due* to police incompetence—I believe we should move directly to a vote on terminating Frank Bennett's contract *immediately*."

This speech ignited a buzz of debate among the crowd, which continued unchecked as Reid Burlingame succeeded in taking back the lectern from Clyde. The shriek of feedback produced when Reid adjusted the microphone silenced the group enough for the president to be heard.

"Now just hold your horses, Clyde. Not everyone knows what's been going on. We need to hear a report from Frank before there's any vote taking."

Reid's statement met with a general murmur of approval, not out of any loyalty to Frank, but because everyone was afraid that they might have missed some new details of the Harvey case.

With a nod from Reid, Frank took his place behind the lectern and looked out at the sea of faces. In the past year, he had come to know and like most of them. Now the benign Presbyterian parish hall looked more like the Roman Coliseum. He half expected to see lions burst through the swing doors that led to the church kitchen.

"The man we apprehended during our stakeout at the lean-to on the Mount Henry trail is named Jason Klein," Frank began explaining. "He's a twenty-five-year-old law student at SUNY Albany. On the morning that Janelle disappeared, Mr. Klein was studying in the library in Albany with a group of other students. At least seven people can verify his presence there."

Clyde made a great show of grimacing and rolling his eyes during this explanation, as if arranging for seven witnesses to back a story was the oldest game in the book.

"Mr. Klein is an exemplary student, with no criminal record. As far as we can determine, he has no knowledge of, or link to, Janelle Harvey."

"Then why was he there picking up the ransom money?" someone shouted from the audience.

"He says he wasn't. He had been hiking in the area the day before and lost a small pack. He came back looking for it, saw something resembling his pack under the lean-to, and pulled it out. It was the ransom money, but he didn't know that."

"Huh! Of course he would say that when he's caught red-handed," Clyde said.

"Neither Nick Reilly nor Penny Stevenson picked Mr. Klein out of a lineup as the man, known as Pablo, who was seen talking to Janelle in the Trail's End," Frank continued in a monotone as if he'd never been interrupted.

"The fact that's he's not *Pablo* doesn't *mean* he's not the kidnapper!" Clyde shouted from his seat on the dais. "Tell them about the paper. How do you *explain* that?"

"A piece of paper containing a quote from a novel written out in calligraphy was found near the lean-to at the time Mr. Klein was apprehended. It was very similar to a paper found in Janelle's bedroom. We're not certain how it got there, but the paper does not tie Mr. Klein conclusively to Janelle." Frank struggled to keep his voice sounding confident, even as a bead of sweat trickled from his hairline into his right eye. In truth, he was still puzzled by that paper. He hadn't been able to reconcile Jason Klein's innocence with the appearance of that damn quote from *Madame Bovary*.

"Although it seems probable that she did write it, it could have been faked. Calligraphy isn't unique; it can't be matched like handwriting. And the paper could have been left there at another time."

"You are simply *parroting* the claims of that young punk's high-priced lawyer." Clyde pounded his knee. "This town deserves to *know* why you caved *in* to his outrageous demands!"

It was true that Peter Stratton had proved a formidable opponent. Having just finished Stratton's course on criminal law, Jason had decided not to attempt talking his way out of his predicament. Instead, he had sat back and let Stratton make short work of the police allegations. In addition to quickly producing an irrefutable alibi for the time of Janelle's disappearance, the lawyer happened to be quite an expert on handwriting analysis, and it was he who had pointed out that the paper would never stand up in court as evidence linking Jason to Janelle.

"In the absence of any evidence to connect Mr. Klein to Janelle, we had to let him go. The district attorney"—

Frank glanced over at Clyde to emphasize this point—
"felt that we didn't have enough evidence to charge him.
However, we've asked him not to leave the state without
letting us know."

Clyde's snort of disgust was audible to all, but Reid
and Frank chose to ignore it.

"Well, that seems reasonable," Reid said. "So if this
fellow's not the kidnapper, what's your next step?"

This was the question Frank had been dreading,
although he knew it was inevitable. He certainly had no
intention of standing here before the whole town and
confiding his suspicion that the animal murders and
Janelle's disappearance were somehow linked. He would
have to tell them that he intended to keep looking for
Pablo, but he had no ready answer for the next logical
question—How?

Frank drew a deep breath and his hands tightened on
the lectern's battered oak edges. "We'll continue to
search for this man Pablo. It's our best lead to date."

Ned Stevenson rose from his seat in the first row. In
contrast to Clyde's shrill bombast, Ned sounded eminently
calm and reasonable. "Isn't it true, Frank, that you have no
direct evidence that this man Pablo has anything to do
with Janelle's disappearance? As far as we know, he's just a
patron of the Trail's End who Janelle spoke to briefly. Is it
wise to spend so much time trying to track him down?"

"As I think I may have mentioned, Ned," Frank replied,
trying his best to duplicate the younger Stevenson's chatty
tone, "Janelle was having more than just a casual conversation with this man—she was taking notes on what he told
her for her term paper on utopian communities. We've
learned that Pablo has set up some type of community of
his own. Janelle could very well be there with him."

"There you *go* again!" Clyde was out of his seat and

pacing across the dais. "You keep insisting that the child has run *away*. We wonder *why* our police chief can't catch the kidnapper—it's because he doesn't *believe* Janelle's been kidnapped. I say, get rid of him!"

A murmur of discussion began to build again, growing into a crescendo of support for Clyde.

Frank stared straight ahead, his face impassive. No matter what they said about him, how they criticized him, he'd be damned if he showed he cared. If they thought he was going to beg and plead to keep this two-bit job, they were sadly mistaken. He wouldn't stoop to defend himself to these fools—he'd just resign.

Then Jack Harvey stood up, looking from left to right until he was certain he had everyone's attention. "I want Frank Bennett to continue to head the investigation into my daughter's disappearance." His voice rang out through the parish hall without need for amplification. "I'm sorry to disagree with you, Clyde, after all you've done, but, I think Frank's the man who can bring Janelle home to me." Then, suddenly flustered by his foray into public speaking, he jammed his hands in his pockets and muttered, "That's all I wanted to say," and sat down.

"Well, unless anyone has something more to add, I think we can take our vote," Reid proclaimed. "All in favor of keeping Frank Bennett on as police chief, raise your hand."

All the members on the town council raised their hands, except Clyde, who stoically kept his folded on his lap.

"Motion carried," Reid said, as cheerful as if they'd just voted on new Christmas decorations for the green. "I think we'll take a ten-minute break, then move on to a discussion of the new rules for disposing of large objects at the town dump."

As he rose to go, Frank spotted Lucy and Edwin, Earl,

and Jack all working their way toward him through the milling crowd. The expressions on their faces made him walk even faster to his truck. He made it there without speaking to anyone, and took off. Too wound up to endure the confines of his small house, he simply drove.

He had no idea how long he'd been on the road when the Trail's End sign, illuminated by a single spotlight, loomed up ahead of him. Realizing he had hardly eaten all day, he turned the wheel sharply and just cleared the entrance, spraying gravel.

At nine, the parking lot was nearly empty. People tended to dine early, and with no entertainment scheduled, the Trail's End was winding down for the night. Frank entered the nearly deserted bar and plopped down on a stool. "Hey, is it too late for a burger?"

Nick looked up from his cleaning at the other end of the bar. "Not for you, Frank!" Now that Laurel had forgiven him and he knew his job was secure, Nick was quite enthusiastic about the role he had played in the Harvey investigation. "Say, I hope there's no hard feelings about what went down at the lineup?"

"Why should there be? Clyde and Ned Stevenson may be satisfied to pin Janelle's disappearance on an innocent man, but that's not the way I operate. I just have to keep on plugging 'til I find the real Pablo."

"Yeah, Ned didn't seem too pleased with Penny after the lineup. I heard them going at it." Nick shook his head. "I don't know what she sees in him. Penny's got everything: looks, brains, money. She could do better than Ned."

"Penny has money?"

"Yeah, she's not one to brag or anything. But at closing time we'd have a drink, get to talking. Her parents died when she was a kid. Their life insurance, the money from selling the house, it all went into a trust fund for Penny. Her guardian invested it, and when she turned twenty-five, she found herself sittin' on a bundle."

"How much?" Frank asked.

"Oh, she didn't say, but I got the feeling it wasn't chump change." Nick regarded his lone customer. "You know, you don't look so great—are you sure a burger is all you want? Why not have one of the dinner specials."

"Maybe you're right." Frank took the menu Nick offered. "I haven't had a decent dinner all week."

"Get the lasagna primavera," Nick recommended. "That's what I had—it's real good."

Frank looked a little dubious, then shrugged. "What the hell." After Nick sent his order to the kitchen, Frank idly continued to read the menu, his attention caught by the Vegetarian Specialties heading. Under it the entrees began with Bulgur Pilaf, Stir-Fried Vegetables over Quinoa. Frank stopped reading when he reached Pinto Bean and Kasha Casserole; he felt like he was deciphering a menu in a foreign country. "What the hell is quinoa?" he asked Nick.

"It's a type of grain," the bartender explained. "It's not bad. A lot of people order it. In fact, now that I think of it, your man Pablo used to get that sometimes."

Frank looked up. "He's a vegetarian, then?"

"Oh, yeah. Big time. All I had to do was serve some-one a steak or pork chops, and he'd be off on how wrong it was to raise animals for food. You know, they should be living free and all. Like a pig would know what to do with itself if you just set it loose somewhere."

Nick's information hit Frank like a shot of caffeine. He'd been involved with an animal rights protest in Kansas City that had turned really nasty—people throw-ing blood on rich ladies wearing fur coats. He'd been

frightened by the depth of hatred he'd seen on the pro-
testers' faces as the cops pulled them off the shoppers
outside the fur salon.

Did the animal murders in Trout Run fit into this? Did
Pablo kill them, or have them killed, as some sort of
bizarre symbol? Though why would he kill them if he
was a vegetarian? There had to be a connection, he was
certain.

"Where do you buy this stuff—kasha, quinoa, bulgur?" Frank asked. "I've sure never seen any of that at the
Grand Union in Verona."

Nick laughed. "Nah, we get it at a place called the One
Earth Organic Farm. They grow vegetables and herbs, but
they also have a small store where you can buy grains and
stone-ground flour and dried beans—all that kind of
stuff."

"You've been there?" Frank asked.

"Yeah, to pick up orders. It's north of here, on the way
to Wolverton. Why? You thinking of turning veggie?"

"No, but remember you said there weren't many
places in the North Country where a guy like Pablo
would feel welcome?"

"Of course! He must go there! And maybe they know
where he lives."

"I sure hope so." Frank poked around in his lasagna
and held up a stringy green thing on the end of his fork.
"What the hell is this?"

"Swiss chard."

Frank grimaced. "Lucky you came up with the organic
farm lead. Otherwise I'd have to hold this dinner recommendation against you."

21

THE FAINT LIGHT OF DAWN crept cautiously into Frank's bedroom. He awoke instantly, fully, and pervaded with an unusual sense of well-being. Had he been dreaming of Estelle? Sometimes he visited with her vividly in his sleep, and these encounters always left him happy and at peace. But this morning he could not recall dreaming. Then it came to him; the lead on the organic farm he'd gotten from Nick Reilly. Today was the day he would find Pablo, he was sure of it. If he left right after breakfast, he would be in Verona by seven. All farmers, surely even organic ones, were early risers.

A bowl of Cheerios and a cup of coffee served to temper Frank's enthusiasm. He should really talk to Tommy Pettigrew before chasing off to the farm. He wanted to spring this animal rights angle on him and see what kind of reaction he got. Although he had a good feeling about this lead of Nick's, Lord knows his hunches had been wrong often enough lately, and any information Tommy might provide could be useful.

After restlessly dawdling away enough time to be certain that both Jack and Dorothy, who both worked seven to four, would have already left, Frank headed over to the Pettigrew house. Pounding on the door and leaning on the bell simultaneously, he made enough racket to wake both the dead and a teenage boy. Frank had already walked through the unlocked front door, ready to shake the kid awake, when a bleary-eyed Tommy appeared in the living room.

For a moment, Tommy stared at Frank as if he didn't even know who he was. Then, with his thought processes gradually clicking into place, Tommy coughed life into his voice and said, "What're you doing here now? Uncle Jack and my mother are both at work."

"I know," Frank answered. "It's you I want to talk to."

Tommy glowered at him. "My mother told you to leave me alone."

"Tom, Tom, Tom. I never pegged you for being a mama's boy. I just want to have a little talk, man to man." Frank dropped onto the sofa. "Have a seat," he added, as if Tommy were in his house and not the other way around.

Tommy lowered himself to the edge of a chair, as if he expected the arms to reach out and grab him. He stared at Frank and waited.

"We got interrupted the other day in the barn."

"I got nothing to do with that old man's bird," Tommy responded immediately. "My mother told you—I was home with her the night it happened."

"Right, studying. I bet you aced that test," Frank said. "Forget Harlan's emu for the time being. There was something else I wanted to ask you.

"Remember Elinor Stevenson's little dog, Leo? In all those years of coming to work with Elinor, he never left the store. Then one day he takes it into his head to go out into the lumberyard and gets crushed to death under

some boards." Frank paused. Did he see a flicker of concern in Tommy's eyes? He pressed on.

"Now, that was way back in January, long before
Janelle disappeared. In fact it was . . ." Suddenly, the little
connection that had been eluding him clicked into place.
In his mind, he heard the volunteers in the old flower
shop memorializing the date Leo had died. He saw the
cheerleading coach checking her calendar for the date
when she'd noticed Janelle's distraction.

"It was January twenty-first that Leo died," Frank
continued. "The day before the Lake George game. The
day before Janelle's teachers and friends noticed a
change come over her. What do you know about that,
Tommy?"

He had the satisfaction of seeing a bead of sweat break
out on Tommy's upper lip.

"I don't know what the fuck you're going on about,"
Tommy muttered.

"Oh, I think you do. Janelle knew you'd killed Leo. She
was upset about it. She wanted to confide in someone,
but didn't know who to turn to."

Tommy pulled himself up straight in the recliner, as if
to be better prepared to fight or flee. His normally sallow
face flushed to a dull red.

"Why did she run away, Tom?" Frank asked softly. "It's
because of these animal killings, isn't it?"

Tommy examined his large, rough hands with great
interest. "It's not my fault she's gone." His words were
nearly inaudible.

"Tell me everything now, Tommy. Tell me about the
man she sneaked out at night to see. Tell me why you kill
the animals. If you make it easier for me, I'll make it easier for you. There's a chance you could get off with just
probation."

But Tommy said nothing. Frank waited. The silence grew oppressive.

Frank finally spoke. "You're doing it to taunt this character Pablo, aren't you? You didn't like Janelle sneaking out to meet him. I have a lead on where he lives, Tommy. I know he has something to do with these killings, and I'll find it out today. I'll probably be there by this afternoon. I'll find Janelle. Then it'll be too late for you."

Frank watched in amazement as relief seemed to course through Tommy's body. His familiar cocky contempt returned.

"You don't know nothing and I ain't telling you nothing. You can't arrest me 'cause you got no evidence I did anything wrong. Now get out of our house or I'll get my mother to complain to Clyde that you're screwing up again."

The One Earth Organic Farm was easy to find, lying on the main road between Verona and Wolverton. He must have passed it many times before, although he had never paid much attention to the modest, weather-beaten buildings and the struggling plots of vegetables.

Frank pulled in the driveway and followed the gravel path to a door marked with a sign that read SHOP. Opening the door, he was engulfed in the pungent scent of herbs and spices. Large bins filled with dried beans and peas, rice, grains, and flours lined the one narrow aisle. Above them were smaller bins filled with what were presumably herbs, although Frank's knowledge of this subject began and ended with parsley. At the back of the shop, the building widened out enough to accommodate a large wooden table topped by an old-fashioned scale and some plain brown bags.

A woman in her early thirties, hugely pregnant, emerged from a darkened doorway behind the table, just as the front door opened to admit a man about a decade older. "Can I help you?" they both asked.

Frank turned from one to the other and settled on the man, simply because the woman looked so exhausted. "Hi, I'm Frank Bennett, chief of police over in Trout Run." He extended his hand, but the man seemed not to notice as he turned to straighten the lids on some bins.

"I'm working on the disappearance of Janelle Harvey— I'm sure you've heard about it—and we have reason to believe she might be with a man named Pablo. I understand he's one of your customers?"

The rising inflection of Frank's voice indicated that this was a question, but the other man simply gazed at Frank poker-faced, without saying a word.

Frank took a more direct approach. "Do you know where Pablo lives?"

"Can't help you," the man said, and turned to go back outside.

Frank reached out and grabbed his arm. "What do you mean, 'can't help me?' Do you know this guy or don't you?"

The man shrugged off Frank's hand angrily. "He's a customer. He comes in, he buys, he leaves. That's all I know." Before Frank could speak again, the man was out the door.

Reconsidering his strategy, Frank turned to the woman and gave her an "oh well, what can you do" sort of smile. Perhaps it was just as well to have the husband out of the way; he tended to have better luck with women anyway. "You have quite a selection here," Frank began, walking over to the counter.

Just then a little girl appeared from the back room,

tears streaming down her face. "I can't get Amy's hat to stay on her head," she wailed.

Her mother took the doll and tied on the offending headgear. "There you go, sweetie. No need to cry." The child scurried away.

"That's the nice thing about the little ones. You can solve all their problems so easily. Now, when they get to be this age"—Frank pulled one of the Missing Girl fliers from his notebook to display Janelle's smiling face—"then you never know what they might do when they get in trouble."

He noticed a furrow of concern in the woman's brow as she gazed at Janelle's picture. "Her family's worried that she might have been influenced to do something foolish. Well, you're a mother—I don't have to tell you what it's like to love a child and want to keep her safe."

The woman swallowed hard and began twisting the fabric of her dress. "I hope my husband didn't offend you. He just has a thing about authority figures." Her timid voice indicated that the only trouble she had with authority figures was with the one she had married.

Frank pressed on. "Janelle was seen talking with this fellow Pablo shortly before she disappeared. Chances are, he's done nothing wrong. But we just need to talk to him. It's the only lead we have right now." He summoned up a smile that he hoped conveyed benign paternal concern.

The woman nodded, her eyes flicking nervously to the door. "Sometimes we make deliveries to Pablo's compound. I'll draw you a map."

22

FRANK WAS SORELY TEMPTED to head straight for the compound by himself, but common sense prevailed. Pablo's followers could be armed, and if he encountered trouble, no one would even know where he was.

He radioed Meyerson to meet him in Wolverton. Briefly, they discussed the merits of waiting until they could obtain a search warrant.

"Look, Lou, I don't feel like screwing around all day when we're this close," Frank said. "Have Pauline or someone get the process started while you and I head over to the compound. I bet we can talk our way in, but if we can't, we'll just wait there 'til the warrant comes through."

Reluctantly Meyerson agreed, and by noon they were lurching along a dirt track that grew progressively narrower. Meyerson winced as pine and birch trees scraped at the well-maintained finish of the state's four-wheel-drive vehicle. Frank peered into the thick undergrowth that made the woods virtually impenetrable on foot. "It's hard to believe anyone lives back here year-round. How do they store their food? They can't possibly have electricity."

The road seemed about to dead-end into a stand of pines when it suddenly dipped and curved hard to the right. As Meyerson swerved, the truck bottomed out with a sickening crunch of metal against stone. Frank tried not to picture the truck's muffler, concentrating instead on what lay in front of him.

The prospect called to mind a village on the Russian steppes he had seen on a *National Geographic* special—a forlorn outpost of humanity amid the wilderness. The four buildings, made of unpainted wood, had been erected by someone with very limited carpentry skills, and even less architectural ability. Each was oblong, about twenty by forty, punctuated at irregular intervals by windows of different sizes. One building, slightly smaller than the others, appeared dangerously close to collapse, but it presumably wasn't occupied by humans, since a squirrel dashed in and out at will. Smoke wafted out of the cinder block chimney of the building on the right. It was too hot to need a fire for warmth, so someone must be cooking, though no people were in sight.

Frank and Meyerson got out of the truck cautiously. A sudden stab of anxiety wrenched Frank's gut as he thought of those crazed survivalists the Feds were always raiding out west. Nothing he'd heard about Pablo indicated that he was armed, but Frank was not about to walk heedlessly into these dilapidated buildings. "Hello!" he shouted, hoping to get the inhabitants to come to him. "Anybody around?"

His voice sounded pathetically small to his own ears out here in the woods. Still, the compound was so silent, and the buildings so insubstantial, that surely anyone inside would have heard him. Frank and Meyerson waited a moment longer, but when no one came out to greet them, the lieutenant started toward the building on the right, his hand lightly resting on his holstered weapon. The door, made from a large sheet of warping plywood, shuddered under his insistent knocking. "Police!" he barked. "Anyone home?"

This produced a response, although from a different quarter. A sleepy-eyed woman appeared on the stoop of the building across the bare dirt yard. She said nothing but cocked her head at them inquiringly. Frank appraised her with distaste as he and Meyerson approached. Her brown hair, none too clean, was pulled into a lank braid that hung almost to her waist. Long, bony, bare feet, thoroughly coated with dirt, protruded from the hem of her sacky sundress. She raised her hand to scratch her head, and Frank averted his eyes from the dark hair that curled out of her armpits.

"Good morning, miss," he said with forced politeness. "We're looking for a fellow named Pablo. Is he around?"

"Who wants to know?"

Meyerson took the authoritarian approach. "I'm Lieutenant Meyerson of the New York state police and this is Police Chief Bennett from Trout Run. We'd like to ask Pablo a few questions regarding the disappearance of Janelle Harvey. Can you ask him to step out here, please."

The woman looked genuinely puzzled. "Who told you about that?" she asked.

"Her family's been searching for her for weeks!" Meyerson snapped.

Her face cleared. "Oh, really. Well, you'll have to talk to Pablo, but he went out for supplies."

"When will he be back?" the lieutenant asked.

She shrugged.

"What time did he leave?" he continued with elaborate patience.

The woman raised both arms and rotated them to indicate her lack of a watch, then turned to go back into the house.

"Wait!" Frank shouted. "What did you mean by asking who told us about Janelle's disappearance? You know her, don't you?"

The woman merely shook her head and slipped through the door. Frank used his foot to block her from shutting it. "Send Janelle out here. We just want to talk to her, see that she's all right."

"I don't know what you're talking about."

"She's here!" Elation quickly replaced Frank's determination to stay calm. He began to press against the door with his shoulder as the woman threw the full weight of her body against it from the other side.

Meyerson pulled Frank back, and the door slammed shut. "We can't enter the buildings unless they let us in, Frank. Not without a search warrant. We'll radio in and tell them to put a rush on it. If she's in there now, there's no way for her to get away without us seeing her."

Frank answered with an edgy chuckle. "C'mon, Lou, there are ways around that. We can say we had reason to believe she was being held against her will and was in danger."

Meyerson shook his head. "I know how you feel about this case, Frank. I don't want to see you screw it up now. What if she's dead? Have you thought of that? If we go in without a warrant, nothing we find will hold up in court. You don't want this guy to walk, do you?"

Frank jammed his hands in his pockets. "All right, all right. But I'm not leaving this spot until I meet up with

Pablo," he said as they headed back to the truck to begin their wait. "We better hope he's not out eating brown rice and spreading his gospel."

Meyerson, not a man to allow time to pass idly, pulled a notepad from his pocket and began printing neat notes. Frank was so wound up that sitting still in the truck was an act of sheer physical discipline. He knew if he allowed himself to get out of the vehicle to pace, his paces would soon lead him up to one of the many uncurtained windows, and from there, the temptation to infringe civil liberties would be irrepressible.

He satisfied himself with studying the buildings of the compound. The community Pablo had created was a far cry from the shipshape bruderhof's air of domestic prosperity and harmony. If Frank had found Janelle there he could have at least reassured her father that she had been living a decent life with good people in her absence from home.

But this place! What could Janelle possibly see in this forest ghetto to make her want to leave her home in Trout Run? What could be so bad that she felt compelled to seek shelter among these outcasts eking out a subsistence living? He could accept that Janelle felt alienated from Kim and Melanie and their shallow concerns. But could she possibly feel more connected to the slovenly hippie they had spoken to this morning?

He sat contemplating the woman, trying to imagine what her good points might be, when Meyerson dropped his pen, instantly alert. Frank was about to ask him what was wrong when he heard it too—a sputtering, back-firing engine laboring up the dirt road. An instant later, a dilapidated Chevy truck pulled into the clearing beside Frank's. Two men got out: one, barrel-chested with a bushy red beard; the other, blue-eyed, ponytailed, and even to Frank's grudging eyes, far more attractive than the police artist's sketch.

Frank and Meyerson quickly got out of their truck, and the four men faced one another in the still woods. The burly man glowered at his visitors, but Pablo was the soul of well-bred courtesy.

"Good morning! Welcome to our compound. How can I help you?" Pablo passed his clear blue gaze quickly over Meyerson and rested it on Frank.

"Frank Bennett, Trout Run police; Lou Meyerson, state police. We're here about Janelle Harvey," Frank said curtly.

Pablo's only response was a slight elevation of his straight, dark eyebrows. "We will be more comfortable inside. Ben, will you please unload the truck?"

Frank marveled that words that were in themselves polite could sound so offensive. Nevertheless, he followed his host to the building whose chimney still emitted smoke, eager to see the inner sanctum of the compound.

He was amazed to see that the inside of the building was actually quite comfortable-looking. They stood in a large room lined with chest-high bookshelves, above which hung a variety of paintings, some abstract, some representational. Woven wool rugs in Native American designs covered the unpolished wood floor, and several overstuffed armchairs and wooden rockers surrounded the central wood-burning stove. A large trestle table, with benches on either side and straight-backed chairs at the head and foot, stood at the far end of the room. Beyond it lay a doorway, which presumably led to the kitchen. A strong but not unpleasant smell of cooking vegetables permeated the room.

Pablo gestured them toward the chairs, then turned

toward the kitchen and said, "Rosalie," in a voice no louder than he would use in normal conversation. Instantly, a plump woman with a mass of wildly curly graying hair came to the doorway.

"Bring our guests some tea, please." Pablo leaned back languidly in the worn but genuine leather armchair, crossing one long leg over the other and dangling his sandalled foot. "You had a question about Janelle?"

"For starters, where is she?" Frank asked.

Again, the raised eyebrows. "I've no idea."

Meyerson, who had been perched tensely on the arm of a chair, leaped up. "Don't play games with us, man! We have witnesses who saw you with the girl. You're looking at charges of abduction, statutory rape, contributing to the delinquency of a minor . . ."

Pablo's long, finely shaped nose twitched in distaste. "Don't be preposterous. You can't intimidate me the way you routinely oppress the underclass."

"You don't deny that you know Janelle Harvey?" Frank asked.

"I don't deny it." Pablo echoed him with a mocking smile.

"And you brought her here?"

"She came here," Pablo corrected.

"But she's not here now?"

He shook his head. At that moment, Rosalie arrived with the tea, and Pablo took elaborate pains pouring, straining, and stirring.

Frank stared into the clear, rosy liquid in his cup. Unlike Meyerson, he felt surprisingly calm. He could see where this was headed: Janelle had eluded him once again. It was almost what he had come to expect.

"Let's start at the beginning, Mr. . . ." Frank paused to allow Pablo to fill in the blank.

"My name is Pablo."

"That's your full, legal name?" Meyerson interrupted.

Pablo gazed up at an impressionistic painting of a woman with one huge breast and one tiny bump. "The state knows me as Paul Esterhazy," he said contemptuously.

The name sounded vaguely familiar to Frank. "Any relation to the Esterhazy fertilizer people?"

Pablo looked deeply pained. "That some of my relatives engage in unethical pursuits is beyond my control."

Frank, certain that fertilizer money had paid for the land, books, paintings, and whatever other creature comforts the compound offered, restrained his impulse to sarcasm. "Let's start at the beginning," he said levelly. "You talked to Janelle at the Trail's End bar in Trout Run in March. Was that the first time you met her?"

"Yes. I found her to be a fascinating young woman."

Frank suspected that what fascinated Pablo the most about Janelle was her fascination with him. "And I believe after that first meeting, you agreed to meet her again?"

"You seem to know all about it," Pablo said.

"So she slipped out of her house one night to meet you, and then what? You arranged to pick her up on April eighteenth on Stony Brook Road?"

Pablo cradled his tea mug in his hands and sipped at it contemplatively. "I don't know where you got the idea I met her at night. We agreed to meet one afternoon—a few days later, I can't remember the day—at the picnic area that overlooks the brook there in Trout Run. We talked for several hours. Then, about two weeks later I happened to be driving along Stony Brook Road, on my way back from the used book store in Lake Placid, when I saw her walking. I stopped to offer her a lift."

"That was some lift you gave her—all the way out here," Meyerson interjected.

Pablo looked at the lieutenant as if he were nothing more than a blackfly—irritating but inconsequential—and turned his attention back to Frank.

"She wanted to talk some more. We went back to the picnic area. After about an hour, she asked if she could come and live here at the compound."

"Were you aware that an elderly man named Dell Lambert who lived on Stony Brook Road apparently saw Janelle leave with you?" Frank asked.

Pablo shrugged. "What if he did? I wasn't trying to be secretive."

"That man is now dead. He had an unfortunate accident," Frank continued. "What can you tell me about that?"

Pablo cocked his head to one side. "What could I possibly tell you? I don't even know of whom you are speaking."

"Were you back in Trout Run two days after Janelle left?" Meyerson asked.

"No, I didn't leave the compound at all for several days after Janelle arrived. I wanted to give her time to feel comfortable with the others before I left her."

Frank scowled. More like he wanted to keep constant watch over her so she didn't get away. He still couldn't figure out the Lambert angle, and he could see Meyerson was ready to move on.

"So, you encouraged Janelle to walk off and leave her family without saying a word?" Meyerson was having an increasingly difficult time containing himself in the face of Pablo's blasé recitation of the facts.

"I did not *encourage* her to do anything." Pablo made a steeple of his long fingers and balanced his prominent chin on it as he continued in a deliberate voice. "Janelle is a highly intelligent woman. She came to accept the impossibility of living the life of the mind surrounded by petty, venal distractions. She made the logical choice in coming to live at the compound—"

"We'll come back to why she came in a minute," Frank interrupted. "How long was she here? When did she leave?"

"When?" Pablo repeated, as if surprised that this should interest them. "She left Saturday night."

Frank squeezed his eyes shut and bit his lip. His expression was that of a man who has been hit so hard and so suddenly that mere profanity cannot begin to express his pain. While he had been wasting his time interrogating that poor hiker, Janelle had been on her way to another hiding place. If he could have immediately applied himself to locating the compound, instead of being sidetracked by that stupid stakeout, he might have found the girl.

"I wonder why Janelle felt she had to leave in the middle of the night, Mr. Esterhazy," Meyerson speculated. "You weren't holding her against her will, were you?"

Pablo refused to be antagonized. "I imagine," he said, slowly twisting a large silver ring on his right hand, "that she did not want to have to explain her actions to me and the others. It was easier for her just to sneak off."

"Oh yes, much easier to walk four or five miles through the pitch-black woods in the middle of the night, than to ask you to drive her back home."

Pablo turned to face Meyerson and began speaking in a slow, patient tone that he might have used to explain long division to a slow-witted child. "Janelle was here because she wanted to be. But living in a community such as ours is difficult. One must be prepared to make sacrifices. I thought she was mature enough to commit to our way of life. Apparently, I was wrong. Naturally, if she had asked me to take her somewhere, I would have complied. But she did not ask."

Frank listened to Pablo with only half an ear as his mind churned through other possibilities. The timing of her departure was just a little too convenient. Who could have tipped Janelle off? Was there someone in town who had known all along where she was? Or was it Pablo who had been alerted?

"Could Janelle possibly have known that we were on to her being here? Is that why she ran?" Frank asked. "Did she get some sort of message on Saturday?"

"How could she?" Pablo spread his sinewy arms in a dismissive gesture. "We have no phone, no radio, no newspapers, no mail."

"Yes, but *you* come and go. Maybe one of your friends on the outside let you know we were closing in on you."

"I have no 'friends on the outside,' as you put it. My whole universe is here, where we all live in complete isolation from worldly distractions."

"Just what are these 'distractions' you're all hell-bent on getting away from . . . Pablo?" Frank hesitated over the name, hating to give this charlatan even the most insignificant recognition. Still, there was no point in antagonizing him when there was so much yet to learn.

"Money, fame, status, possessions, sex—"

"Whoa, there. What do you mean, 'sex'?" Frank interrupted.

Pablo's full lips separated in a slight smile and his eyelids drooped to half-mast. "Yes, we are entirely celibate here at the compound. The intellect cannot develop fully when one is preoccupied with primal physical gratification and all its concomitant emotional entangle-ments."

"So which of these deadly distractions was Janelle try-ing to get away from?" Meyerson asked. "Money, fame, and status obviously aren't problems, and I wouldn't say she was overloaded with possessions, either."

"Janelle's reasons for coming to the compound are not mine to divulge," Pablo said in a disturbing echo of Pas-tor Bob. He could not have known how this would set Frank off.

"Don't give me that crap! I want to know, once and for all, what this kid is running from. And if I have to haul you into court to find out, I will. Now why don't you just make it easy for both of us, and tell me everything you know about Janelle."

Pablo was obviously torn between his pledge to defy the state and all its emissaries, and his equally powerful desire to be rid of Frank and Meyerson. He decided on the latter. "There was apparently some personal entangle-ment that she wanted to be free of," he admitted.

"Who with?" Meyerson asked.

"She didn't say."

"Do the names Craig Gadschaltz or Bob Rush sound familiar?"

"I can't say they do."

Frank jumped up from his seat in exasperation. "Well, what the hell did you spend all this time talking about?"

"What I always spend my time talking about. Books, philosophy, society, ethics. Janelle's petty personal prob-lems were of no interest to me. I tried to help her under-stand that they should not concern her, either."

"She wasn't pregnant, was she?" Frank asked.

For the first time, Pablo looked disturbed. "I must

admit, that never occurred to me. Rosalie would know."

The woman had apparently been unashamedly eaves-dropping, for she entered the room the moment her name was mentioned and proceeded to answer the question.

"Janelle wasn't pregnant. I had to help her when her period came." Seeing the puzzlement on Frank's face, she elaborated. "She was used to relying on unnatural and unsafe products created by the drug industry to exploit women."

It took Frank a moment to realize she was talking about tampons, which Estelle had regarded as the most significant scientific breakthrough of the mid-twentieth century. Not caring to dwell on what the alternatives could be, Frank moved the questioning along. "Did Janelle confide in you why she left home?"

Rosalie hesitated, glancing over at Pablo. "Tell him anything you know, Rosalie. Now, if you'll excuse me, I have some reading to do."

"Just a minute." Meyerson placed a restraining hand on Pablo's shoulder. "We're going to want a complete tour of this place, and we'll need to talk to everyone. After all, we have nothing but your word that Janelle really left here."

Pablo jerked away from the lieutenant's grasp. His eyes narrowed in anger as he considered this outrageous invasion by the state. "Do you think you're going to find Janelle tied to a bed or buried outside the kitchen door?"

"It won't take us long to get a search warrant," Frank reminded him.

Pablo spun away from them and stalked out the door, calling back over his shoulder, "Fine. Rosalie will escort you."

Despite her initial deference to Pablo, Rosalie proved

quite chatty. "This is the kitchen," she said, displaying with pride a room more primitive than the kitchen in Frank's grandmother's house, which hadn't been electrified until after World War II. "I do most of the cooking because Pablo feels we should each contribute to community life according to our talents."

"And how did Janelle contribute?" Frank asked.

"She helped me in the kitchen and Charles in the garden."

"So you spent some time alone with her. Did she tell you why she left home?"

Rosalie lifted her mop of hair, damp with sweat, from the back of her neck. "She wasn't specific. I just remember she said she was relieved to be free of . . . she used an odd word . . . *coercion* . . . that was it."

"Who was coercing her to do what?"

"She didn't say."

"Didn't you *ask*?"

"Oh, no. When you come to the compound, you start a new life. You leave your old life behind entirely." Rosalie removed some rolls from the oven of the woodstove. "We never question each other about our pasts."

"Could her father have been the person coercing her?" Meyerson interjected.

Rosalie cocked her head to one side in consideration. "I don't think so. When she first arrived, she was very anxious about contacting him to let him know she was okay. Of course, that was impossible."

"Why?" Frank and Meyerson asked simultaneously.

"We have no way of reaching anyone on the outside," Rosalie said with the same incredulity she would have shown if they had asked her why she didn't visit Mars.

"Pablo goes out into society. Surely Janelle could have

written her father, and Pablo could have mailed the letter for her."

Rosalie shook her head so adamantly that, for a moment, her hair completely obscured her face. "Pablo refuses to accept any services of the U.S. government."

"Convenient," Frank muttered. He opened the back door. "Come on, Rosalie, continue the grand tour."

"We raise much of our own food," Rosalie said as she led them past a weedy-looking garden to the next building. "This is the women's house. It's where Janelle, Lark, Catherine, and I sleep."

The room was set up as a large dormitory with four twin beds, all of which were unmade. Pegs on the wall held a collection of ratty dresses, T-shirts, and jeans. A cloudy mirror propped up on a small chest was the only concession to feminine vanity. The woman they had seen earlier sat at a table by the window, a mass of tiny beads spread out before her. She looked up at Rosalie, but said nothing.

"Lark is making porcupine quill jewelry, which we use to barter for goods we can't grow or make ourselves. This was Janelle's bed," Rosalie continued, anticipating Frank's next question.

Frank lifted the covers and looked under the mattress, but Janelle had left nothing behind. "Where did she keep her things?"

Rosalie pointed to the pegs. "We each have just two sets of clothes. This is her dress, so she must have been wearing her pink shirt and her jeans when she left." Frank checked the pockets of the dress while Meyerson opened the trunk, the only other place in the room where anything could be hidden. But it contained only sweaters and blankets.

Frank continued the tour with Rosalie, leaving Meyer-

son behind to question Lark on her knowledge of
Janelle's whereabouts. The men's dormitory was almost
identical to the women's, except it was slightly smaller.
After poking distastefully through the gray bed linens in
the main room, a flash of movement outside the window
caught his eye. "That must be Charles out in the garden,
huh? Why don't you introduce me, Rosalie."

But Charles, although friendly and cooperative, had no
insights on what had brought Janelle to the compound
and what had made her leave. Their conversations, he
reported, had been largely confined to horticultural mat-
ters. Meyerson had had even less luck with the inaptly
named Lark, Ben, and the herbalist, Catherine. But he
had made one find.

"Look at this," he said, leading Frank behind the
men's dormitory. Before them sat a vintage Japanese
compact car, so tiny it seemed toylike. "According to Ben,
Pablo makes some money as a trader of used books, and
this is what he drives when he's making his rounds."

Frank peered through the window. Every inch of space
in the car, except the driver's seat itself, was filled with
books. "Well, that certainly explains why Janelle left the
gas can behind. It's a wonder Pablo managed to squeeze
her in here."

Frank stood back and surveyed the compound from
this angle. "What the hell . . . ?" He suddenly started
trotting around to the front of the building, calling
back to Meyerson over his shoulder. "There's another
room in this building! Rosalie showed me the men's
quarters and I noticed it was slightly smaller than the
women's. But from the outside the buildings are the
same size."

He charged back into the men's dorm. Maybe he had
given up too easily—maybe Janelle was being held here!

He spotted a small door, concealed by the men's clothes that hung from pegs above it. He reached out to yank the door open, and practically fell on his face.

Pablo made an exaggerated gesture of ushering Frank in. A neatly made double bed entirely consumed the floor space. The windowless walls, covered with bookshelves and art, seemed to offer no possibility of concealment.

"So, you don't sleep with the hoi polloi, eh?" Frank said, slightly out of breath. Nothing and no one was hidden here.

"This is my inner sanctum. I need a place where I can read and meditate."

"I imagine you do," Frank said. Turning to leave, a thought occurred to him and he reversed direction. "Say, Pablo, how do you feel about animals?"

"Animals are our kindred spirits on earth. They must be allowed to live their lives without interference from humans. That is why we consume no animal products here."

"You lived at the Silas bruderhof for a time. They're not vegetarians, are they?"

"No, they exploit animals for their own purposes. I tried to get them to see the error of their ways, but I failed."

"How do you feel about zoos?" Frank continued.

Pablo shuddered. "An abomination! Imprisoning animals for human entertainment—it's barbaric!"

"And keeping pets—I imagine you frown on that?"

Pablo grew quite animated, warming to his subject. "Did you know that cats will revert to their feral state in just one generation? They can easily live outdoors as hunters, instead of being confined to houses and beholden to humans for mass-produced, unhealthy food full of chemicals and dyes. There's no reason that all animals should not be living free."

"What if a few animals had to die in order to achieve this freedom? " Frank probed.

"You mean, some that were weakened by domestication might not survive the transition? That's true, but—"

"No," Frank interrupted. "I meant what if a few animals had to be sacrificed to make your point about living free. That would be justifiable under the circumstances—a sort of holy war, right?"

Pablo's caution snapped back into place. "What are you getting at? All war is immoral."

"You wouldn't consider killing a pet or an animal in a zoo? You know, to release it from bondage and sort of make a statement at the same time?"

"I've never killed anything in my life. What are you going on about?"

"Someone's been killing animals in Trout Run: a dog, a rabbit, a cat, an emu. Do you happen to know anything about that?" Frank sat on the edge of the bed, casually blocking the door with his outstretched legs.

"Don't be absurd! Of course I don't!"

"Is there anyone else around Trout Run you've been spouting your theories to? Maybe someone . . . misinterpreted . . . them."

"This is a typical tactic of the police state. When you can't entrap me on one charge, you trump up another and try again!"

"Don't blow that left-wing hot air in my face, Mr. Esterhazy. I suggest you think long and hard about why Janelle came here, why she left, and where she went. And when something comes to you, just step out of your front door and let us know—the state police will be camped on your doorstep until we find that girl. "

On the teeth-rattling ride down the dirt road, Meyerson speculated on their plan of action. "It doesn't seem possible that Janelle could have contacted anyone to pick her up. If she really walked out of here, she must have hitchhiked once she got to the main road. We get that out on the news, and set up a roadblock—maybe we'll find the person who gave her a lift."

Frank nodded absently. It now appeared Janelle could not have been the one to have sent the ransom note. And Pablo claimed he wasn't the person she sneaked out to meet at night. Of course he could be lying, but to what purpose? He had admitted taking her to the compound, why deny that he was the man she sneaked out to see at night?

Frank sat in silence for the rest of the trip down the dirt track. As they finally turned onto the paved road, he said, "Asshole."

"Excuse me?"

"That fraud, Pablo. I'd like to roust him out of that stupid compound of his just to wipe the smirk off his face. But if his story checks out, we can't even charge him with anything."

The hint of a smile played over Meyerson's stony features. "Maybe no criminal charges, but we might be able to make it a little difficult for him to stay the guru-in-chief."

"What do you mean?"

"Oh, I just happened to notice a few things that other branches of the government might be interested in. Like Pablo's outhouses seemed kinda close to that little stream. Human waste contaminating a watershed preserve area—the Department of Environmental Protection tends to frown on that. And then that wood-burning stove didn't seem to be properly vented, did you think?"

"I believe you're right, Lew," Frank agreed. "That would be a building code violation. And certainly driving a car with the rear window obscured with books could result in a person receiving a citation. And speaking of those books, does Pablo strike you as the type of fellow who would report to the IRS any profits made from the sale of books?"

"He may not be diligent in that regard." Lew smiled serenely. "Funny how one little problem can lead to another, isn't it? Yes, I think our man Pablo may be in for an unfortunate run of bad luck."

"Pity."

23

MINUTES AFTER A PLEA for information was broadcast on the Tuesday evening news, a truck driver called to report that he had picked up a young woman a quarter mile from the spot where the dirt road to the compound joined the main road very early Sunday morning. He had driven Janelle as far as a truck stop near the entrance to the Northway, where he left her with five dollars.

A waitress at the diner confirmed that the driver had departed without Janelle. She had noticed the girl making a phone call, then hanging around outside. When she had looked out again after the lunch rush, the girl had gone. Try as he might, Frank couldn't prod her to remember how or with whom Janelle had left.

He left state police headquarters at noon on Wednesday, with nothing to show for his efforts but a splitting headache and a sheaf of printouts from the phone company listing every number that had been dialed from the diner's two pay phones. When he got back to his office in Trout Run, Earl was waiting for him.

"Mrs. Guttfreund called again. She wants to know if you found out who was tailgating her on Sunday."

"Oh, let me see . . . Sunday, Sunday . . . wasn't that when I was interrogating that poor hiker? And why didn't I do it on Monday? Oh, could that've been when I was getting my ass chewed out by the Council? Tuesday I was discovering that I just missed finding Janelle at the compound. And this morning, well, I've just been sitting around scratching my butt, haven't I?"

Earl, uncertain whether to be amused or wounded, simply said, "It's the third time she's called."

Frank flung the phone reports on his desk, where they narrowly missed upsetting a two-day-old Styrofoam cup of coffee. "I tell you what, Earl. Why don't *you* take over the Guttfreund investigation. You're always wanting to be in charge of something—here's your big chance."

Earl said nothing, intuitively sensing that this was the best way to preserve what little dignity remained to him. He went over to his desk, and in a few moments, Frank could hear the strident tones of Mrs. Guttfreund's voice floating across the office from the receiver of Earl's phone.

As he stared at the list of phone numbers, Frank assuaged his guilt by telling himself it was really time that Earl showed a little more initiative. Suddenly, a number on the list leaped out at him—it had the same exchange as every number in Trout Run. Quickly, he dialed it.

"Hello," a man's voice answered on the second ring.

"Jack?"

"Yeah, who's this?"

Frank recovered from his shock and identified himself. "Janelle called you Sunday morning. Why didn't you say something?"

"What the hell are you talking about? Janelle didn't call me!"

"I have a telephone report here that shows a call from the diner where she was last seen, to this number. Could Dorothy have answered?"

"Right, and then it just slipped my sister's mind that *Janelle* called? No, she must have got the answering machine and not left a message. I only bought the thing since she's been gone."

"The call lasted two minutes, Jack. That's too long for someone to just listen to your greeting, then hang up."

"What are you insinuating? That I talked to her and told her to stay away?

"Maybe Clyde was right after all. You've gone off the deep end. You have your own ideas and you just twist the facts to fit them. If Janelle called me once, she'll call again, and this time I'll make sure she doesn't get some stupid machine. I'm just going to sit here by the phone and wait. Now don't call me again and tie up the line."

Frank sat studying the receiver after the line went dead. Earl watched from his desk, waiting expectantly to be filled in on the latest development. Instead, Frank immediately dialed Meyerson.

"Lou? Frank here. Hey, tell me what you make of this. Janelle made a two-minute call to her father Sunday from the diner, and he denies ever getting it." He beat his pen against a notepad, listening intently. "All right, I'll hold."

Frank's eyes were fixed on the Idaho-shaped water stain over the file cabinets as he pondered the significance of Jack's lie. And it had to be a lie.

Somewhere he heard a voice, but he was so lost in thought that it took several seconds to process the sounds into meaningful words. "What?" he asked Earl. "What was Janelle wearing? Jeans and a pink shirt. Why?"

"Because Mrs. Guttfreund says the truck that was following her . . ."

"What are you talking about, Earl? What's Agnes Guttfreund got to do with what Janelle was wearing?"

"Well, if you'd let me finish, I'd explain," Earl said with an edge in his voice that was entirely unfamiliar to his boss.

"Mrs. G. says a red pickup was tailgating her, then it passed her. A little later, she came around a bend and she saw the truck pulled over, and two people were starting off into the woods."

Forgetting that he had been waiting for Meyerson to come back on the line, Frank hung up the phone. "Jack Harvey drives a red pickup!"

"No, it couldn't have been Jack. Mrs. Guttfreund went on and on, calling the guy a young punk."

Dismissing this objection with a wave of his hand, Frank headed for the door. "Oh, Agnes is so old she thinks anyone under fifty is a young punk."

"No! Don't you *see*?"

The frustration in Earl's voice brought Frank up short. He spun around to face his assistant and saw Earl recoil. "What is it, Earl? What don't I see?"

"I . . . I didn't mean it like that. I just—"

"It's okay. Tell me . . . please."

"Tommy drives Jack's truck sometimes. If Jack says he never got Janelle's message, maybe it's because Tommy answered the phone and talked to her."

Somewhere deep inside himself, Frank felt the coiled spring of anxiety unwind a few turns. This damn case was on its way to being solved. "Earl, I do believe you're right," he said as he reached for the phone. He paused before dialing and met Earl's eye. "Absolutely right."

"Hello, Mrs. Guttfreund. Frank Bennett here. Just fine, ma'm, and you? Well that's what I'm calling about. I just wanted to clarify something. When you passed the truck . . . when it had pulled off the road . . . can you describe the two people you saw go into the woods?" Frank held the receiver away from his ear as Mrs. Guttfreund's tetchy voice boomed over the line.

"It was dark and I just saw them from behind. If I'd recognized them I wouldn't be asking you to trace the truck, now would I?"

"No, I know you didn't recognize them, ma'am, but I wonder if you noticed any details of their appearance. Height, clothing, hair color?" Frank listened, tapping a pencil. "Yes, ma'am, I understand. You certainly couldn't take your eyes off the road. But would you say it was a boy and a girl?"

"How should I know?" Mrs. Guttfreund had worked herself into a state of high umbrage. "Today the girls wear jeans and work boots and the boys have long hair. They all look the same."

Frank clenched the receiver and counseled himself to patience. "That certainly is true, ma'am, but maybe something about their size, their build . . ."

"My night vision isn't good. That's why I don't like driving late, even at dusk. All I can say is one was taller than the other, and they were both thin."

"Okay, Mrs. Guttfreund. That's a help. We'll get right on it."

"Do you know who was tailgating me?"

"Yes, I think I do. I'll take care of it, I promise."

"So Tommy was helping Janelle hide out in the woods, huh?" Earl asked as they went out to the car.

"Maybe. Maybe not."

"But what else could it be?" Earl asked.

"The other possibility is Tommy wants to be sure Janelle never comes home."

"You really think Tommy would *hurt* Janelle?"

"I'm afraid he could." Frank gunned the engine.

"But Tommy's her cousin," Earl protested.

Frank didn't bother to answer. Earl turned his head and leaned against the passenger side window. Frank could see him blinking furiously. Discovering that Janelle was definitely still alive had boosted everyone's morale; now he had taken that reassurance away.

Frank felt the all-too-familiar stab of remorse. But Earl annoyed him. He thought being a cop meant strutting around with a gun on your hip, telling people what to do. He needed to find out that too often it meant finding out things about people that you just couldn't believe were true, but were.

They didn't speak until Frank turned into the drive leading to Jack's and Dorothy's houses. "Don't say anything about how we know Tommy and Janelle were together," Frank warned as they walked up the steps to Dorothy's front porch.

Frank's insistent pounding brought Dorothy to the door, looking like a mole who had been flushed from her hole into unfamiliar daylight. She squinted up at Frank. "Jack's home, you know. Maybe he didn't hear you knocking."

"I didn't come to talk to Jack. Where's Tommy?"

Instantly, her face contracted with fear. "Tommy? He's . . . he's . . . not home."

"Earl, go check the back bedrooms." Sharing none of Meyerson's concerns for civil liberties, Earl did as he was told.

"What is it?" Dorothy asked, her voice quavering pathetically. Frank ignored her as he marched through the kitchen and headed down to the basement. "He just went camping for a few days with a friend," she called down after him.

When he got back to the living room, Earl was waiting. "He's not back there. I checked the closets and everything."

"When's the last time you saw him?" Frank asked.

"I tried to tell you. He and Dennis Treve left for a camping trip on Snowshoe Mountain Monday morning. They had three days off school for teachers' conferences. Why? What's wrong?"

"Was Tommy driving Jack's truck Sunday evening?"

"Well, I suppose he could've been. Jack and I went to dinner at Malone's in my car. Tom didn't want to come. Said he had to get ready for his trip. Maybe he took the truck to go to the Store or something. Why? Was there an accident?"

"When do you expect him back?"

"Well, tonight sometime. He didn't really say—you know how boys are . . ." Her voice trailed off.

"Is this his hat?" Frank picked up a dirty Yankees cap from a small table by the door. When Dorothy nodded, Frank shoved it in his pocket and left without any further explanation. Dorothy stood in the doorway and watched them drive off.

"Do you think it could have been Dennis that Mrs. G. saw go into the woods with Tommy?" Earl asked.

"It's easy enough to check—we'll go over to the Treves' right now. But even if it was Dennis, there's something mighty convenient about the timing of this campout." Frank thumped the steering wheel. "I should have pressured Tommy more, right from the start. I should have taken him into custody until he told me what was going on with those animals."

A brief conversation with Mrs. Treve confirmed that Dennis had indeed been away since Monday morning, when her husband had dropped them off at the Snowshoe trailhead.

"What about Sunday evening? Was Dennis with Tommy then?"

A hard-faced woman with two toddlers clinging to her fat legs, Mrs. Treve did not seem particularly concerned with the whereabouts of her eldest. "How should I know? He's eighteen. He comes and goes as he pleases."

"When's he due back?" Frank asked.

"He has school on Thursday. He better be home by then."

"Are we just going to wait 'til Tommy and Dennis come home?" Earl asked once they were back in the car.

"No way. I'm done with waiting. We'll go back to the office and I'll call the park service to send some rangers and a dog over to meet us at the Snowshoe trailhead. You fill up our water bottles and get some sandwiches to put in the packs. We'll need food if we're going to search from now 'til sundown.

"And Earl," Frank called when he was halfway through the door. "Pack some hand shovels."

At three, Frank and Earl met three young rangers from the park service at the spot where Agnes Guttfreund had seen Tommy and his companion enter the woods. The trail that led up Snowshoe from Route 51 was a steep one. The rangers had brought walkie-talkies, and gave one to Earl. Frank eyed their medium-size, shaggy dog skeptically. "That doesn't look like a trained bloodhound to me."

"Sam's a very good tracker," a young ranger with the name tag RUSTY claimed.

Frank scowled. He found it hard to take a man with bright red hair and freckles seriously. "All right, you and the dog come with Earl and me." Frank nodded toward the two older rangers. "You two cover the north side of the trail. Get way off the trail and bushwhack. Look for signs of their campsites. Radio us if you find them."

Frank watched dubiously as Rusty showed the dog Tommy's hat and discussed it with him earnestly. Sam set off ahead of them, nose to the ground, guided by something only he could smell.

The dense shade of the trees made the day seem pleasantly cool, but as soon as they started climbing the exertion quickly drenched them with sweat. This in turn attracted the scourge of the Adirondacks, vicious little blackflies that made mosquitoes seem compassionate by comparison. The men crashed through overgrown parts of the trail, wiping the stinging sweat from their eyes and swatting furiously at the carnivorous insects.

The dog never hesitated, only occasionally veering off the trail, then returning to continue the progressively more vertical ascent.

After two hours of searching, they paused to rest and eat. Sitting on a flat rock, Frank surveyed the woods they had just walked through. At this elevation the trees were mostly white oak and birch. The woods were very still. The only sound was that of water in a little stream rushing headlong down the mountain to join Stony Brook. Frank found it hard to reconcile the beauty surrounding him with what he believed he would soon find: Janelle hiding out in the woods because she was somehow involved in Tommy's animal murders; or Janelle dead, her cousin's victim.

Try as he might, he couldn't imagine a happy ending to this whole sorry mess. But he did know one thing—he couldn't bear to be out here for one more day. The need to find Janelle, to have the whole thing resolved one way or the other, infused him with a rush of energy.

"Let's go!" Frank bounded up from his seat and set off again with renewed determination. But after another two hours of trudging uphill, down, and back up again, blindly following that silly dog, Frank felt the seedling of despair growing. "Are you sure this dog is really following Tommy's trail? How do you know he's not just tracking a squirrel or something?"

"He's never lost the scent," Rusty reassured them. "We're on the right track."

Now the only way Frank could force himself to go on was by picking out a certain tree or rock and swearing he would not lift his eyes from the ground again until he reached it. He dragged himself up a steep outcropping of rock and practically stepped on Sam, who lay panting in the middle of the trail.

"Well, Rusty, it looks like your dog's pulling a work stoppage," Earl said. "Guess he's not going any farther 'til he gets a dog biscuit."

Frank was in no mood for jokes. "C'mon, Rusty, get that mutt moving again."

Rusty looked worried. "I think he's lost the trail. Maybe it picks up again on the other side of that stream. C'mon, Sam."

The dog followed his handler dutifully through the water, but soon sat down. Rusty led him off to the other side of the trail, but Sam stubbornly returned to the trail, where he plopped down again.

"This is it," Rusty said. "This is as far as Tommy came."

"Don't be ridiculous!" Frank snapped. "There's no sign that they camped here. It's too steep to even pitch a tent. I suppose you think Tommy just jumped off the side of this mountain."

"He must have gone back down the way he came up," Rusty said.

"He just hiked to this particular spot, turned around, and went back. Okay, I think I've had all the help I can take from the park service. We'll get some state troopers in here tomorrow and do this search right."

Earl warned that they had better start working their way back down the mountain if they wanted to be back at their cars by dusk. He checked in with the other team by radio. They too had found nothing, and agreed to head back.

Rusty, who was used to long hours of hiking, soon drew far ahead of Frank and Earl. Although the trip down the mountain was easier on the lungs and heart, it required strength to brace your legs against the steep descent. They struggled along slowly, concentrating on getting back to the trailhead. The dog ran back and forth between them, taking circuitous routes under bushes and down into gullies. Sometimes they would lose sight of him, but they could always hear him barking. Then he would tear back into view and sit below them on the trail, waiting.

They tramped along silently, eyes cast down, for a good ten minutes. Suddenly Earl stopped. "Where's Sam?"

"Oh, great. It's not enough we can't find Janelle. Now that stupid dog is lost, too."

Earl called, "Sam! Sam! Here, boy!" At once, behind them they could hear his faint answering bark. They called some more, and Sam barked some more, but the sound was not getting any closer.

"We'll have to go back to look for him," Earl said.

Frank, desperately tired and outraged at the thought of having to backtrack up the mountain, followed. The last thing he needed was to lose Earl in the bush.

About a hundred feet up the mountain, they spotted Sam. He was standing to the left of the trail, below them in a little gully. "Get over here, Sam," Frank bellowed, but the dog just stood staring at them, barking insistently.

"Here, Sam, here boy," Earl cajoled. But still the dog refused to come. Instead he began running back and forth over a five-foot stretch.

"Jesus H. Christ," Frank muttered as he left the trail and scrambled down to the dog. He picked up momentum as he went, and his legs, rubbery from so much walking, could not slow him down. He felt his toe catch on something and he fell facedown about a foot from Sam.

"Goddammit to hell!" Frank's face was almost purple with pain and rage.

Earl had scrambled down the slope and was pulling on his elbow to help him up, but Frank shook him off and pulled himself up. "I'm going to strangle that dog!"

Sam wisely sat a few feet away, watching the proceedings with his sharp brown eyes. Then, as if unable to restrain himself, he began to run circles around Frank and Earl.

"Grab ahold of him, would'ya," Frank directed Earl. Even through his thick boot, his big toe throbbed with the force of his stumble. "What the hell did I trip on, anyway?"

And then his eyes fell on it: a piece of bright copper pipe about three inches in diameter, sticking straight up from the ground about four inches, like a marker. Frank moved closer to examine it. He tugged on it, but it didn't budge. He looked up and his eyes took in the whole scene: Earl struggling to hold the frantic dog, who was trying his best to break away and pawing the earth at the same time; the abundance of dried leaves that seemed to have oddly settled in this section of the gully; the broken branches of the small berry plants that grew on the far side of the gully.

"Something's buried here," Frank said. He swiftly kicked away the thick mat of leaves, and the freshly dug earth became apparent.

He'd known this was a possibility, but seeing the grave when he had come so close, so very close, to finding Janelle alive was almost more than he could bear. He cradled his head in his hands.

But when he spoke his voice was steady. "Let's get to work, Earl. I'll radio the other rangers, you get out the shovels."

With shaking hands, Earl started digging at the downhill end of the grave. "I bet it's just one of those animals he's been killing, don't you think?" he asked.

Frank was about to scoff at this, but one look at Earl's pathetically hopeful face changed his mind. Besides, the kid had a point. Every other time he had thought he was about to find Janelle he'd been wrong. Why not now?

He was digging at the top of the grave, near the copper pipe. "Why the hell did he put this here?" Frank muttered half-aloud. "He went to such lengths to hide the grave, and then he seems to have left this pipe as a marker, almost like he was planning on coming back."

Sam, relieved that his human companions had finally got his message, sat panting quietly a few feet away, watching the men dig. Then, for no apparent reason, his ears pricked up, his hackles rose, and he raced to Frank's side. He sniffed at the pipe, cocked his head, and began a peculiar half-whine, half-growl. Frank observed his behavior with a wrinkled brow. Then he gently nudged Sam away, and laid his own ear next to the opening of the pipe.

What he heard sent a shiver of terror and revulsion through his body. He leaped up as if the pipe had burned him. "Jesus Christ, Earl! Whatever it is, it's still alive. Listen." And he pushed Earl's head down to the pipe so he could hear the sound, too. Frank listened again: soft, labored breathing. Human breathing.

Earl, who had been digging rather gingerly, none too eager to come into contact with a body, now sent dirt flying furiously. His shovel was the first to hit the box. As they cleared dirt and rocks from a wider area, the crude wooden structure was revealed: about three feet wide and five feet long, it was big enough to hold a good-size dog. Hastily knocked together, many of the box's nails had not been driven in straight and protruded from the edge of the cover. They tried to pull the cover off, but they hadn't dug enough around the perimeter to free it. They returned to digging, their progress maddeningly slow.

Finally they created a clearance of several inches around the box, enabling them to lift the lid straight off.

Inside lay Janelle Harvey.

She was on her right side. Her terrified left eye regarded them for one brief moment before she squeezed it shut in protection against the light. Even the fading daylight in the deep woods was too much for eyes that had seen total blackness for almost two days.

Her knees were drawn up to her chest to allow her to fit in the small box. As Frank and Earl carefully lifted her from her prison, she gasped with the pain of being moved from the position her joints had been locked into. She drank desperately from the water bottle they offered her, and Frank noticed that the inside of the box had been fit-ted with a small water dispenser of the type used in hamster cages.

He'd fantasized about this moment: a triumphant rescue; a joyful reunion. Instead, Frank looked at the frail forlorn figure slumped against a tree, her dirty pink shirt half torn off. This was not the Janelle he had carried about with him in his mind's eye. That Janelle was pretty and smart and loving and headstrong. He wondered if the girl he had found would ever merge with the girl her father had lost.

Frank sat down next to Janelle and began to talk softly. "Earl radioed the rangers, and soon they'll be here with a stretcher to carry you down the mountain. They'll take you to the hospital to make sure you're all right. In a few days, when you feel up to it, you'll tell me everything that happened, okay? But right now, I have to ask you just one thing. Who did this to you, Janelle?"

Janelle had been looking off into the trees the entire time Frank was talking, and her gaze did not shift now. At first her lips moved soundlessly, but then she said softly, "Tommy."

24

FRANK STRODE ALONG the long green hospital corridor, trying to keep focused on his destination, but against his will he glimpsed the tableau in each dimly lit room: a stricken person lying in the bed, a TV blaring, a relative sitting uselessly in a chair, waiting to be freed by the end of visiting hours. As Frank put his head around the doorway of Janelle's room, he expected to be met by the same scene. But the bed was empty, the TV silent, and a weak beam of sunshine came through the open curtains. The room was filled with flowers and cards. Janelle sat in a chair by the window, leafing through a magazine. Frank observed her silently. It had only been twenty-four hours, but already she looked much better. Although still drawn, her face had regained its rosy color; her strawberry blond hair gleamed in the light.

"Hello, Janelle."

She jumped in her chair and the magazine fell to the floor.

"Can I come in?"

She nodded but did not smile. Her solemn hazel eyes

followed him as he crossed the room to sit in the chair beside her.

"How do you feel?"

Janelle shrugged and looked down at her hands. "Okay, I guess." Then she brought her head up sharply and looked Frank straight in the eye. "Daddy says you always said I hadn't been kidnapped or murdered. How did you know?"

"Well, I wasn't positive," Frank said. "First it was the gas can that made me doubtful you'd been taken against your will. It seemed like you intentionally set it behind that bush, then got into a car and rode away. Then, the more I talked to people, the more I believed something had been troubling you."

Janelle averted her eyes. "You were right about the gas can. I meant to come back for it, but then I never did . . ." Her voice trailed off as she gazed out the window.

"Did you plan to leave with Pablo that day?"

Janelle shook her head. "We just got to talking, and suddenly it seemed like a good idea. I guess you think I'm a real idiot."

"No, I don't." Frank paused to choose his words carefully for once. For his own satisfaction, he wanted to hear Janelle's whole story. But more important, he needed Janelle's cooperation to find Tommy. Despite massive search efforts by the state police, Tommy was still on the loose.

"You know, Janelle," he continued slowly, "sometimes when people are scared, they do things they wouldn't necessarily have done if they had the . . . the luxury to think their problem through."

They were silent for a moment, then Frank spoke softly. "Do you want to tell me what made you so scared?"

Two tears slipped down her cheeks, but she did not sob. "I'm so ashamed."

Frank longed to put his arms around her and brush away her tears, to rub her back as he had rubbed Caroline's so many times over the years, even when she was grown. But he sensed that she would not want that from him—would not even want him to pat her hand. Instead Frank put on his no-nonsense voice.

"Janelle, you did not commit a crime. Tommy committed the crime, and I intend to get to the bottom of it. I know you didn't run away from home for a little change of scenery, and I know Tommy didn't bury you in that box as a practical joke. I want you to tell me why, in your own words. Now, I'm going to turn on this tape recorder, and I want you to tell me everything that happened between you and Tommy, starting at the very beginning."

Frank clicked on the little recorder, then held his breath, hoping his strategy had not backfired. But Janelle took a deep breath and with her head bowed, began talking.

"It started in January. I came home from school one day and I was going to bake some cupcakes, but we didn't have any eggs so I went over to my aunt's house to get some. My aunt was at work, but all my life we've just walked in and out of each other's houses, so I went into the kitchen." She stopped and closed her eyes, as if calling up the scene that day. Her delicate features twisted in pain at the memory.

"I heard this horrible, high-pitched screaming. It wasn't loud, but it seemed close. I looked out the kitchen window into the backyard . . ." Janelle stopped, mouth open but paralyzed.

"What did you see Tommy doing?"

"He had a raccoon. It was . . . nailed to a board. It was

still alive, struggling to get free, hurting itself more and more every time it moved. And Tommy was just standing there, watching it." Janelle shuddered, breathing heavily. "Smiling."

"I ran outside, yelling for him to stop. At first when he saw me, he seemed scared. Then he just started to laugh."

She stopped, her breaths coming in rapid, short gasps. Then she calmed herself. "He killed some other animals after that. He left things for me to find. Then, I met Pablo."

"How many times did you see him?"

"Three. Once at the Trail's End, and twice at this place where there's a picnic table over near Stults' farm. We talked for hours. He was so intelligent. He had read all kinds of books I've never read. He knew about philosophy and theology and ancient history and Greek and Roman and Indian myths. It was great—I had never talked to anyone like that before. I never even knew people like him existed. I mean, up to then, Mrs. Carlstadt is probably the most intellectual person I knew, and she only knew about English literature. Eventually I kind of hinted about my family problems. He never asked for details or told me what I should do. He just started talking more and more about the life at the compound.

"He said that most people were just made of what he called 'the raw elements' and that God had created them simply to reproduce and create workers to keep the world functioning on its most basic level. Then he said there were a small class of people who rose above their basest instincts to live the life of the mind. He said God put them on earth to think and create and produce art and music and literature. He said a lot of great minds had been ruined by sexual temptation—people like Nietzsche and Byron and Van Gogh. That's why Pablo created the compound—so people could realize their creative potential and be protected from the distraction of sex."

Janelle looked at him with a combination of sheepishness and defiance. "I know it must sound stupid to you now, but he made it seem so right. It just seemed like sex was all anyone I knew ever thought about. All Kim and Melanie ever wanted to talk about was guys, and who was going with who, and who was breaking up with who. It got real old. Before Craig and I broke up, he was always on me about it. And then . . ." Janelle's eyes glittered with tears, but she did not cry.

A great feeling of compassion welled up in Frank. Every so often, a child was born who rebelled against the reality she found herself in. Who knew that some other life existed but didn't know where or how to find it. He believed these children were headed for certain glory, or certain disaster. There was rarely any middle ground. Janelle had narrowly escaped the ultimate disaster; he wondered if she would rebound and go on to some wonderful achievement.

"So," he said gently, "you thought it would be nice to go off and live the contemplative life with Pablo and his friends."

Janelle nodded. "Pablo told me that I could learn more reading in his library than I could in high school. He said I could go off to college later if I wanted to. He told me it was important that I be totally committed to the notion of leaving my old life behind. He said everything I would need would be provided for me at the compound, so there was no need to bring anything, or make any preparations to leave. He said there would come a day when he felt I was ready to make the move, and he would come for me."

Frank scowled. He had suspected that Pablo had downplayed his role in Janelle's flight. "And that day came on April eighteenth, when he drove up alongside you on Stony Brook Road."

"That's right. I set the gas can down, just like you said. I meant to just go for a little drive and talk, but Pablo said this was the day, and I decided he was right."

"You didn't feel bad, leaving your father to worry about what happened to you?"

Janelle looked away and her voice pleaded for understanding. "I did. I begged Pablo to let me call or write just to tell him I was okay, but Pablo said it was important to my spiritual growth that I stop clinging to the past. I tried to think of a way to get in touch with Daddy anyway, but there were no phones at the compound, and I had no money for stamps, and no way to get to a mailbox."

"So it wasn't you who sent the ransom note after you left?"

"Ransom note? What ransom note?" Janelle looked genuinely perplexed.

"Never mind. So what was it like, living at the compound?"

"Well, it was a little hard to get used to—no TV, no radio, no phone, no hot water. But I kind of got to like that part. We would wake up early and eat breakfast together. We all had chores to do, like planting the vegetable garden and fixing up the buildings. We'd meet again for lunch, then in the afternoon we were supposed to read or work on our creative projects. After dinner, we'd sit around and have these conversations that were supposed to help us exchange ideas and do what Pablo called 'feeding each other's spirit.' But mostly it was Pablo talking and everyone else just agreeing with him.

"You know, when he first told me about the compound, I thought I wouldn't fit in there because I'm not any kind of creative genius. I thought the others would all be like Pablo, but after a while, I realized they weren't too smart. I mean, I liked Catherine and Rosalie. But they all seemed to depend an awful lot on Pablo, and to not have much to say for themselves. Still, I was happy enough, because for the first time in months, I had nothing to worry about."

"So why did you leave?"

As she looked up at him, he saw a face shaped by bitter knowledge.

"It happened before breakfast. No one else was up yet. I went into the kitchen, and while I was leaning over the counter, measuring out the tea, Pablo came and put his arms around me and started kissing my neck." Janelle clenched her fists.

"I knew he wouldn't force me. But it was catching him like that, hearing him use that same soft, reasonable voice he used when he was trying to explain Kierkegaard, that made me see him for what he was. A fake. A bullshitter. I knew then that there was no place on earth to run away to. That I had to come home and tell Daddy and face whatever happened. That night after everyone was asleep, I just walked away. I came with nothing; I left with nothing.

"I was so mad, I wasn't even thinking about how I would get home with no money. The sun was coming up and a truck was coming, so I stuck out my thumb, and he stopped right away. I got in, and it wasn't until a few minutes later that I realized it was pretty dangerous to be hitchhiking."

Frank bit back the impulse to point out it was no more dangerous than going off to live in a religious commune with a man you met in a bar.

"Anyway, the guy who picked me up turned out to be a really nice man. He said he wished he could take me all the way to Trout Run, but he was headed north. He dropped me off at the rest stop on the Northway and gave me money to call my father and get something to eat.

"I was really scared to call my dad, but excited too, you know? So I decided to eat something first. After that, I had a dollar left. I forgot how far away I was, and that it was going to cost more than a quarter. It ended up being ninety cents, so then I only had a dime left. Anyway, the phone rang four times and then I heard Daddy's voice say hello. I started talking right away, and then I realized it was a recording—that Daddy had got an answering machine. I almost hung up, but then I remembered I didn't have any more money, so I told him on the machine where I was and to please come get me, that I was all right, and that I loved him. Then the phone company cut me off.

"After that, I sat down to wait. Hours went by, and I was convinced that he wasn't coming. I thought about calling again collect, but I figured he wouldn't accept the call because he was so mad he didn't want me anymore. I was hot, and hungry again, and depressed, and I didn't know what I was going to do, or where I could spend the night. Then I saw our truck pull up.

"I ran up and opened the door before it had even stopped. It was Tommy driving. The strange thing is, I was so glad to be going home that I didn't even care. I wasn't scared—I just figured he wanted to head me off before I talked to my dad. You know, to work out what my story should be. He didn't say much while we were driving, but he never was much of a talker. I figured anything he had to tell me, he could say right before we pulled in the driveway."

She paused, as if to gather strength to tell the last part of her story. When she spoke again, her voice was so soft he had to lean forward to hear her.

"Even when he pulled off on the side of Route Fifty-one, I wasn't scared. I, I just didn't get it." She shook her head, and the face she turned toward Frank still showed her disbelief. "After all, he's my cousin. We played together . . ." Janelle's voice trailed off.

Frank tried to help her along. "He tied your hands? He made you walk into the woods with him?"

"No, nothing like that." She hesitated. "You see, the woods are like, magical, to Tommy. After his dad died, he'd spend all day there and just come home to sleep. It's comforting to him. So I just figured he couldn't talk unless he was there. And I knew we had to talk.

"Anyway, we climbed and climbed until we finally stopped at that little dried streambed. Tommy started clearing away these leaves and branches, and underneath it was . . . that box." Janelle shivered.

"I was afraid he had some dead animal in it. When he opened it up and it was empty, I was actually relieved." She let out a bitter laugh.

"He finally started talking. He told me about Miss Noakes's cat and the emu. He said you came and talked to him and you knew what was going on. He said now that I was back, everything was going to have to come out, and that he'd be arrested."

Janelle's eyes welled up with tears, whether in sympathy for Tommy or fear of him, Frank wasn't sure.

"He told me he couldn't bear to be shut up in prison, even for a day. He'd go insane if he couldn't be outdoors. So his plan was that he would run away. He had some money saved and he wanted to go out west and see the Rockies. And I sat there smiling and encouraging him, saying that would be great, thinking that he sounded really normal and happy for the first time in a long while. I still had no idea what the box was for. And then he told me."

Janelle and Frank stared at each other for a long minute; she, clearly reliving that awful moment of knowledge; he, imagining her terror.

"He said I had to stay in the box for three days while he got away. He said he'd call my dad after that and let him know where to find me. He actually showed me the little water bottle and the food he had for me, all proud of himself for having thought of everything." Janelle stopped abruptly, the look in her eyes a million miles away.

"You tried to reason with him?"

Janelle jumped, as if surprised to see that Frank was still there. "I said I could camp out in the woods for three days to give him a head start before I went home. There was no need for that box." Janelle turned to Frank, amazed even now. "He didn't trust me. He didn't believe I would do that for him.

"I tried to run, but he caught me right away and dragged me back. And then he punched me in the jaw, and it was like one of those cartoons—I actually saw stars. I fell down and hit my head." Janelle gingerly touched some stitches closing up a nasty-looking cut on her temple. "I guess I passed out. When I came to, I heard the sound of the shovel going into the ground, and the dirt hitting the top of the box.

"I cried. I begged him, 'Just kill me and get it over with.' And he said, 'You'll be all right. I kept a dog in there for four days.' And then I heard him walk away."

"Janelle, we haven't found Tommy yet. Dennis Treve turned up yesterday and said that when he woke up at their campsite, Tommy had packed up and left. Do you have any idea where he might have gone out west?"

Janelle examined the cuticle of her left thumbnail intently.

"Janelle, if you know, you must tell me. Tommy is a dangerous person. He needs help. You don't want him to hurt anyone else."

Janelle sighed. "He's not out west. He would never leave these mountains. When I was lying in that box, I knew I was going to slowly starve to death. Because the more I thought about it, I realized he would never be able to leave here. He never understood why anyone would want to go away from here, even on vacation.

"He's probably in his secret hiding place. We discovered it when we were kids, and no one knows about it but me. There's a trail that leads into the woods at the back of our property. It's not marked, but it's pretty easy to follow. About a quarter of a mile in, there's a big rock with a tree growing on top of it. The trail goes to the right, but if you just work your way through the trees to the left, you come to a ledge where there's a cave. Tommy always goes there to hide whenever he's upset."

Frank sat quietly, his tape recorder still running. "Anything else?"

She shook her head vigorously. "That's the end of the story. You found me. That's it."

Frank smiled. The proverbial two-thousand-pound elephant was in the room with them and Janelle was doing a damn good job of pretending she hadn't noticed. "What about Mrs. Stevenson's little dog, Leo—did you know Tommy killed him?"

Janelle nodded. "I guess that's when I got really worried."

"So why didn't you tell your father?"

Janelle's eyes had the flat, deadened quality of a badly executed portrait. She said nothing.

"Maybe," Frank said softly, "Tommy said if you told on him, he'd tell on you."

Janelle remained stubbornly silent, her face as impassive as the blank green hospital walls.

"Did you not want him to tell your father about the person you were slipping out at night to see?" There, the elephant was acknowledged!

Janelle's face was now bright red. Breathing rapidly, she struggled for air.

Frank had seen people hyperventilating before, and knew it was nothing serious. But what if it was more than that? Just then, a nurse entered the room. "What have you been doing to her? She's still in a very fragile state."

"She's just a little short of breath—she'll be okay."

The nurse did not take kindly to his diagnosis. "You'll have to leave now."

Frank hesitated.

"*Right* now, before I call Dr. Ericson."

"It's Bob Rush you're protecting, isn't it?" Frank asked Janelle.

But the nurse pushed him out of the room before he could see the reaction on Janelle's face.

Frank insisted that Earl stay at the office while he and Meyerson and two other troopers went to look for Tommy in the hiding place Janelle had described. The path, overgrown with lush, late spring growth, had been hard to locate at first, but once found it was exactly as Janelle had described.

They came to the large rock with the tree on top and paused to discuss their strategy.

"The underbrush is awfully thick here," Meyerson said. "There's no way he won't hear us coming."

"Do we know if he has a gun?" one of the other troopers asked.

"Jack says none of his hunting rifles are missing, but a kid like Tommy—who knows? He might have been able to get one from somewhere else," Meyerson answered.

"He's never used a gun on any of the animals he's killed. Janelle said he only had a knife," Frank reminded them. "I'll go in first, Lou can back me up, and you guys stay here. You'll be able to hear if we need help."

Without waiting for Meyerson's agreement, Frank set off through the brush to the left of the rock. The going was steep and rough and he was soon out of breath, but within ten minutes he heard the faint sound of moving water. The plant growth thinned in the sparse soil, and Frank saw a rock ledge with a small stream cascading over it, splashing its way downhill. At first glance, the ledge seemed a solid wall of stone, but then he noticed a small opening, partially concealed by a low bush. Directly in front of it were the remains of a campfire.

Silently, Frank pointed the cave out to Meyerson. With his gun drawn, he approached the entrance. "Tommy, it's Frank Bennett. Come on out, son. We've found Janelle. You and I need to talk."

They waited, but the only sound was the wind stirring the treetops. Frank crept a little closer, listening for some small noise that would tell him Tommy was there. He had no desire to poke his head into that cave.

"Tommy, you can't stay in there forever. Your cousin isn't hurt. We can work all this out."

Still nothing. Dropping to his knees, Frank crawled closer to the entrance, curious to see if the campfire remains were still warm. He reached his hand out.

"Frank!'

Meyerson's shout threw Frank into recoil. Immediately, he brought his gun into firing position.

"No, look over here."

Meyerson stood on the edge of the ledge, peering down the sheer drop to the creek below. When Frank joined him he saw a crumpled figure on the rocks, two waffle-soled hiking boots pointing straight up.

"Christ, I hope he didn't fall when he heard us coming!" Frank said as they scrambled down the slope.

But when they reached Tommy, his body was cold and stiff. Dried blood blackened the hair on the crown of his head, which rested on the large, rounded rocks of the creek bed.

"Do you think he fell, or jumped?" Meyerson asked.

Frank shook his head, looking up to the ledge twenty-five feet above them. "Who knows? It's not a sure-fire way to kill yourself, but the kid was panicked."

Despite his size, Tommy looked pathetically young in death. He had been sick and dangerous, but he was still just a kid. A kid who'd been abused by his own father, taunted by other children; who'd found power the only way he could—by tormenting creatures that were weaker than he was. Prisons were full of men who'd started out like Tommy and grown more twisted over time. But maybe with help, Tommy could have straightened out. They'd never know now. Tommy's options were all used up.

"You take care of this, Lou. I'll go tell Dorothy." He looked up at the rocky outcropping he would have to climb to get back to the trail. "I saved one child in the family but lost the other."

25

DORIS GLANCED UP as Frank entered the Town Office, but did not stop typing. "The coroner called while you were out. I gave the call to Earl. And George Fisk just reported that his truck was stolen out of Stevenson's parking lot."

"In broad daylight? I suppose he's one of those fools who leaves the keys in the vehicle." Doris merely smiled, so Frank kept going into his office.

"So what did Doc Hibbert have to say?" he asked Earl, unwrapping a roast beef sandwich for an early dinner at his desk. He had a meeting at six-thirty with the Town Council to plan for security at the July Fourth fireworks display.

"He says he can't sign Tommy's death certificate. He has to get a second opinion from a pathologist. It'll take two days."

"What, he can't figure out if Tommy's dead?"

"He can't confirm that Tommy died from accidental causes." Earl picked up a message pad and read what had been dictated to him. "The depth and position of the head contusions are not consistent with a fall from that height."

Frank swallowed with difficulty. "What the hell are they consistent with?"

"Being struck forcefully from behind and above with a heavy object."

Earl's words hung in the air between them.

"Janelle says she was the only one who knew about that cave," Frank said.

"Tommy might have told Dennis. Janelle wouldn't know if he had. The coroner says Tommy died sometime between noon and midnight, Wednesday. Dennis turned up around two P.M."

Frank nodded but didn't seem to be listening. "I have to go somewhere. If I'm not back by six-thirty, you go to that council meeting. Just agree to do whatever they want."

Frank pounded insistently on the door of the Harvey house. When no one answered, he tried the door and found it unlocked. He stepped inside with trepidation—could he be too late?

Suddenly the hall light flicked on and he found himself face-to-face with an irate Jack Harvey.

"What are you doing here?"

"Where's Janelle?" Frank asked.

"Over at Dorothy's."

"Are you sure?"

"Of course I'm sure! Where else would she be?"

Frank snorted. "You could ask that?"

"Look, Frank, I appreciate all you've done, I really do, but Janelle's home now and we're just trying to put all this nightmare behind us. Why do you keep trying to stir things up?"

"Because the nightmare's not behind you, Jack. I'm afraid there's more to come."

A large bouquet of roses on the hall table caught Frank's eye. He read the card: "From all your friends at Stevenson's lumberyard."

"When did those arrive?" Frank asked.

"Ned brought them over to the hospital. What's that got to do with anything."

"Daddy, what's all the noise? Who's here?"

Janelle stood in the front door, her pink sundress billowing slightly in the breeze.

Frank heaved a sigh of relief. The girl was still safe.

"Janelle, did you happen to mention Tommy's hiding place to anyone who visited you in the hospital?"

Janelle stared at Frank, her face blank as a stone.

"Janelle, the coroner thinks Tommy didn't die from falling off that ledge. He says your cousin was hit over the head several times with a heavy object; he was dead when he went over the edge. No one knew where Tommy was but you, and you were in the hospital."

As if in slow motion, Janelle began to sway. Her hand reached out for the door frame but came nowhere close. Frank rushed forward to catch her as she crumpled to the floor.

A whiff of kitchen ammonia brought her around. As her glazed eyes brought Frank and her father into focus, she turned her head and rested it against the wall. "Daddy, could you leave me alone with Mr. Bennett, please?"

Jack opened his mouth, as if to protest, but backed silently out of the room.

When Janelle spoke her voice was surprisingly steady, but she kept her head resolutely turned away. "I've known Ned all my life. He always treated me like a kid sister. When I was having so much trouble getting Daddy to let me go away to college, I thought maybe Ned could help. I asked him to talk to my father, but he said the best thing to do would be to apply for scholarships to a few different schools. Then when I got one, my dad couldn't possibly not let me go. Ned said he'd help me with the applications because he knew what the admissions people looked for. He even said he'd loan me the money for the application fees. We agreed to keep it secret, so Daddy wouldn't interfere."

Frank could see where this story was headed.

"We had a system. I would stop by the lumberyard every Monday and Thursday, and if Ned had a certain red pen in the cup on his desk, it meant he'd be waiting for me that night in his Jeep. He'd park it behind some trees in the field beside our drive. Daddy always goes to bed early because he starts work at seven, so it was easy to sneak out.

"At first, we really just worked on the applications. Then, we started talking about other stuff. Ned told me about going to college at Penn . . . living in Philadelphia . . . working in California . . . traveling in Europe. Ned was the only person I really knew who'd ever been places or lived far away from here."

Janelle sat on the edge of the hall stairs and set to work systematically unraveling the hem of her dress. Her hair fell forward in a curtain before her face. "I know what I did was wrong. Ned is *married*. But he knew how to . . . Craig was so . . ."

"Never mind. I get the picture." Yes—finally now, he saw what had been there all along. It was as if he'd been looking at one of those trick pictures, where the same lines make two entirely different images. He had never considered Ned as a candidate for the other man in Janelle's life. Not because he couldn't imagine that she would be attracted to him, but because he couldn't fathom that any man married to a woman as beautiful and vibrant as Penny would be tempted by a few moments of contorted sex with a teenager in a parked car.

"I didn't know Tommy had seen me leaving the house at night," Janelle continued. "He must have followed me, and"—she shivered in revulsion—"and watched us. That day in the backyard, Tommy told me he knew what I was doing with Ned, what a slut I was. And he said if I told my father or anyone else about the raccoon, he would tell about me and Ned. He said everyone in town would care a whole lot more about me breaking up Ned Stevenson's marriage than they would about some little animal. I knew he was right, so I kept quiet and just tried to push the whole thing out of my mind. But then things started getting really awful."

"Tommy killed Mrs. Stevenson's dog the day before the Lake George game?" Frank asked.

Janelle nodded. "I went to the lumberyard that day and everything was in an uproar. Leo was missing, and then they found him dead under that stack of boards. Mrs. Stevenson started screaming and crying. We all just thought it was an accident.

"Then I got home and Tommy was waiting." Janelle hugged her knees and rested her head on them, making herself into a tight little ball. Her voice was muffled but still audible. "He was smiling—gloating, like he had just won a prize or aced a test or something. He said, 'Aren't you going to thank me? Now you won't have to worry about picking up any dog hairs when you're out there in Ned's truck.' And he laughed.

"That night I met Ned and I told him what Tommy had done. I said we had to do something to stop Tommy. I said I was going to talk to my dad. But Ned got angry. I'd never seen him mad before. He said we couldn't risk anyone finding out about us. He said Clyde could be very unreasonable, and that he would probably fire my father because of what I did with Ned."

Janelle lifted her tear-streaked face. "I couldn't let that happen. Daddy's worked his whole life there. It's all he knows. I seriously considered killing myself, but that's a terrible sin," she said without irony.

Frank put his head in his hands. "Oh, Janelle, you honestly think your father wouldn't have believed you, wouldn't have helped you?"

Janelle sighed. "Even after what Ned said, I still thought about telling Daddy. But I couldn't bear thinking about how disappointed in me he would be. He was always going on and on, warning me not to make the mistake my Aunt Dorothy made. He really thought I was a virgin. And then I thought if I did tell him and he believed me, then what? I didn't want Tommy to get arrested. It would kill my Aunt Dorothy, and I love her. Then I met Pablo and realized I could go to his compound, and it just seemed like the only solution."

Frank looked at Janelle's slumped figure. There was still one more thing he needed to know.

"Janelle, what did you and Ned talk about when he visited you in the hospital?"

"He acted all happy to see me, but I don't think he really was. And I wasn't happy to see him. I told him it was over between us, and he agreed. But he wanted to know if I had told anyone about us—you, my father, my aunt. I told him no, but he kept asking."

Janelle sat silently, pausing for breath before the final hurdle.

"And then he asked me about Tommy. He said he supposed it would all come out once Tommy was found, and he only cared because of the pain it would cause Penny and his mom. He said, 'If only I could talk to Tom. Maybe I could get him to agree not to say anything. Maybe I could offer to pay for a lawyer to get him out of this mess.'"

Janelle's voice cracked, and she began to cry. "That's when I told him where to find Tommy. I thought Ned might really be able to help him. I thought there might still be a chance that no one would have to know. Oh, God! What have I done?"

She grabbed Frank's hand. "No, Ned can't possibly have killed him. He wouldn't. Please tell me that's not what happened!"

Gently, Frank pried her fingers loose. "We'll get the final pathologist's report in two days. Until then, don't tell anyone what you've told me. Not even your father. Stay with someone at all times, and keep the doors locked. I'll have a trooper parked outside."

Janelle's eyes widened. "You don't think he'd kill me, too?"

"I don't know—it would be awfully risky. He must realize that if something happened to you now, even if it looked like an accident, I would never let up 'til I got to the bottom of it. Still, you can't be too careful."

Frank drove away, abusing himself roundly for his own stupidity. He had been so obsessed with finding some romantic connection between Bob Rush and Janelle that he'd completely overlooked the other obvious candidate for her affections. Finally he understood the Stevensons' extraordinary interest in this case. Janelle's running away must have been a godsend to Ned—the perfect way out of an affair that couldn't possibly have ended well. He had a vested interest in promoting the kidnapping theory because he knew it would throw everyone off the real reason for her flight. And Tommy had been in exactly the same position, for an entirely different reason. Neither one of them knew where Janelle had gone; they just both wanted her to stay away. And keeping each other's secrets had been the best way to keep anyone from finding Janelle.

It must have been Ned who sent that lame ransom note. And the excerpt from *Madame Bovary* must have been a little love note that Janelle had once given him. Ned had planned all along to drop it at the stakeout to make it look like the "kidnapper" had been there but had been scared off. When that poor hiker had stumbled into the setup, Ned must have been amazed at his own luck. Frank's mouth twisted. The cocky bastard was probably sorry Janelle hadn't died in that box.

And no wonder he had made Ned so nervous by telling him Dell Lambert had seen him driving up and down Stony Brook Road—Ned hadn't been spying on Dell, he'd been going to his trysts with Janelle. But Ned hadn't known Lambert had seen him until Frank told him about it, so it looked like the old man's death had been an accident after all.

But for Ned to actually kill Tommy to keep the affair secret—that seemed incredible! Protecting Penny hardly seemed a powerful enough motive for such a drastic action. After all, if he loved her so much, he wouldn't have been screwing around with Janelle in the first place. Perhaps Ned was worried that Clyde would disinherit him. Frank couldn't imagine the old man taking such a hard line, but who knew?

The real problem was how to come up with enough evidence to arrest the sonofabitch. Ned had motive and opportunity, but without any physical evidence to link him to the crime, he would easily beat the charge. And Trout Run wouldn't take kindly to wild allegations against one of its leading citizens.

Frank was so deep in thought that he hardly knew where he was. A call over the radio brought him back to the here and now.

"Frank, there's a report of a serious accident on Farnham Road. A car went off the road at the hairpin turn. Caller didn't see it happen. Just says there are car lights shining up from the side of the road."

"I'm on my way." Frank turned the patrol car around and turned on his lights. It never rained but it poured. He had wanted to get back to the office and call Meyerson to discuss strategy; now he'd be messing around with this accident for hours. But nothing could really be done until the coroner's suspicions were verified, anyway. Tomorrow he'd return to Tommy's hideout and see if there was any shred of evidence indicating Ned's presence. Until then, it might actually be better to have something else to occupy his mind.

Frank knew exactly where the accident must be. Farnham Road was a narrow, twisting mountain road that the locals used as a shortcut between the main road to Lake Placid and the west side of Trout Run. One turn was particularly bad, and if you were going too fast in the dark, you could easily leave the road.

When he arrived at the spot, the only signs of an accident were some broken tree branches, two deep tire marks in the mud on the side of the road, and the eerie glow of lights shining up into the trees. Frank looked down the hill and saw it: a small car turned on its back like a bug. Its rear end was pointed down the hill. The only thing that had stopped it from rolling all the way down into the ravine was a large maple tree that wedged the hood of the car against the hillside.

Frank scrambled down the slope, pointing his flashlight at the wreck. As he grew closer, he could see that the car was red. A few more steps and he could make out the insignia on the hood. A jolt of fear hit him. A Mazda Miata—the kind of car Penny Stevenson drove.

He shined his flashlight through the shattered passenger side window. A dark-haired woman was trapped in the compressed front seat. Her face was turned away from him, but the left hand was flung out. A familiar diamond solitaire glinted in the light.

Frank moaned, paralyzed by the pain of this new tragedy for a moment. Then he snapped to attention. He needed help. Even opening the door could send the car tumbling down the hill. Gingerly, he reached through the broken window and picked up the limp hand. Forcing himself to concentrate, he placed two fingers across the wrist. Maybe it was just wishful thinking, but he thought he felt a flicker of pulse. He dropped Penny's hand and charged up the hillside.

An hour later, with the help of two tow trucks and an ambulance and with the Medievac helicopter hovering overhead, Penny Stevenson was pulled from the wreckage of her car. Frank watched in agony as the paramedics labored over her. To his eye she looked remarkably unscathed, except for a trickle of blood running from the corner of her mouth.

But the paramedic shook his head. "Goddamn Japanese tin cans. They crumple right up. And she wasn't wearing a seat belt."

"It's too late?" Frank asked.

"No, she's alive. But just barely. She's got some serious internal bleeding. She's going to have to go to Burlington for surgery. Tell the helicopter to land at the baseball field and we'll meet him over there."

The procession to the baseball field was ominously like a funeral cortege, and Frank watched as the chopper carried Penny away. He tried to convince himself that she was young and strong and would pull through this. He grimaced. Pull through and wake to the news that she was married to a murderer.

A cold rain fell, making the early May day feel more like late October. Frank and Earl trudged through the meadow behind the Harvey house on their way back from watching the state police forensic team unsuccessfully scour the area around Tommy's hideout, looking for evidence to indicate foul play. Frank had known they would find nothing, but having his suspicion confirmed irritated him intensely.

As they drew near the patrol car, Frank suddenly tossed the keys to Earl. "Here, you drive."

Caught by surprise, Earl let the keys bounce off his arm and drop into the mud. Wiping them off on the seat of his pants, he climbed into the driver's seat and set the car on course for the office.

"Say, I forgot to ask—did you call the hospital this morning to check on Penny?"

Frank nodded, gazing out the window, as if the passing scenery were all new to him. "She made it through the surgery. She's in intensive care. They said her condition is extremely critical."

"Is anyone with her?"

"Ned and his mother went over last night."

"What about her folks? Are they from far away?"

"No, her parents died when she was young. She's got no family but the Stevensons."

"I wonder what made her go off the road like that? It was dry last night," Earl speculated aloud. A squirrel darted in front of the car and he slowed momentarily. "Probably she swerved to avoid an animal. Girls are like that. They'd sooner run their car into a tree than take down a stupid possum. Too bad she wasn't wearing her seat belt, though. That time I stopped her for speeding, she had it on."

Frank, who had been listening to Earl's prattle with only half an ear, turned to face his assistant.

"You say she did have it on when you stopped her?"

"Yeah," Earl said, nodding vehemently. "Otherwise I would have given her a ticket for that, too."

Frank pictured Penny getting into her little red car that afternoon he had met her outside the post office. His mental image clearly included Penny buckling her belt as soon as she sat down. And she had been headed home, just a quarter of a mile away. Why would she not have been wearing the belt on the long, dark drive back from Lake Placid?

Frank opened his mouth to say something, then changed his mind and returned to staring out the window, until they reached the office.

They entered in time to catch the tail end of Doris's phone conversation.

"Well, I'm glad it turned up. Thanks for letting us know. I bet you won't do that anymore."

"Thanks for letting us know what?" Frank asked as he reviewed his message slips.

"George Fisk called to say his truck turned up."

"Any damage?"

"Just a dent in the front bumper. He was so glad to have it back, I don't think he even cares about that. Says he'll never leave his keys in the truck again."

"Too great a temptation for the kids," Earl said. "Hope they had fun on their joyride. Where did the truck end up?"

"Over at that little parking area by the trailhead to Mount Dyson," Doris replied.

"Strange destination," Earl commented.

Frank shrugged, already focused on his need to call state police headquarters and check on the progress of the pathologist's report.

But the pathologist could not be rushed, and Frank hung up unsatisfied. He walked to the window and watched the rain slamming against the glass. The green was deserted except for a few cars pulling up in front of the Store, men on the early shift at Stevenson's already breaking for lunch. Facts that had been floating in his mind began to form into ideas.

"Where did Doris say they found George's truck?" Frank asked.

"At the trailhead to Mount Dyson, why?"

"Isn't that on the road that intersects Farnham Road, just past where Penny had her accident?"

"Yeah," Earl said without much interest. "It's about a mile away."

"And didn't George's truck have a dent in the bumper?"

"So?"

"You think that's a coincidence?" Frank demanded.

Understanding dawned in Earl's eyes. "You think the kids who stole George's truck caused Penny's accident?"

"I think whoever stole that truck ran Penny off the road, and I don't think it was kids. Come on—we're going over to Al's Sunoco."

Both Penny's crushed Miata and George's dented truck had ended up at Al's Sunoco, the only garage in town. Without a word of explanation to the incredulous Al, Frank flung himself down in front of the large Ford truck's dented bumper and peered up at the damaged edge.

"Ah, I knew it! Red paint!" Frank emerged triumphant from under the truck. "This thing is so much higher than

Penny's car that the tires did most of the work pushing her off the road. But the back of her car caught under the truck's bumper and left some red paint. Now, let's go look at Penny's car."

Frank barely paused to look at the rear end. The Miata was so thoroughly damaged on every side from its tumble down the hill, it was impossible to determine if any of the scratches on the back came from the truck. Instead, he pulled open the driver side door and knelt down to examine the seat belt mechanism. The belt still moved freely, but when Frank attempted to insert the tongue into the clasp, it wouldn't hold. "Give me a flashlight," he demanded.

Al produced one and Frank soon uttered a grunt of satisfaction. "There are scratches on the clasp end of this. I'll bet money that it was tampered with to make the seat belt unusable."

Frank strode back to George's truck, with Earl and Al in his wake. He gazed into the pristine interior. The truck still had that new car smell. "I can prove that this truck ran Penny off the road. I can prove that it was premeditated. But how the hell am I going to prove that bastard was the one who did it?"

"Who?" asked Earl and Al in unison.

"Al, don't let anyone near these vehicles, including their owners. *Especially* their owners. I'll have the state police forensics guys over here this afternoon."

As they got back to the patrol car, Frank commanded Earl to drive.

"Where to?"

"Just around. I need to work this all out."

Once they were alone, Earl asked, "So who do you think was driving George's truck? Who would want to hurt Penny?"

"Ned."

"Get outta here! Why?"

"This is what I think: Ned killed Tommy to keep him quiet, but then he must've realized he'd taken away part of the hold he had over Janelle," Frank continued, talking more to himself than to Earl. "Without the need to protect Tommy, Janelle might eventually have told her father or her friends why she ran away. Once Penny found out about the affair, she'd have left Ned for sure."

"That doesn't make any sense! Why kill your wife if you don't want her to divorce you?"

"Remember I told you Penny said she was an orphan? Nick Reilly says her parents left her a trust fund. That's why Ned was so panicked that no one should find out about him and Janelle. If Penny divorced him, he could kiss that money good-bye. So he had to kill her now and inherit it, before any gossip about him and Janelle could get out."

"But the Stevensons have their own money," Earl protested.

"That's the part I have to look into. You know, when Ned joined the business full-time, they put old Bertha Calloway, who did the books for years, out to pasture. Ned computerized everything, started expanding and modernizing. I wouldn't be surprised if he's in over his head. And Clyde probably doesn't realize it—Ned has him bamboozled with computer spreadsheets and *Wall Street Journal* jargon."

"So Ned figured if he killed Penny and made it look like an accident, he'd inherit all the money and straighten everything out," Earl said. "I guess he figured an accident with Janelle would look too suspicious, huh?"

"Right. First, he damaged Penny's seat belt, so he

could be sure she wouldn't be wearing it. Then he took George's truck—everyone up there probably knows the keys are always in it. It was risky, but Ned's about George's build. They all wear khaki pants and Stevenson's shirts. Put on a cap like George always wears, and from a distance anyone would think it was George. Then he waited for Penny to come by on her way home, forced her off the road, and dumped the truck at the trailhead." Frank paused. "Shit. I wonder how he got home from there? He was home when I went by that night to tell him about the accident."

"I bet he left his bike hidden over at the trailhead. He's got one of those fancy mountain bikes. I see him out on it all the time," Earl offered.

"Good, Earl. That adds up. Now, how're we going to prove it was Ned driving the truck?"

"Fingerprints?"

Frank snorted. "I suppose there's a chance Ned was so cocky that he didn't bother to wear gloves. But it seems like too much to expect."

"Maybe they'll find something else in the truck."

"That's our only hope. It helps that the truck is brand-new. At least they won't have to sift through a decade's worth of dirt." Frank sank into a glum reverie.

"Hey, Frank?" Earl broke the long silence as he parked the patrol car in front of the office. "Maybe it's not so safe that Ned's over at the hospital with Penny. Couldn't he, uh, pull her plugs or something?"

"Oh, shit! You're right, Earl."

But when Frank called the hospital, the ICU nurse assured him that there had been no change in Penny's condition. She was still alive, although just barely. She also reported that Ned and his mother had left an hour ago to go home for a much-needed rest.

"Just one more thing," Frank said to the nurse. "Is there always a nurse able to see Penny at all times?"

"We're watching her very closely, sir," the nurse replied patiently, used to dealing with distraught relatives.

"I know, but if her respirator stopped or her intravenous . . . fell out . . . you'd know that right away?"

"Yes, sir, all the patients' monitors are right here at the nurses' station."

"Good, good. Thanks."

Frank hung up and began explaining to Earl as he dialed again. "I'll call Meyerson and he'll have to arrange for the Vermont state police to send someone over to the hospital. It could take a while."

"But if Ned's on his way back here, it would take him two hours to get back over there again, even if he didn't stop to rest," Earl said.

"If he really is headed back here," Frank replied.

It took nearly half an hour of discussion and explanation with Lieutenant Meyerson to arrange for the forensics team to examine the vehicles at Al's, and to set up the guard at the hospital. When he finally finished, Frank stood up and reached for his hat.

"Where are you going?" Earl asked.

"I think I'm going to stop in and see Ned."

26

THE STEVENSON FAMILY owned a large tract of land behind the lumberyard, and all along the road that bisected it were the homes of various Stevensons. Ned and Penny lived in the original stone house, a rambling two-story affair with a wraparound porch. Anticipating the day when stairs would become a problem, Clyde and Elinor had built themselves a brand-new ranch house next door. Across the way lived Clyde's sister, and quite a few of her many children had built homes farther down the road.

Frank sat in the patrol car for a moment, staring at the row of Stevenson mailboxes by the edge of the road. Poor Penny had been attracted by all this togetherness, thinking she'd finally found the family she longed for. He only hoped that longing wouldn't be the death of her.

Frank walked up to the front door and leaned on the bell. There was no response from within, but Ned's Jeep was in the driveway, so he had apparently told the nurse the truth. Frank pressed on the bell again and heard the old-fashioned chimes reverberate. The curtains on one of the front windows moved, and Frank saw the face of a black cat staring out at him. A moment later, the front door opened.

Ned stood before him, red-eyed and unshaven, wearing sweatpants and a T-shirt.

"Did I wake you, Ned? Sorry about that," Frank said as he walked in without waiting for an invitation.

Ned's eyes narrowed in irritation, but he smiled nevertheless. "I just got back from the hospital. I was up all night. The nurses told me to get some rest. They'll call if there's any change."

Frank marched through the front hall and headed for a big overstuffed chair in the living room. Ned had no choice but to follow.

"It's too bad Penny didn't have her seat belt on," Frank commented as he plopped himself down. "She might have come through the crash with hardly a scratch."

Ned nodded sadly.

"I'm surprised she wasn't wearing it. Seems to me whenever I saw Penny driving, she always had it on," Frank continued.

"Usually she did. The one night she was careless, was the night she really needed it."

"So you think she was just careless?" Frank asked. "Is there any chance the seat belt wasn't working?"

Ned seemed to grow more alert. "She never mentioned she was having problems. Although, come to think of it, I remember reading something about a seat belt recall in certain Japanese cars."

"Well, we'll just have the state police mechanics look at it. You might have grounds for a lawsuit there. Not that any amount of money could compensate you if Penny didn't pull through this," Frank added.

Ned's hand tightened on the sofa cushion. Just then, a white cat came charging into the room and leaped into

Ned's lap. In a reflexive motion, Ned flung the cat away from him. It landed next to its black compatriot, and both animals stood eyeing their owner malevolently.

Ned gave an edgy little laugh. "I guess Yin and Yang are trying to tell me they're hungry. Penny always feeds them. She's had them for years."

"They say animals can tell when something's not right," Frank said as he rose from his chair. "I don't know if I believe that, though, do you?"

Ned glanced out the window at a passing car rather than meet Frank's eyes. "Beats me. Was there anything else?"

"Yeah, just one little thing. You know George Fisk's truck was stolen out of your parking lot yesterday afternoon. It's turned up again, so I doubt George will press charges. But I really ought to find out who did it. Talk to them, shake them up a little. You wouldn't happen to have noticed anyone around his truck, would you?"

Ned was headed purposefully toward the door. "No, I didn't. I don't spend much time looking out the window when I'm at work."

"Of course not." Frank stood on the threshold as Ned held the door for him. "Stick close to home, Ned. Get some rest. You don't look so good."

Frank pulled away from the Stevensons' and headed over to Al's Sunoco to check on the forensics team. He might never get the evidence he needed to convict Ned, but at least he'd had the satisfaction of watching him squirm.

When he arrived, the garage was a hornet's nest of police activity. Al had been unceremoniously barred from his own workplace and stood by the gas pumps, complaining to anyone who would listen. Frank looked for Meyerson to give him an update.

"There are definite signs of damage to Penny's seat belt that wouldn't be caused by normal wear and tear," Meyerson reported. "Now the men are going through the truck."

Al's workbench was covered with sealed plastic bags, each containing some crumb or fiber or speck from George's truck. Frank stood around watching, knowing he was just in the way, but reluctant to leave.

He heard footsteps behind him and turned to see Meyerson returning from the rest room. "What's that all over the back of your pants, Frank?" Meyerson asked.

Frank looked down. Intermingled black and white cat hair clung to his beige pants. Yin and Yang had apparently been sitting in the same chair he had chosen at Ned's house. Frank brushed at his pants in irritation, then stopped and swiftly reached out to grab a clump of the fluff as it floated through the air. His smile soon turned into a full-fledged laugh as he scanned the plastic bags of evidence.

"Cat hairs, Lew," Frank said as he held a bag up for inspection. "Ned may have a little trouble explaining how fur from Yin and Yang got into George Fisk's brand-new truck."

Arresting the scion of Trout Run's leading family for murder and attempted murder was not a matter to be undertaken lightly. Frank spent the next day preparing to strike.

He spoke to Janelle again to confirm that she had told Ned, and no one else, about Tommy's secret hiding place, and also that she had given Ned the excerpt from *Madame Bovary* as a love note. He verified that Jack, Dorothy, Dennis Treve, and even Tommy's boyhood friends never knew the location of Tommy's hideout. He clarified that George Fisk had never given any member of the Stevenson family, or anyone who'd ever been in Ned and Penny's house, a ride in his week-old truck. Then, when he was certain he had all his ducks in a row, he got a search warrant to seize Ned's computer and sent in auditors to review the books at Stevenson's Lumberyard.

After two days of agonized waiting—two days that Frank had spent holed up in his office, refusing to offer explanations; two days that Ned spent under the watchful eyes of the state police—Frank had what he needed to make his arrest.

Walking into Stevenson's Lumberyard and uttering the words, "Ned Stevenson, you're under arrest for the murder of Tommy Pettigrew and the attempted murder of your wife, Penny," had been a moment of pure vindication for Frank. Ned, of course, had known this was coming, had even hired the lawyer Peter Stratton to represent him. Still, Frank had the pleasure of seeing the flicker of panic in Ned's eyes when the words were spoken. After all, no rich white man with an Ivy League MBA ever expects to be led off in handcuffs, no matter what he's done.

Now Frank, Ned, and Stratton sat in Frank's office reviewing the evidence. Ned was no more ruffled than he would have been if Earl had pulled him over in the speed trap. Frank had an annoying tickle in the back of his throat from breathing in the fumes of Stratton's high-priced aftershave.

"Ned, the audit reveals that Stevenson's went from profits of three hundred thousand dollars last year to losses of more than two hundred and fifty thousand dollars this year," Frank began.

"If overexpansion and ill-conceived stock market investments were a crime, Chief Bennett, half the executives in America would be behind bars," Stratton said without lifting his head from a file folder he'd opened. "Tell us what else you've got."

Frank continued to direct his comments to Ned. "You

were having an affair with Janelle Harvey and you didn't want Penny to find out. She told you where Tommy was hiding. No one else knew."

"It's her word against my client's, Bennett, and the young lady's recent exploits would lead me to say she's not a very reliable witness," Stratton replied.

Ned stretched out his legs and smiled slightly.

Frank took a long drink from a glass of water on his desk. "How did cat hairs from your client's cat get into the truck that ran Penny off the road?" he demanded.

"Ned's office is full of cat hair. Fisk probably picked it up in there."

"You're not suggesting Fisk tried to kill Penny!" Frank said.

"It's not my job to find out who did do it; only to prove my client didn't. I think we need to start talking to the D.A. about reducing these charges," Stratton said as he began to pack up his briefcase.

Stratton was a cool character. He was bluffing, Frank knew, but he thought he was winning the war of intimidation. So far.

"Just one more thing needs explaining, Mr. Stratton," Frank said. "You remember that ransom note that I thought your other client, Mr. Klein, wrote? Well, I was sure wrong about that. Because our investigators found the computer document of that note on Ned's computer."

Ned sat straight up. "But I deleted it!" he shouted. Then he clapped his hand over his mouth.

"Shut up, Ned!" Stratton barked.

"Geez, I'm not one much for computers," Frank said, "but even I know that when you delete a file, it just goes to the trash can. You forgot to empty the trash, Ned."

And that's when Ned started to cry.

27

FRANK APPROACHED THE DOORWAY of his office. Earl sat with his back to him, feet propped on the windowsill. He knew if he spoke Earl's name now, the kid would leap up in guilt, and that's not the way he wanted to start this conversation. So he backed out past Doris's empty desk—really, that woman must have the weakest bladder in the North Country—and reentered the building, slamming the door and whistling "A Mighty Fortress Is our God." When he reached the office door this time, Earl was typing a report, both feet flat on the floor.

"Morning, Earl."

"Morning." Earl stopped typing, then with a deep sigh, resumed his two-fingered dance with the keyboard.

"What's wrong?"

Earl peered up through his bangs. "Nothing. Things just seem—"

"A little dull, now the Harvey case is closed," Frank finished Earl's sentence. "I know what you mean. The whole time we were working on it, all I wanted was for it to be over. Now that it is, I'm a little let down. Kind of like the day after Christmas."

"I guess, but—" Earl looked away.

"But what?"

"Nothing."

Frank walked over to the window and looked out. Behind him, the computer keys began to click again. "Earl," Frank began, his eyes still riveted to the unremarkable sight of Augie Enright putting up this week's sermon title in the church signboard. "I want to thank you for all the work you did on the Harvey case. I couldn't have closed it without you."

The typing stopped.

Frank turned around, expecting to see Earl's sweet, goofy smile. Instead the kid looked as foul tempered as a Thruway toll-taker on Labor Day weekend.

"You're just saying that to be nice. I'll never be a real cop. I'll just be your, your sidekick"—he spit the word out with surprising vehemence—"forever."

Frank didn't know what the right response to that was supposed to be. He'd kind of assumed Earl wanted to be his sidekick forever—this was the first he'd heard of grander ambitions. "Well," he ventured, "you could be a real cop. Of course, you'd have to go to the Police Academy."

"You think I don't know that?" Earl snapped. "I can't get in."

"Can't get in? Why not?"

"Because I'm too dumb!" Earl yelled in the tone that Frank usually used on him. "I flunked the entrance test, all right?"

"Wait a minute, you're telling me you've already applied to the State Police Academy and you failed the test? When was this?"

"Back in February."

"This past February? How come you didn't mention it?"

Earl shrugged. "I thought you'd laugh."

Frank sank into his chair. Is that what Earl thought of him? That he was the kind of man who would mock another person's dreams?

"Earl," the word came out choked. "Earl," he began again, "I would never laugh at you. I'm very impressed that you want to do this."

"Yeah, well, it doesn't matter 'cause it's not going to happen. I can't get in."

"Earl, lots of people flunk these tests the first time they take them."

"Did you?" Earl demanded.

"Well, no. But that was years ago. They're harder now," Frank improvised. "Look, you can take it again."

"What's the point? I'd just flunk again."

"Not if I prepped you for the test, you wouldn't. I'll help you study."

For the first time in this whole crazy exchange, Earl looked him straight in the eye. "You'd do that for me?"

"Yes. I would really like to—if you can put up with me. Okay?"

Finally, that loopy grin. "Okay."

Frank knew it was a bad time to be going to the Store, but the magnetic pull of the coffeepot reeled him in.

The morning meeting of the Coffee Club was in full swing. Augie Enright pulled up a chair, and Reid Burlingame patted it invitingly. "Come join us, Frank. Have a donut."

There was no avoiding it. Frank sat down and prepared to be grilled.

"When do you think Ned's case will come to trial, Frank?" Bart Riddle asked.

"The D.A.'s ready. But Ned's hired the lawyer who

was up here when we arrested that hiker. He's filed for all sorts of extensions, so it'll probably be a few more months."

"I hear Clyde didn't want to put up the bail money, but Elinor made him. They say he's plenty pissed off, now that he got Bertha back in to go through the books. Apparently the lumberyard is one hundred thousand dollars in the red," offered Augie.

"I heard it was more like a quarter of a million," contradicted Bill Feeson.

"Plenty of talk that Stevenson's will have to close down," Augie said.

This is what Frank had dreaded. He knew most of Trout Run would rather have a murderer walking free among them than lose the three hundred–odd jobs that the lumberyard provided. If Stevenson's closed its doors, somehow Frank would be blamed, not Ned.

"That's nonsense." Reid banged his coffee cup for emphasis. "I want you to nip that rumor whenever you hear it. I've talked to Clyde myself, and he assures me that Stevenson's can pull through this."

Augie knew when he had been rebuked. "So, Frank, have you heard from Penny?"

"Yes. They moved her to a rehab facility. She had some nerve damage to her left leg, but she should be walking fine soon. Then I think she'll move to New York City. She oughta be a whole lot safer there."

"Will she testify at the trial?"

"She'll be able to state that the truck intentionally ran her off the road. She didn't see who was driving."

"So it all hangs on the cat hair, and that computer file thing, huh?" Bart inquired. "Think that's enough to get a conviction?"

"On the attempted murder charge, yeah. On Tommy's

murder . . ." Frank shrugged. "It's all still circumstantial. It depends on the jury." The trouble was, Ned didn't look like a murderer. The jury might think the evidence was sufficient to convict the kind of man you'd cross the street to avoid on a dark night, but not to put away a clean-cut young businessman like Ned. Frank stared at his companions. He wondered if anyone at that table would have the guts to vote to convict Ned Stevenson.

"Attempted murder—that'll only get him a few years. He'll be out by the time Clyde's ready to retire," Bill scoffed.

"He might get out, but I doubt he'll have the nerve to come back to Trout Run," Reid said. "However the trial turns out, I think that's the last we'll see of Ned Stevenson."

"And to think the whole thing started with Janelle Harvey disappearing. Who woulda thought that Ned and little Janelle . . ." Augie began.

Frank stood up, rocking the table. He wasn't about to go down that path. "Thanks for the donut, guys."

"Bye, Frank," they all chorused.

Walking across the green, something caught Frank's eye. He paused before the town bulletin board, then fumbled in his pocket for his keys. The smallest key on the ring opened the glass door. He reached in and removed a flier. Janelle's sweet face beseeched him one last time. Then he crumpled the paper and threw it away.